1984

THE WORLD WE LIVE IN

THE
WORLD
WE
LIVE IN

STORIES BY

LOUIS BROMFIELD

The Blakiston Company

PHILADELPHIA

CONTENTS

THE POND   1

DEATH IN MONTE CARLO   28

THE OLD HOUSE   81

TRUE LOVE   123

THE MAN WHO WAS IN LOVE WITH
     DEATH   136

DAUGHTERS OF MARS   172

THE GREAT FAÇADE   207

UP FERGUSON WAY   240

THOU SHALT NOT COVET   273

THE WORLD WE LIVE IN

THE POND

IT WAS A STILL NIGHT WITH THE STARS VERY BRILLIANT OVERHEAD. You could see them shining through the fronds of the tall slender betel palms like diamonds set in filigree against the dark velvet of the tropical sky. The two boys, one stripped to the waist, the other clad only in a pair of bathing trunks, sat leaning against the trunks of two of the palm trees. One of them was fair. He looked a little like a Swede, young, tall, good-looking and fresh with rather large features. The other boy was small and dark, tough and wiry. The tall blond boy was the one who wore the bathing trunks.

In the tents under the coconut palms behind them someone was playing a banjo. In the stillness of the night the only other sound came from the lazy beating of the surf on the beach a little way off. The air was hot but here on the knoll beneath the betel palms there was a breeze which kept off the mosquitoes.

Sometimes the two boys talked and sometimes they merely sat there, relaxed and silent. They were both fighter pilots on rest and the stillness of the night was like a sedative. Every now and then the boy in the bathing trunks would go down to the edge of the Pacific, throw himself headlong into the warm water and swim lazily for a while and then in a circle return to the white beach.

They both knew what it was like to be close to death but they were young and much of their talk was very young. And now in the stillness of the night they had time to think lazily and they were homesick.

"Funny," said the dark boy, "I never dreamed when I was growing up that some day I'd be way out here in the middle of the Pacific Ocean. I used to go down on Saturdays to Long Beach and go swimming and kind of wonder how far it was to the other side but that's about as far as it went."

1

"What were you going to do when you grew up?" asked the blond boy.

The other boy laughed, "I never thought anything about it. I was just going to work in my father's garage when I grew up and some day inherit it . . . and that was about all."

"It must have been swell to have the ocean so near when you were a kid."

"I never thought anything about it. It was just always there, about half an hour from the house. Sometimes when it was foggy in winter we wished we lived a little farther away."

Then they fell silent again and presently without saying anything the tall blond boy rose and went down to throw himself into the water and swim for a time. The other boy lay supporting his head on one arm, vaguely conscious of the beauty of the spectacle. The water was full of phosphorescence and when his companion threw himself into it, it was as if he had thrown himself into fire. The splash was like flame, every drop of water sparkling and glowing like a jewel. And then as the blond boy swam lazily he seemed illumined by light. At each thrust of his arm the water sparkled and shone and at last as he came close to the beach, stood up and walked out of the water, his whole body was outlined in phosphorescence. He was lean with lithe muscles and strong arms and broad shoulders.

The dark boy thought suddenly, "That's the way a fellow must look arriving at the Gates of Heaven." And then quickly, half-ashamed, and half-frightened he put the thought out of his mind. It was a crazy thought. It was one of those thoughts which was taboo. It might bring Tom bad luck. It was funny what this island country and the life did to you, making you think crazy things you'd never think of back in Long Beach.

His companion rejoined him, sitting again to lean against the trunk of the betel palm. He shook the phosphorescent water from his fingers, took a cigarette from the package on the ground beside him and lighted it, leaning back lazily and tilting his blond head to inhale and savor the goodness of the cigarette.

The dark boy, whose name was Jimmy, said, "You never get enough of that water, do you?"

"No," said Tom. "You see, I was born and brought up in Dakota. I never saw the ocean until a year ago."

"Funny," said Jimmy, "about the kids from the Middle West. Porky was tellin' me the other night that about three-fourths of the guys in the Navy come out of the Middle West —kids that never saw the ocean in their lives until they joined up."

Tom stirred and looked out toward the beach where the water rolled up slowly, flickering, iridescent and glowing in the darkness.

"It's a funny thing," he said, "if I ever crash I want to crash in the water and not on land. When I'm over land I'm always kind of uneasy and queer, but when I get out over the ocean everything's okay and I feel fine."

The banjo went on tinkling in some distant tent and after a little while Tom continued, "All the water I ever saw until I was fifteen years old was a pond on the farm. It wasn't much of a pond—just a couple of acres and sometimes in hot weather it very nearly dried up . . . wasn't much more than a mud puddle." He laughed suddenly, "But it was the only water for miles around. The country's kind of flat up there, no trees to speak of . . . it just stretches away as far as you can see. It's kind of lonely. A pond like that made a lot of difference. When I was a little kid it was like a whole ocean to me. I used to wade in it and sail boats on it. When I began to learn geography I used to pretend it was the Atlantic—one side was America and one side Europe. I used to pretend the boats were ocean liners. When I got a little older I saw an advertisement in a Chicago newspaper saying to send for information about trips to Europe. I wrote and sent for it and they sent me back a lot of pictures of ocean liners—inside and out. They were wonderful and after that I built little boats that looked like ocean liners."

He was talking suddenly as if he were alone and talking to himself.

"In spring and fall the wild duck and geese used to stop there sometimes. It was way off their course and I don't know why they came except that when the first ones came my mother used to take wheat and corn out to them. She always had to slip out and do it at night because my father didn't want to see good feed wasted on wild birds. She'd take it to the far end of the pond where it was hidden by the cat-o'-nine-tails and the hazel bushes. The birds would eat it up early in the morning and my father never found out. And so they got to stopping at the pond on the way north and south."

The dark boy yawned and said, "Yeah, it's funny the things you think about when you get homesick. I always think about my old man and the garage."

The blond boy lighted another cigarette. "I think about my mother and my wife . . . and the pond."

"I ain't married. I never had a real girl friend. I used to run around a lot but I didn't go steady."

They were talking suddenly like old experienced men.

The sound of the banjo died away with the final whirring vibration of a string, and there was only the velvety black silence and the sound of insects and the lazy lapping of the surf.

"What's your wife like?" asked Jimmy in a sleepy voice. You could tell he wasn't really very interested. He was half-asleep.

"She's not very big and kind of shy. I've known her ever since I was a kid. Her folks have a big farm about ten miles from us. It's a nice place but it hasn't got a pond. When she was a kid, she was always beggin' to come over to our place to see the pond."

Jimmy didn't say anything and after a long time Tom said, "My wife's going to have a baby."

"When?"

"Any time now."

"It must make you kind of nervous."

Tom laughed, "It seems kind of funny . . . havin' a kid of my own. It don't seem true."

Again the silence intervened and Jimmy said, "I suppose you want a boy."

Tom laughed again, "I don't really care much. I'd kind of like a boy to begin with. I'd like to think of him growin' up there and playin' around the pond like I did when I was a kid."

Jimmy stood up, yawned and stretched and said, "I'm goin' to turn in."

"Okay. I'm goin' to have another swim."

Sleepily Jimmy asked, "Don't you ever get enough of that ocean?"

Tom only laughed and Jimmy walking off toward the tents said, "Don't let the sharks get you."

But Tom was already running down the slope to the sea. He called out, "I'm not scared of sharks or anything in this whole damned ocean."

Jimmy turned to watch Tom's entry into the water in a ring of light. He stood there watching, a little bewildered again by the beauty of the sight. He found himself thinking, "It's like a sea god returning to the sea." And then he turned away and went slowly back to the camp thinking, "I must be going nuts—thinking screwy things like that. It's these damned Pacific islands. I'd better get back to the garage in Long Beach before I really go nuts."

. . . . .

Three times Tom made the lazy circle in the warm phosphorescent water and when he came out he stood there on the white beach looking across the channel toward the dark mass of the island opposite. There was no moon but in the brilliance of the night, there was enough starlight to silhouette the rims of the palm fronds. As he stood with his feet planted in the warm sand he was aware of a faint sense of ecstasy, as if he were no longer himself, an individual, a man standing there on the white beach but only an atom, an infinitesimal particle belonging to this whole universe of palm trees and white sand and space and stars and phosphorescent water, an atom forever immortal and indestructible because he was part of something far greater than himself.

And then quickly the sensation passed and he was himself again—a man, strong and young, who might even now be the father of a baby who would live and grow and become a part of this same universe and go on long after he himself was dead. The fact of death was always there, quite near at hand, but now it seemed to have no great significance, being lost in this greater thing. He felt a sudden desire to weep, not out of any personal sorrow, but out of a sadness that was vast and incomprehensible—the sadness of the whole human race.

A great coconut crab crawled across his foot, rousing him with a start. He did not attempt to kill it or even to touch it. He only stood there watching it waddle ridiculously up the bank toward the knoll where he and Jimmy had been sitting. There was something clumsy and comical and important in its queer gait, something out of a world which had existed before there was any man on earth. He found himself smiling in the darkness.

Then slowly he shook himself and walked up the knoll and back to the tents. They were silent now and dark for all the other boys were asleep.

He did not fall asleep at once for he could not shake off the excitement of the moment on the white beach and he was tormented by homesickness. Lying there in the darkness, beneath the mosquito netting, he kept seeing again the pond and his mother and Sally. But he saw the two women always in relation to the pond. They were standing beside it feeding the ducks which swam there or Sally was cutting the wild iris that grew on the edge of the pond, or they were watching the wild ducks which came to join and feed with their tame cousins. And sometimes he saw Sally and himself as children playing on the shallow, muddy edges of the pond, pushing out their small boats, building little harbors and ports where the tiny boats might tie up. It was a whole ocean—that muddy little pond—a whole universe over which he and Sally were God and Goddess. And he thought how much the pond had been a part of his life and Sally's, how they had grown up there beside it taking each other quite for granted until one day his body told him what love was and how different it was from friendship. Vaguely the pond seemed to have a part in that too. It was beside the pond he had first touched Sally's hand in a new way. It was beside the pond he had first kissed her, knowing that they belonged to each other as simply as the

birds on the pond belonged to each other. It was beside the
pond that he had said, "I'm going to air cadet school. Maybe
we'd better be married before I go away."

He could not say what made him say it just that way, why
he'd asked her to marry him when he was going away almost
at once to leave her alone. Something more powerful than himself, something more powerful even than his conscious love
for her. It was something that had to do with that strange
sensation he had experienced a little while before on the beach,
a sense of being only an infinitesimal part of something vast
and splendorous which had to be carried on. There had been
a kind of fierce urgency about it, and a sense of time running
short. Perhaps that was the reason so many young people were
getting married all over America, why so many young people
were having babies when in ordinary times they didn't get married and if they did, they didn't have babies right away.

And he thought about a lot of other things too, among them
the conversation he had had with Jimmy as they sat there
against the betel palms on the edge of the sea. He didn't think
about what they had said but what they had not said, ponder-
ing what it was that shut men off from each other so that
they could not reveal what lay deepest in their hearts. What
had happened to him just now there on the edge of the phosphorescent water, for example—that he would never be able
to tell anyone, and never would he be able to tell anyone really
how he felt about the pond, how much he loved it, how much
it was a part of himself, how much it had to do with his life,
as if he himself had been born out of its very depths.

While he and Jimmy talked there in the darkness the communication had been through halting, inadequate words.
Jimmy was a tough little guy, but for all that or because of
it, much shyer than himself. Jimmy had talked about Long
Beach and the garage and his father but he hadn't really said
anything at all. The things that were important were the
things they had not said, but *felt* there in the darkness—that
it was good to be young, that it was wonderful to fly, that
being in love was wonderful even for a Don Juan like Jimmy,
that both of them were thinking it would be wonderful to
have their girls there with them, there in the warm starlit dark-

ness—he, his own Sally, Jimmy just any pretty warm-blooded girl.

And he wondered whether men who weren't fighting ever had these feelings without being able to communicate them. Perhaps back home in the daily round of civilian life there wasn't time to think or *feel* things like these, or perhaps all feelings and emotions were blunted by the daily round of monotonous living. Maybe it all had something to do with flying, with fighting, with being near to death. He knew that he was too young to know how it would have been to marry in the monotonous times of peace, to have a wife you loved who was going to have a baby, your baby, in the next room instead of far away from you on the other side of the world.

Maybe it was good—all this he was going through now. Maybe he was lucky to be young and healthy and to be a flier. Maybe if you got through a thing like this you'd know things which other men didn't know—the stay-at-homes who weren't so lucky. What had happened in the last six months he knew suddenly and without doubt would make all the rest of his life richer and bigger.

Sleep wouldn't come and he went on thinking about the things he and Jimmy hadn't said to each other. Jimmy hadn't mentioned his mother at all. Maybe she'd died when he was a kid or maybe, worse than that, she left his father to run off with another man. Of course he hadn't spoken of his own father because there wasn't much he could tell Jimmy. He wouldn't say that his father was a hard man who squeezed every penny—a man who didn't seem to have much human feeling. He'd never understood about the pond or why his wife and his son loved it so deeply. He'd always talked about draining it and using the land to grow crops. No, there wasn't much he could say about his own father.

And presently the humming of the insects made him drowsy. He turned and quickly went to sleep.

·　·　·　·　·

The pond had always been there, little more than a depression in the endlessly flat prairie, stretching away to the horizon

—a depression where the water from the surrounding flatness collected. Before the appearance of the white man the buffalo had come there by the thousand to find water. Indians pitched their tepees beside it during the hunting season, and when the first covered wagons began the long trek across the continent they stopped there to camp and water their horses and cattle. None of them stayed there for they were bound further west, none of them until Abner Wade claimed four sections of land and built a sod house for himself and his family. It was good grazing land with deep soil that would raise wheat, acres and acres of wheat stretching away as far as one could see.

But it wasn't the richness of the land so much as the pond that led Abner to settle there. It was the only piece of water for two days travel in any direction and around it grew a little grove of big cottonwood trees. And all around the edge of the pond there was a little thicket of wild shrubs broken only by the ancient buffalo trails. It was like an oasis in the vast flat desert of buffalo grass.

Abner left the farm to his son who in turn left it to a daughter. The daughter married a Swede, a newcomer into the country, and the Swede was killed a little while afterward, leaving a son who became Tom Peterson's father. The sod house beside the pond became in time a two-room wooden house and at last the farm house where Tom was born and grew up and met Sally and married her. The good land still held out and raised good crops of wheat two years out of three. Tom's father was a good man with cattle and with wheat. He drilled wells and had no more need for the pond.

His wife, Tom's mother, didn't come from the wide, flat prairie country. Axel Peterson, Tom's father, found her at the Iowa State Fair when he went to buy cattle from her father. He was a good-looking, strong, straight-backed fellow of twenty-eight with cold blue eyes and a hard jaw and Annie Wallace, daughter of one of the best cattle breeders in the state, fell in love with him. A half dozen times he went south to court her and at last she married him and went to live in the house by the pond in the bleak, rich wheat country. The first year she bore him a daughter and a year later she had a son they named Thomas after her father and then the doctor told her she could never have any more children. When the little girl was four years old she died of diphtheria. And by that time Annie Wallace no longer loved her husband. By that time she discovered that she came fourth in his heart. His land, his cattle, his bank account all came before her. She knew by then that she had married a peasant very different from the stock she had come from with its comfortable way of life among the streams and rolling, wooded green hills of Iowa.

It was, she knew, a tragedy, but she was a strong woman and made the best of it. When she looked across the table at her husband she understood what had happened to him. The jaw had grown harder, the lips thinner. He was meager and wiry and the long hours he worked in the fields and barns had given him the wrinkled, weather-beaten look of a man ten years older. Being a strong woman, she understood that she was a disappointment to him. He had wanted a peasant for a wife, a big-buttocked woman who would bear him many sons and daughters and, drawn by her pretty face, he had married a woman who came of people whose women had never worked in the fields, a woman who bore him two children and then went barren. She knew what he would do with a Hereford cow who went barren after two calves: he would fatten her up and send her off to the market. Because he was a good Lutheran and a religious man he could not do that with his wife.

And so she tried to fill her life with church work and sewing and a garden, but it was a bleak life. Really all she had in it was the boy Tom and the pond. Tom was a tough little fellow, always tall for his age like his father. He looked like his father's Swedish ancestors but without the hardness in the jaw and mouth and eyes. He had a good hand with cattle and he worked hard in the hours out of school. Very early he had the feeling that he must somehow make up to his father for the brothers he would never have.

But it was the pond that made life endurable for Annie Wallace. She didn't belong in this bleak, flat, treeless country. At home there had been groves of trees and springs and streams and hills. In hill country one lived always with mys-

tery and romance, for over each hill there was a new and unknown world. In this prairie country there was nothing,
nothing as far as one could see, nothing to break the horrible
monotony but the pond. Sometimes Annie thought but for
the pond she would go mad. Beside the streams and lakes of
her Iowa hill country, the muddy little pond wasn't much,
really nothing at all, but in the interminable unbroken flatness
it was a miracle. On moonlit nights its surface turned to silver
with the cottonwoods surrounding it black against the vast
dome of the sky. In June it was rimmed by the blue and yellow of wild iris. Thrushes and quail hid in the shrubs that
bordered it, and in the spring and fall the wild birds came—the
ducks, the geese, the herons and once a pair of wild swan.

When Tom was sixteen he went to Des Moines to school.
She paid for his education out of her own money as well as
for the services of an extra hired hand to replace him, since
that was the only way his father would permit him to go. The
father asked, "What education does a boy need beyond how to
run a farm and know how to raise cattle, especially when he's
going to have this farm some day?"

She knew that whatever it cost her she must save her son
from being forced into the mold of his father.

When Tom went away to school, the pond became the
center of Annie Wallace's whole existence. Sometimes she
would sit in the grass, dreaming, very still, half-hidden in the
bushes watching the wild birds for hours at a time. And then
when she thought of her husband, she was filled with a sudden rush of pity that he was so hard and so narrow, that he
knew and understood so little of the richness of life, that he
never saw the beauty that lay in the sheen of a mallard's wing,
in the lettuce green of the cottonwood leaves in spring or the
warmth that came of a calf's nose nuzzling your hand. He had
made all of his land and the animals that lived upon it no more
than a factory.

When Tom was seventeen her husband first began to talk
about draining the pond. It was, he said, good land going to
waste. The cattle were watered from wells on the range, they
didn't need it any longer.

When she heard him say it the first time she thought wildly,

"If he drains the pond, I'll go away and never come back. I couldn't live without the pond."

But she pretended indifference for she knew that by now his resentment of her had turned at times into a cold hatred because she was so useless. She no longer went near the pond when he was in the house or the barn for fear that simply out of contempt for her and her feelings, he would drain it and stifle all the life that centered in it. She pretended always that she had lost interest in the pond. But secretly, when he did not know it, she still fed the birds and sometimes on hot nights she would leave the house and spend half the night there lying in the grass listening to the croaking of the frogs and the sounds made by the night birds.

The pond was somehow tied up with Tom and Sally. They had played there as children and slowly fallen in love by its side. Sally was a good girl. Annie knew that she couldn't have had a better daughter-in-law, nor one whom she could have known better. When Tom finally went away looking very straight and handsome in his flier's uniform, both she and Sally turned to the pond because it made his absence seem less painful. So long as the pond was there a part of Tom still remained. After Sally found out that she was having a baby they sat together beside it in the long still northern evenings. It meant almost as much to Sally as to herself. She knew that Sally came from her mother's home as much to see the pond as to see her mother-in-law.

And then a month before Sally's baby was expected the two of them went on a visit back to Annie Peterson's home down among the hills and streams and woods of Iowa. It was August and the wheat harvest was over and all that flat dusty country lay hot with an aching heat. It was hot in Iowa but the country was green and the woods and streams made everything different and more bearable. It was the first time Sally had ever seen that lovely, rolling, wooded country and it was like Paradise to her.

They stayed there for three weeks—longer than they had planned because Sally loved the Iowa country so much. They would have stayed and let Sally have the baby there save that her mother wanted so much to have the baby born at home.

Annie Peterson didn't protest. Sally's mother deserved that much satisfaction. Back in the flat country she didn't even have a pond.

They had a letter from Tom every week or two, telling them not very much. He didn't write about what it was like to fly, or how he felt about shooting down Japs. He couldn't tell them where he was. But he did write about the islands and the sea, and a little about the life on a flat-top. He wrote mostly about the sea—what it was like close at hand when the great moving ship left a long trail of fire behind it in the dark waters, about the flying fishes that darted like arrows of silver through the green foam, how from high in the air it was blue and purple and green and around the coral reefs translucent like jade. And almost always he wrote about the pond. Sometimes it seemed ridiculous to them that with all that water around and under him, he should think of that poor little muddy pond there in the flat plains of Dakota.

And so when Annie Peterson thought they couldn't risk waiting any longer, they left Iowa for the Dakota farm. The long trip was hot and wearing and when they arrived at last at the little depot ten miles from the farm, there wasn't any pleasure in returning home. The country stretched away flat and brown as far as the eye could see, trembling a little drunkenly in the heat. Even the Ford which Sally's mother drove to the station was brown with the prairie dust. They climbed in and as Annie Peterson settled herself in the rear seat she thought, "Anyway, there'll be the pond. It'll be cool there tonight. I'll go out and sit by it and listen to the frogs and the birds."

Sally's mother drove slowly and carefully while Sally talked about her visit and how pretty it was down in Iowa. Sally's mother was a tired woman, from the outside world, beaten down by work and the monotony of life in the flat country. Looking at the back of her thin neck under the dusty black hat, Annie Peterson thought, "When Tom comes back, he'll have to take Sally away out of this country. It's too hard and lonely a life for any woman." Then she thought, "If they go I won't have anything left but the pond." But she was a strong woman. She was prepared to face that. In any case she was middle-aged now, getting old. She mustn't stand in the way of young people. Whatever was life in her was passing on through Tom into the baby that was being born soon. It was like a cycle, like the cycle of the life of the pond. There was order and rhythm in it.

The old car rattled slowly along through the dust, past the Heinrich place, past the Downings, past the Lausches. In a moment against the horizon she would be able to see the tall cottonwoods that grew beside the pond. They passed the Gertner place and turned at right angles along the section road. In a second now the feathery cottonwoods would come into view against the gray sky.

The second passed while the old Ford moved slowly along and Sally told her mother about the streams and hills. Then another second and another, but no trees appeared against the horizon. Annie Peterson leaned forward and then actually rubbed her eyes. She thought, "It must be that I need glasses. I've been afraid of that."

She looked again but still there were no trees. She started forward to interrupt Sally and ask her to look and then suddenly she checked herself, terrified, because she already knew what had happened.

Quietly she covered her face with her hands. The tears ran silently down the dry Dakota dust that coated her cheeks. Her face burned with shame for the moment Sally would stop talking and look for the trees which she had loved since she was a little girl, the trees she had begged to be taken to see as a child.

In a little while they turned in at the Petersons to drop off Annie Peterson.

The odd thing was that neither Sally nor her mother said anything about it. They acted as if the ancient trees had not been cut down, as if they did not see the scars in the brown soil where they had once stood nor the ugly gashes in the sunburnt grass where the caterpillar tractors had moved about their ruthless task. They never spoke of the baked mud where the lovely water of the pond had once been.

Annie Peterson got down and pulled her suitcase out of the car after her. The suitcase seemed filled with lead. Sally leaned down and kissed her. "If anything happens," she said, "I'll send Mama over to get you."

Still she did not say anything but her eyes were brimming with tears. Annie Peterson stumbled into the house. That night there was no sound of croaking frogs or night birds. In all the hot interminable flatness there was only an oppressive silence.

．　．　．　．　．

Tom found it good to be back on the ship again. After a time the lazy life in the islands had become tiresome and the men had grown bored with each other. Back on the carrier, there was nothing but the sky overhead and the sea all around, that sea that was blue and purple and emerald and jade colored. On the carrier the wind blew all day and all night, smelling clean of salt and spray.

The carrier turned north among the reefs and atolls. With her went a whole fleet of ships, big and small, cruisers, destroyers, tenders. They moved northward, spread out on the blue sea, looking from high in the air like the fleets of little boats which Tom had once sailed on the pond. After two days a big bomber came out of the clouds from the south and dropped bags of mail on the big deck of the flat-top. A little while later Tom and Jimmy and the other boys stood waiting for letters from home.

There were two for Tom, one from his mother and one from Sally. The one from Sally he read first. It was a long letter, filled with the account of her trip to Iowa with his mother. She wrote of the trees and hills and green pastures. Toward the end she said that she was feeling well and that the doctor said there shouldn't be any trouble about the baby. There wasn't anything to worry about—absolutely nothing at all. As soon as it was born she would send him a radio. She missed him. She loved him. She wished he could be there to see the baby as soon as it was born. She said his mother was writing by the same mail. She enclosed a picture of herself and Annie Peterson standing in front of the big red brick house under the maple trees of Iowa where his mother had been born and had lived as a girl.

The letter from his mother wasn't very long and there was a kind of deadness about it, as if somehow each word had caused her a great effort. It was a tired letter; and slowly as he read it, he felt depression creeping over him. And then at the very end he found the reason. She wrote simply, "Your father drained the pond while I was in Iowa." And then, after her name she had added, "You must not worry about the pond. It makes less difference than I thought it would."

But he didn't believe the lie. He knew why she had written a tired letter. The last thing she had to hang on to was gone from her life. There was Sally and there would be the baby, and perhaps the baby would help take the place of the pond. Suddenly sitting there with the sea wind in his face he found himself praying. "Please Lord, don't let anything go wrong with the baby. They need it so badly—more than I need it. Please, Lord, let everything be all right." And then he thought, "The kid won't have any pond. He won't have any trees or birds or water or mud to play with. He won't have anything but that God-forsaken flat country!"

He felt a sudden wave of hatred for his father and then it seemed to go away, swept clear by the fresh salt air of the sea. It was growing dark and behind the flat-top the sea was becoming alive again with light. The crest of each wave sparkled with light.

Then suddenly Jimmy was standing there behind him. He said, "What's the matter? Not bad news, I hope?"

"No," said Tom, "nothing. I'm just kind of homesick."

"It's wonderful to get letters," said Jimmy, "if they only didn't make you think about home."

Tom thrust the letters into the pocket of his shirt and stood up.

Jimmy said, "Looks like we'd get some action tomorrow."

"How do you know?"

Jimmy grinned, "We didn't come all the way up here just for an airing."

It turned out that Jimmy was right. They got their briefing a little after noon the next day. Their job would be to protect the bombers in an assault on an island that lay a little way off, still too far for the range of the land-based fighters. Tom was glad of the prospect for action. The news about the pond had left him alternately depressed and furious. Late that night he had written an angry letter to his father and then torn it up, believing it would do no good and only perhaps make things worse for his mother. Instead he wrote a letter to his mother saying that when the war was over and he returned, he would take her and Sally and the baby back to Iowa, to the country she loved. That he knew would be the best thing he could promise her; that would give her hope. It would make it a little easier to go on living on that bare, treeless, plain.

That night he dreamed of the pond.

. . . . .

It was three o'clock when the attack began. The empty deck was filled suddenly with men hurrying here and there, with the roar of motors tuning up as the great ship turned round and headed into the wind. And then one by one the planes took off.

In Tom, standing there, waiting for his fighter to move up into line, the old excitement came burning back into his veins. He was one of those who were made for flying. Something happened to him, something queer and unearthly. From the moment the plane started into motion, he became a man no longer earthbound who entered upon another level of existence. It was the take-off and the landing which he loved best —that moment when suddenly you were free of the earth and the moment when returning out of vast heights, out of the clouds you once more came back to the ship. It was like being a god descending among men. Flying for him wasn't just a matter of gasoline and engines and steady nerves and quick reactions. He had the nerves and the reactions to make him a good flier but it was more than that. A first-rate flier became one with his plane so that nothing separated them until one or the other was wounded or failed.

It was different with Jimmy. He felt a plane the way he ran an earthbound automobile, skillfully at high speed, but in his heart and mind the machine was something he drove, always apart from it. When he climbed aboard it was like jumping into the old coked-up jalopy which he used to drive in races along the city block back in Long Beach.

Just now he was standing near Tom, his legs spread a little to balance himself against the gentle rocking of the big flat-top in the long ground swell of the Pacific. He was watching the curious expression on Tom's face and suddenly he shouted above the wind and the roaring of the motors. "What are you lookin' at?"

The rapt expression disappeared and Tom grinned. "Nothing," he shouted back, "just thinking."

Then Jimmy thought, "It must be the hick in him. Everything is always new and wonderful." Then he moved forward to his ship.

At the same moment across the deck came running a boy called Skippy. He was one of the radio operators. He'd worked in W.T.A.M. in Cleveland before the war. He carried a bit of paper in his hand and came running straight for Tom who didn't see him. Skippy had to come quite close and shout in his ear.

He handed Tom the paper and shouted, "She came through all right, Pappy! Thought you'd like to know!"

Then it was Tom's turn up and as he ran he read what was typed on the bit of paper. It was brief enough. It read: "Fine boy. Everybody okay. Love Sally."

He thrust the bit of paper into his pocket, climbed aboard and opened her up. She gained speed, reached the edge and leapt off into the air above the brilliant blue water, banking a little and climbing to reach her place in the formation.

Below on the deck Skippy the radio operator stood shielding his eyes against the sun as Tom's ship climbed toward it and disappeared into the brilliance of its light. Then he turned and said to the sailor standing next to him, "It was against the rules . . . givin' him that message but Hell, goin' off like that and maybe never comin' back, I thought he'd like to know about the kid."

Higher and higher the plane climbed toward the sun until Tom found his place in the formation. Then he turned and over his shoulder watched the last few planes leaving the deck. It was a pretty sight—like the barn swallows coming out at dusk to dart over the pond, hunting insects. The big ship slowly churning the dark green water into a pale jade color grew smaller and smaller and more remote.

Then he heard a voice speaking to him: "This is Jimmy . . . Jimmy. Not bad news, was it?"

He answered back, "No. Good news! It's a boy—everybody's fine."

Then he heard Jimmy relaying the news exuberantly to the others, and then the Commander's voice, "Congratulations, Peterson . . . and now let's muffle all the gossip."

But Tom, high above the sea, alone in his plane, pulled out the bit of paper and read the message again. He couldn't quite believe it. He felt warm all over and then thought, "What's there to be proud about? You're not the only father in the world." And then suddenly he experienced a curious feeling of awe and fright. He was responsible for another life in the world . . . he and Sally together. It kind of scared you.

High up now, all the air about him was filled with clouds, those great white, lazily drifting clouds that hung over the blue South Pacific night and day. Suddenly one by one the ships in the formation would plunge into the mist and be lost for a time as if they had gone out of this world into a white, still misty, eternity. And then suddenly, one by one, they would emerge again into the brilliant light of the sun.

Tom's heart and body were singing.

.   .   .   .   .

The target showed up after a little over an hour. It was a little cluster of islands grouped haphazardly about a bigger green island with a small bay on one side and the white streak of a runway made of broken coral rock. In the little bay there was a big ship and what looked like a destroyer and a lot of barges.

The orders began to come in out of the air. He was aware suddenly that the clouds about them seemed bigger and there were more of them. Then out of a cloud on the left appeared three Zeros. They darted at the bombers but two of the boys ahead, breaking formation, went after them and drove them off. Then suddenly Tom's turn came and he let her drop straight down, leveling off at just the angle to catch a Zero full in the middle with a burst of fire. The burst seemed to break the back of the Jap plane. It exploded in flames and then plummeted downward, falling in two smoking bits of debris.

After that it became a general dog-fight, the fighters darting and dodging like hawks while the bombers did their work. Now and then he had a sudden glimpse at a freakish angle of what was going on, like pictures in a kaleidoscope—the big ship burning, bombs falling on the long white runway going up in great flowers of flame and smoke, bombs falling among the barges and on the crescent of the white beach. And in the midst of all the fighting there was a lot of flak. Sometimes it came quite close and again it was far away.

And Tom, a part of the plane itself, kept wheeling and turning and diving and climbing. He was laughing with excitement and thinking now and then, "Tommy. Your pappy is up here in the clouds having a grand time." There was no sense of time. It was as if everything was happening at once. There were more planes and more flak than they had expected.

Then suddenly he was again on the tail of a Zero in the long darting swoop of a bank. It brought him in low over the island. The Zero swooped into a cloud and Tom followed. It was a big cloud and in it he lost the Zero. It seemed impossible to get out of it, out of the swirling, drifting veils of mist. The few minutes seemed like hours and then suddenly he was in the sunlight again directly over the island and there was a violent explosion close beside him which turned the plane over on its side and then another which came all at once with the shattering of the instrument panel in front of him. The plane started to slip and he pulled her back and then he realized that something was blinding him and wiping the back of his hand across his left eye he discovered that blood was running into his eyes. He knew too that the radio had gone dead and that something was wrong with the left wing of the plane. It wouldn't respond.

He thought, "It can't be very bad if I don't feel anything." And then, "Hell, I'd better get out of here. I'm in no shape to fight anything." He looked back over his shoulder and high above coming toward him there was another Zero. It was the Jap's turn now.

He acted quickly. Softly he said, "Come on, honey" and turned the ship toward the great cloud. He was nearer to it than the Zero but the Zero was coming at terrific speed. He couldn't turn and fight back now. That thick, white, soft, fleecy cloud was safety, life. The plane responded. He turned sharply. The Zero fired but the angle was wrong. It dropped close beside him, so near that his plane shuddered a little.

Then suddenly he was in the cloud.

It was thicker than the other clouds had been. He drove the plane straight forward, deeper and deeper into the white drifting mist. Crippled, his plane could not possibly hope to fight. There was only one course, to drive straight ahead until he was out of range of attack and then turn and limp back to the others or the carrier. And then he remembered suddenly—the instrument board was smashed and the radio dead. He could not talk to the others. He did not know his direction. He was alone.

After a time he veered a little to the left thinking he would swing round in a wide circle. The cloud thinned for a moment and he came out into the sunlight. Ahead of him only a little way loomed another great cloud painted rose by the light of the setting sun. He thought, "I am lost and the sun is going down." Down below there was nothing but water, dark now, almost lead-colored.

There was only one thing to do—drop down out of the cloud and hope to find one of his own squadron or a ship or an island. Quietly in a long slow dive he dropped out of the immense cloud into the gathering darkness.

Down below there was nothing but the sea as far as he could see—not a ship, not a plane, not a piece of land. He did not even know where he was. Only the sun, slipping down to the edge of the horizon, showed him where the west lay.

"We came out of the sun," he thought. "If I fly back into it I will be going in the right direction."

The blood no longer ran into his eyes. He was alone in the universe above the darkening sea. Ahead of him the red sun slipped lower and lower, quickly, as it does in the tropics. He thought quite calmly, "I must get back. I've got to get back somehow on account of the kid."

Below him the water grew first red and then purple and as the sun slipped below the horizon it was suddenly black and the stars came out overhead.

For a moment he had a strange sensation of being already dead—as if he and his plane had become no more than a spirit speeding toward the sun. Quickly he experienced again that strange feeling he had known for a moment on the beach, of being only a part of the universe, no more than a grain of the powdered coral beneath his feet.

Then he was aware that the motor was sputtering and thought, "The gas line must have been hit. The gas must have been leaking. She's running out of gas." And then quite calmly, "This is it! This is where I go over the line."

He wasn't afraid. He felt very calm and still and his head ached a little. The plane was dropping lower and lower, pitching forward a little. He thought, "Now I'll never take Ma and Sally and the baby away to Iowa." And he thought suddenly of the pond, seeing it very clearly as he had seen it as a boy with the tall cottonwoods breaking the dreariness of the flat plains, the water ruffled a little by the hot breeze of summer, glittering in the Dakota sun. And then he remembered that it was no longer there—that his father had drained it. He thought desperately, "The boy must have a pond! The boy and Ma must have it back again!"

Then the world crashed about him in utter blackness as his head struck the metal of the shattered instrument board.

In the dark sea beneath the stars there was an uprushing of water as if it sought to embrace the stricken plane and its pilot. Like flame the leaping water glittered and flared with phosphorescence, scattering tiny jewels over the surface of the sea. Then all was still again with only the stars overhead. And far off on the horizon a lonely new moon.

· · · · ·

The baby was born a week after Annie Peterson and Sally returned from Iowa. Its coming made the disappearance of the pond a little less awful for Annie. In the days of waiting she never looked out of the windows on the side of the house where the pond had been, and in the hot nights when she could not sleep, there was no longer any place for her to go to listen to the rustle of leaves and the croaking of frogs and the sounds made by the night birds. Outside there was only stillness like the stillness of a dead, empty world.

For three days before the baby was born, Annie went every day to the house of Sally's mother, staying late so that when she came home it was too dark to see the place where the pond had been. In the hot sun, the mud had dried quickly and Peterson was already breaking it up to plant winter wheat.

The baby came early on a Thursday morning and the first thing Annie did was to drive into town to send a radio to Tom. The telegraph office hadn't even opened by the time she got there and she had to wait outside for nearly half an hour.

Impatiently she asked Olaf Jensen, the operator, how long it would take for the radio to reach Tom and he said he didn't know. It depended on where Tom was. Sometimes it took only a day or two and sometimes a week. They'd have to find out where Tom was.

Then Annie went to the drugstore and got a roll of films and when Sally felt well enough to sit up Annie took three pictures of her holding the baby and then three pictures of the baby naked save for a diaper. He was a fat baby with a little blond fuzz on the top of his head and Sally said he looked like Tom and had Tom's blue eyes, and Annie, although she knew you couldn't tell what a baby looked like at that age or what color his eyes were going to be, agreed with her because she knew that was what Sally wanted. Each day they speculated a good deal as to when the radio message would reach Tom and what he would say in his reply.

The thing happened five days after the baby was born. It was a hot night and Annie Peterson wakened at the still hour of the morning when tired, old people die, conscious of the faint light from the new moon shining through the window across her bed. For a long time she lay there trying to go back to sleep, but her mind kept her awake, darting here and there to thoughts about Tom, far away in the South Pacific, to Sally

and the baby and the baby's future and now and then to
memories of the vanished pond. And presently when she grew
drowsy again it seemed to her that she heard the sound of
lapping water among reeds as she had heard it so many times
before the pond had vanished.

Rousing herself she put the notion forcibly out of her head
but she still kept hearing the sound despite everything. After
a time she thought, "Maybe it's just something I dreamed.
Maybe he didn't drain the pond. Maybe it was only a nightmare." But when she thought back, she connected it up with
many things and how she had always come home from Sally's
mother's house after dark so she wouldn't see the bare dry
place where the pond had been. She knew, sadly, that it wasn't
a dream but she still kept hearing the lapping of the water although it was a still night without the sign of a breeze.

When the experience became no longer bearable, she rose
and in her nightdress walked the length of the house and
looked out of the window on the other side where the pond
had been.

And there in the moonlight was the pond like a burnished
sheet of silver, just as it had been before save that the cottonwoods were gone and the bushes and the reeds. Slowly as if
in a trance, Annie Peterson walked down the stairs, opened the
door and barefooted crossed the burnt grass down to the edge
of the pond. She was crying now and still she could not believe it. She did not believe it until she had walked into the
water and stood there, still weeping hysterically, wet with
cool water half-way to the waist. She thought, "How glad
Tom will be! I must send him a radiogram." He would be
almost as happy as he'd be about the baby.

.   .   .   .   .   .

The news of the miracle spread quickly over the county.
The words "Peterson's pond is back" went from mouth to
mouth and by nine o'clock people were driving from all over
the countryside to look at it. The miracle was even greater than
Annie Peterson had guessed, for this time the pond was a *live*
pond. Somewhere in the bottom a spring had come to life. It

wasn't any longer just a seepage hole. Living water had filled all the depression and was running over, making its own channel across Peterson's wheat ground into the ditch that bordered the long straight highway. There was running water in the county where before there had never been any water but Peterson's muddy pond surrounded by cottonwood trees.

Among the onlookers the speculations grew. Annie Peterson was among them telling over and over again of how she had wakened in the middle of the night to go out and find the pond. And Sally was there, who should still have been in bed, for Annie had hurried over at daylight to fetch her.

The county engineer said there must have been underground water there all the time and that Peterson's blasting of the cottonwood stumps had loosened the shale underneath so that the water worked its way upward. But most people thought that a fishy explanation which was the only one the county engineer could think up. A lot of people said, "Tom'll be glad to hear about this. He always liked that pond."

The whole crowd was filled with the kind of mystical awe and excitement which touches dry-country people at the sight of running water, for water is a source of life and ties all living things together. Only one man among them all was disgruntled and that was Peterson himself. The new spring had wasted all his good land and all the money he had spent clearing and draining the pond. He wouldn't try it again. It wasn't any good fighting a spring.

A week later came Tom's letter saying that when he returned he would take his mother and Sally and the baby away from that dry, flat country now that there wasn't any more pond. Reading it, Annie Peterson paused and looked up at Sally, saying, "He must know about the pond coming back by now. He must have got my radiogram by now. He's sure to know about it."

The baby was doing fine and Sally had come over to spend a week with her mother-in-law. They spent a lot of time making plans about the pond. You couldn't get back the cottonwoods. It had taken God a hundred years to make them. But you could plant other trees and shrubs and iris to replace the wild iris Peterson had killed so ruthlessly. They sent for nursery catalogues and marked the trees and shrubs they would buy in the spring to plant around the water. This time they'd plant a little grove where thirsty people from all the dry flat country around could come for picnics by the edge of the pond. They wanted it well started before Tom came back. Peterson couldn't stop them now. He could never drain the pond for God had taken a hand in the matter.

Henry Orr was the postman for their part of the county. He was an old man with a huge mustache and he was very slow in delivering the mail because he was a gossip as well as a postman and stopped to talk at every house along the way. There wasn't anything Henry didn't know about the county— when a cow died or a girl got into trouble or how Grandma Beattie's rheumatism was. He read postcards and had a power of divination concerning the contents of letters he never quite dared to open. And so he was the first to know that Tom Peterson was dead. He knew it as soon as he saw the envelope, and all along his route he hinted darkly that there was bad news for Annie and Sally Peterson.

It was noon by the time old Henry arrived at the Peterson Place and found Annie and Sally Peterson outside by the edge of the pond planting something, with the baby in the carriage by their side.

At sight of them old Henry lost his courage. As they called out, "Good morning" to him, he carefully rearranged the packet of mail. There was a letter from Iowa and two nursery catalogues and some advertising from a mail-order house. Carefully old Henry placed the awful envelope in the middle and retied the bundle, knotting it so that it would take them a long time to undo the string. That would give him time to get away, so he wouldn't have to see their faces.

Annie Peterson was coming toward him now and he got briskly down and went to meet her.

"A mighty fine morning," he said. "It's sure fine to have the pond back again. Always makes me feel good to see it."

Then he gave Annie Peterson the packet of mail and turned toward his battered car, hurrying but trying not to run. Once in the car he drove off as if the devil were after him.

By the edge of the pond the two women sat down again on

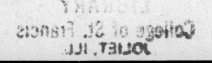

the grass and Annie picked out the knots old Henry had tied so tightly. By the time she had it open, Henry's old car was far out of sight in a cloud of dust.

Almost at once Annie saw the envelope and almost at once she *knew*. She wanted to make the envelope vanish out of sight into thin air for Sally's sake, but Sally was watching, hoping there would be a letter from Tom. And Sally knew too.

Slowly, as if the slowness made it easier and more casual, she tore open the envelope and read what she knew she would read.

Neither she nor Sally said anything nor looked at each other. They simply sat there looking at the pond where the little waves of clear spring water danced and glittered and sparkled in the autumn sunlight.

And then Annie, as if unbelieving, looked at the bitter sheet of paper again, and presently a strange look of wonder came into her face. Her eyes seemed suddenly to shine and slowly she turned to Sally looking at her for the first time.

"Sally," she said in a quiet voice filled with awe, "it happened on September 16th . . . that was the night of the new moon— the same night the pond came back."

DEATH IN MONTE CARLO

THE GREAT SQUARES AND CANALS HAD BEEN STILL NOW FOR DAYS with the stillness of death. The boats which at this time of year usually went to and from the Lido filled with duchesses and millionaires and ballet dancers and gigolos, moved back and forth empty save for a few middle aged and elderly porters and waiters and beach servants. It was a curious frightening stillness in Venice in July, like the hush before an earthquake or the eruption of a volcano. The exodus of foreigners had begun a week earlier, the rich English and Americans fleeing like lemmings to Genoa and Naples to wait for boats that would carry them to a luxury in the new world which still was not menaced. They were all rich or they lived off the rich, a whole world of people who sought only pleasure and had no loyalties and in reality very little nationality save that attached by the accident of birth or marriage to the passports they carried with them, the passports of a protection provided for them by the men and women who stayed at home and worked to create great and solid nations. Mrs. Pulsifer who knew nearly all of them and had lived in the midst of them for nearly fifty years, always contemptuous and aloof, called these lemmings "International White Trash."

She had lived among them most of her life because as a young girl she had fallen in love with a London banker and married him, and so from the respectable life of Beacon Hill and the North Shore of Massachusetts, she had been translated suddenly into another world which in the beginning frightened and confused her by its irresponsibility and its ruthlessness. After twenty years she had come to accept it, as a fact if nothing else, and after thirty she had come to find entertainment in it, but always with detachment as a spectator, never as a part of it. And always she kept as a thing apart, like a precious jewel in a casket, her own integrity and the conviction that work and honesty and responsibility were not quali-

28

ties to be made the objects of mockery. Sometimes in the world in which she lived, her secret convictions left her a very lonely woman, isolated even from her own husband whose behavior even her love for him could not, sometimes, condone.

When her husband died (and she loved him despite all the evil she knew of him as an international banker until he died) she tried to go back to Boston to live. But it was no good; she found it was too late to turn back. She missed the scandals, the skullduggeries, the immorality, the intrigues of the world in which she had spent nearly the whole of her life. Without the "International White Trash" she found life very dull. And so she sold whatever property she had in Boston, closed the great London house and turned everything but a few jewels into cash, and set out to live what remained of her life as a nomad— not living in a tepee and cooking her meals in a pot over an open fire, but as a luxurious nomad camping only in the great *hotels de luxe* all over the world, traveling in a rather high old-fashioned Rolls-Royce that had belonged to her husband and driven by a rather remarkable Cockney driver called 'Ennery who had driven her husband for twenty years. 'Ennery like a good many of the "International White Trash," spoke pidgin versions of a half dozen languages. He knew the great hotels of Paris and Moscow, Venice and London and Bucharest and Deauville. He understood the art of bribery and knew evil and incriminating facts about a great many famous people, bankers and millionaires, politicians and statesmen. He could have been a blackmailer but he was not because, like his employer, Mary Pulsifer, he found life a spectacle in which experience had taught him to accept everything and find nothing very surprising.

'Ennery and Mrs. Pulsifer got on very well together, and together, in a little more than ten years, they had covered thousands of miles of Europe, Asia and North and South America. The Rolls-Royce had ample trunk room on the top and a built-in bar for the entertainment of Mrs. Pulsifer's friends among the International White Trash. They were always turning up everywhere—in Egypt, in Singapore, in Hong Kong, even in such unlikely and out-of-the-way places as Kansas City and Houston, Texas.

Always on their travels the conventions between servant and mistress were respected scrupulously, for Mrs. Pulsifer was not among those women of her world who changed the color of their hair, and stood on their heads and had their faces lifted in order to preserve an unconvincing illusion of youth. God gave her a spare, thin figure, and her old-fashioned dignified carriage defied the piling up of years. She wore expensive, rather old-fashioned clothes made for her in Paris by Worth and about her thin throat a narrow black ribbon. Her hair she wore on top of her head with a slight suggestion of a pompadour, and on top of the hair, rather high, she wore Queen Alexandra hats, adorned in summer with a bunch of violets and in winter with a bird. She had a style of her own, a great style which nothing, not time, nor disasters, nor great dressmakers, could alter, a style recognized by those—the great dressmakers, the headwaiters, the head porters—who knew the signs of a rich woman, of impregnable position and unassailable character.

In all the world, out of hundreds of acquaintances among the great, the rich and the notorious, 'Ennery, the Cockney driver, remained her closest friend after the death of her husband. He was a beefy man with graying hair, a broad face and small, shrewd blue eyes. Most of Europe and half the world knew the rather high old Rolls-Royce with 'Ennery at the wheel and Mrs. Pulsifer sitting rather high, like royalty or a bird on a perch, in the back.

When the German army swept over the border and across France, Mrs. Pulsifer and 'Ennery were at the Ritz in Paris. They stayed there until the last minute partly because Paris was allowed no news of the gravity of the situation and partly because both Mrs. Pulsifer and 'Ennery liked the excitement. They left Paris only the day before the Germans entered it in the high Rolls-Royce bound southward with the vast and pitiful mob of refugees. After Orléans, they disappeared and no news could be found of them, either by the officials of her late husband's bank or by ambassadors, or any of the many relations, English and American, most of them International White Trash, who hoped to inherit from her and so followed her curious nomad life with a more than normal interest.

The last news to be had of Mrs. Pulsifer and 'Ennery before the débâcle was from a bank official fleeing Paris for the South in a car filled with bank records. He had seen the old Rolls-Royce in the Square at Orléans. In it, besides Mrs. Pulsifer and 'Ennery, were three peasant women and seven children, and on the roof lashed among Mrs. Pulsifer's expensive Vuitton bags and trunks were a perambulator, three mattresses, a goat and a large cheese. In the Square, jammed with women and children and nuns and old men and women, which had been machine-gunned by a German dive-bomber a few minutes before, Mrs. Pulsifer had opened the built-in bar and, aided by 'Ennery, was passing out brandy to the wounded.

. . . . .

The Princess D'Orobelli awakened in Venice having dreamed of Mrs. Pulsifer. She could not think why for she had not seen Mary Pulsifer for years. The Princess herself was a nomad, restlessly following the seasons from capital to capital and resort to resort, and in the past her path and that of Mary Pulsifer frequently crossed. They were friendly, although never very intimate, because there was nearly twenty years difference in age and there was something in Mary Pulsifer, rigid and unbending like her own Edwardian figure, which checked the loose, easy-going sort of relationship which passed for intimacy in the amoral, devil-take-the-hindmost world in which they both lived. In other words, the Princess was International White Trash and Mary Pulsifer, although she frequented the same world, was not. Mary Pulsifer, like her driver, 'Ennery, was always outside, aloof, watching the show but taking no part in it.

As she wakened and pulled the bell-rope above her gilt baroque bed, the Princess was aware of a feeling of strangeness. It was as if the city outside her palace had died. There were no sounds of life, no jubilation, no shouting, not even the ordinary familiar cries and laughter of Venice out of season in peacetime. Then as she yawned and raised her arms above her head, she remembered that Venice had been deserted in full season by the lemmings and that a declaration of war might only be a few hours distant. It might already have happened—that Frenchmen and Italians were fighting each other at the border. It was all fantastic and unreal and annoying, but at the moment it concerned her less than the consciousness that her arms, as she raised them above her head, were no longer firm and round and solid. As she raised them she was aware that the muscles sagged away from the bone. They were flabby. Someone—it was Mary Pulsifer herself—had once referred to that sort of arm cruelly as "kimono arms."

At forty-eight the Princess still looked remarkably handsome but it was the kind of look which led people to say of a woman that she was "remarkably well-preserved." It was not the youthfulness born of a placid life, of good humor, of balanced living, of a genuine, primitive kind of happiness. It came out of bottles and jars and hot towels and ice and violent physical exercise taken earnestly every morning in a routine fashion. For in her own life there had never been any of the natural well-being that breeds youthfulness. Since she was eighteen years old and married Count Pavloff, it had been a stormy and corrupt life.

With disgust she lowered her arms, scratched the tip of her nose where she felt a small irritation, and sat up propping the lace pillows behind her. She touched her nose carefully with one lacquered nail for her face was covered with grease and she hated the feel of it on her fingers. She hated the feel and smell of it because both things were associated with the knowledge that she was growing older each night. And she was fanatically concerned with personal cleanliness, bathing always twice a day, as if like Lady Macbeth some dark inward part of her were conscious always of some filth which might be washed away if only she bathed often enough.

Then the door opened and Serafina came in. Serafina was a fat Italian woman of about the same age as the Princess with hair still black and black eyes that were like gimlets. Unlike the Princess she had never made any attempt to make herself "smart." Although she went everywhere as the maid of the Princess and knew the servants of the richest and most notorious people everywhere, she still remained a provincial Italian woman from Padua, her ample form dressed always in rather rusty black bombazine. She had character and so she became well-known all over Europe as May D'Orobelli's Serafina. She liked the varicolored existence she led; she liked the luxury, the scandals, the gossip. She was at heart a peasant, earthy, shrewd, eternal and indestructible. She was attached to her mistress through long habit and association, but she had no illusions. She knew that she held her job and had held it for thirty years because she knew much too much about her mistress and because when her mistress got into a tight place of one sort or another (which she was constantly doing) her own courage, wit, ingenuity and advice were indispensable.

She came in carrying the tea and as she entered she said brightly, "*Buon giorno! Principessa.*"

"*Buon giorno*, Serafina." The sight of the maid's thick, stalwart figure cheered her. So long as she had Serafina everything was all right. Lovers could come and go. Wars could rage, disasters occur, but so long as they were together they made an unbeatable team.

"Any news?" she asked as Serafina placed the tea tray across her thighs.

"No news!" said Serafina. "No war yet, but things are going very badly for the French."

The Princess laughed. It was a hard, bitter, brittle sound. "Not badly enough yet for the jackals to attack the wounded lion."

Serafina's face became grave. "You should not speak like that, Excellency. I do not mind. My feelings are like your own . . . like all the honest people in Italy. It isn't that, but someone might hear you."

She poured out the tea, doing it as she had done it every morning for thirty years past, with just the right amount of milk and sugar. "It's all very well to trade on being an American and having the Embassy get you out of the troubles you make for yourself, but it's different now. This is practically wartime and this is different. In Italy you're still the wife of his Excellency and his Excellency is Italian, so by law it makes you Italian too." She gave a deep sigh, "And this is different from other wars. This is a war of desperation. The Italians have been misled, but they're so far along on the wrong path that they have to fight and win to survive."

She was aware that the Princess was listening with only half an ear, but she went on just the same as she crossed the huge pink and gilt bedroom to pull back the curtains and let in the sunlight. It was a bright morning and Venice should have been crowded with foreigners. There should have been laughter and the sound of music in the canals and the squares when Serafina drew back the curtains. But there was only silence.

"And money is not going to help you any more. They'll just take it away from you and don't argue about it. That's what all the rich in Italy and Germany thought—that Mussolini and Hitler were going to save them and their money, and look at them now. They've taken all their money and their property and their factories and turned them into the streets or chased them out of the country."

The Princess stopped listening altogether about the middle of the speech. She was sick of talk about Hitler and Mussolini and Communism and Fascism and sanctions and all the other things which made the world an unpleasant place. She had been sick of it all for years now. Serafina was always expecting calamities which never came. For thirty years she herself had done as she pleased, living outside the law, because she was rich. And always she had gotten away with it, so what reason was there to worry now?

Impatiently she asked, "Were there any messages?"

"No," said Serafina, knowing perfectly well what her mistress meant by "messages."

Before the maid went into the bathroom to turn on the bath, she paused, filling the whole doorway with her stalwart figure. "Venice is silent," said Serafina, "because all the foreigners have gone. Without foreigners, Venice is a dead city. Without foreigners, half of Venice will starve. And Venice is silent because her sons have been called off to a war they don't want and don't understand. The mothers and sisters and sweethearts grieve without glory. Venice will be a dead city as she was before the foreigners came. We may not see them again for fifty years. Horrible as they are, they meant prosperity to Venice."

The Princess poured another cup of tea. "If I did not know you so well, Serafina, I would say you were being insolent."

Serafina stood her ground, "Perhaps I am," she said and disappeared into the bathroom.

By "messages" the Princess had meant only "message" and that only from one man. He was the reason she remained behind when all the other lemmings had fled. He was in the army now. She didn't know where he was although she thought it likely that he was north of Milano. He was very precious to her, not so much because she loved him as because attractive lovers were no longer easy to find at her age. He might be the last lover she would ever have. She did not know whether he had sent her no message because he was not permitted to, or because he was indifferent. The reason did not trouble her; she was far beyond suffering through pride or the softness of her feelings. She had no illusions. They were fond of each other, but no more than that. She found him attractive because he was young, but she was not exigent; she had seen too often in her world the amorous disasters which engulfed exigent women. She had been married to His Excellency, the Prince, for ten years and had not seen him save occasionally in the distance for five. Nor had she any illusions about the lover. He was like herself, sensual and vigorous, and from her he had rich presents and fine uniforms for which she paid, and a speedboat. Some people might have called all this "keeping" him, but the thought did not trouble her; she had been independent and disillusioned for too long.

And yet, as she sat up in the baroque bed, drinking her tea, she was aware of an ache and a faint sense of terror. What if he should be killed in this idiotic war? At thirty-two he was too young to die, too young and too beautiful even if he had nothing whatever to do with her. She liked good-looking young men; there were times when watching a troop of *Bersaglieri* or Alpini passing on the street, she had seen among the common soldiers a boy whose beauty produced the same curious ache and tightness in her throat. She could not think of Tino as wounded or dead. He was the only thing in the world she loved almost as much as her jewels.

As she had grown older the jewels had become more and more important to her. It was as if she could only compensate for each new wrinkle or gray hair by adding another clip or bracelet to the slow fading of her beauty. They were famous jewels; not ten women in the world, not any queen, had more wonderful emeralds and diamonds and rubies. She loved them not only for their brilliance and beauty but because as she had grown older, she had become more hard and avaricious. They represented a fortune, but they represented more than that, for they were the perfect symbol of wealth and the power of money by which she had always lived, arrogantly, lawlessly. When she wore her jewels she had a strange feeling of safety; with money you could buy what you wanted; with money you could buy your way out of any crime, out of any disaster.

Bending over the bathtub Serafina knew what her mistress was thinking—that she was worried over two things, Tino and her jewels and most of all over her jewels. "She can," thought Serafina, grunting as she leaned far over, "buy herself a new lover anytime, but there are two or three diamonds and emeralds and rubies she could never replace."

In their brief exchange of words over the "message" question, neither of them had been specific or mentioned names. There was no need to and Serafina had the perfect tact of the perfect servant, always pretending that she was blind, deaf and half-witted even on those occasions when she had come upon her mistress in remarkably compromising situations. All that was Her Excellency's problem, and Serafina wanted none of it for herself.

She threw a spoonful of verbena bath salts into the tepid water, gave it a stir or two with her big peasant's hands and turning to the door said, "The bath is ready, Excellency."

*   *   *   *   *

At noon there was still no "message" and May D'Orobelli, nervous, irritable and a little tired, sat down alone to eat an

orange and a few leaves of lettuce at a table in her bedroom
overlooking the silent canal. She was in a bad temper and
so instead of descending to the big dining-room she had
Serafina bring the lettuce and orange and a cup of black coffee
to her bedroom.

She did not speak to Serafina at all and presently Serafina,
as if talking to herself, muttered, "There is no use in people
being bad-tempered because their plans are upset. Today nobody is any better than a pea dropped out of a pod in the
middle of the road. One kind of people has had everything
their own way for years and years and now all that is changed
and they're going to be like everybody else." She clattered the
dishes indignantly and added, "Nobody knows what is going
to come of it but anyway the world is going to be different."

The Princess said, sourly, "You're turning Communist and
Fascist just like all the rest."

"I'm not turning anything, Excellency. Only I can see a fly
on the end of my nose. What's going on is going on, from
China to Hollywood and nothing is going to change it. I'm
an ignorant woman but God gave me as much sense as a horse.
A lot of Romans once thought Rome could never fall." And
with that dark insinuation, Serafina cleared away the remnants
of lettuce and sailed out of the room.

The prophecies of Serafina did nothing to raise the spirits
of the Princess. When the maid had gone she lay down on the
chaise longue and closed her eyes. She did not fall asleep because some part of her consciousness kept listening, for a laugh,
for a shout, for the cry of a peddler, for any sound which
would break the deathly unnatural silence of the empty
melancholy city outside her window. And as she lay there she
considered herself and her history in relation to Serafina's dire
prophecies, with a detachment that was remarkable and rare
in a woman so egotistical and selfish.

She knew what Serafina meant by her "cracks"—that her
mistress was one of those who had been born with everything,
who had never had to work, nor to fight for anything save the
desires of her own idle, voluptuous body. She had been born
rich, cradled in the wealth piled up out of railroads and steel
and banking by a ruthless and unscrupulous father who, she

admitted to herself, with all the cynicism and disillusionment of a hard woman, should have spent his whole life in jail. And she had married two husbands who had wanted her for her money as she wanted them as façades behind which she could lead the life she chose. She had never had any illusions about them, even as a girl of eighteen. She had always bought what she wanted, as her father had bought Senators and governors and Congressmen in his day. She had even paid her husbands to keep out of the way.

And now Serafina was making dark slurs and insinuations and there was no message from Tino and all her jewelry was in a safe deposit box in a foreign bank in Rome and she was tired but (she thought) "still stubborn and hard." They couldn't defeat her. They couldn't break her, not all of them together. She would be no "pea dropped from the pod in the middle of the road." The money, the jewels, this palace, like the house in Newport and the villa in Rome, and all the money tied up in good American tax-exempt bonds, were hers. Her father had worked for them and left them to her; how dared the riff-raff of the world to threaten what was hers, what gave her power and the right to lawlessness.

Out of the half-conscious, dreaming state, she was roused by a knock at the door. Drowsily she said, "Come in," thinking, "Damn it, can't I ever have any peace?" And then quickly, her heart beating a little more rapidly, she thought, "Perhaps it is a message from Tino or Tino himself."

It was not Tino. Through the crack in the door appeared the broad face of Serafina, glum as ever.

"It is His Excellency, General Rizzo."

"Why in the name of God did he come now, right after lunch?"

"He says it is important, Excellency. Otherwise he would not have disturbed you at this hour."

The Princess frowned, "Tell him to come back later."

But Serafina did not obey and go away, closing the door to leave her in peace. She came in, closing the door behind her.

"I think it unwise to send him away, Excellency. He appeared agitated. If you take my advice, you'll see him. Things are not the same as they were. . . . Even His Excellency, the General, is not the same."

The Princess knew what Serafina was implying—that something had happened to the General. He wasn't any longer simply a docile ex-lover who would come and go at her whim. Something had happened to him as it had happened to Tino, to all the lemmings who had fled, to Serafina, to Venice itself. She had a sudden swift sensation of bewilderment touched with fear, a sudden sense of her world collapsing, all about her.

"Very well," she said, "tell him to come up here."

She took out her mirror and reddened her lips and put a touch of shadow under her eyes, and then lay back again, more irritable than before. Then the door opened and the General came in.

He was oddly unlike an Italian in appearance. He came from north of Milano and was lean and straight and blond although there was a good deal of gray in his hair. He was, she knew, about fifty years old. The sight of him made her heart flutter a little at the memory of what he had been, of what she had been, of what they had been together. That was a long time ago, so long that the very ashes were cold. They had been cold for a long time, ever since he took up the Fascist nonsense and turned fanatic. As he crossed the room his rather wintry face relaxed in a smile, perhaps born of the same memories of the days before she was a woman with "kimono arms."

He kissed her hand and said, "You are looking very well, May."

She told him to sit down and then said, "Why did you come at this ungodly hour?"

He sat very straight, very rigid, like an Inquisitioner backed by fanatic moral convictions. In him there were signs of the same disease which had afflicted Serafina.

"I came," he said, "to warn you. I had to come quickly and when I could find time from my other duties. I'm leaving for the frontier tonight at six."

"To warn me about what?" she asked bluntly.

"To get out of Italy. You should have gone with all the others."

"I don't want to go."

The eyebrows of the General raised a little and she knew that he was thinking of Tino. She had never made the least effort to conceal her love affairs. There was never any need. Her money had always made her position impregnable.

"Of course," he said, "the decision is entirely up to you. My advice is to go—today, as quickly as possible."

"I am an American," she said, as she had said a hundred times before. "I can do as I please."

He smiled again and the smile had a curious quality. There was nothing friendly in it, nothing even to hint that once, long ago, they had loved each other. It was a smile which washed its hands of her, a smile almost of triumph as if he had been waiting with all those others, for this moment when they could say at last, "Now it is our turn." Even as she sat there looking at him, she wondered whether he had always been like that, even long ago when he had lain in her arms. Had he been hating her then in his heart, hating her money and power and arrogance, only waiting. . . .

He said in his peculiar soft voice, "Whatever you choose to do, May, is entirely your own affair. Only I must remind you that in Italy you are not an American. You are married to an Italian and you are Italian. Nothing will change that or make it any easier for you than for any Italian peasant woman. To-morrow or day after there will be war . . . a war unlike the last war or any other war since Rome itself fell. If you are thinking your money will protect you, that you can buy what you want, let me point out that those in command, those who will be in power, are not corrupt politicians or small customs officials. You cannot buy them because they have set out to do something and they mean to do it. They will kill. They will be ruthless."

He paused for a moment, but when she did not speak, he said, "I do not mean simply Fascism or Communism or any-thing else like it. It's something bigger than that, going on all over the world. It's one big thing and it doesn't matter which side you're on. It's the war of the 'Have-not's' against the 'Have's'. It's the war of millions of people against those who have always taken everything and given nothing. That, my friend is what the war is about from one end of the world to the other. There are 'have's' and 'have-not's' on both sides but before it is finished the 'have-not's' will all be on one side and there will be no more 'have's'. It will not be a nice war." He sighed suddenly, "That is why I advise you to go."

"What if I choose to stay?"

He shrugged his shoulders, "I should hate to think how miserable you will be . . . you who have never even poured yourself a cup of tea."

She did not answer him but sat staring out of the window into the silent city. She heard his voice presently, saying, in a mocking way, "If it is the thought of Tino that is keeping you, I doubt that you will see much of him."

Quickly she turned her head as if she meant to speak angrily, rebuking him for his insolence and mockery, and then quickly, as if she felt that speech was futile, she fell silent. The General sat very stiff and straight on his chair.

It seemed to her that he was a stranger whom she had never known at all. There was even a kind of vengefulness in his voice and manner. It was frightening, if the world was filled with people like him, who had been waiting for a long time, for years, for this moment.

"I did not come entirely on my own," he was saying. "His Highness telephoned from Rome, ordering me to advise you to leave the country."

She sat up and looked at him. If the Crown Prince himself had taken that trouble the situation must be serious. She said, "You're not lying?"

"On the soul of my mother I am speaking the truth."

Quickly she said, "I cannot go. All my jewels are in Rome."

"Staying behind will not save your jewels. They will be taken from you sooner or later. When the time comes they will be taken from you as they were taken from women in Russia and Germany who did not have the sense to escape while they had the chance. Staying behind to save your jewels will not save them."

"It's outrageous! It's vile!" she said. "How dare they?" And then suddenly, very quietly, she said, "How do you know all this?"

He smiled again, "I know it with my bones. You must not abuse me, May. I am only one man, a fly on the face of the universe. Who am I to change the whole destiny of civilization and the human race? I can do nothing. If you would change it and save yourself appeal to the symbol of it all, the Austrian house-painter who spent half his life in shelters for the poor, sleeping on vermin straw—the king of the 'have-not's.' Or to his friend the blacksmith's son who as a child never had enough to eat or his friend who starved in Siberia and robbed trains and was beaten and imprisoned and had to flee for his life. Go and appeal to them. I doubt that they will hear you." He stood up and bowed, this time making no sign of kissing her hand. "I am going now. Having known you very well and for a long time, I do not much care what happens to you or your kind. But as an old friend, I advise you to leave now, this very afternoon and make your way as rapidly as you can back to your own country of which you have seen so little. It is the last refuge of those who take everything and give nothing. It is the last place in the world where they are protected. Good-bye and good luck."

He turned and went out of the door and as the door closed she had a sudden feeling that she would never see him again and that the world in which they had once been happy was gone, forever. She would never see it again. The odd thing was that in his coldness, his vengefulness, *he* was happy, with the curious tense happiness of fanatics.

· · · · ·

The knowledge that very likely she would not see Tino again and the anxiety for her jewels tormented her and presently she rang and said she wanted the gondola to go to the Piazza to do some shopping. Perhaps, if she went there, she would have news. She could at least find war bulletins and perhaps some news less gloomy than the intimations of the General and Serafina. Perhaps France had already made peace and there would be no war or perhaps a miracle had happened and France had turned the tide and was fighting back, driving the hordes led by the Austrian house-painter back into their own dull bloody country.

At the great damp gateway of the palace with the dirty water of the canal lapping the steps, the gondola was waiting. But not with Beppo and Paolo at the oars. There was only an ugly misshapen old man whom she had never seen before. Beppo and Paolo she had chosen for their good looks; they were the handsomest gondoliers in all Venice and each time she touched their hands as they helped her into the gondola, she felt a sudden quick delight in their beauty. But they were gone now, long since mobilized somewhere in the north. When she rudely asked the old man who he was he replied that he was the uncle of Guiseppe the concierge. He did not even give her his gnarled hand as she stepped from the damp stone into the wobbly boat.

She told him to take her to the San Marco landing and he replied, "Very well." He did not even address her as "Excellency."

The canal was empty of boats and still, like the whole city. The terrace of the Grand Hotel was empty; no gondolas bobbed about the painted posts. There was no gay launch waiting to take millionaires and tarts and princesses and adventurers to the Lido. The lemmings had all fled and the hotel was still.

The Piazza near the church was empty save for a few pigeons strutting and preening themselves on the great flags, but on the far side there was a great congregation of people, dressed in black as Venetians always were, without a single note of color which foreigners always brought with them.

As she stepped from the gondola, the old man still made no effort to aid her but only stood in the far end of the boat watching her with eyes that were dead and without expression.

As she walked slowly across the great square, the pigeons fluttered out of her path, cooing and giving small cries of alarm. She had known this square for nearly thirty years, during fetes when banners and lights garlanded the heavy buildings, on hot sunny days when Venetians and foreigners mingled at the tables before the restaurants and cafés. This was the heart of Venice, the soul of Venice, beautiful, gay, heavy with history, and Venice to her was home, as much home as any place she had ever known. But she had never in all these years seen the great square as it was now, the vast expanse empty and silent save for the crowd all in black at the far end.

She was halfway across when she was seized suddenly by fear, fear of a kind she had never known before, the terror of a vast open space empty save for her own insignificant tiny figure. It was as if she were utterly alone, the last creature alive on earth, yet she had too the impression of being surrounded by ghosts, of figures whispering and pointing at her, figures whom she could not see save with her mind. Why they were whispering and pointing at her she did not know.

Her footsteps wavered and her legs felt weak and for a minute she felt as if she were about to faint but she pulled herself together quickly thinking, "I cannot faint here in this vast empty place. No one would ever find me. I should die here."

Then suddenly as if she had no control over her body, she began to run. She had no consciousness of direction. She only knew that she must run somewhere, anywhere, away from this great empty place into some shelter where she would not be alone, exposed and helpless. And at the same time she was aware of the ludicrousness of the situation—the spectacle of the fashionable, almost notorious Princess D'Orobelli, running, panic-stricken as a frightened rabbit, toward the shelter of the heavy arcades.

Before she stumbled and fell prostrate on the low steps at the edge of the square it seemed to her that an eternity had passed, in which she lived again all her long bitter life. Then for a time she appeared to lose all consciousness and when she opened her eyes again she discovered standing over her a hideous old woman dressed all in black with an evil face. Hair grew on her chin and lips and out of a great mole on her cheek.

The old woman was screaming abuse at her in a low Venetian dialect. "Evil woman! Foreigner! Prostitute! Go back to your country! Leave us in peace! Corrupt us no longer with your vile ways, flinging your gold into the streets for honest citizens to scramble over! You and your kind are doomed! Get gone from us! You who have brought war and doom!"

Then suddenly she spat full in the face of the Princess.

Scrambling to her feet, the Princess ran again, this time back to the landing steps where the gondola and the old man awaited her. The old crone followed her, making remarkable speed, keeping close to her heels all the long way across the open square. The pigeons, now genuinely alarmed, rose and flew for safety in a panic, high among the byzantine glories of the church of San Marco. At last she reached the landing stage where the gondola rode idly on the lapping water. The old man, his head sunk far down beneath his shoulders, was asleep like an ancient turtle. Jumping aboard, her heel caught in the gunwale and threw her prostrate into the bottom of the boat. The shock of her body against the boat wakened the old man who stared at the hag who remained screaming from the stairs. He made no move to help the Princess to her feet but merely shoved the boat away a safe distance and yelled back obscenities at the old woman.

Suddenly from nowhere appeared two other crones who joined the first one in screaming foul names and accusations across the widening stretch of water. The Princess scrambled to her feet, climbed inside the tiny gilt and black cabin ornamented with the flamboyant arms of the House of D'Orobelli and pulled the heavy black curtains together to hide herself.

·　·　·　·　·

Serafina helped her to remove the clothing soiled with spittle and pigeon dung and the dust of the great square. With a perfectly dead and expressionless face she listened to the story of what had happened. Even as the Princess told the story she could not herself quite believe that this had happened to her in her beloved Venice. It all had an unreal nightmarish quality. Only her torn stockings and bleeding knees and the filth on the white silk dress gave the adventure a sense of reality.

When she had finished Serafina only said, "It is bad, Excellency. The General is right. It is finished forever. You had better go."

She was frightened now and hysterical and ready to flee. There remained only one thing to hold her. Tino did not matter. In her terror she discovered now how little he meant to her, that he was no more than a convenience who could be replaced. She could buy another Tino. The thing which held her were the jewels. Those she could not buy again. With a sudden flash of bitterness she saw that she had reached the age when avarice was stronger than love. The jewels she could not leave behind, and they were in Rome. If she went to Rome to get them herself she might never escape. She might not even save the jewels themselves.

She saw them very plainly laid out in their cases bearing the names of the great jewelers in Bond Street and the Place Vendôme, in Fifth Avenue—the great emeralds and glittering diamonds and the rubies that were like lovely prisms of pink flame. To lose them would be to lose a part of herself. Without them she would no longer be the famous Princess D'Orobelli; she would only be an ageing, hard woman like any of the others who haunted the hotels and night clubs. No one would turn to say, "Look, there are the famous D'Orobelli emeralds!" or "See! That is the most famous necklace of diamonds in the world!" They had never been so desirable to her. She would not leave them to be seized and broken up and dispersed here and there among common vulgar people.

To Serafina she said, "I cannot go with the jewelry in Rome."

And Serafina, still impassive, replied, "I could go to Rome and fetch the jewels if your Excellency trusts me."

The mind of the Princess turned suspicious. "Do you want to flee with me? You don't want to stay in Italy?"

Serafina made a surprising answer, "Excellency, why should I want to stay behind in this doomed country? Why should I choose to starve and be cold and suffer obscene, unnameable experiences. I mean to go with your Excellency. You will go where the last luxury remains. With your Excellency I shall be warm and comfortable and well-cared-for, and have plenty to eat. I'm getting old. I've been spoiled. I do not face the prospect of misery with joy. If your Excellency will trust me I will go to Rome and fetch the jewels. No one will suspect a poor ugly woman like me to have jewels hidden in her bosom and between her legs. No one will stop me. No one will search me. It is much better that way."

"But how will you cross the border?"

"Excellency," said Serafina, "between us we can accomplish anything. We have accomplished some dark and difficult things before now. If there is any difficulty I will send you a message, somehow, and we can work together, you with your money and powerful friends and I with my brain."

Then for the first time did Serafina's heavy face show any expression. As she stood up from putting fresh stockings on the Princess' legs, a glint of humor, almost of triumph, came into her beady black eyes. The glint was the clue to their whole relationship through the long years. It was the look of one clever criminal to another with whom he has been working successfully. It was not affection which had held her all these years in the service of the Princess D'Orobelli. It was the excitement, the adventure, the luxury, the sense of being a collaborator with a clever and shameless and ruthless woman. The look said, "Together we can accomplish anything."

. . . . .

Serafina found her way alone to the Rome Express, dressed in black, looking like any peasant woman or small shopkeeper. The letter and the key to the safe deposit box she kept tucked away in her capacious bosom where the letter crackled with every breath she took. The farewell between mistress and servant was unemotional with very little said. It was as if they were both turning the key in the lock of a house, a well-beloved house, which neither of them would ever again see.

The Ventimiglia train left a little later than the Rome Express and there was only the gondola with the old Choron, uncle of the concierge, to take the Princess to the station. In all Venice there were no lights save here and there beneath the landing stages of a damp palace where a dim blue light had been hung to mark the outline of the canal. And the silence which hung over the city was deeper than by day. On the bridges and on the pathways no voice was heard but now and then a shape, dressed in black, passed against the colonnades and doorways hurrying on some mysterious mission. The only sound was the lapping of the water and the faint grunts of Choron as he poled the boat slowly and cautiously along the canal. Twice the gondola struck another in the darkness and for a moment there was an exchange of hushed cursing and then the two boats backed away from each other in the thick darkness. There were moments when the gondola seemed not to move at all and at other times it seemed to float not upon water but in thick black air, lost and timeless in eternal space.

In the tiny cabin, the Princess sat, tense as a coiled spring, frightened and angry and vindictive. She was thinking of all that had been left behind in the Palace—the great wedding picture by Titian, the Michelangelo fountains, the great Tintoretto ceilings that were like a blaze of light, the priceless furniture—all those things which she had collected bit by bit, shrewdly but which none the less cost her fortunes. Long ago the Government had forbidden her to take them out of the country. Now they would take them from her. They were *hers* she thought bitterly. She had bought them with *her* money, the money left to her by her father. It was thievery!

All she could take with her she had hidden in her luggage—a bag and a dressing case—and these contained only a few baubles worth nothing.

But as the gondola crawled on its way through the blackness, one sensation drowned out all others, blotting out into blackness itself the resentment, the bitterness, the anger. It was a terrible feeling of being alone, utterly alone not only here in a dead city but in the whole world. Tino was gone, the General had revealed himself as hating her always, even in the beginning. Serafina was on her way to Rome from which she might never return. And she herself was going off into the blackness into a strange world in which she had neither home nor friends. For suddenly she saw that she had no friends, but only acquaintances out of that gawdy world in which she had spent a whole lifetime seeking only to escape boredom, a world in which "friends" felt toward each other as the General had revealed he felt toward her only a little time before.

But always the thought kept coming back to her, "I have my money and my jewels if Serafina can save them. I can buy what I need and want."

The gondola brushed into a stone stairway and out of the darkness came the voice of the old man, "We are here!" Again he did not address her as "Excellency." He lifted the heavier of her two bags on to the quai, and then as she stepped out, he shoved the boat off into the blackness without so much as even "*addio*" or a wish for a fortunate journey. She had turned toward him, taking a bank note from her handbag to give to him, not out of gratitude nor for a service, for he had been cold and insolent, but to bring herself luck on the journey. But when she turned he was not there. In his place there was only the darkness and the faint lapping of the water in the silent canal, and out of the darkness came again to her, more sharply than before, the chilling sense of being utterly alone. In the darkness it was like being the last creature left alone on earth.

In the station, behind the closed doors, a few faint lights left most of the big room in shadows out of which emerged hundreds of dim, almost ghostly faces, faces with fear in the eyes and at the corners of the mouths. They were the faces of the last refugees, not the lemmings and the International White Trash; those were gone already. They were the faces of small humble people, servants and bank clerks, small shop-keepers and tourist agents, fleeing across the border before the trap closed to ruin and imprison them there perhaps forever. Around them clustered their frightened wives and children.

At each ticket grille, there was a crowd of frightened men and women bereft of decency and self-control, fighting for the bits of paper that would put them safely out of a country which at any moment might be at war with their own. This war was no concern of theirs; some of them had Italian wives and half-Italian children; most of them loved Italy, but now suddenly their small individual worlds had fallen into ruins. They had to flee with their wives, their babies, their pitiful bundles, anywhere, outside Italy.

The Princess went from window to window only to discover that at each window the same riot was taking place, and at last she turned to a policeman, a dark good-looking fellow (she noted that even through her fear) thinking, "I will vamp him into helping me."

She said, "I am Princess Ugo D'Orobelli."

Without changing his expression, he said, "*Si, Eccellenza.*"

"I must have a ticket. I must leave on the Ventimiglia Express." She became utterly helpless and feminine, "I cannot fight my way through the crowd."

She waited for him to soften, either before her femininity or the prestige of her wealth and title, but his expression did not change. He merely said, in an indifferent voice, "I am sorry, *Eccellenza*, you will have to take your place in line with the others."

It was as if he had said, "There are no more princesses or millionaires. There are only people." There was even in the cold look in his black eyes a hint of what she had found in the General—the faint sense of vengeance and triumph, as if he, like the General had been waiting all this time to humiliate her. Bitterest of all she understood that she was no longer young and beautiful. To the policeman she was simply another middle-aged woman, no more remarkable than any of the other frightened women huddled in the shadows.

Their terror was slowly, like an infectious disease, communicating itself to her. As she turned from the policeman, she thought, "I must get hold of myself. This is all ridiculous." And then something of her father, the buccaneer, came to life out of her anger and fear. She thought, "I'll show them that I'm as good as the next woman. I'll take care of myself." And plunging her handbag tightly in the crook of her elbow and using her valise as a kind of battering ram, she attacked the group of struggling refugees at the nearest window.

Here it was true that she was only "people." Even the men took no notice of her sex. Being the Princess Ugo D'Orobelli meant nothing. She pushed and kicked and pinched and was pinched and kicked and pushed in turn. She was called foul names and hurled back foul words in exchange. And after ten minutes she found herself standing before the ticket grille facing a small ugly bald man.

Quickly she said, "I want to reserve a compartment on the Express to Monte Carlo."

The man gave her a quick glance of astonishment. Then his eyes narrowed until they were slits. This gave him a curiously venomous look like a snake.

"*Signora*," he said, with obvious satisfaction, "the train does not cross the border. It does not go to Monte Carlo. It goes only as far as Ventimiglia. And there are no reserved compartments."

For a second she was silent, but almost immediately from behind her rose rude cries of "Get on with your business! Hurry up! Give us a chance!"—followed by a chorus of obscenity and evil epithets.

The little official behind the wicket had shoved a bit of paper toward her—a humiliating, ordinary third-class ticket. She opened her handbag and as she pushed the price of the ticket toward him, she held in her hand in full view a thousand lire note. The eyes of the little official opened a little way. Then he said, "*Signora*, I could take your money, but if you gave me a million lire I could give you nothing in return."

Before she had time to reply she was pushed violently from the window by the man behind her, who said, "Get out of the way! Give the others a chance. Bribery won't help you or any other millionaire criminals."

With the ticket crumpled in her hand, she forced her way through the crowd, seeing nothing but the snake-like eyes of the petty official with the glitter of contempt in them. And she could hear the bitter edge of scorn in his voice as he refused her bribe. There was something terrifying in the very spectacle of a Latin petty official refusing a bribe.

She found herself a place to sit on the edge of the luggage truck. She did not like children and the platform and the truck at her back was filled with them—children of all ages and sizes, most of them whimpering or crying with fear. The men and women near her regarded her with suspicion, as if she wore some label which set her aside from the others.

They *knew* what she was because most of them had been

servants at some time to International White Trash, or had cashed checks for them, or sold them souvenirs. They knew the rudeness, the selfishness and the annoyance of people like herself who wore expensive clothes and carried expensive luggage. And it was stamped on her face. In reality that was where they found the betraying label which marked her. The hard eyes betrayed her, the hard line of the sensual lips, compressed now with anger and resentment and humiliation. A mother picked up her child and drew away from her. Then another made the same gesture and then another and presently she found herself sitting alone on the truck like a leper.

Then the gates to the train platform were thrown open and as she stood up, she was caught by the rush of frightened refugees and carried, now on her feet, now on her knees, through the gateway halfway down the platform until the mob began to disperse as they climbed on the train fighting for places. There were wild cries and curses and the screams of frightened children and the tinkle of glass as windows along the train corridors were broken in the struggle. Police fought and shouted and cursed, but they too were only carried forward helplessly in the wild struggle.

When it was over she found herself in a third-class compartment on a hard wooden seat. With her on seats built to hold a maximum of ten were three old women, one of them with a cancerous lip, six children, three of them lost and frightened, wailing for their parents, two middle-aged men, a young girl and a fat man. The compartment smelled horribly of garlic and old sweat. Then one of the frightened children began to vomit recklessly. The Princess tried desperately to unwedge herself and escape, but the corridor of the train was jammed with refugees. She could not even move from her seat. At last, in a blur of distaste and horror, she was aware that the train was moving.

. . . . .

All through the night the darkened train crept like a slow-worm across the flat plains of Northern Italy burdened with its cargo of sweating, frightened, crowded humanity. Trains loaded with troops and cannon and ammunition thrust it aside on their way to the border, and as each train passed, fear tightened its hold on the hearts of the refugees until in them one by one it reached that point where it no longer had the quality of fear but that of despair in which misery deadened even the fear of death. Bewildered children cried and fell asleep at last in the stinking crowded compartments. An old man died and was thrust aside in a corner, propped up with a newspaper covering his face because, sitting up, the body occupied less space. In a spot cleared precariously in the corridor of one car, a woman gave birth to a child.

In the compartment which the Princess shared with thirteen other people, the stench and the heaviness of the air became suffocating, and now and then she slipped into unconsciousness, waking again to the dull misery and discomfort with a start, wondering where she, who had always been so luxurious, could be and how she had come to find herself in surroundings so sordid. Twice when the train stopped and she wakened with a jolt she determined to make her escape even though she found herself in the midst of wild, open country, but each time, even before she could extricate herself from the tangle of arms and legs, the train went on its way. About two in the morning she found herself weeping, out of fury and discomfort and hatred for the human animals with whom she found herself imprisoned. It was a cold, savage hatred for less fortunate people who until now had never played any part in her existence save as servants or conveniences.

Just before dawn the train reached the border station at Ventimiglia. A cold fog obscured the platform and the *Douane*. When cries of "Ventimiglia Frontier! Last stop!" arose from the outside, only a few among the refugees stirred. They were like animals numbed and deadened by too long imprisonment in a confined space. And then after a little time, like terrified sheep they all tried to escape from the train at the same moment, trampling each other, screaming and fighting, shattering windows and falling as they were pushed from the steps to the platform. Outside the cold freshness of the air was like a slap in the face.

But the misery was not finished. After a long delay began the examination of papers and of baggage to prevent the carrying off of gold or precious *objets d'art*. The refugees were forced into a long line, to pass between two small and mean officials, swollen now with authority and arrogant and brutal. They took an endless time, examining each man, woman and child, now and then dragging from the line a man or woman whose papers were not in order, to thrust them into a station waiting-room where they were kept prisoners by four bullies in black shirts, their shouts and screams and imprecations silenced presently by the blow of a club or a kick. The woman who had had the baby lay on a baggage truck and on the station platform near her lay the body of the old man who had died. The corpse lay on its side in the grotesque sitting position into which it had frozen during the long night on the train.

Twice the Princess attempted to pass the others and go to the head of the line and twice she was thrust rudely back with shouts and insults and even blows. And when at last she reached the official examining the papers, he read her high-sounding name and then grinned insolently at her.

"Did you have a pleasant journey?" he asked.

She did not answer him and he said, "No doubt it was a new and interesting experience for Your Excellency."

She wanted to insult the pock-marked little man who a few weeks earlier would have groveled before her, repeating over and over the word "*Eccellenza*" with a different intonation. So she wanted to slap him, to spit in his face, but her desire to escape out of this mad, crumbling world was far greater, and she held her tongue although the self-restraint made her ill to the verge of vomiting.

He could not stop her, for her papers were in excellent order, but he took an interminable time before he stamped them, turning the passport this way and that, examining the signature insolently as if to imply that he suspected forgery, and comparing the passport photo with her own face, to say finally, with the air of a critic, "You were much younger, Excellency, when that was taken."

Behind her in the long weary line refugees shouted evil names and called out to hurry, that the frontier might be closed at any moment.

But the torment was over at last and she walked through the station gateway to find a conveyance to take her across the line. There was no conveyance. The short strip of white road outlining the Mediterranean was empty in a foggy gray light, save for two men, a woman and a child, carrying their belongings, who walked ahead of her.

This was a road she knew well, like her hand. She had crossed and recrossed the border perhaps a thousand times in her life. It was one of the highways of the world that was frequented by the rich and the fortunate. Winter and summer, the year round, this road had been filled with expensive motors, going from Italy into France and from France into Italy—kept women, Indian princes, international bankers and munitions manufacturers, gamblers, idlers—all the International White Trash who frequented what Mary Pulsifer had once called derisively the Côte d'Ordure—the Garbage Coast, making a pun on that name Côte d'Azur which once one saw everywhere advertised as a paradise on earth.

And now on this foggy morning the white road was empty but for the figures of five refugees, stumbling along carrying their own luggage, two of them working men, two of them a lady's maid and her child, and one the Princess D'Orobelli.

. . . . .

On the French side, the contamination, the fear, had not yet touched the petty officials. For days now their country had been overrun. From hour to hour they did not know whether it had been conquered, nor when they would be at war with the little men on the far side of the white strip of road. But they shrugged their shoulders and stuck to their jobs.

There was a thin, lugubrious one with drooping mustaches and a pleasant, short, red-cheeked one with bright blue eyes. They were more courteous and less insolent than the officials on the other side. When the Princess showed them her papers, they examined them carefully but with indifference. When they had finished, they returned them to her and bade her walk through the doorway to the soil of France. They were used to princesses and millionaires, and they were good republicans who looked upon such gawdy individuals merely as citizens of a free state. They did not address her as "Excellency" or "Princess" but merely as "Madame." There was no change in this, it had always been the same. They did not insult her as the Italian *douaniers* had done.

As she passed through the doorway she felt a sudden relief. She had never liked France in the way she had loved Italy; in France people of the streets sometimes shouted mockery or insults at people driving past in rich motors. They did not step aside respectfully almost in awe as Italians did when the automobiles of the rich and fashionable drove through a street. They could, like the Italians, be sometimes bought, but they did not grovel before the buyer; they showed frank contempt for him. But now in this shattered world, they did not turn arrogant and savage, hating and insulting her. They still addressed her as "Madame" and displayed as much politeness as they had ever done. And behind these two figures, the tall lean one and the short chubby one, she sensed a world free, at least for a little longer, of that thing she had encountered on the great square of Venice. It was odd that she should be glad to be out of her beloved Italy on the soil of a country where democracy was still the existing order.

On the outside of the station the little square was empty save for a single battered *fiacre* driven by an old coachman with one eye. Around it had gathered the refugees who had crossed the frontier ahead of her and two or three others. They were quarreling among themselves and bargaining with the coachman. They were all small people with very little money with whom bargaining had always been a part of the daily struggle for existence and now, furiously quarreling, they were bidding against each other for the services of the lone conveyance, raising their bids a few centimes at a time while the evil coachman waited for the best price.

The Princess divined almost at once what was happening and her heart brightened. She was tired, her clothes torn, her feet swollen and aching, the stench of the train still clung to her. But she still had money—more money in her purse than perhaps the rest of them had all together. Her whole being experienced only one desire—to reach Monte Carlo and the

Hotel de Paris, to have a hot bath and a bed with clean linen.
She knew what to do now. It was an ancient procedure, well-
tried. It was safe here. In France even here on the frontier,
life remained sane. Bargaining was still the order of things.
Money still had power.

Quickly she went toward the little crowd of bargainers and
opening her handbag she took out the thousand lire note. The
evil old coachman saw her with his one eye as she came
toward the crowd across the little square. He saw her raise
the thousand lire note and wave it above her head and at the
same time he struck his bony horse with a whip and drove
through the bargaining crowd toward the Princess. Before the
little group of refugees understood what had happened she
had climbed in the *fiacre* and said to the driver, "Hotel de
Paris, Monte Carlo." The evil old man grinned and struck
the horse again with his whip. This was like old times. This
was a world he understood.

Behind the *fiacre* one of the men refugees started to follow
them, shouting curses. The woman and child began to cry
and then the man gave up the chase.

.   .   .   .   .

It was a long journey along the white road above the sea, a
journey much longer in the broken-down old *fiacre* to someone like the Princess who had been used to traveling it always
at high speed in a luxurious motor. The old broken-down
horse clattered along the paving, the hoof beats echoing back
and forth between the empty villas. The sun had come up
and was burning the chill mist, but as it cleared away it revealed a dead and empty world, house after house, pink,
yellow, white and pale blue, blind and shuttered. Even along
the edge of the road, the shops were shuttered save for one
or two where an old woman or an old man stood in the doorway to stare at the spectacle of the Princess being driven past
in a broken-down *fiacre*.

The old man on the driver's seat never spoke and that suited
the Princess. She was in no mood for conversation. The old
man had understood the language of money and that was

enough for her. It made her feel secure again at least for a little time. Two or three times he turned rheumatically in his seat to leer at her with his single eye. She tried to avoid his gaze but about the cold eye there was something hypnotic. Slowly he became like the old man who had replaced the gondoliers, like the old woman who had spat at her in the Piazza San Marco. His oldness frightened her.

They passed through Mentone, dead and deserted and as they turned past a jutting rock and came in sight of Monte Carlo, he turned and said, "You got through just in time. That was the last train. They have closed the frontier." His voice was weak, high-pitched and dim with age.

The old horse went more and more slowly and it was nearly noon before the *fiacre* entered the realm of Monaco with Monte Carlo looming colorless and empty and ugly on the steep and rocky mountainside—Monte Carlo which was so ugly by day and so fantastically beautiful by night. Now empty, with shuttered windows, it was drearier than ever. The new Casino seemed blank and modern and out-of-place, the old one—garish and grotesque. A sudden panic seized her lest the Hotel de Paris, like all the villas, should be closed, lest there should be no one to take her in. She had told Serafina she would stay here until the maid sent word of her where-abouts. The news of the closed frontier was discouraging. Serafina might never escape now with the jewels. She might never see them again.

The hotel was open, after a fashion, although there were few people in it. A handful of servants and the assistant man-ager remained.

He was a paunchy fellow, very dark, with a shrewd eye, a Monegasque by birth. His eyes brightened at sight of her. He said, rubbing his hands, "What a surprise and a pleasure, Excellency!"

The hotel was not really open, he said, but she might have a room and food. The food would not be excellent as the chefs were gone, called to the army or evacuated. There was no water for the baths but the servants could carry hot water to her room. All the foreigners had gone and a good many of the natives. Monte Carlo was a ghost city, too near the border.

If there was a war it might be shelled and bombed. The servants who remained were volunteers, securing double wages for staying behind to guard the property.

"But I suppose," he said, "you'll be staying for only a few hours."

"I am waiting here for my maid. It may be two or three days. It may be longer. She is in Italy."

The dark little man looked alarmed. "But the frontier is closed, Excellency. No one can come through."

"It has been closed before and opened again. I would like a bath as quickly as possible and some tea and orange juice."

"Certainly, Excellency."

The great hall was empty, the dining-room closed. The sound of her footsteps echoed along the great hallways as he led her to a room. She had never seen the Hotel de Paris like this even in the deadest part of the off season. From her window the little harbor was empty of yachts and pleasure boats. Only a few fishing craft remained. Only the water of the Mediterranean was the same, opalescent and blue.

After tea and orange juice and a bath she fell asleep. It was dark when she wakened, three in the morning. When she rose to look out of the window, still half-asleep, she looked out over a dead city. No light shone anywhere in the city where there had always been light and at this season of the year there had never been any night. Standing there in the darkness she was frightened again in spite of all her hardness, and for a moment she fancied that she heard again laughter and the sound of music. But there was nothing, not even the ghost of laughter.

. . . . . .

On the evening of the third day a small and very dirty little boy appeared at the hotel with a message. It was brief, simply to say that an individual called Serafina had arrived in Ventimiglia. The frontier was still closed. More news of her could be had if her Excellency would come to *numero dix sept* rue de la Port and ask for Madame Lestrade. When questioned the boy knew nothing more. He was, he said, given five francs to deliver the message.

When the Princess asked the assistant manager if he knew Madame Lestrade of 17 rue de la Port, his plucked eyebrows rose. Madame Lestrade he said, was the proprietress of an establishment which was certainly not respectable, a place frequented by sailors and the servants of the rich who lived in the hotels and villas on the hill. The rue de la Port ran along the edge of the outer harbor. He looked at the Princess with a faintly curious expression. Having spent all his life, since fourteen, in *grand hotels de luxe* he knew a great many strange things about rich and fashionable people.

The Princess answered the quizzical look by saying, "I have business with Madame Lestrade. It concerns my maid."

"Perhaps I'd better send someone to accompany your Excellency," he suggested; "it is certainly not a savory place."

She answered him bluntly, coldly. "It isn't necessary. I shall wear no jewels. I am quite able to take care of myself." She had no intention of telling what the business was. Until she was safe in New York, no one must know of the jewels but herself and Serafina.

Then she went to her room and when she had put on the simplest dress she had, she set off down the hill toward the port. Her heart beat rapidly and there was in her eyes a curious glittering look which had become more common of late.

She thought, "Things are going better. If Serafina has sent the message, she must have the jewels. If she is at Ventimiglia, there must be some way of getting her across the border. It will only be a question of money."

As she walked down steep ramps and bits of stairway she kept seeing the jewels again, the lovely green emeralds, the cold glittering diamonds, the rubies the color of blood. She wanted them desperately, to touch them, to hold them up to catch the light, shining and glistening. Without them she was naked. Now they were nearly hers once more, only a few miles away on the other side of the border, beyond two lines of troops waiting the order to kill each other. She must get them quickly, before it was too late.

Once she reached the level of the old port she had very little trouble finding the rue de la Port. It was a short street of not more than twenty houses, a street of bars and small brothels and tiny shops. Number seventeen was the largest house in the street, three stories high with narrow balconies overlooking the harbor. The street and harbor had a curious empty and desolate air.

When she pushed open the door she found an empty room with a bar at one side, a great many mirrors with red plush seats all around the edge of the room. She knocked on the bar and waited but no one answered the sound. The mirrors made her nervous for they sent back her reflection many times —the reflection of a middle-aged woman, smartly dressed, hard, a woman with the rather battered remnants of good looks. The horrible night on the train had done something to her. Here in the mirrors of a brothel, she realized it for the first time. Youth was gone forever. No amount of peace or rest, no amount of massage or dieting would ever bring it back. Never again would a man look upon her with excitement or desire. She had crossed a frontier and it like the other frontier was closed. She felt a sudden stab of bitterness as if acid were corroding her heart. Then she straightened her tired body and went to the door leading into another room. There she knocked again and after a moment she heard the sound of footsteps coming down a stairway. The sound was that made by feet stuffed into slatternly slippers. Then the door opened and a woman came in.

She was about the same age as the Princess but her hair was dyed a shade of orange gold and carefully set in tight waves. She wore a sleazy *peignoir* with a black knitted shawl over her shoulders. She was heavier than the Princess for she had not starved her sensuality. Her eyes were blue and hard, the nails of her dirty fingers lacquered a brilliant red. She looked boldly at the Princess and said, "You are Princess D'Orobelli."

"Yes."

"I am Madame Lestrade. *'La Goulue'* they call me down here. Sit down. Join me in a brandy, Madame?"

The woman went over to the bar and took down a bottle. The place had a strange smell, compounded of cheap perfume and powder, of stale beer and lavatories. As Madame Lestrade took down the bottle she stared boldly at the Princess. Princesses did not impress her. She had had strange experiences with rich people who came down from the great hotels and villas of the upper town seeking bizarre adventures. Clearly she regarded her merely as an equal, as simply another woman experienced and hard like herself. In a chatty way, she said, as she poured out the brandy, "I have sent the girls away. It wasn't fair to keep them here in case we were bombed. And in any case there was no business. I found good places for them in a house in Marseilles. Business is good there. The port is full of warships." She spoke as though she were discussing the marketing of vegetables. She raised her glass, and said, "Your health, Madame."

The Princess raised her glass. The brandy was hard and burned her throat.

Madame Lestrade asked, "You came about the individual called Serafina, I judge. You must be very attached to her."

"Yes," said the Princess, "I want to get her across the border." In spite of herself the vision of the jewels made her voice tremble. "I must get her across. That is why I came to see you."

"I can perhaps help you," said Madame Lestrade. She poured herself another brandy and added, "I have a small boat and two sailors. Quite frankly we used it for smuggling. They know their way about in the dark. They could perhaps bring back this individual for you." She coughed, "It would take money, of course."

"Naturally," said the Princess. "How much?" Her hands were still trembling, a fact that Madame Lestrade noticed. At the sight she mentally doubled the price.

"Ten thousand francs," she said, "paid in advance. It is a very risky business. I may lose my boat and Vincenzo and Pierre may be captured or killed. In that case I must keep the money whether they rescue the individual or not."

"Yes," said the Princess. It was worth many times that. What was three hundred dollars to recover jewels worth more than a million. What did it matter if two men she had never seen, common working men, were killed. "Yes, that is satisfactory."

"And I shall need two cartons of American cigarettes and two bottles of brandy."

"Very good. When can you send for the individual?"

"Tonight after the moon has gone down into the sea."

"I will send the money and the stuff within an hour."

"*Bon jour*, Madame."

"*Bon jour*, Madame."

The Procuress and the Princess parted as equals. The long climb up the hill exhausted the Princess. It was quite dark by the time she reached the Hotel de Paris.

At the doorway, miraculously, there stood a huge old-fashioned Rolls-Royce. Two of the garrison of servants who remained and a stocky hard-faced driver, were unloading from the roof a strange assortment of luggage—a couple of battered tin trunks, a mattress, a sewing machine and a goat. There were many more things but these few she identified by the faint light from the hotel doorway.

Wearily she climbed the steps and went into the vast and empty hallway. There, coming down the grand stairway, toward her, walking very straight, an Edwardian hat perched high on her old-fashioned pompadour came the last person in the world she had expected to meet in the Hotel de Paris in Monte Carlo in wartime. She thought suddenly, out of the depths of the superstition that so largely ruled her life, "That is why I dreamed of Mary Pulsifer. She was coming into my life!"

.   .   .   .   .

It had been a long slow journey, full of discomfort for a lady so old and so used to luxury as Mary Pulsifer. Without 'Ennery she could not have made it; even her liking for adventure and excitement could not have provided sufficient stimulus to carry her through. But 'Ennery was magnificent. Sometimes, as she rode, sitting up very straight as if she were in a coronation procession instead of a refugee fleeing before an invading army, she wondered at the curious involutions of her life—that she had married Vivian Pulsifer and loved him despite the evil she knew of him as an international banker, that she had gone on through all these years in the great house in London, sitting at the head of his table, welcoming his shady guests, famous, important men like himself—munitions manufacturers, politicians, oil kings, bankers, currency speculators, all engaged in immoral and dubious undertakings, striving always to bolster up and preserve that crooked structure of their own creation which had shown the first signs of collapse in 1914, and now was doomed forever.

Riding in the back of the old-fashioned motor with two French peasant women beside her, two more at her feet and a weary child asleep in her lap, she sighed at what now seemed to her the lost opportunities of a long life. Once she might have exposed the game of her husband and those "distinguished" men who had frequented the great house, a game designed for only one purpose—to subjugate all humanity to the will and profit of a small conniving class. They had been without nationality. Among them were Germans, Americans, Englishmen, Frenchmen, Dutchmen. Their only bond was not nationality but their will to power and wealth a million times beyond the need of any man. It was these men who had created this world and in their over-reaching greed, brought about its destruction.

Mary Pulsifer, old and wise and tired, saw it all very clearly even in the moment when the dive-bombers were machine-gunning 'Ennery and herself and killing women and children and old men along the road beside her. They were the helpless victims of something too great for humanity to deal with, too vast for people to understand, unless, like herself, you knew the inside and were old enough to feel detached and outside all the misleading passions which obscured the truth. When the Stukas had dived low over the car, she had not been afraid because it did not matter to the world or to herself whether she died or not. She was too old, it was too late, for her to do anything about the infamies to which she had been a complacent witness. In a way she had been as guilty as the others, for in a way she had been an accomplice. She had known the evil but had been too comfortable, too indifferent to denounce it.

What was it those men wanted, at the expense of human happiness and civilization? Now, as an old woman, she was no more able to find the answer than she had been thirty years earlier when the pattern of the whole monstrosity had begun to become clear to her. They had been driven by devils; anyone of them would have been happier and have lived longer if their lives had been more simple and easy. Her husband had killed himself long before his time by straining always for more power and more wealth. 'Ennery, sitting there before her, his heavy figure black against the dim light from the stars, was a happier, more honest man. She and 'Ennery had always understood each other from the first day when 'Ennery, home from the Boer War, had come to work as coachman. Now she saw that both 'Ennery and herself had loved her husband, because he was a lovable man, but they had never respected him. In some ways it seemed to her that, during the long years they had been together, she was closer to 'Ennery than to her dead husband. When her husband died and she told 'Ennery that she meant to give away all her great wealth to make the world a more decent place—all that wealth accumulated in so evil a fashion by her husband— 'Ennery had approved at once, saying, "Yes, Madame, I think your plan an excellent idea!" But shrewdly he had added, "But keep ample for yourself, Madame. You are too old, if you will pardon my saying so, to change your ways now. You'd be very uncomfortable—not being free to come and go as you like."

She had followed his advice, but after all she needed very little—only a small fraction of the great fortune. Now and then she had smiled to herself at the thought of the fury that would rise on her death, when all those useless people who hoped to inherit from her, those members of the International White Trash, discovered that she had given the money away. It had been perhaps a small gesture, perhaps a great one; she did not know. She only knew that giving away all that evil money had made her feel more decent, and at moments had given her a feeling of satisfaction at having dispersed the wealth and power which the men who once gathered around her table had so cherished.

In all the terror and confusion in the square at Orléans and on the road afterward, it had all become very clear to her— what was happening. The Stukas, the terror and misery of all Europe, the dead and dying along the road, were all part of a fury that was sweeping the world and in the end would destroy the men like her husband, who had created it. Her husband and the men sitting at her table in the great house in London had tried to destroy the German Republic because they were afraid of the people. They had financed and encouraged the man who had brought this misery and terror along the quiet roadsides of green, fertile France, because they had thought he was their friend and thought as they thought. But in the end they had not killed the monster; they had merely forced him to take another shape, the shape of a new monster who hated his creators and protectors more than the people they had feared. It would not be a quick decisive misery, all this blind aimless fury, she thought bitterly, it would go on and on until it found shape and meaning as the fury which ended feudalism had found shape and meaning, but in the end it would destroy the men like her husband and those who sat at his table—the ones who took everything and gave nothing. That much, with an inner wisdom, she knew was certain.

It was a tiring journey. 'Ennery drove day and night, down, down across France with rumors never far behind, that the Germans were in Tours, in Blois, in Orléans, in Bordeaux, in Lyons. There was trouble about gasoline, but the rebuilt old-fashioned Rolls had been made for crossing deserts and mountains on their long tours and once her tanks were filled, she was good for eight hundred miles without replenishing. In a village outside Orléans 'Ennery filled her tanks to capacity, paying the keeper of the tiny filling station a small fortune for all the gasoline he could supply.

It was Mrs. Pulsifer who decided to head for Monte Carlo. When she asked the women she had picked up along the road where they were bound, they replied pitifully that they did not know. They had been driven from their homes and ordered to take to the road. No one told them where to go; no one had provided any way of transportation. Each of them had a little money.

She chose Monte Carlo shrewdly. The roads through that part of Provence would be empty; the advancing Germans would not trouble to bomb and machine-gun roads where there were no refugees. She divined that people would be fleeing away from Monte Carlo rather than toward it, since it was so near the Italian border. In Monte Carlo there would be plenty of food and shelter.

So they drove all night and all the next day, stopping only for bread and cheese and wine. And growing weary, Mrs. Pulsifer fell to thinking about death, really for the first time in her life, because she had always been very fortunate, not in being rich, but because she had always loved people and found life an entertaining spectacle. So because her life had been full she had no dread of death. And she was old now and this new war bore down upon her; another war was too much to ask of anyone—especially a war which need not have happened save for those men who had gathered round her husband's table.

It was evening when the over-burdened old Rolls came over the pass and into the light of the setting sun, with the whole of the Mediterranean spread far below beyond the white fringe of pleasure resorts. At sight of it the peasant women and children who had never seen so vast an expanse of water began to exclaim and chatter among themselves, forgetting for a moment the memory of their menfolk and their shattered houses.

Smiling, Mary Pulsifer listened to them. This was a very ancient sea and the sight of it gave her a sense of peace. It had survived wars and revolutions. Civilizations had risen and fallen and disappeared on its shores. And for her it had many pleasant memories of the villa where she had come in winter with her husband, sold when she disposed of everything and owned now by a cinema actress. There were memories of yachting parties, of the ballet and Monte Carlo itself where she had come with her husband so many times to dine with Zaharoff, the Levantine pimp, the great munitions operator, the man responsible for the deaths and misery of millions. In the old days it had been a happy luxurious life so long as you did not lift the cover and see what was going on underneath.

As the car descended the long, winding, empty road, the

purple air grew darker and with the darkness no blaze of light appeared from the harbor, the Casino or the city itself.

"It is a dead place," thought Mary Pulsifer, "and it will never again come to life in our time."

At the Monaco border, a little man in fancy dress costume stepped into the dim lights and warned 'Ennery. There was a law. No lights at all were permitted.

The order gave Mary Pulsifer a sudden shock. In the last war, it had been different. Places like Monte Carlo with its Casinos, its banks, its great villas owned largely by the men who sat about her husband's table—had been protected. By mutual agreement, by secret arrangement they had managed to have their own property spared. The houses of the humble might be destroyed but no army attacked or bombed *their* chateaux, *their* castles, *their* munitions factories. She thought, "No, it is different this time. It is more desperate. The people are wiser. They no longer have patience. This time even the appeasers, the bargainers, the shrewd and the greedy will be destroyed." She had come to Monte Carlo because she had believed it was safe for those poor women and children traveling with her, and now it was not safe.

.   .   .   .   .

At the hotel they received her with astonishment and pleasure. Like the Princess she was a symbol out of the old rich life, but the pantomime of welcome was more genuine in the case of Mary Pulsifer, for she was kind and generous and humorous, and she was always a little ashamed of being so rich. She was a simple woman and she loved people, and in consequence people loved her, even the humblest. And she was important too, they knew, because she had so often been the guest of Zaharoff.

The idea of receiving the peasant women, their children and the goat, created a shock in the heads of the assistant manager and his staff, but Mrs. Pulsifer insisted, and in times like these her word was law. And she was, they knew, excellent pay.

So the women and children, startled and a little frightened by the splendor all about them, were taken off to the great bedrooms once occupied by Grand Dukes and super-pimps and millionaires and kept women. They had baths and a good meal and then Mary Pulsifer went downstairs to see about the goat whose owner was worried over what had become of it. And going down the stairs she had to her astonishment seen May D'Orobelli, looking tired and hard and old, coming in the door. In her depression and weariness she was the last woman in the world Mary Pulsifer wanted to see, for the Princess D'Orobelli somehow symbolized all the sick world which Mary Pulsifer knew could not be saved. In all that world May D'Orobelli was the final symbol of those who took everything and gave nothing.

．　．　．　．　．

They had many things to tell each other. They had never known each other very well, for although they frequented the same dying world, the Princess had always looked upon Mary Pulsifer as stuffy and Mary Pulsifer had looked upon the Princess as a singularly vicious representative of her class. But now, having dinner together in Mary Pulsifer's sitting-room, alone in the dark and silent resort, a kind of intense but false intimacy sprang up between them, as if they were the last two people in the world.

It was a good dinner, a dinner like those of the old days, with champagne and fish and a bird, and as Mary Pulsifer talked the weariness went out of her. As she grew older she slept less and less and now she knew, as she sat there, that she was not going to sleep, and so she drank more champagne than usual and at midnight they were still talking.

The Princess told the story of her last day in Venice and of the frightening change which had come over Italy and Mrs. Pulsifer told very quietly the story of her flight from Paris, of the dive-bombing and machine-gunning which showed no discrimination for the widow of a famous international banker but attacked her as well as the peasants and children and nuns fleeing along the road.

"I headed for Monte Carlo," she said, "as the safest place I could think of."

It was the disillusioned Princess who gave her the answer to the shocking change which made Monte Carlo no longer safe. She said, bitterly, "There is no place safe in Europe for people like us, Mary. In the last war one's property was safe. In this war nothing is sacred. They have taken everything I have but my jewels."

Then she told Mary Pulsifer what she had told no one else —of Serafina's rescue of the jewels and her arrival on the other side of the border. Mary Pulsifer knew of the famous jewels. Some of them she had seen. But now she heard all about them, in detail, the story of each one of them that was famous—the great Royal diamond, the Queen's ruby, the emeralds which had once belonged to Pauline Bonaparte. And Mary Pulsifer listened fascinated and a little frightened, because as the Princess talked, the jewels seemed to acquire life, to become much more than jewels. May D'Orobelli talked of them as an insanely doting mother talked of her children, or a brilliant scientist talked of his ideas. A fire came into her eyes that had never been there before, even for a lover. In her voice and manner there was a kind of madness.

Mary Pulsifer, listening, thought, "They are all she has left. She has lost her lover. She has no real friends. She has no friends on whom she can depend. She is terrified by what she has been through. There are only the jewels."

The sudden naked gauntness of May D'Orobelli's life was a dreadful revelation, but because Mary Pulsifer was a nice person, she felt pity for the woman sitting opposite her, drinking glass after glass of expensive brandy.

At one in the morning she was still listening to the tale of Madame Lestrade and her plan of smuggling Serafina across the border when a waiter knocked on the door.

When he came in, he said, "There is a woman downstairs who wishes to speak to Your Excellency."

A look of relief and delight came into the strained, hard eyes of the Princess. "Tell her to come up at once."

When the waiter had gone away she said, trembling, "It is Serafina. She has come with the jewels."

But it was not Serafina. When the door opened the woman who came in was Madame Lestrade. She wore a hat that partly covered her face, throwing a shadow over her eyes. In a glance Mary Pulsifer fixed her station in life. The Princess rose and went eagerly toward her.

Madame Lestrade remained by the door. She said, "Madame, I have bad news."

At the speech the Princess stopped suddenly and leant against a chair.

Madame Lestrade said, "The boat is lost and with it the two men. Vincenzo was killed as they tried to land. Pierre managed to get back but he is dead. He died a few minutes ago." The woman spoke in a voice so cold and dead that, out of her experience, Mary Pulsifer divined that there was some special bond between her and one of the men.

"And Serafina and my jewels?" cried the Princess. "Where are they? What have you done with them?"

In the same dead voice, Madame Lestrade said, "To hell with you and your jewels. My lover is dead!"

The Princess began to scream, "You have cheated me! You have tricked me! You have stolen the jewels!"

The woman stared at her in silence while she screamed hysterical accusations. Then very quietly she called the Princess the foulest name she could summon up, a word so foul that one woman rarely used it to another even in a Marseilles brothel. She said, "You and your lazy kind and your precious jewels are at the bottom of everything. May God curse you and your damned jewels to eternity!"

Then before the Princess could begin to scream again, the Procuress was gone out of the door.

Alone in the room with Mary Pulsifer, she returned to the table. She no longer screamed. She sat there sobbing and trembling while Mary Pulsifer tried to comfort her. She felt no contempt but only a curious sort of pity, born of her weariness and perhaps of her nearness to death. To her the woman opposite was not simply an unspeakable creature whose avarice and selfishness were monstrous, who had shown no emotion save fury for having caused the death of two men she had never seen. To Mary Pulsifer, this was a human creature upon whom the Furies were closing in with all the inevitability of a tale of Greek mythology. The fading hysterical woman opposite her was a horror, but once she had been young and beautiful; once all of life had been before her. She was the product of her age and her society, of its thievery and ruthlessness, its vulgarity and greed. Her story had begun long ago before she was born. It began with the thievery of her father, his bribery of Congressmen, his wanton destruction of smaller people who got in his way, with the vast and vulgar house he had built in New York so that his wife and daughter might become "fashionable," with her marriage to a degenerate European nobleman. Mary Pulsifer, old, and with the touch of death upon her, felt less scorn than compassion. The age which produced this monstrous woman opposite her had been an ugly vicious age, but it had planted the seeds of its own destruction. For a moment, it is true, she did feel a kind of delight and triumph that retribution was closing in. This woman opposite her was frightened; that was why the jewels had become more important than anything in life. They were all that was left her; they were the symbol of a security founded upon the precarious power of money alone. Mary Pulsifer had always been rich but not in this fashion.

After a time, she said, "You mustn't behave like this, May. They aren't lost. There is still hope of getting them."

The Princess sat up straight and began to make up her face, "I'm sorry, Mary. It must be because of what has happened to me the last two or three days. Nothing like it has ever happened to me before."

"You had better get some rest. We'll think up a way. My driver is very good at such things. He'll have ideas. It's all right so long as actual war doesn't break out."

"You're very good to me, Mary. I don't see why you should be."

Mrs. Pulsifer laughed, "I don't see why either, but I am. So leave it at that."

.   .   .   .   .

But when Mrs. Pulsifer had gone to bed, she did not sleep. Her heart beat wildly and thoughts and memories raced in a muddle through her tired brain. She relived fragments of the past, out of the life which had always been pleasant but somehow without savor until her husband died and she set out with 'Ennery to roam the world and get to *know* people and the goodness that was in them. She knew somehow that she would never leave Monte Carlo, that the whole thing was coming to an end here. At last she fell into a restless sleep, half-wishing as consciousness slipped away from her, that she might never waken.

At ten o'clock when she wakened and had had her tea, she sent for 'Ennery.

He came in, square and stocky and solid, looking, with his broad red face and graying hair, a rock of security. She bade him sit down and then she said to him, "I've not been very well lately, 'Ennery."

"I'm sorry to hear that, Madame. Perhaps the strain 'as been too much."

"There're one or two things I want to settle just in case anything should happen to me suddenly."

'Ennery's blue eyes blinked and he said, "You mustn't talk like that, Madame."

"It's only common sense," she said briskly. "In the first place, you're taken care of in my will, so you needn't worry."

He knew that already because he knew Mary Pulsifer, but he said, "That's very good of you, Madame."

"I'm leaving a check with you to take care of the poor people we brought with us here. I could leave it with my lawyers or my bankers but they might think it foolish to waste good money on humble people in a foreign country. I prefer to trust you. We've been together for a long time and we understand each other. We feel the same about things. I want you to act as if I had adopted all of them. I want you to keep in touch with them and see that they do not starve until this war is over and they are back again in their own houses. I know I can trust you."

"Yes, Madame. Of course."

She gave him an envelope and then said, "The Princess D'Orobelli is here."

"Yes, Madame, I saw her. She looks very badly."

"She is frightened and unhappy." Then she told him the story of the jewels and as she talked she found herself making excuses, explaining the frightened, raddled woman. But 'Ennery understood. He interrupted her presently to say, "Yes, Madame, I'm sure there is a way out for 'er Excellency and 'er maid. You and I have been in just as tight fixes, like that time we ran the frontier between Iran and Afghanistan on the way to Kabul. You leave it to me. I'll think up something."

She sent him away then to see that her refugees were all right and to find out what news there was. Then she went back to bed and fell asleep once more. She did not waken until nearly six o'clock when the Princess appeared accompanied by 'Ennery.

The Princess was in a strange state of exaltation. 'Ennery had thought out a plan. It was simple enough, very like the plan of Madame Lestrade. He would bribe his way through both the French and Italian lines. He needed money, four or five bottles of brandy and some American cigarettes. He asked permission to use Mrs. Pulsifer's old Rolls-Royce and he needed an American flag.

He would cross over and find Serafina and bring her and the jewels back. The plan would need to work swiftly during the time one set of soldiers was on guard. As soon as it was dark he would cross over. He thought he could leave about nine o'clock and be back in Monte Carlo by midnight.

As he told his plan he looked at Mrs. Pulsifer, seeking her approval, for he trusted her shrewdness and judgment. He related the details in a flat dull voice. The only sign of animation was the glint which came into the clear blue eyes. Otherwise there was no hint that inside this dull, solid, respectable, elderly man there was the same spirit of adventure that had moved Drake and Morgan, that same spirit which had been a bond for so long between himself and Mary Pulsifer.

And as he talked, a faint envy rose in the heart of the Edwardian old lady. It was an adventure she herself would have enjoyed. When he had finished, she said to the Princess, "I'd like to speak to 'Ennery alone for a moment, May, if you don't mind." And when the Princess had gone into the next room, she said to 'Ennery, "You are to take no risks, 'Ennery. You understand that. It isn't worth it—for a pile of trash that might just as well be glass. Remember, that if anything happened to you, I should be lost."

"You needn't worry, Madame. I'm not doing it for 'er Excellency but because I'd like to see if it could be done."

"I shall be waiting up for you. If I should be asleep wake me when you come in. I shall want to hear about it."

. . . . .

Luckily there was a moon. 'Ennery had to run without lights but it was easy enough because so many of the villas along the edge of the winding road were white and showed up with a kind of phosphorescence against the dark Mediterranean. As he drove, 'Ennery calculated all the dangers, all the possibilities he could summon out of his imagination. He had no illusions. Success depended upon the soldiers he encountered at the two frontiers. Being a cosmopolitan he knew what to expect of Latins. They would either be good-natured and easy-going or they would be pompous, officious and impossible. If he fell upon the officious kind the mission would be difficult or impossible. If not, it would be easy enough, for he had prepared a good story.

His mistress, he would say, was caught on the Italian side of the closed frontier. He was passionately in love with her. He wanted only to spend an hour with her and return. If, on the Italian side, they had any doubts he would suggest that a couple of soldiers accompany him to the house where she was staying, remain in another room while he visited her, and return with him to the frontier. There would be, of course, money and cigarettes to bribe them, and brandy to make them drunk. If they drank enough they would not be troublesome. He would get Serafina into the back of the car, hide her on the floor under a blanket and set out for home.

There were many things on his side. It was great luck that neither frontier was guarded by efficient and unromantic English or German soldiers. The Latins would want to believe in the story of a mistress. That was something they would understand. The fact that he was an elderly man would only make them more sympathetic, because the situation would touch their sense of humor and make them laugh. A couple of drinks and a package or two of American cigarettes and they would laugh more. He knew exactly what he would do: he would clown his part. He would act as if devoured by passion to reach the mistress awaiting him on the other side of the frontier. He would describe the ardor of their love for each other and the impatience of the mistress. That he was ugly and old would make it all the funnier. He would even pretend that he suspected her of being unfaithful to him. Unless he ran across a pompous non-commissioned officer, the plan was certain to work. The old-fashioned high-rumped Rolls-Royce made it all the more comic.

Only one thing could go wrong. On his return, the French customs men might want to search the car for contraband. If that happened, he would have to run for it, taking a chance on a stray bullet hitting him. That was a chance he would have to take. On his return there could be no delay, no turning back.

As the car passed through Mentone, he slackened speed knowing that somewhere not far ahead he would be stopped. Then out of the darkness he became aware of a barrier across the road just ahead and at the same time he heard a sharp cry of *"Halte!"*

He stopped the car and out of the shadow of a house by the road stepped a sergeant and three soldiers. Opening the door 'Ennery stepped down on to the road and at the same time he saw in the moonlight the lower part of the sergeant's face. The rest remained hidden in the shadow of his steel helmet, but the lower part was all 'Ennery needed to see and he grinned to himself with relief. It was the lower part of a good-looking face with a firm chin and sensual lips partly covered by a black mustache, carefully waxed and tended. The lips and chin were those of a sensual man who liked women and good food. The mustache showed that the man was a lady-killer. He would understand. So far so good.

Quietly he said, *"Bon soir, mon ami!"*

. . . . . .

The two women dined again together, very well on the best the hotel could offer. The Princess, greedy by nature, liked good food and Mrs. Pulsifer with the presentiment of death upon her, thought, "It may be my last meal." In any case whether she lived or died, it would be a long time before any one in Europe would live as they once had lived. It might be a lifetime before there would again be famous restaurants and grand dinners, a long time perhaps before there would ever again be enough of such common things as soap and sugar. Here in the Hotel de Paris they were dining on the last remnants of the Grand Era.

The Princess was fidgety, her mind absorbed with speculations regarding 'Ennery's success or failure, and when at last they had finished the long extravagant meal, Mrs. Pulsifer suggested a game of six-pack bezique to kill time and divert her companion's mind from the rescue of the jewels. But even that did not go well. The Princess' mind continued to wander; she played badly and Mrs. Pulsifer who had played millions of games with her husband, won seven thousand francs very quickly—seven thousand francs which she would give to her refugees.

Ten o'clock came and eleven and finally midnight and at last Mrs. Pulsifer, feeling suddenly weak, said, "If you don't mind, May, I'll go to my room and lie down. I'm feeling very odd. I shan't take off my clothes. I'll only need a wink or two. If I should happen to be asleep call me when 'Ennery comes back."

Then she climbed the stairs.

When she had gone the Princess ordered more brandy and sat down to wait for the sound of the returning car. In the whole of the hotel everyone had gone to bed save for a boy who slept upright in his chair by the door. The great hall and reception rooms with their gilt chairs and tropical plants were full of empty shadows. Once or twice as she sat drinking, the disordered mind of the Princess peopled the shadowy place with phantoms—Zaharoff and Edward VII and Lily Langtry and Old Leopold of the Belgians with his dyed black beard, Serge Diaghileff, Liane de Pugy, a whole procession of grand dukes and rich Moscow merchants, all the ghosts of those who once frequented these great rooms, all the figure of a Europe which was now dying. And suddenly she would waken with a drunken shudder and think, "I must be going crazy. There is no one here but myself and that boy asleep in his chair by the door. I am alone here waiting for Serafina and the jewels, and I am getting older every moment." And she would pour herself another brandy and as she drank, she would sit staring at nothing while the phantoms returned out of that world which had been so pleasant for people like herself and so evil for people like Mary Pulsifer's refugees. And from among the phantoms now and then would appear the lean grim face of the General and the curious glitter of hatred and contempt she had seen in his eyes.

Outside the night had the stillness of death and so she heard the motor of the old-fashioned Rolls long before it arrived at the door. She heard it from the moment it started up the long hill below the Sporting Club. The sound creeping into her brain suddenly dispersed the phantoms and she thought, "They have come!" Standing up quickly she knocked over the bottle of brandy. Without troubling to salvage it she ran toward the door and out into the square past the boy sleeping in his chair.

She was waiting there in the dim light of the doorway when the car drove up. It came to a sudden halt, so violent that the brakes cried out, and almost at once 'Ennery stepped out. He moved uncertainly for he was a little drunk from all the brandy he had been forced to drink in order to carry through his plot.

The Princess cried out, "Did you get her? Have you got the jewels?"

The old driver balancing himself unsteadily, regarded her for the space of a second in silence and into his shrewd eyes there came that same look of hatred and contempt she had met before so many times in the last few days.

"I got her, Excellency. I do not know about the jewels."

"Where is she? I don't see her."

"Something has happened to her, Excellency. At the border I had to run for it. They machine-gunned us."

Then he opened the door and stood back with great dignity, almost with pomp as he had done so many times waiting for Mrs. Pulsifer to descend in all her Edwardian splendor. But

no one came out of the car. On the floor half-covered by
the carriage robe, huddled the body of Serafina. She was lying
with her face down. A thin trickle of blood, black and glistening in the dim light, ran down across the step.

·   ·   ·   ·   ·

With the help of the boy and a porter who came in his
nightshirt with a jacket over it, they got the body out of the
old-fashioned Rolls and into the hotel where they laid it on
a sofa, the hat pushed grotesquely over the face of the dead
Serafina.

And then an extraordinary thing happened. While 'Ennery
and the two servants looked on, the Princess began tearing off
the clothes of the dead woman, and as the black cloth gave
way, there came to light a wonderful array of jewels—glittering bracelets, rings, necklaces, clips, pendants of diamonds
and rubies and emeralds, all removed from their cases and
fastened to the old-fashioned bodice and drawers of the dead
woman by safety pins. One by one the Princess tore them
loose, sobbing and laughing hysterically as she worked.

'Ennery, sickened, turned away to find his mistress and
report to her. As he walked up the stairs, he heard the Princess cry out, "They're all there! They didn't get one of
them—the swine!"

·   ·   ·   ·   ·

Upstairs 'Ennery knocked gently on the door of Mrs. Pulsifer's room. Twice he knocked, each time with a little more
violence, and when there was no answer, he pushed the door
open and went in. The room was in darkness and twice before
touching the button of the light he called her name respectfully. Still there was no answer and when he turned on the
light, he saw the old lady fully dressed lying on the bed. She
was very still and even before he touched her he knew that
she was asleep forever. The tears came into his eyes and a
lump into his throat.

In the hallway, the body of Serafina still in the torn

clothes, lay on the sofa covered by a green baize cover from one of the tables and in the room overhead the Princess sat at the dressing table in her bath room, a great pile of jewels before her. One by one she lifted the pieces of jewelry and scrubbed them carefully with a toothbrush to wash away the blood that dimmed their glitter.

Out of the stillness of the dawn from the direction of Ventimiglia came the dry bark of cannon. The Italians had attacked at last, but the Princess, absorbed in her task, heard nothing.

THE OLD HOUSE

PEOPLE SAID MRS. LINTON WAS FOOLISH AND STUBBORN ABOUT the Old House. It was bad enough living there through the winter in peacetime but there was no excuse for putting up with the isolation and discomfort in time of war. When the first raids began to happen and people talked about invasion, the stubborn attitude of Mrs. Linton only irritated and alarmed her friends throughout the neighboring countryside. Certain friends argued with her; others, according to their temperaments, threatened her or attempted to cajole her into leaving the Old House and moving inland into some safer area away from the seacoast and the threat of invasion; but none of them had any effect. Mrs. Linton only said that she was happy there or that she did not mind the discomfort or the isolation, or to the more aggressive pleaders she said (for she could be tart when occasion called for it), "Please mind your own business. I may be seventy-six years old but I am in my right mind and in perfect health. I can still work ten hours a day in the garden and not notice it."

At the beginning of the second year of the war, the situation so wrought up the countryside that a spontaneous delegation arrived from Vintner's Green, the nearest village which was twenty miles away, to plead with her to abandon the Old House and go inland until the war was over. She received them and with the help of the old manservant, Peterman, served them with tea, stout or beer according to their tastes and made them a little speech. She told them that she appreciated their kindness and interest, but that she meant to remain. Turning her work-worn old hands over and over upon each other shyly as she spoke, she said, "I was born here. I have lived here all my life. It is too late to go away now. It would be like dying before my time. Please don't worry about me. If there should be such a thing as invasion, I shall go away. But I am certain no such thing will happen. Even if it did happen the Old House would be of no use to anyone. They will sweep over and past it. How could tanks ever get through the marshes?"

And old Mrs. Simpson, the greengrocer's mother, spoke up and said, "What if it should happen during the neap tides? What would you do then?"

"I'd wait till low tide to get out," said Mrs. Linton. "The tide goes down just as much as it comes up. At neap tide you can take a short cut and walk right across Filmer's reach on dry land."

Such an argument was sound, the hard-headed villagers agreed. Exchanging glances which implied that Mrs. Linton was certainly courageous and stubborn, if not a little mad, the villagers gave it up and, after having a look at Mrs. Linton's rose garden, went back to the mainland in a strange assortment of vehicles ranging from the baker's ancient and wheezing delivery truck, to the horsedrawn cart of Mr. Murgatroyd, the big hop-grower.

One more effort was made to pry Mrs. Linton loose from the Old House and transport her to an area more secure. This time it was made by Sir Horace Danby, the squire and a hardshell Tory who had connections in the War Ministry. He was a bluff man, nearly as old as Mrs. Linton, who disapproved of the divorce law reform and still held the tenacious belief that women—especially old or very pretty women—should be protected and told what to do. Long ago, within his memory, Mary Linton had been a very pretty woman and now she was an old woman, so in both categories he felt that she was his victim. He proceeded without consulting her, and as a result of his activities, a rather officious young Major arrived one morning at the Old House to notify Mrs. Linton that the zone for a considerable distance inland from the coast had been declared a combat zone and that she would be required to vacate the Old House before the first of the coming month.

But Mary Linton, although she was an old woman and once had been a very pretty one, was not without character or influence. In the great days when she had traveled about the world as the wife of Derek Linton, the diplomat and later foreign minister, she knew many people and brilliant people and even though nearly twenty years had passed since she had spent a season in London, the legend of her beauty and her wit still persisted.

So after the visit of the officious young Major, Mrs. Linton put on town clothes and made the tiresome journey into London to interview certain old friends in the Government. When she returned, she settled down again in the Old House with the certainty that no more efforts would be made to dislodge her. She had always been an honorable woman and refused to take advantage of the privileges to which the long, distinguished, lives of herself and her husband entitled her, but with the Old House it was different. To separate her from it would be like taking the blood out of her veins. To stay there was all the reward she had ever asked. It was said in the village that the Prime Minister himself saw her point and agreed with her.

. . . . .

In a way the neighbors and friends were quite right in their concern for Mrs. Linton. In the first place they felt for her the solicitude which a community feels for one of its members who is a distinguished and worthy citizen. Mary Linton had always recognized her responsibilities and so people came to her with every sort of problem, from difficulties with teething babies to how to manage an obnoxious mother-in-law, and she never refused to do what she could to help, for inside Mary Linton there was a curious conviction, so profound that she never thought of it, that she was a part of these people, that for all the former glory and brilliance of her life, she was different from none of them. She and they were all part of a community to which fate or luck or circumstances provided a lively variety of character and station in life. She might, she thought, just as well have been born old Granny Taitus with her over-fondness for the bottle as Mary Wentworth Linton. It was only a matter of luck like the cards in a game of bezique.

And so the whole community from Sir Horace Danby to Granny Taitus returned the feeling. That is why they were all so concerned over rescuing her from the Old House. Mrs.

Linton represented something very special to them, something which antedated the great mills and factories and shareholder aristocracy of modern England, something which ran far back into remote and mysterious time, something as old as the ancient earth of the hop fields and orchards beyond the marshes. Without quite knowing what it was, they *knew* that Mary Linton symbolized somehow the thing upon which their lives were founded, the thing for which they had lived and fought, for which their ancestors had lived and fought for more than a thousand years. Mrs. Linton was something they had to preserve. This they *knew* without thinking about it at all.

And it must be said that the Old House was an isolated and perhaps a dangerous place, remote and lonely. It stood on an island in the great marshes which fringed the coast. Once, in almost prehistoric times, the island had been a part of the mainland, but for more than a thousand years, the mainland had been sinking slowly, and gradually it had become marshy land and the marshy land in turn had been turning slowly into sea. When the first house had been built by a Roman on the "island," the "island" was a low hill connected with the mainland by fields and forests. By the time the first Norman built a kind of fortress-castle upon the foundations of the Roman dwelling, the fields and woods were already soggy with sea-water and turning into marshes. At neap tide there was a wide expanse of shallow water between the "island" and the mainland.

By the time Mary Linton was born in the Old House, the "island" was separated from the mainland by ten miles of impassable marsh filled with sedge and pink-flowered mallow, haunted in November and March by great flights of wild fowl. The only means of reaching the mainland was along a troublesome and expensive road for the upkeep of which the people of the Old House were responsible. It was troublesome and expensive because it was forever disintegrating and sinking lower and lower by infinitesimal degrees into the marshes. After the neap tides, when the sea covered all the marsh and lapped its way across the road, there were always expensive repairs to be made. At the time of the neap tides there was usually fog which, with the rising sea, cut off the house altogether from the mainland so that it seemed strangely dreamlike and intangible like a ghost house emerging out of water and mist.

The little island, rising damply above the marshes, possessed an almost unbelievable fertility. Behind high walls, sheltered from the east wind which sometimes blew in chill and bitter from the North Sea, grew vegetables and flowers which none of those produced by the neighbors on the mainland could rival in quality and beauty. The walls were important. Some of them had been there since the Norman days and others were built upon the ruined foundation of crumbled Roman walls. The ancient cedars which thrust their branches above them were all twisted and distorted by the winds, bald on the seaward side with long green fingers reaching out on the landward side as if in an effort to regain the shelter of the mainland. From a distance across the marshes on a clear bright day the house gave the impression of bleakness; it was only when one entered the great gate that one discovered inside the walls the lush green lawns and the borders of flowers and the neat beautiful rows of vigorous vegetables.

The very history of the Old House was written in its walls, from the heavy vaulted arches of the damp cellar where at neap tide the water sometimes rose to the third step of the ancient stone stairway, to the odd Victorian Gothic study and conservatory erected by the rich mill-owner's daughter whom Mrs. Linton's grandfather, Cecil Wentworth, had married in the beginning of the nineteenth century. The main part of the house was built sometime at the end of the reign of the great Elizabeth when a Wentworth had been a merchant-trader of the Cinque Ports and a partner with the Queen in piratical enterprises against the Spanish. And there was a small wing built under James the Second and a kind of guest house, very weathered, in the Georgian style built to house the Wentworth offspring in a more vigorous age when one numbered grandchildren by the score. The Wentworths for a hundred years had undergone many ups and downs of fortune, but they had always been a distinguished family and even in the most desperate situation had clung to the Old House. The whole history of the family was written there, in the Lely and Reynolds and Raeburn portraits, only five of which remained, in the old deeds and documents which Mrs. Linton kept in a great chest in the library, in the still stained spot on the stone flagging of the great hall where a drunken wastrel Wentworth had shot himself in earlier Victorian times, in the decaying stump of a great oak long since dead and overgrown with ivy from which Oliver Wentworth had caught a first glimpse of the Dutch fleet on its way to sweep up the Thames with broomsticks lashed to the masts. History lay in the paling yellow photographs of Mrs. Linton's brother killed at twenty-one in the Boer War and in the drawing by Sargent of her son Herbert killed at Mons when he was twenty-three.

Mary Linton's roots grew deep in the soil of the little island. All her life she had returned to it—from Berlin, from Washington, from Delhi, from Tokyo, from London. And now, at last, she had returned to stay there until she died and was buried at last in the burial ground near the old half-ruined Norman Chapel.

As far back as anyone could remember, as far back as any record could show, it had been called the Old House. It may have been called that even by the Romans. In its walls, in its crumbling stones was written not only the history of the Wentworth family but in a way the history of England as well.

.   .   .   .   .   .

At sight of Sir Horace's ancient Rolls picking its way carefully along the causeway road from the mainland, Mrs. Linton said, "Damn!" She saw it as she sat for a moment resting from her labors in the garden, in the Victorian gazebo built on the top of the old Roman wall. From the gazebo you had a view across the marshes to the mainland, and now in the August afternoon heat the distant mainland faded in and out of the haze like some indistinct desert landscape.

She knew that her appearance was untidy. The old gingham frock was patched and stained with the fresh good earth of the kitchen garden where she had been kneeling all the afternoon pulling weeds and digging with the stout steel trowel which lay by her side. This vegetable business was important. The rich ancient soil not only provided the people of the Old House with vegetables and fruits for eating and preserving but it supplied an excess which she gave away to old Granny Taitus who was too old to care for her own garden and for the nursery where the hop-pickers' children were kept while their mothers worked in the fields. There were no longer any young or middle-aged men to be had and there was no one to care for the gardens but herself and old Hicks. Of the two she was the stronger for old Hicks had attacks of rheumatism which during the dampness at the time of the neap tides put him altogether out of the running. Both of them worked sometimes as long as twelve hours a day. Old Hicks had been born a week earlier than herself in the same little cottage where he still lived, and like herself he had come to think of the little island as a kingdom which should always have well-stocked cellars and stillrooms against a time of scarcity or siege. Like herself he rarely left the island any longer.

From the gazebo she could see the old man, his gnarled bent old body bending down over the fresh green of the latest planting of carrots. She should, her conscience told her, be there beside him, fighting the weeds which threatened to choke the young plants, and she was ashamed of herself for indulging in what Hicks called "a spell of rest" here in the summer house where the breeze from the sea could reach you. The walls which protected the garden from the harsh east winds of February and March also shut out the cooling breezes of summer. Sometimes, inside the walls, it could be devilishly hot.

Hicks, she thought, must not overwork himself. If anything happened to him, she would be defeated. There was no one to replace him. If, one day, he tottered and fell on his face, she would be alone for Peterman and Cook could not help her in the garden. It wasn't only that they had their hands full already with the Old House—keeping it in order, painting and repairing it, now a pipe, now a cornice, now a cracked pane—but they had no feeling for plants or flowers. The house itself was all they cared for . . . like mill workers, like manufacturers, she thought, they did not value the earth as the beginning and end of all else.

But Sir Horace's car was quite near now. She could hear the dull chugging of the ancient motor as his driver maneuvered among the ruts and holes in the half ruined road. She thought, "I should go and change my frock and redo my hair and freshen up for the old humbug." And at the same time she thought, "But I'm not going to. I'll wash my hands—that's enough."

As she rose she looked down at the hands, smiling, at the callouses, the broken nails, stained with the good rich earth of the little island. Bismarck, who never paid compliments to women, had once, long ago, called them the most beautiful hands in Europe.

On the way into the lavatory she stopped outside the window of the kitchen to call in to Mrs. Hicks, the cook, "Sir Horace will be here for tea. Very likely he'll want a whiskey. Tell Peterman to bring it to the rose garden."

Mrs. Hicks smiled at her. She was a fat woman ten years younger than old Hicks. She wasn't really a good cook but she did all right and it was much better to put up with the monotony of her puddings than to attempt bringing in someone, perhaps no more competent, who did not feel about the Old House as they all did. Mrs. Hicks went to the mainland only two or three times a year.

After she had scrubbed the earth from her hands, she walked through the great hall to find Sir Horace already crossing the lawn toward her.

His plump round face was red with the heat and he puffed a little as he walked. In a way he was a fine looking old man with his white hair and white Guardsman's mustache and pink face and china blue eyes. She could remember that once he had been a very handsome young man, but now as he moved across the lawn toward her, she felt a wild inclination to laugh. He looked, in his carefully shabby tweeds, exactly like Colonel Blimp. Why she had not thought of it before she did not know, perhaps because she had known him as a young fresh-cheeked boy at Harrow and then as a handsome young Guardsman— handsome in the peculiar English blond way—and then as a middle-aged man with a Guardsman's carriage. It had all happened very gradually, imperceptibly—the transformation from the handsome, stupid young Guardsman, whom England was still rich enough, fortunate enough, to afford, into the puffing plump, stupid old man. The comedy of the idea softened a little the irritation which had risen in her at sight of the old car chugging along the causeway and still remained gnawing at her sense of tranquillity. It made it easier to face the prospect of a wasted hour or two which might have been spent with old Hicks among the carrots.

As he saw her he said, "Good afternoon, Mary. I thought it was about time I paid you a visit." She held out the work-stained hand and smiled at him and said, "I was wondering what had happened to you."

She had not wondered. She had known that he had not dared to face her after she had defeated his effort to have her sent away from the Old House for her own good. "You're looking well."

He sighed, "I'm feeling as well as anyone can in these times."

She knew what he meant—that he had given up his comfortable new car, that good whiskey was difficult to find, that his special brand of Havana cigars could no longer be had, that there were no servants in the house in London, that service in his club was wretched, that there were too many radicals and labor people making trouble, that all a man's money was being taken from him, that the working classes no longer had a proper respect for men of property.

She said, "I told Peterman to bring us tea in the rose garden. The roses are lovely just now and it will be cool under the big cedar."

They started toward the rose garden across the velvety lawn they had crossed perhaps a thousand times together in various stages in their existence since they were children, when Sir Horace was a tow-headed boy, then as the handsome young Guardsman, then with his bride, and later as a rich middle-aged man, and now as Colonel Blimp. Mary Linton, thinking of this, also thought, "I suppose we should feel very tired and old and useless, but I don't. I feel remarkably young and well."

The Old House had, in a curious way, given her back her youth. When she became a widow and left London and the world—that insane world which for forty years she had seen dancing crazily toward disaster—the Old House, even with no servants to speak of, with herself doing part of the household work and helping Old Hicks in the garden, had made her feel young again. It was as if she had tossed away all the rubbish and come back again to the beginning of things, to the good English earth and all the long line of stout-hearted tradition which the Old House represented.

As they neared the rose garden, Sir Horace took from the pocket of his tweed coat a small packet of letters.

"I stopped at the post office and brought these over for you," he said. "I thought it might save you a trip."

"That's very good of you, Horace. I haven't gone to the village for a fortnight. The trip is so tiresome with a horse after one has become accustomed to automobiles. It takes nearly the whole day."

Horace laughed, "It takes nearly as long by car over that road of yours. Another high tide and there won't be any road." He looked at her slyly, "But I suppose you would like that . . . to be cut off altogether."

She did not hear him at first for she was going through the packet of envelopes trying to recognize the handwriting of each one. She succeeded on only two—one was from a cousin and the other from her granddaughter Ellen. Most of the others were, she knew at once, of no importance in any case . . . bills or appeals for money for this or that charity. Perhaps she could find the money for the bills, but for the charities it would be difficult even to squeeze a very little. Through these thoughts she became aware of what Sir Horace had said and replied, "No, I shouldn't like to be cut off altogether but it's impossible to find money for the repairs and even if I had the money there is no one to do the work."

The rose garden was built about a fragment of mosaic pavement which had once been the floor of a Roman bath and lay four feet below the level of the garden above. Here no biting wind ever seared the blossoms or froze the delicate plants. In one corner grew a great Cedar of Lebanon. Beneath it

Peterman had put out the tea things on a weathered ancient table. She had been right about the whiskey. That was what Sir Horace wanted.

When he tasted it, he said, "Ah! That is real whiskey again. There isn't any more like that."

"It is from what is left in the cellar. I'll give you a bottle to take home. I have only one drink a day of it—just before I go to bed. Sometimes Mrs. Hicks has a 'poor spell' and it puts her back on her feet."

"They're sending all the good whiskey to America nowadays," grumbled Sir Horace.

Then Peterman, very old and dignified, in his shabby clothes, brought the tea and while he talked for a little while, respectfully, in an old-fashioned way with Sir Horace, Mrs. Linton said, "If you don't mind I'll look at this letter from Ellen. I haven't heard from her for such a long time."

So while Sir Horace and Peterman talked, she went quickly through Ellen's letter. It was not long, only two pages, written in Ellen's cool, quiet hand, so easy to read, so remarkable in a woman so young. There was very little small talk, simply facts about her work in London and finally in the third paragraph, she wrote quite simply, "I am getting married on Thursday next to a young man you have probably never heard of. His name is John Searles and his father is a builder—quite a big builder—in Liverpool. I met him in the canteen three weeks ago. He will have a fortnight's leave and I am wondering if we might come on to stay with you. It will be quiet there and I think John will like it. I always love the Old House. I am not asking you to come all the way to London for the wedding. We're getting it over as quickly as possible at the registry office and it wouldn't be worth while asking you to leave the Old House and come to London just for that."

Mrs. Linton picked up the envelope to look at the date of the postmark. Yes, clearly Ellen meant *this* Thursday. The letter must have lain at the village post office for nearly a week. Only a telegram could reach her in time.

Mrs. Linton was aware that her heart was beating more rapidly at the prospect of seeing Ellen and meeting her young man. She could hear Sir Horace's voice above the drone of the bees, as he talked to Peterman, and she was aware of his manner and the quality of his talk. He was patronizing old Peterman whom he had known all his life. His whole attitude toward Peterman was that of "my good fellow." There had always been something inexpressibly stupid and vulgar about Horace.

Then Peterman went away and she said, "Ellen is getting married."

"Well, well. That's good news. Whom is she marrying?"

Mrs. Linton watched him carefully. "She says that his name is John Searles and that his father is a builder in Liverpool. They met in her canteen three weeks ago."

Sir Horace did not answer her at once. The expression on his face was rather silly. Then he said, "Very strange things are happening in England nowadays—marrying after three weeks acquaintance!" It was as if he said, "The Empire is going to pieces when a child with the blood of the Wentworths and the Lintons in her veins marries the son of a Liverpool builder . . . after knowing each other for only three weeks."

There were many things she could have said—biting, devastating things about Sir Horace's own ancestry only three generations back. Sir Horace was rich, but he was, after all, a mill-owner. It was not the calling which had formed his point of view; it was merely money. With money he and his father before him had bought everything he was or possessed. She could have annihilated him, sitting here in the shadow of the Old House, beside the Roman pavement, her roots deep in the soil and the glorious past of England, but she only said quietly, "Very likely it is for the good of the country."

"Possibly," said Sir Horace. "He'll turn out to be one of those damned radicals."

"Queen Elizabeth was a rip-snorting radical," said Mary Linton and let it go at that. It did not matter because Sir Horace did not even understand what she meant.

He said, "I really came over to apologize, Mary, for interfering in your affairs, but I did it from the best of motives. I thought and I still think it isn't safe for you to live here alone."

"I'm not alone. There's Peterman and the Hicks'."

"A lot of help they'd be if raiders or parachutists descended on the Old House."

Mrs. Linton smiled, "What could they possibly want with a place like this? In any case it's been knocked about a good deal in the past—the Romans, the Danes, the Normans all had a crack at it but it has survived despite everything."

Sir Horace refilled his whiskey glass and looked at her obliquely. He did not approve of her cosmopolitan speech and the queer idioms and expressions she sometimes used. After a moment he said, "There's another thing, Mary. I've always felt very close to you . . . like a brother, you might say. I've always felt a kind of responsibility."

"Thank you, Horace."

"I know that Derek died leaving very little, that he spent a great deal of his own money in the service of his country."

"He spent practically all of it," said Mrs. Linton.

"That was what I was driving at. I imagine you must be rather pinched. I just wanted you to feel free to call upon me anytime you really need money. I'm not as rich as I once was, with the Government taking everything with their damned taxes, but I can still help out an old friend."

She felt the color coming into her cheeks, because suddenly she was angry, why she did not know since Horace was only trying to kind and generous. Her anger was born of something far deeper than his kindly, bungling offer to help her. It came out of the past. It was as if her husband had returned and stood there behind Sir Horace, wiry, clever, able, devoted only to his country, giving his life and all his fortune to it. He had been a singularly loyal person. He had married her, poor as the Wentworths were, because he loved her, when he might have married any brewery heiress as Sir Horace had done. She thrust back her anger, moved by the wisdom born of a long rich life, thinking, "People cannot help being stupid. One should forgive them. One ought only to crush out the stupid ones when they make life cruel or impossible for others." That was why England was in desperate danger now —because the stupid rich had been in power for too long.

So quietly she said, "Thank you, Horace, but I'm all right. I manage to get along, to have everything I want. That's one of the reasons I stuck by the Old House. While I'm here I need very little. If I went away I should have all sorts of expenses I couldn't possibly meet."

"I just wanted you to know."

Then above the buzzing of the bees there arose another sound, remote and distant, but pervading and dominating all the hot stillness of the rose garden. It was the sound of distant gun-fire.

"They're at it again," said Sir Horace.

"The wind is from the south. Otherwise you don't hear it," said Mrs. Linton.

They spoke no more of the sound. For most people on the coast it had long since become a part of their lives, like the east wind in winter or the great tides in spring and autumn.

Presently Sir Horace said, "Things seem to be going from bad to worse."

Mrs. Linton did not answer him. It was not that she too wasn't troubled; she had lain awake hour after hour in the Old House, worrying about what had been happening in Europe, in Africa and in the East.

"Those damned Malays betrayed us after all we've done for them, and then the Burmese. Not a share of rubber is worth a tinker's dam. And now oil shares are going the same way. It'll take years to restore the plantations and refineries that have been destroyed by our own people. It's a bloody business —forgive the language, Mary—but I don't know what we're coming to."

"I've heard the word 'bloody' before, Horace."

"Did Derek have any rubber shares?"

"Yes, a few."

"They're worth nothing now."

"No."

She was glad about the rubber shares. She had never wanted Derek to buy them. There had always been something unclean about them, something unclean about the whole business of exploitation, of cartels, of big money, of all the things which had built up this war that was threatening the very existence of England. Horace thought himself a business man but about these things she knew much more than he knew for she had lived all her life watching their rottenness, their greed, grow and expand now in Singapore, now in Berlin, now in Washington, now in Shanghai, cornering this pocket of wealth, this pile of resources, shutting each other out from markets, supporting and encouraging traitors and dictators, exploiting helpless people. She had watched them at work—these great business men, like maggots corrupting the greatness of England for their own selfish ends, as the same sort of men had done long ago in Rome. She knew it all—the whole long sordid story—better than poor stupid Horace or any of his kind could ever know or understand it. It had led in the end to Munich, with its conniving and groveling and to the sound of guns rumbling against the distant horizon, drowning out the sound of the bees. She had known so much that she had tried to forget it all and hide away from it here in the Old House where the real greatness of England was written in every stone. But one could not escape it any more than one could escape the stupidity of Horace or the sound of the distant guns.

Poor Horace, who thought business men were clever and knew how to rule. It was a business-men's government which had brought this all about, fostering and coddling a mongrel upstart from a frontier village in Austria because they thought he would serve their ends.

Horace went on talking and she listened with only half her attention. What he said was of no importance. It was all the old stuff in essence—"the old school tie" and "the playing fields of Eton." Horace never saw that these symbols were worn and played out, that what they stood for was no longer the same. Her dead husband, Derek, had come from the playing fields of Eton, so had her father and grandfather before him, but they had believed in the greatness of England that lay in the stones of the Old House and they had fought for it, not for fat revenues from shares in rubber and oil companies. That was why all of them had died without fortunes; that was why today she was a poor woman and the Old House was slowly crumbling. But it was no use talking to Horace; he would not even understand what she was saying, just as he could not understand that to send her away from the Old House would mean her end. He was like all the stupid, well-meaning, dull people, soggy with material comforts, who thought Chamberlain a God when he returned from Berchtesgaden "bringing peace in our time."

The rumbling of the distant cannon grew a little louder as the wind turned more toward the south. Old Peterman, stooped and dignified, came and took away the tea things and Sir Horace stood up, saying, "I must leave now, Mary. It takes such a long time to maneuver your awful road."

She too rose and asked, "Could you take a telegram for me to the post office?"

"Of course."

"It's to Ellen. She wants to come here for her honeymoon."

"That will be nice for you."

"Yes . . . but I'm a little afraid."

"Why?"

She hesitated for a moment. "Never mind. I can't exactly say why. Come, I'll go into the house and write out the telegram and address."

He followed her into the great hall and the small library where she sat down to write. The telegram was brief:

Letter delayed. Delighted have you here. Love. Impatiently
Mary Linton

She counted up the words and then opened a little drawer in the old desk. In it were a heap of small coins and two or three pound notes. The drawer was her treasury. Out of it came the money which paid the Hicks and old Peterman.

Horace said, "Don't bother, Mary, I'll pay it."

"No. This is private business. You can do me a favor, though. They'll be married on Thursday so it's likely they'll take the train to Crosby Downs the same day. You could open any telegram addressed to me and make certain when they're arriving and it would be a great help if you could send them over in your car. It's a very tiresome trip in a dog-cart."

"Of course, Mary."

He flushed and added, "I'll try and pay you another visit soon, but it's very difficult on petrol rations, even for a warden."

"I understand. Come when you can arrange it, Horace."

But she wished he would not come at all. His visit had disturbed and depressed her.

"And I wish you could bring yourself to leave the Old House and go somewhere inland."

She smiled, "I'm afraid I won't."

"It's very old and very big. You must find yourself uncomfortable here."

"It's very old and it's very big and it's falling to pieces but I belong to it. Thank you just the same, Horace, when the Old House goes down I shall go with it."

She walked with him as far as the ancient Rolls and then bade him good-bye, standing in the gateway to watch the car bump its uncertain way along the half-ruined causeway to the mainland. Then slowly she pushed shut the heavy gate and walked across the garden to the back of the house where she had left her trowel and gloves. Picking them up she returned again to where old Hicks, bent over the young carrots, was still fighting the weeds.

.　.　.　.　.

At night it was lonely in the Old House, but Mrs. Linton did not notice it. The Hicks and old Peterman slept in the Victorian Gothic wing which meant that Mrs. Linton was left quite alone in the old part of the house. People said there were at least two ghosts in the Old House, one a soldier wearing an Elizabethan ruff and the other a woman of no identity who appeared in a night dress, and one or two others, who came and went. There were also stories that the Victorian relative whose blood still stained the flagging of the great hall sometimes returned. Guests in the house claimed to have seen them and Mrs. Linton was never quite certain whether she had seen them or not. There were moments sometimes in broad daylight, when she experienced an overwhelming sense of someone standing just behind her. Occasionally she found herself speaking in the half-conscious conviction that it was Peterman or one of the Hicks in the room with her, but always when she turned in expectation of an answer there was no one there.

The idea of ghosts did not disturb her; she did not really know whether she believed in them or not, but her instinct told her that there was no reason why they should not exist, and certainly it would be very odd if a place as ancient as the Old House did not have them. Indeed, at times it seemed to her there was something friendly about the idea of having one's ancestors always in the house. The place would have been unnatural and horrible if there had not been ghosts about, if the Old House were simply an *empty* place. She was never lonely because she always felt them all about her, especially at night when candles and oil lamps were the only means of illumination and every corner was black with shadows. She always had the half-realized conviction that the old shipowner who had connived with Elizabeth was still there, and the Wentworth who had spent half his life at the Court of Catherine de Medici, and the radical William Wentworth who had organized what amounted to a rebellion among the cotton spinners of the Midlands. And she was quite certain (without thinking about it) that her husband Derek was there all the while. Although he was only remotely a Wentworth, he had loved the Old House as much as she herself loved it.

She had no more fear of the physical than of the supernatural. In her long life she had experienced many perilous adventures; as a young woman she had been shut up in Peking during the Boxer Rebellion; she had walked the quais of St. Petersburg when there was a machine gun in every doorway, and once in Basutoland she and her husband had spent forty-eight disturbing hours in constant expectation of being run through by spears. So the idea that any intruder might come to the Old House and murder her in her bed, if it ever occurred to her, did not disturb her. The marshes were impassable and the only way of reaching the Old House was by the old causeway road. In any case, everyone in the whole countryside knew that she was too poor to be worth robbing. The only things left in the house which might be stolen were the Lely and Reynolds portraits and they were too bulky to cart away. Derek had always said, "Never possess anything which you would mind having stolen nor anything which people can steal from you and you will never need to lock a door." There had never been a locked door in the Old House as far back as she could remember. No one could steal memories, or honor, or self-respect, or conscience and in all of these Mrs. Linton was an immensely rich woman.

In the evening when the darkness came down and the mist rose from the marshes Mrs. Linton had dinner and then went into the library to work. By the light of a paraffin lamp she sat at the big Jacobean desk to write in her diary.

Nothing ever happened at the Old House. What she wrote in the diary were memories of the past and reflections which grew out of her long rich life.

Tonight she wrote: "Sir Horace was here today for the first time in many months. He came, of course, for my own good, wanting to give me the benefit of his all-superior wisdom and intellect. It occurred to me for the first time that he must have sat for Low's portrait of Colonel Blimp. I must have been very stupid not to have noticed it before. Perhaps fondness and long habit blunted my perceptions. Because I am fond of Horace no matter how stupid he may be. That is what makes him dangerous. At times he seems so nice and plausible.

"It occurred to me after he left, while I was working beside Hicks in the carrots, that stupidity was not the only element which made Horace tiresome and dangerous. There are also great lacks in him—a lack of pride, a lack of dignity, and a lack of all sense of distinction and love and pride in one's country . . . the kind of pride we once had in England as the champion of freedom, of government, of justice and tolerance. There are so many people in England like Horace . . . people who are not really evil, but stupid and material and compromising and sadly without pride and honor . . . the people who made Munich possible. It is better to lose one's property, even one's life, than to compromise, to abandon the things which have always made the true glory of England. The nineteenth century with its factories, its cheap tin trays and cotton shawls, its vast fortunes, its undernourished, enfeebled working class, has cost us dear indeed. If we have lost our honor and our pride, we have lost everything. We had best go down into oblivion."

She wrote a little more and then locked away the journal, put the desk into order and picking up the lamp passed through the great hall and up the worn stairway. She was very tired. She would sleep well.

Once in her room, she pushed open the window and looked out toward the sea. The night was clear but a cloud of mist lay flat and white like cotton wool across the marshes. From high up overhead came the faint drone of planes, the curious rhythmic beat which marked them as German. There were fewer of them now. Once the droning sound had filled all the sky in a canopy of sound.

. . . . .

All the morning of Thursday Mrs. Linton was like a child. Early she went to work in the garden, pinching and tying the tomato vines which Hicks had planted against the wall facing south where they would catch all the sun and feel, during the night, the heat that came back from the ancient stones. It was a good year, Mrs. Linton thought, with satisfaction. Everything grew well; the espalier peach trees were heavy with fruit. Perhaps it is an omen, she thought, that God after all is on our side. The reports from Germany were of a poor harvest, of potatoes frozen in the ground, of wheat withered in the fields. But the thought of a poor harvest, even in Germany, depressed her, for the soil was dear to her wherever it might be. The earth was made for fertility, to be cared for and cherished.

But above the depression rose the feeling of excitement over the prospect of seeing her granddaughter. Like a child, she felt spasms of terror lest, after all, something had happened and Ellen would not appear. Like a child she left her work in the garden a half-dozen times, to climb the steps to the gazebo and look toward the mainland. It was foolish for she knew well enough that there was no possible train until the late afternoon.

The day dragged on until nearly five when from the gazebo, she saw far off Sir Horace's Rolls picking its way along the causeway. Quickly she left the gazebo and went to her own room. There she scrubbed the work-stained hands and covered them with cream to soften them. She did her hair, usually tossed up casually, with the greatest care, and at last she put the faintest touch of rouge on her cheeks. It was not only that she wanted to look well for Ellen, but for Ellen's young man.

She met them half-way across the lawn and at first sight of the young man she thought, "It's going to be all right. He has a nice face."

He was dark, which she had not expected, as if he had Cornish blood, with dark eyes and a firm chin and a full generous mouth. He was tall and walked rather loosely—the walk of a physically strong confident man of balance, without fear. Beside him, Ellen, who was by no means a small girl, seemed slight and almost fragile. They were both dressed in mufti and for a moment Mrs. Linton experienced a swift sense of joy, as if the war were already finished and young people like them could go on with their lives and have children and lead happy lives such as she herself had led long ago here in the Old House.

Then Ellen's arms were around her, young, strong confident arms, and Ellen was kissing her cheek and saying, "It's wonderful, Granny, to be back here. This is John."

He smiled at her and she saw that there was more in the dark face than she had noticed. The smile was irresistible but the eyes remained grave and a little sad. So many young people had eyes like that nowadays—the young people who were paying for the folly of men like Sir Horace, the young people who seemed darkly aware of the heavy burden they would have for the rest of their lives. The jaw was square and firm.

"Oh, yes," she thought, "he'll do! He'll do!"

    .   .   .   .   .

She put them in what was called the Admiral's Rooms above the great hall not far from her own bedroom. It was pleasant having some one in the house again after so long. Houses were made to be lived in; they lost their characters when they stood

empty for long. Her own memory carried her back to late
Victorian times when people still had big families and the
Old House was always filled with cousins and uncles and aunts.

Because the occasion seemed one meriting a certain festivity
even in wartime, she changed her frock again, and as she
dressed her thoughts kept returning to John Searles and the
serious dark face. She understood why Ellen had married him;
she herself was already a little in love with him—not with
John Searles himself but with the kind of man he was. A little
sadly she envied Ellen; it would be nice to be young again and
in love, even in such hateful times as these.

Downstairs she encountered old Peterman and saw that a
faint glint came into his eyes at sight of her best frock. The
glint increased when she said, "I think we'll have cocktails
tonight. There's still gin in the cellar, isn't there?"

"Yes, Madame."

"And vermouth?"

"Yes, Madame, if it isn't corked. Vermouth doesn't keep
very well."

"Tell Mrs. Hicks we'll have dinner at eight."

There would be no tea. She had no desire to disturb them.
Ellen would hear the old bell which rang for dressing and
know what it meant. She left Peterman and walked out into
the garden, dressed and behaving as ladies had behaved in more
leisurely luxurious times. In Victorian novels they "drifted"
through a garden. That was what she was doing now, "drifting" uselessly in a flowered frock. And she was aware in a
little time that she did not like the role. She saw so many
things to be done—a bit of pruning here, a bit of weeding
there, vines which needed tying against the old walls. The
carefully scrubbed hands, covered with cream to hide the
dryness and callouses, itched to be back again at work. "Drifting" was certainly not her role.

For a while she went and sat in the gazebo watching the
lowering sunlight across the beloved marshes, and as she sat
there she was aware again of the distant sound of guns and
at the same time she felt a deep satisfaction that Ellen and John
Searles had elected to come here to the Old House. While she
sat there, life was beginning again within its old walls; it was

going on and on. After she was dead Ellen and John might elect to live there and bring up their children. She experienced, against the sound of menacing cannon fire, a swift and passionate sense of immortality. She was aware that she herself as an entity, an individual, was of importance only as one link in a chain of great length beginning long ago in misty remoteness and continuing far into the haze of the future. That she died was of no importance for she would go on and on in Ellen and the children of Ellen and John Searles and in their children. She would go on in a different manifestation in the Old House itself and in the garden, in the changes she had made in the house, in the trees and shrubs she had planted in the garden, just as the men who had laid down the ancient mosaic pavement of the rose garden were still, after a fashion, alive whenever one noticed the mosaic and speculated upon its creator, what sort of man he had been—that he must have been rich, that he must have been a cultivated man of taste. For a moment, it was almost as if he were there in the garden with her, a pro-consul of a great Empire as her husband had been, a great Empire long since vanished. And there were others there too, the ancestor who had been a partner of Elizabeth, the Admiral, the Prime Minister under George the First, the first Normans who came to fortify the island and build the heavy vaulted cellar over which the Old House was built. Presently she herself would join them and their immortality, to become one of those who had helped to build the Old House, who had helped to build and maintain the England she loved so much. After her would be the children of Ellen and John Searles, born of the eternal mating of the new and the old which had always been the strength of England. It all went back into the past and far into the dimness of the future, and she herself was only a part of the whole pattern and therefore indestructible since in the end only the whole pattern was of importance. The woof must never be torn, the pattern never destroyed.

She fell into a kind of revery, lulled by the warmth and perfume of the garden and the monotonous, hypnotizing throb of the distant guns, and presently through the quiet of the evening the sound of the old bell roused her—the bell which had called so many people who were now ghosts to dinner in the Old House.

In a little while she saw Ellen and John Searles coming through the door of the great hall and she rose and went down the steps that led from the summer house to the shaded lawn. They saw her and Ellen called out, "Oh, there you are!"

She thought, "How happy they look. How lucky they are to love each other." And again she was aware of a faint, distant pang of envy. Aloud she said, "We still have a few minutes before the second bell. I'd like to show John the roses."

Ellen laughed, "Granny's very proud of the roses. In the old days she always carried off all the prizes at the flower show. She's a demon gardener. She really takes care of everything here."

John really liked the roses and appreciated them. He said, "I wish my mother could see them. She has quite a rose garden of her own."

And out of her knowledge and experience, Mrs. Linton suddenly saw the rose garden of John's mother—a little ordered plot in the suburbs of Liverpool behind an ugly, rather pretentious new house filled with stuffed, expensive furniture all a little vulgar but strong and new and sure of itself. If there had ever been any snobbery in Mrs. Linton, it was long since dead; she did not vision the rose garden of John's mother with condescension but only abstractly, with detachment and realism because that was the way it would be. That was the way it should be; there would be no ancient Roman pavement there in that Liverpool suburb. It would all be new, and because of that John Searles would be strong and vigorous, and Ellen would be happy and have strong, handsome children, and there would be new people, strong and young in spirit as well as body, to take over the Old House and keep it alive and safe from the dangers of decay. It was a lucky moment when Ellen looked across the table of the Canteen and her eyes met those of John Searles. He was what the Old House needed, what England herself needed, now, desperately. But for this war, Ellen might never have met him nor anyone like him. She would have met only young men of her own class (how Mrs. Linton in her wisdom hated that vulgar word "class"), young men who were tired, with no aim, with no place to go. In the old days it had been a very long way from the Old House to the house in the suburbs of Liverpool. For nearly a lifetime England had forgotten where her strength came from.

Then against the distant sound of the guns, the old bell rang again and John Searles said, "I'm glad to hear that, I'm fighting hungry."

"I hope you'll like the dinner," said Mrs. Linton. "We're having roast capon, and lots of green vegetables. There'll be trifle for a sweet." And aware of the cook's deficiencies she added, "Mrs. Hicks is very good at it."

· · · · ·

After dinner they went again to the rose garden and had coffee and brandy there under the old cedars. The sound of the guns had died away again and in the long still northern twilight, life seemed to return again to the old half-forgotten pattern of ease and gentle living. And while they sat there John Searles at last told her what it was he was doing in the war. The deepening twilight seemed to loosen his tongue; it was as if shyness or modesty had kept him silent up to now. It was wise of Ellen, old Mrs. Linton thought, to allow him to tell his own story, where and when it suited him; she did not urge him to tell it nor attempt to tell it for him as many foolish women would have done. You could not do that with a man like John Searles. He was a masterful, serious fellow.

And he did not tell his story easily or glibly. He told it because, Mrs. Linton understood, he was aware of her curiosity and was being kind and obliging. And as she listened she felt a chill steal round her heart not because of what he told her but because of what he did not tell. What he told was simple enough. He said quite simply that he was a Captain in the Commando service. He had volunteered for it because it suited him. He did not say it, but Mrs. Linton understood, that to him there was something horrible and inhuman in a war between machines in which men slaughtered each other without even being seen. She saw what she had known at once from his face—that he was a romantic and a man of action. And as he talked, quietly, in response to her gentle, tactful prodding, of raids in Libya and on the French Coast, she saw that there was in him the crusading hatred of which only a romantic is capable. He hated the Germans, not because they were abstractly the enemy, but because they were a people of profoundly evil intent, set upon destroying all that was good and gentle and civilized, and because they were bent upon destroying this England, this little island, the Old House itself. It was only in personal combat that his hatred could be satisfied. Firing a cannon, dropping a bomb, or even firing from one plane at another, left him feeling cold and dead and unsatisfied. He was, she divined, of the old breed, of a courage and dignity and fire which had nothing to do with machines. He was near to reality and to the earth to which all of them must return when machines had made life impossible. Sir Horace, she thought, with his vulgarity, his lack of dignity, his willingness to compromise, was a perfect product of machines which destroyed the self-reliance of man, his courage and his dignity. For too long man had confused machinery with civilization. They had nothing to do with each other.

John Searles, she saw, was like the men who had destroyed the Armada, who had fought at Waterloo and with Wellington in the Peninsular War, the men who had built England. Somehow in the body of the son of a Liverpool building contractor, the old spirit had returned; if there were enough men like him England would be safe. Men like Sir Horace would compromise England for the sake of a little profit for themselves, but men like John Searles would accept no half-loaf.

In the long northern twilight she could see that Ellen was watching him with shining eyes and Mrs. Linton, with the chill still round her heart, thought, "She knows. She understands. Even if something happens to him, she has had for a little time what few women ever have!"

Presently the chill of the marshes rose and began to flow in over the ancient walls and they left the rose garden and went into the house, where in the drawingroom by the light of paraffin lamps, she and Ellen taught John to play six-pack bezique. While the lesson went on, Mrs. Linton, her heart so filled with satisfaction that she wanted to laugh aloud, thought, "Of course, John wouldn't know bezique. Bezique was a game of the gentry." It was not the tired gentry who would save England. It was the stout men who had fought with Drake long ago here in sight of the Old House itself. Elizabeth herself had known that, long ago, in her own glorious day.

· · · · ·

For ten days more Ellen and John Searles stayed on at the Old House, slipping back out of their bruised young lives into the dreamy quietness of the garden and the marshes. Once in the dog-cart drawn by the old horse which Hicks cared for, they drove to the mainland to make a round of calls in the village because Ellen knew that people like Mrs. Hipshaw, the postmistress, and old Granny Taitus and many others would want to see the man she had married and because she was proud to show him to them. And on the last day Sir Horace kindly sent his car to take them and their luggage to the station. Never once during the whole visit had Ellen said to her grandmother, "I think you should leave the Old House and go inland to some safer, more isolated place," not even on the last day when out of nowhere there appeared suddenly a strange plane marked with a swastika which came low and circled three times over the little island before British planes appeared to dive low and drive it off in the direction of the North Sea.

John Searles said, "I wonder what the fellow could want. Probably came to have a look around for gun emplacements."

"There's nothing here to bomb," said Mrs. Linton. "They've never bothered us. Once they dropped some bombs a couple of miles off in the marshes. Sir Horace said it was just an accident—that they were chased back from somewhere and were just unloading on the way home."

Ellen looked at her but said nothing. Ellen understood.

· · · · ·

When they had gone away, life at the Old House settled back once more into the drowsy rhythm of fading summer. The night began to come down over the marshes a little earlier each day, slowly, imperceptibly. In the garden the roses burst into an extravagant second blooming. The little carrot seedlings, freed of their weeds grew into sturdy bright colored roots topped with great tufts of lacy fern-like foliage. Against the warmth of the old walls tomatoes and peaches ripened. The moon of August went through the four quarters, died and was reborn again in a lonely glittering sliver of light. This was the moon which in its fullness brought the great neap tides which some years rose so high that they covered the whole of the causeway.

During the day and sometimes in the night when the wind was from the south, one still heard the distant thunder of cannon. Once the sound of guns was very near when in the early morning a convoy slipping along the coast was attacked only a little way out to sea, just beyond the rim of the marshes. Overhead fewer and fewer planes droned inland high in the sky. Some nights none at all passed over and across the marshes and over the Old House the old stillness of peacetime returned, broken only by the faint sound of lapping water or the cry of a wild bird.

As the moon went into the first quarter, the first wild swan appeared quite near the house in the water that filled the ancient moat. The villagers said that it was a sign that the winter would be early and hard. Mrs. Linton thought it odd that the swan arrived alone. It had never happened before. The swan stayed on and on, feeding on the crumbs of bread Mrs. Linton threw into the moat.

One afternoon while she was feeding it, old Peterman came on to the terrace to say that he had spied Sir Horace's old car coming along the causeway. Leaving the swan to devour the remainder of the crumbs, she went into the house and washed and creamed her hands and changed her frock and redid her hair. She was not quite certain why she took all this trouble but it had something to do with the feeling that for a long time past she had been rather rude to Sir Horace and snubbed him. It was a kind of atonement because she lacked the humility to tolerate stupidity.

Watching him from the doorway as he crossed the lawn, it occurred to her that he seemed tired and that somehow the rotund Colonel Blimp figure appeared to droop as he walked. She felt a sudden impatience with the slowness of his gait not because she wanted to see him quickly but because he carried letters in the pocket of the expensive tweed coat.

As he came nearer he said, "I thought I'd pay you a call, Mary, before the neap tides. About one more good tide and nobody will be able to use that old road of yours. Then you'll be cut off altogether."

She thought quickly, "That wouldn't be so bad as it might seem." But she did not say it. She said, "I see you've stopped at the post office. That was very good of you."

He took the letters out of his pocket and gave them to her and as they walked toward the rose garden, she went quickly through them.

None held any special interest save a letter in Ellen's clear, strong writing. Her fingers itched to open it and read it at once but she waited until Peterman brought the tea and the whiskey and then said, "There's one here from Ellen. Do you mind if I skim through it?"

While she read Sir Horace talked to old Peterman who wanted news of friends in the village. As she tore open the letter her hands trembled a little from the fear she felt in her heart. "Oh, God! Don't let it be that anything has happened to John Searles."

It was not death which greeted her as she read, not death but life. The letter was not long.

It read: "Dear Granny: I'm writing in haste to tell you a bit of news I know you'll want to hear. I'm going to have a baby. I didn't write before now because I wasn't certain. The doctor says that I am very healthy and that there shouldn't be any trouble. I wanted you to know at once. There isn't any way of telling John because I don't know where he is. He was sent away a fortnight ago, I don't know where, but I think to Libya. I've had no news of him yet. The doctor says it will be perfectly all right for me to go ahead working at the Canteen. I'm glad of that because I don't know what I would have done otherwise. Nowadays you just can't sit around thinking.

"I'm still enjoying the stay at the Old House. There was something especially wonderful about it. I always feel that I belong there, but the wonderful thing was that John felt the same way, as if it was a place he knew very well, where he had been before. We had a long talk about that on the way home—about the strange feeling one sometimes has about having known and loved a place in some earlier existence. He asked me especially to tell you that, and that when the war was over and things were going well again, he wanted to come down and go over the whole place and set about doing all the things which needed to be done. Being an architect and a builder he was very interested in all that.

"You were a great success with John. He said it was a pity that your kind of woman seemed to be dying out in England. I told him I didn't believe that. I said that there were still women like you only they didn't seem the same because everything was so different. Don't you agree with me?

"There is not much news to write. The Canteen goes on just the same. I'll let you know immediately I have any news of John. Do write. I know you always say that nothing happens at the Old House but I like to hear even the news about the carrots and the roses. Give my best to Sir Horace and thank him again and if you go to the village say hello for me to Mrs. Hipshaw and all the others.

"Much love as always—Ellen."

Sir Horace had finished his talk with Peterman and Peterman had gone away. As she put down the letter, she said, "Ellen is going to have a baby."

"She lost no time, did she?" asked Sir Horace.

"Young people don't have much time nowadays. It isn't as it used to be."

His face was serious and although his eyes were turned toward her she knew that he was not seeing her at all. He was looking far beyond and suddenly she knew what he was thinking—of the time he was young, of his own children, one son killed at Amiens long ago, one grandson missing. She

felt suddenly sorry for him, a dull, material fellow without
much imagination, who could only suffer without the compen-
sations of imagination or of fantasy or of faith. He would
never know that feeling of immortality she had known for an
instant in the summer house on the wall when she herself, with
all her sorrows and disappointments, became utterly unim-
portant and only a part of something far greater and more
enduring. She had been contemptuous; now suddenly her heart
was filled with pity.

She heard herself saying, "Would it amuse you to stay for
dinner, Horace?"

His pale blue eyes narrowed again out of the vagueness of
the tired empty stare and focused upon her face. "That's kind
of you, Mary. I'd like to. There's no one to return to. I'm
quite alone at the house."

"I'm not having much—an omelette and salad, and pudding
for a sweet."

"That suits me. I'm dieting on doctor's orders. My blood
pressure is not good."

"We'll open some wine. There's still quite a lot of good
Chablis left. There's nothing better with an omelette."

. . . . .

As she sat there she decided to make the evening as gay as
possible. A little later she excused herself and put on another
frock and her pearls, and as she dressed she thought about
him, understanding suddenly that he was worried about his
factories and the returns on his rubber and oil shares because
these things were to him all-important, not alone to himself
but to England as well. If rubber plantations and oil refineries
were destroyed in far-off Malaya and no dividends came in, it
was the end of the world. He did not see that these plantations and refineries could rot the very security of England and
destroy the world of which England was a part. He did not
understand that they did not make the greatness of England.
They only came out of the greatness of her people; they did
not make that greatness. They had come about only because
there had been Englishmen in the past like John Searles, like

the Admiral and the old man who had been a partner of Queen Elizabeth. When there were no more Englishmen like them, men who did not bargain or compromise in the illusion that they were saving their comfort and security, the Empire would fall apart. It was not money which had made England great but the quality of Englishmen. She was aware that she could never make him understand this, for he believed not in men but in machines. Out of machines had come his own wealth and importance, and now the machines were failing him.

So at dinner they talked mostly about the past, about their early youth and how motors and planes had changed everything. Only the Old House had remained the same.

Looking about him, Sir Horace said, "It is almost exactly as it was fifty years ago, with the candles on the table and the lamps in the drawingroom."

"That's why I like it," said Mary Linton. "It's as if it had stayed here all the time while a lot of the rest of England moved away from it."

After dinner they played two games of bezique by lamplight and then Sir Horace said, "I must go now. The servants will be wondering what happened to me. I've loved the evening, Mary. It was as if the war didn't exist. It's so quiet here that the war seems a nightmare."

She went with him to the gateway where the driver waited with the car. There was a brilliant moon and the old Cedar of Lebanon cast long black shadows across the flat lawn. Sir Horace stopped for a moment to look toward it.

"They'll be coming over tonight."

"Not many of them come nowadays."

He paused to light an expensive cigar. "It's wonderful how the weather has held up this year. Usually there are storms before now."

She sighed, "Nothing is the same any more."

Then out of the air drenched with moonlight came the sound of a plane. Both of them were silent for a moment looking up but seeing nothing. The plane came very low and circled over the house and then went away again into the distance.

"It's German," said Sir Horace. Then he too sighed and said, "Well, good night again, Mary, and thank you. I'll be over again after the tides." As he stepped into the old car with its air warden flag, he said, "I don't suppose I could tempt you over to dine at the Priory some night. I could send for you."

She smiled, "Perhaps. Let it go until after the tides."

Then he spoke to the driver and the old car jolted down the paved roadway from the gate toward the causeway. Slowly she turned and walked back toward the house. In the moonlight the ancient shadows fell black and clear. The lamplight glowed softly through the mullioned windows of the drawing-room. The air was filled with the heavy odor of night-blooming jasmine. From somewhere near the rose garden a nightingale was calling to his wife.

Beneath one of the cedars she stopped for a moment and leaned against the rough bark of the trunk, pressing her face close to it in a moment of pure happiness. It was no longer simply her house; she was a part of *it*, of the stones, the light, a part of this very tree. And now Ellen was married and was to have a baby and all this would go on and on long after she was dead. There in the moonlight, it was almost as if already she had joined those other ghosts.

It was a breathless night and as she wrote by lamplight in her diary the Old House was still save for the faint creakings and rustlings which affect old houses, and these sounds she had long ago come to accept so that they became a part of the silence. When she wrote, she lost herself in the past so that she was no longer in the house but in China or far-off Singapore or St. Petersburg or Berlin and did not even hear the occasional roar of the guns or the sound of a plane going overhead.

Tonight she found herself writing passionately, furiously, in a continuation of that mood of ecstasy which she had experienced as she pressed her face against the trunk of the Cedar of Lebanon.

She wrote: "I have always been a very fortunate woman, and now as an old woman I can understand a little that my good fortune was not merely luck. I myself, and my husband, had much to do with it; for in a way both of us were gamblers. The very marriage was fortunate for it was not only that we loved each other but that we shared a common philosophy and faced whatever came with the same spirit of adventure. I think I can say honestly now that we never looked for the main chance; we never placed our faith or our energies upon the material things which can vanish and in vanishing, leave one destitute, because they are the only resources one possessed. Ah, we were poor at times—poorer than a Whitechapel beggar—because we had to keep up a position, not for ourselves, but for what we represented. And sometimes it was painful. Sometimes I wore a frock, made over and over, for five long years, at dinners and balls and receptions, and that was not easy for a woman who was pretty and liked to appear well. But it was a small thing, of no importance. I was fortunate in knowing that, even as a girl. In the end when my husband was dead and life was finished, I found that I possessed not shares and bonds, but an immense fortune in those things which are indestructible—things like friendships and wisdom, memories and knowledge of people and of the world, a good conscience and a sense of having done one's duty honorably toward one's fellow men; things which remain forever there in the chest of treasures, to be taken out and used and returned again to safekeeping in the deep recesses of one's mind. Now when one is old, these things are more valuable than gold, more nourishing than food, for they sustain the mind and one's courage and supply the very spirit with sustenance. I know now that my husband and I, long ago, made the proper choice."

She lay down the pen and leaning back in the chair closed her eyes thinking back into the remote past which returned now in a long and splendid procession of rich experiences from the time when as a bride she had left the Old House never to return to it again for much time until she was an old woman.

She was thinking of a night in St. Petersburg in the eighties when the certainty came to her that there was someone in the room beside herself. In her memories it was a snowy night and she was returning with Derek in a droshky through the wide streets as the snow fell softly and the bells of the droshky jingled in the early morning stillness. And now all at once she was aware, although her eyes were closed, that there was someone standing quite near her. Dimly in the confusion of her mind she thought, "Perhaps it is one of those ghosts people are always seeing in this house, only tonight he is being more tiresome and persistent than usual."

And then she heard a man's voice, a young, very real voice, saying, "I beg your pardon, Mrs. Linton." And opening her eyes she saw that the owner of the voice was a man in German uniform. He was young, with hard blue eyes and a lean, square-jawed face, not bad-looking but hard.

For a second she thought, "I'm dreaming. This is a result of all the conversation with Horace." But he spoke again, saying, "I am sorry to disturb you but there was nothing I could do about it."

Sitting upright she managed to ask, "Who are you and how did you come here?"

He bowed, a stiff German bow which started all the dim memories racing again. "I am Lieutenant Erich von Rintelen. I came here by parachute. We have taken over the place. The servants are locked up."

She said, "Be careful of them. They are old."

"They are merely locked in two rooms and well guarded. There is no intention of harming them."

Then she said, "Won't you sit down?"

It seemed idiotic that he should go on standing there so stiffly. Because she had lived in so many places and knew well so many people of so many races and nationalities, it was difficult to think of any one man as "the enemy." Now she could not feel any special hatred of this strange tense young man with the hard eyes and the bitter face. She was so old that she felt a kind of pity for him, thinking with a remote part of her mind, "It must be horrible to live with all the things that have gone to make up such a face. It must be a kind of Hell."

He said, "Thank you," and sat down, and she asked, "What is it you want here?"

"That I cannot tell you. I can only tell you that we are here and that there must be no signaling from this house."

She smiled, "People told me something like this would happen."

"I regret to say that we shall have to put you under guard."

He spoke coldly and politely, with a certain mechanical respect, but without the warmth which she usually felt in young people. Then she remembered that he had addressed her by her own name and a strange thought, born of the old memories, came to her. She asked, "How did you know my name?"

"We know these things," he said, "but I know about you myself—anyway." He spoke excellent English with only a slight accent. "I have seen pictures of you as a young woman. I have even seen pictures of this house, of a tennis party here."

"You have seen the pictures in Germany?"

"In Germany . . . in my grandfather's house."

His grandfather's house . . . von Rintelen . . . Things began to come together now, slowly, like the pieces of a picture puzzle. She managed to say, "Are you any relation to Chancellor von Rintelen?"

"He was my grandfather. He was a very methodical man. He liked taking pictures. In all the old albums they are carefully labeled."

Again for a moment she had the feeling that all this was something that she was dreaming, born out of the talk of Ellen and Sir Horace and John Searles.

She said, "I understand now. The Chancellor was a great friend of my husband and myself." As much a friend as any German had been. They had stayed in his shooting-lodge in Silesia. Once he had come here to the Old House on a week-end visit. That must have been when the photograph of the tennis party was taken. Then quite suddenly she remembered the week end with an astonishing clarity. She remembered all the people who had come down to stay. The Prince has been staying at the Priory with Sir Horace and came over for dinner on Sunday evening. Mrs. Langtry had been there too and an attractive American woman called Mrs. Parkington whose husband was one of the richest men in the world. It was a happy time, when all the world seemed rich and pleasant and war seemed something that would never happen again. On that Sunday evening, after dinner, her husband and the Prince and the Chancellor had started what they thought was a plan for eternal peace.

She smiled again, "It is very odd how things go wrong." And then she realized that he could not understand what she meant not only because he could not have read her thoughts but because he belonged to a generation, a world so different, and she added, "I was thinking back. I remember the picture very well."

"My grandfather was a dreamer," said the young Lieutenant. "He made a great deal of trouble for our generation. He worked for things that could never be. All that is changed now. There is no place in Germany for dreams about peace. We had to learn that."

Somewhere in her mind the speech roused memories of the raucous voice screaming over the wireless from Nuremburg and Berchtesgaden and Munich and the wild insane answering roar of the disciplined mob, and she felt suddenly sick as she had felt listening to that voice until she shut off the wireless for the last time, never to listen to that voice again because afterward it haunted her, filling all her whole being with faintness and disgust. "We will destroy France!" the voice screamed. "We will crush England!" And the insane answering roar like the chorus of a mad house, "*Sieg Heil! Sieg Heil! Sieg Heil!*"

"And so," she thought, "I am a prisoner in my own house —the Old House! And what they said would happen, has happened! And this world is all mad insane melodrama and opposite me is a young man with a hard cruel face who hates and could destroy everything that I have worked for and loved all my life."

Slowly and with dignity she rose and said, "No doubt you have things to do. I will leave you now. I have only two small requests to make."

He stood up and bowed again. It was extraordinary the desire of the Germans to formalize everything, to put the appearance of good manners even on rape and slaughter and destruction.

"What are they, Mrs. Linton?"

"I should like to be confined in my own room where I shall be more comfortable. And I should like to take with me my journal and some ink and a pen. It will stave off boredom. I am used to a very active life."

"I can see no objection to either request. Of course I cannot allow you a light or anything which could be used in signaling to the mainland."

She smiled, "I am not trained as a secret agent. I would not know how to signal. Come, I will show you the way."

She took up the small reading lamp and moved toward the door. He followed her as she crossed the great hall and climbed the brown stone steps of the stairway. At all the doors stood German soldiers clad in rather clumsy gray uniforms. At the door of her bedroom there was already a sentry posted. She opened the door and turned, "There is another door on the far side of the dressing room leading into the back hall."

"Yes," he said, "we know that. There is already a man posted there." He bowed again, "The lamp, please."

She gave him the lamp and he said, "I must remind you again—no attempt at signaling. We shall have to shoot immediately anyone who attempts to make a signal. If an alarm is given it means the death of all of us."

"I understand that. I suppose you have found a place to sleep."

"Yes . . . just across the hall."

He had chosen the Admiral's Rooms.

"Good night," she said.

"Good night."

He bowed again and with his free hand closed the door. There was no key in the lock. There were very few keys in the Old House. If there had ever been any they were lost long ago. The people who had lived there were not suspicious people, nor did they suffer from bad consciences.

When he had gone she sat down in the chintz-covered armchair near the window looking out over the marshes drenched with moonlight. In the old days from this window you could see on a clear night the lights of the village on the mainland, but now there were no lights.

She thought, "How odd that I who came here to retire from the world, to have a little peace before I died, should be thrust suddenly into a position which demands action—perhaps violent action."

For she did not doubt her responsibility. She did not know why young von Rintelen and his soldiers had come here, whether the action was part of a plan of invasion or merely an isolated raid. *Why* they had come was not of the first importance; the only important thing was that people on the mainland should know they were here. Out of her long experience she knew that this was not the moment to attempt any rash act which would not succeed. Whatever she did must be certain of success. And again as she sat there, she was overcome by the feeling of ecstasy she had known as she pressed her face against the rough bark of the ancient cedar. She was a part of this, a part of the very tree itself, of the earth, of the walls.

And she thought suddenly of what Ellen had written—"John felt the same way, as if it was a place he knew very well, where he had been before. We had a long talk about that on the way home—about the strange feeling one sometimes has of having known and loved a place in some earlier existence."

That was very odd. Could it be that John Searles *had* once lived here long ago in another existence? Was that why in the very moment he crossed the lawn toward her, she had had that feeling that he was right, that he belonged here. Had he been in some other life the Admiral or perhaps the shipowner of the Cinque Ports or the one who had fought with Wellington in the Peninsular Campaign? They were very odd and dangerous—these strange intimations of the past. They were paralyzing as too much tradition, too much past could sometimes be.

She thought, "I must not sit here moonstruck and paralyzed. I must act."

Then suddenly the wild swan beneath the window cried out above the lapping of the water in the moat. Why had it come here alone to stay on, alone, mateless? She knew, out of her deep love of the earth and the trees and all nature that Nature herself, perhaps God, had a way of sending signs which men could not always read. Again and again she had been aware, during her long life, of times when she was very near to understanding many strange things that remained always just beyond the reach of her perceptions. Sometime perhaps she would pass over this line, thrust aside the veil which held her back . . . like Saint Francis of Assisi perhaps . . .

And she was no longer alone in the room. The others were certainly there, unseen, but quite real, their presence pressing in upon her—the Admiral, the boy who had gone with Wellington, the ship-owner, the Prime Minister, even her own brother dead in South Africa and her son killed at Mons. They were certainly there all about her, pressing her to act, as if they were a council called together.

The swan, disturbed by the step of the German sentry, cried out again in the stillness, and the presence of the others in the room became overwhelmingly real, so real that softly, she found herself saying, "What is it I must do? What is it you want of me?"

But there was only silence and the curious feeling that all the while the room was becoming more crowded. That part of her mind which had always been acute and brilliant said, "You must pull yourself together. You are being paralyzed." But a deeper instinct cried out, "No. Be very still. Listen! Listen! And you will understand." and then all at once she *knew*. Although the stillness remained unbroken, she heard what they were saying. What they asked was a terrible thing, the most terrible thing they could have asked of her. They were saying "You must do it. It will not matter so long as the greater thing—the thing for which all of us lived and some of us died—is kept alive."

For a moment she felt a chill in her hands and feet and about her heart as if she were dying, and thought, "No, I cannot die now, not until I have done what must be done." The swan cried out again in the stillness and she found her lips moving although no sound came from them. She was saying softly, "Very well . . . very well."

She stirred and sat upright and suddenly she was alone again in the room, alive, her will strong now and sure.

Quietly she went to work by the light which spilled in at the open window. She went first to the chest where her old, rather ratty, furs were kept and, opening it, she began to take out the tissue paper in which they were wrapped during the summer. She worked swiftly but quietly, stilling the rustling

of the paper lest it alarm the sentry outside the door. Then
she took the paper from the drawers where her other clothes
were kept, and at last she went to the shelves of books where
she kept only those books which she loved, which had helped
her at some time or other to understand the complexity and
beauty of living; and one by one with a firm hand, she destroyed them, tearing out the pages as quietly as possible.
There was a moment of weakness and pain when it seemed
to her that she was tearing out her own heart, but the moment passed quickly. What she was doing had to be done
quickly while there was still time, before she joined the others,
and like them, became a legend.

Quietly she crossed the room and opened the door of the
great cupboard where more frocks, old and rather shabby,
hung neatly encased in paper, and when she had opened the
door, she heaped the rest of the paper inside the cupboard.

.   .   .   .   .

It was Mrs. Hipshaw, the postmistress, who gave the alarm.
Her liver had been troubling her for days and in the middle
of the night she got out of bed to find her medicine. As she
opened the door of the kitchen where she kept it in a bottle
on a shelf near the stove, she saw the glow in the sky and
when she went outside she could see the flames leaping up
toward the full moon.

She acted quickly, first telephoning old Hibbard who led
the firemen, then Sir Horace at the Priory and finally the
orderly of the Colonel in charge of the Coast Defense. In
the excitement Mrs. Hipshaw quite forgot about her liver.
In ten minutes the firemen assembled, all of them old men
or boys or men who were crippled. Sir Horace, the warden
appeared in the old Rolls, and because the Old House was a
long way off they fetched rope and attached the hand-drawn
pump to the back of the old car. In that fashion they would
arrive there more quickly. Then the firemen climbed into
the Rolls or clung, perched precariously, to the pump itself
and the strange procession with the rear brought up by a

troupe of children and half-grown boys, set out across the half-ruined causeway road.

What happened was very simple.

The old Rolls with Sir Horace in his tweeds beside the driver bumped and rocked rapidly along the half-ruined road toward the Old House. The neap tides had already begun to come in and in places along the road the ruts and holes were filled with water. Splashing and careening, the car and the little hand pump reached the foot of the cobble-paved incline leading up to the gateway when suddenly out of the moonlight came a burst of gunfire. In the front seat of the Rolls the driver fell forward and the automobile turned sharply and came to a stop suspended on the edge of the causeway. The pump crashed into the side of the car, dislodging at the same time the elderly volunteer firemen clinging to it, thus saving their lives, for most of them were thrown clear into the water alongside the causeway out of range of the bullets.

By water or along the causeway in the wild light from the burning house most of the men and all the boys made their way back toward the mainland and only when they arrived there and troops appeared did they realize that Sir Horace, their air raid warden, was not with them.

For eleven hours, well past the middle of the day, the battle went on. The fire burned itself out and toward evening, the men of a territorial regiment, scaling the old Roman wall near the chapel, wiped out the last of the Germans. Lieutenant von Rintelen was the last to die, with his back against the wall of the rose garden where his grandfather, long ago, had tried to plan peace for the world.

When the fighting was over they found Sir Horace, the air raid warden, slumped forward against the shattered windshield of the old Rolls, an expensive cigar by his side, and in the garden beneath the ancient Cedar of Lebanon they found Mrs. Linton lying on her face, one arm extended. The fingers of the hand were closed together tightly as if they held something precious she had tried to save. When the grasp of the cracked, work-stained fingers was loosened they found inside only the earth of the little island.

TRUE LOVE

IT WAS ALL HERBY'S FAULT TO BEGIN WITH. HE USED TO BE STAGE manager for one of the Shubert road companies. He was a pink-faced, white-haired shrewd specimen who knew all the answers along Broadway. You wouldn't have thought it of him. He wasn't impressive-like; he looked more as if he might be a doorman instead of a stage manager. His face was young and unlined like the faces of people that don't worry about nothing, but his white hair—his wife used to keep it very white and put bluing in the water he washed it in—made him look older than he was. You couldn't tell how many years of age he was but he was older than he looked. I know that on account of Momma.

Momma was Herby's wife. They had a house way out at Bay Shore and that's a long way to commute but it didn't matter much to Herby because he was always with a road company. So when he was in town he could live out there all right except when a new company was rehearsing. Momma musta bin about fifty-five. When she came to town she got herself all horsed up with a near-mink fur coat, a fancy hat and all the fixin's, so she looked like one of those club women from East Orange that buys seats in a bloc to see a show. But she wasn't like that at all out at Bay Shore. She was nuts on fishin' and most of the time she wore dungarees and was out in a boat and she even went out with a commercial fisherman when she got a chance. Her and Herby didn't have any children but they was always bringin' up some relations' kids. They had a little house with the prettiest flower garden you ever saw around it, about a block away from the Great South Bay. Momma and Herby was as happy as could be. Herby really hated the show business all the forty years he was in it but it was the only business he knew and he was in it just to save enough money to get out of it and stay down in Bay Shore and spend the rest of his life fishin' with Momma.

I tell you all this just because I want you to understand that Herby's interest in the girls in the show was purely fatherly. I guess it was because he didn't have any kids of his own. He was always lookin' after other peoples' kids. Twenty or thirty dumb girls can get themselves into a lot of trouble, especially in a road company because the smarter, better-looking girls is likely to be taken up by the New York company and we was always left with the residue. Usually if there was smart girls with a lot of talent they didn't stay long with a road company. They got their selves into better jobs.

A lot of people called Herby "Whisperin' Herby." It was on account of a habit he had of never raisin' his voice. I never heard him get mad or yell. I guess that's why he never had any lines in that pink face of his, and his affect on the company was always soothin'—a valuable thing in the theatre. And Herby never had loud-mouthed conversations. If he wanted to talk to you, he takes you into a dark corner of the stage and practically whispers to you. A stage manager on the road doesn't have any office of his own and so Herby had to hold his conferences in a corner behind scenery or a lot of trunks. Half the time Herby seemed to be in the shadows somewhere on the stage whisperin' to somebody, usually one of the girls who was broke or in trouble with some guy. If you didn't know Herby and the way he felt about Momma and the house in Bay Shore, you'd have thought he was on the make. But it wasn't like that. He never made no passes at the girls. He was kind of like a Mother Superior, workin' out their troubles for them.

That's how I knew that Daisy was in some sort of trouble when I seen her and Herby off in a corner whisperin' together. It kept happenin'—in Syracuse, in Rochester, in Columbus, in Indianapolis—right along the whole tour. We was tourin' with the *Student Prince* then. I knew somethin' was cookin', but I couldn't quite figure it out because Daisy was one of the smart girls who never got herself into scrapes. She'd have been out of the road company long before then but for one thing. If you didn't look at Daisy's mouth she was gorgeous. She had gams like Dietrich and a façade like Turner and black hair and big blue eyes with long black lashes and a natural complexion that was like a beauty advertisement, but some-body when Daisy was a baby, had neglected her adenoids. She had buck teeth that stuck straight out. The girls who were jealous of Daisy because she was smart called her "squirrel puss."

It was a shame, on account of if Daisy hadn't had them buck teeth she could have been gettin' big money in New York from Ziegfeld or George White as a show girl. It was all right in a road company. She could hold her lip down over her teeth when she was on stage and in a chorus, most of the audience didn't notice anything about her but the gams and the façade. But of course there wasn't no good tryin' that when she went to see Ziegfeld or George White. If she held her lip down over her teeth it looked as if she'd been badly stung by a bee and was all swollen up, and if she answered questions, out popped the teeth and they'd say to their secre-taries, "Take this young lady's name," and to Daisy, "You'll hear from us," but she never did. Daisy was ambitious and year after year she'd be sent away, until when they was castin' for show girls, they'd say, "if that buck-toothed girl comes around, just tell her we're all set."

So year after year, for five or six years, Daisy would turn up in our road company. As I said, she was smart, and she got to be the oldest girl in the company and the one who used to take over puttin' the girls through their routines. She was good. Herby and I used to think she was better than the director himself. She could have made a good living that way but that wasn't what Daisy wanted.

We had a company electrician named George Harrington who was a good happy-go-lucky kind of fellow. He was smart too and he could have got along a lot faster in the world but I guess he just wasn't interested. He made good enough money and he liked the life. He'd rather sit in the basement and play rummy and pinochle and drink beer with the boys than fuss around gettin' ahead. There wasn't any-thing he didn't know about lighting, and he had a pretty good education, but he just wasn't interested. He was a hell of a good-lookin' kid with that easy-goin', kiddin' manner that goes big with the girls when you're good-lookin' along with it. He was the Irish lookin' kind with black hair and blue eyes and big square shoulders and a fine physique. I guess he had pretty much what he wanted until Daisy came along. He had enough money and an easy rovin' life and all he wanted of everything. He had more girls than he could use. They used to get into fights over him and make us a lot of trouble.

Now the funny thing was that George had never thought about ever marryin' until Daisy came along. He went nuts over Daisy, buck teeth and all. They'd go out together night after night when the show was over and be together always on the train. George, who'd always been carefree as a grasshopper takin' it where he could find it, wanted to marry Daisy. He told her (what she already knew) that he'd had plenty of girls but that she was the only one he'd ever wanted to marry. He was always talkin' to her about marryin' him, givin' up the show business and settlin' down to raise a family. It just changed his whole character and it saved us a lot of trouble because when he began goin' for Daisy it stopped the fightin' over him among the other girls.

But Daisy wouldn't marry him. She was a funny girl, not a bit like the usual chorus girl. She was in love with George, I think, all the time because she used to talk to him by the hour about havin' more ambition and betterin' himself. But George was good-lookin' and lazy and good-natured and it didn't make any impression. I don't know how far things went between them, but I guess it went pretty far, because George wouldn't have stood faithful for a couple of years just like he was—worshipper from a distance and he stayed faithful all right. If he hadn't of, we'd have known it by new outbursts of disorder among the girls.

I could never make out what it was that made George so crazy about her but Herby, who used to read a lot, took me off in the corner one day and whispered to me the explanation.

It was Freudian, he said. "George is crazy about her not in spite of the buck teeth but on account of them." Now, I couldn't figure that, but Herby said that people was like that, that love had a funny way of being tied up with all sorts of things like feet and hands and hair and a lot of other stuff. He said George had been runnin' around like a goat since he was fourteen but he'd been waitin' all the time to really fall in love until a girl with buck teeth came along and Daisy was it. Herby says it was on account of George's bein' brought up a half-orphan, his father having cooled when he was three years old. His mother, Herby said, brought him up and educated him, and Herby said he bet that George's mother had buck teeth. I bet she hadn't and we put up ten dollars on it. So one day when we was all gassin' about family and stuff like that, Herby asked George if he had a picture of his mother and George opened his wallet and brought out a picture.

It was the picture of a nice-lookin' woman about fifty, and by George she had terrible buck teeth just like Daisy.

I paid Herby the ten bucks but I told him that he'd gypped me because he musta seen the picture before, but he swore he hadn't, and I guess he was right on account of Herby is the honestest guy I ever met.

It was about this time that Daisy and Herby began to have those whisperin' conferences in dark corners on the stage or at private tables in restaurants. I didn't find out what it was all about till later but what they was talking about was Daisy's teeth.

It seems that Herby had found out there was a dentist in New York who could make over your teeth any way you wanted 'em. He'd been makin' over teeth for Hollywood stars, changin' the look of 'em altogether and changin' the whole of their careers and their lives even. Herby had got the idea that Daisy ought to have her teeth made over—that the teeth was her only handicap and that, with that beautiful façade and them beautiful gams, there wasn't any place she couldn't go if she had beautiful teeth. Herby had been findin' out about it and was tryin' hard to persuade her to get 'em fixed.

It cost a lot of money and it took a long time, something like four or five months and it meant that Daisy would have to hide away for a long time and it was kinda painful. She couldn't make up her mind and Herby just kept after her in his persistent whisperin' way. He knew what was the matter with Daisy. He knew a lot about women, more than George, with all his runnin' around, would ever know. He knew that Daisy was et up with ambition and that she'd never settle down until she satisfied that ambition or it soured on her. He was fond of Daisy and fond of George. He wanted to see 'em married and settled down and happy but he knew it wasn't any good as long as Daisy's ambition was gnawin' at her. And the buck teeth stood between her and that ambition. So Herby wanted to get her teeth fixed and let her get the ambition out of her system and then everything would be all right. It was Herby who loaned her the money to get it done.

When the show broke up in the spring, Daisy told everybody she was goin' out to Minneapolis to visit her aunt and get rested up. George was for goin' along with her but she wouldn't let him. What she actually did was to stay right in New York and have her teeth made over. George didn't find it out because she sent letters to her aunt to be mailed from Minneapolis and he wrote to that address. He might have gone out there to surprise her and find out, but he couldn't get away from the East long enough on account of he took a job in a summer theatre and by the time the season finished we was rehearsin' a road company again.

Only Daisy didn't show up for the first time in five years. The letters from Minneapolis said the doctor said she was run-down and she ought to take a couple more months vacation. She said she'd join the show on the road. She knew we needed her and would fire some girl if necessary to give her a place.

Ziegfeld was gettin' a Follies into shape at the same time and there was a lot of new girls as usual gettin' their pictures in the paper, wrapped in a scarf or with just a bunch of flowers where they had to be on account of the Vice Society. They had one new girl called Lillian LaVerne that was really a top looker. I noticed a couple of the pictures specially because there was something about the girl that kind of haunted me. I was sure I knew her face someplace but I couldn't figure out where. She was a blonde with a wonderful figure the press agents showed off plenty—she had the most wonderful façade and gams I'd ever seen except on Daisy.

One day during rehearsals I took the *Daily Mirror* with a picture of Lillian LaVerne stripped but holding a guitar with a big bow of ribbon on it in front of her over to Herby and said, "This girl is drivin' me nuts, Herby. Has she ever worked for us?"

Herby looked at the picture carefully and then said, "I never seen her before. She's sure got something . . . a lot of things. She's too good ever to turn up with us. She's for Ziegfeld." And then he sort of grinned in a way I didn't like because it seemed to make a fool of me. I looked at the picture again and said, "If I didn't know Daisy was brunette and had buck teeth, I'd say she looked like Daisy."

"You're nuts," said Herby, "Daisy's in Minneapolis. I had a letter from her yesterday."

"Well," I said, "it's mighty peculiar."

And then one day at rehearsal just before we were leaving for Pittsburgh on tour—it was *Blossom Time* that year—a dame comes walking across the stage. There wasn't anything but a house light on and you couldn't see very well but I noticed one thing—she walked like Daisy who always had a show-girl walk even with a road company. She was dressed like a million dollars with a mink coat and a couple of orchids pinned on it.

I'd have sworn it was Daisy except she was a blonde and Daisy was always a brunette when she was with us. Then she called out to me "Hello, Spike!" And I knew it wasn't only Daisy. It was that new Ziegfeld girl they'd been givin' the build-up called Lillian LaVerne.

It was the mouth that threw me. The buck teeth was gone and it changed her whole look and expression. Instead of havin' a funny lookin' mouth she had what they called "rose-bud" lips. She certainly was a looker—the lush kind. You know, the kind that puts ideas in your head on sight. With the buck teeth she'd always kind of looked like a kind of sour and a little mean—the kind of dame that teases you and holds out on you. Honest, you couldn't believe it was the same girl.

I said, "Well, you sure look in the money, kid." I didn't
say anything about the teeth because I thought she might be
sensitive-like about them. She said, "I sure am, Spike. Nothin's
too good for me." And then she laughed and showed the
most beautiful set of pearly white teeth you ever seen. Honest,
it made her into two other wimmin.

And then Herby came up in that undertaker's way of his
and said, "What about her?"

I said, "You knew all the time that girl in the picture was
Daisy."

"Sure," said Herby, "only I couldn't tell yet." Then he
said to Daisy, "Has George seen you yet?"

"No," said Daisy, "I ain't been in circulation much."

And then I seen George coming out from behind a bunch
of lights they was packin' up. None of us said anything and
just waited to see the effect. He came right over—he was
goin' to ask Herby something and in the dim light he couldn't
see very well. He never guessed Daisy was there until he was
right on top of her. Then he looked at her and gave a double-
take. Daisy didn't say anything. She just grinned.

A funny thing happened. I never seen George lose his
temper but after the double-take when he realized who and
what the dame in the mink coat and the orchids was, he got
red in the face like he was goin' to have a stroke and said, "Oh,
it's you, is it?"

"Sure, it's me," said Daisy.

"I thought you was in Minneapolis," said George.

"No. I was havin' my teeth fixed."

He just stood there starin' at her. I could see Herby was
kinda worried. I thought George was goin' to hit her.

"So you wasn't in Minneapolis at all?" he said.

"No, honey," said Daisy. "I wanted to surprise you."

George's face was still as red as a beet. He said, "Well,
it's a lousy surprise. And it ain't improved you. You look
just like any other broad. When you get to look like a human
being again, let me know."

And then he just turned and walked away back to the
bunch of lights.

"Well!" said Daisy, but you could see what happened had

upset her, because she was fond of George and always had it in mind to marry him some day. Herby was sure right about it bein' the buck teeth that made George fall in love. Never before did I ever see love walk out on a man the way it did when George discovered the good-lookin' blonde was his old pal Daisy. He just didn't want any part of Lillian LaVerne. It was buck-toothed Daisy he was in love with.

So what happens? Well, we go on the road and never did we have a worse time with George and the girls. They was fightin' over him all winter and all the time George was as ornery as a man could be. He made it worse than ever by playin' first one girl and then another, settin' 'em all against each other. Once Herby almost wired back to New York to have George fired.

And Daisy? Well, as Lillian LaVerne, she did all right. There was Rolls-Royces waitin' for her every night outside the New Amsterdam and she got an ermine coat along with the mink and she had herself a flat on Park Avenue and she was in all the gossip columns. They called her "that new lovely" and a lot of bologny. When we got back to town she looked us up. Success never turned her head that way. She'd been in show business too long. She asked for George but he wasn't around and somehow he never was when she showed up. I guess he kept an eye kind of out. Her and I went down to Bay Shore for a week end with Herby and Momma. She was nice as could be. She was around town all that summer and I seen her now and then.

In the fall we started gettin' ready for the road again but George didn't show up. Just disappeared clean out of sight. So we went on the road without that Irish he-goat and had a peaceful winter, hardly any fightin' among the girls at all. And along about May just before comin' back to town and foldin' up, Herby comes to me one day with a newspaper in his hand and says, "I just want to show you what you could do for yourself if you'd get your teeth fixed."

Then he opened the paper and there was a big picture of Daisy wearin' nothing but a silver fox and the picture of some jerk who didn't look quite bright and over the top it said, "Follies girl marries bathroom-tile heir."

It seemed Daisy under the name of Lillian had copped herself a guy with about ten million bucks and they was off to Europe on their honeymoon.

At this point, four years pass and the scene changes. We are in the middle of the depression. Again newspaper pictures and headlines—"Lillian LaVerne—ex-Follies girl divorces bankrupt bathroom-tile heir." Just the old familiar story about the Follies' girls. I don't see her and Herby don't see her and nobody knows where she is. We played all the rest of that winter on the road with *The Desert Song* and business was pretty lousy and we come into town early and I went down to Bay Shore and boarded with Herby and Momma.

We talked about Daisy and Momma said, "Too bad Daisy ever got her teeth fixed. It sure wrecked everything. Somebody saw her last week and said she was on the bum proper—not only drink but hopped up."

Then she turned to Herby and said, "It's all your fault—puttin' ideas like that in her head. That girl had common sense as long as she had them buck teeth. And now look at what's happened to her!"

Herby didn't take that layin' down. He said that all this stuff about the Follies was somethin' Daisy had to get out of her system and that there was no two ways about it. She had to fulfill herself, he said, and that all he'd done was to help her.

Momma said that was high-falutin' talk and that Herby read too many books and his head wasn't strong enough to take in their real meaning. And with that a fight began—the biggest fight Momma and Herby ever had in all their lives—and Momma packed up and went to town to stay with her sister that kept a fur store. All over Daisy's teeth that had already messed up George's life and made him disappear.

Well, I stayed on with Herby and after a couple of days Momma came back again never mentioning the argument but sayin' that she had seen Daisy and she was pitiful. Not only was she drinking but she had three teeth missing—three of them pearly white teeth that had changed her whole career.

· · · · · ·

That autumn we didn't go on the road. Business was too lousy. But Herby and I got a job with a revival they was puttin' on of *Maytime*. We had a pretty good-lookin' set of chorus girls because there wasn't much work. We'd just got 'em lined up when we got a telephone call that they was sendin' over a woman dance director. We didn't like that much. There was always trouble when we had a woman runnin' other women.

But it was all right. Who should walk out on the stage but Daisy, and so help me God she had dark hair again and squirrel teeth, lookin' a little thinner and older but just about the way she looked when she left us. I guess maybe the figure wasn't so good, kinda propped up here and there, but she looked pretty good. Only of course she was dressed kind of plain after the mink and orchids.

I could see Herby's face and I guess he was feelin' just the way I was—that he was seein' things.

But, boy, was she chipper. She just said, "Hi, fellows! When do we go to work?"

Well, she always was a good director. She could handle the girls and had a lot of good solid routines—nothin' very original but good enough for a revival. We wanted to ask her what happened to her teeth but both Herby and me was kind of sensitive about it, and it wasn't till after the show opened that she broke down and told us.

It was like this. She had had her old teeth sawed off all right and new ones pegged on and everything was all right for three or four years. She got her minks and ermines and millionaires and then things began to happen to her teeth— not the false ones of course that was screwed on but the roots they were screwed on to. It seemed that the doctor Herby sent her too was just learnin' his business when Daisy went to him and kind of experimented on her. That's why she had so much trouble. In the end all of them expensive screwed-on teeth had to come out and then Daisy didn't have any at all, so she had to have a plate made. And then the trouble began all over again on account of Daisy wanted a plate made with teeth on it like Lillian LaVerne had—beautiful, regular pearly teeth. But it wouldn't work on account of the Lord and Daisy's adenoids had made her a mouth for squirrel teeth and only a plate with squirrel teeth would fit her mouth and stay in. They tried and tried but in the end Daisy had to have a Daisy plate with squirrel teeth and not a Lillian LaVerne plate with perfect ones. The Lillian LaVerne plate would just fall out at just the wrong moment. So she had to come in the end to bein' the way God meant her to be, with squirrel teeth.

She was kind of funny about it. She said, "I guess that's one of the reasons my marriage didn't turn out so good. I had a Lillian LaVerne look and a squirrel teeth personality all the time, and that would kind of confuse anybody."

Of course the false squirrel teeth wasn't as bad as the real ones. The dentist managed to cheat a little on the plate, but they was buck teeth just the same.

Well, one day about the middle of the season, Daisy comes to Herby and says, "How's about usin' your influence to get George his job back?"

Herby didn't get it and he says, "What George? What job?" And Daisy said, "Why George Harrington—you know, the electrician."

"I thought George was dead," Herby said, "I ain't seen him or heard of him for six years."

"Well, he ain't dead," said Daisy. "You'd be surprised how alive he is."

"Are you goin' around with him again?" asked Herby.

"Yes," said Daisy, "he's just as nuts for me as ever."

"Okay," says Herby, "as long as he's mad for *you*. But I don't want that he-goat around here like he was before. Too much trouble with all the girls."

"He ain't gonna bother the girls," said Daisy. "We're gettin' married."

"And none too soon," says Herby. "You've both lost the better part of six years."

"It was them damned teeth," said Daisy.

As soon as Daisy went to George, Herby got on the telephone to call Momma and tell her about how she was right all along about the teeth.

Well, it seems Herby was right too. As soon as Daisy got

her buck teeth back, George went for her again in a big way. It seems this fella Freud, Herby talked about, has got something. It was like George was more in love with Daisy's buck teeth than with Daisy's gams and figure.

Again the scene changes. It is ten years later in Bay Shore. George and Daisy is married and they've got two kids, a boy and a girl and they're livin' in a house right next to Herby and Momma, and you never seen a happier couple. The kids is nice brought up kids, about seven and nine years old. When I went down to visit George and Daisy, the kids come runnin' down the walk to meet me. They was both grinnin' and yellin' and both of 'em had braces on their teeth. I suppose Daisy, what with her and George's mother both havin' squirrel teeth, wasn't takin' no chances.

Later that night we was all together, Daisy and George and Herby and Momma and me. We'd been celebratin' and everybody was kind of frank, so I said to Daisy, "Daise, are you ever sorry you had your teeth changed that time?" And Daisy said, "I sure am. All that mink and stuff wasn't worth what George has got." And she threw her arms around George and gave him a big kiss.

Now, if that ain't true love, I don't know what is.

THE MAN WHO WAS IN LOVE
WITH DEATH

IT WAS THE MUSIC WHICH DID IT—THE STRAINS OF THE
"Intermezzo" from *Cavalleria Rusticana* played drearily by a
tubercular, sallow-faced young man, an elderly pinched woman
with eyes too near together and wearing pince-nez attached to
her shirtwaist by a black ribbon, and an old man who had been
fat in the happy days before the war and whose skin now
hung in wattles over his collar. The young man played the
violoncello, the woman the violin, the once fat man played
the piano.

They were hired, he knew, by the hotel without any choice
in the matter. It was the order of the local *Gauleiter* that all
first-class hotels must have music. It was considered good for
the morale. *Das macht freudig.* Music gave the illusion of
gaiety in a conquered beaten city. For whom the show was
put on he could not imagine, unless it was for the foreign
correspondents who lived in the Grand Brunswick Hotel.
Certainly it was or had once been a first-class hotel. Once it
had been a brilliant *hotel de luxe* frequented by rich and fashionable foreigners who came for the *Festspiel* or to see the
architectural glories of the ancient now ruined city.

Certainly there was nothing about the music which "made
gay." The three dreary people pounded the piano and sawed
on the cello and the fiddle, mournfully, behind their screen
of tired dusty palms. It was evident how they had been
selected. The young tubercular fellow was unfit for a labor
camp or to work in the munitions factories. He had not the
strength to do a quarter-day's work. The woman was over
fifty. From her appearance she had perhaps been a music
teacher in the days before the Germans swarmed in to the
country to destroy its property and its soul. The old man at
the piano had possibly played in a *bierhalle* and grown fat on
"treats" from the patrons who liked his music. But those

days were passed. There were very few patrons in *bierhalles* nowadays and the beer they drank was so weak it would make no one fat. And so the skin of the old man who was almost thin now, hung in yellow folds. Naked, he would be frightening—a picture of "famine overtakes the Pilsener drinker."

And so the three of them, ordered by the *Gauleiter* to practice the art which once all of them had respected and loved, sawed and pounded drearily away at the music of Mascagni's "Intermezzo." There was not enough of rebellion and bitterness in their souls to make them play badly, with deliberation. There was only the despair of people whose lives were wrecked, who were too near to death to care about anything any longer beyond a crust of bread and a cup of *ersatz* coffee.

"Music," he thought idly as he watched them, "might be written or played by unhappy people but never by people in despair."

It was like the Germans to believe the mere presence of these three dreary figures making mournful sounds would deceive the correspondents into believing the city was still prosperous and gay. The Germans always had theories and plans for everything, regardless of the spirit or of the realities. It was one of the reasons why always, sooner or later, they failed. He wished for a second that he had the talent of Raemaekers to sketch in bitter lines the picture of the musicians. He would call it, "The *Gauleiter* says that music makes gaiety."

Although he had never seen them before, he knew them the moment they began playing the "Intermezzo." They had been with him for a long time, always in the back of his consciousness, like people he had encountered in another life. It had needed only the music to make him look up from his newspaper and notice them, sitting there behind their screen of dusty palms against the stained glass of the window depicting the Triumph of Bacchus. He knew exactly how they would look. He knew the palms and the design of the atrocious window. The whole lobby of the hotel, he saw suddenly, was exactly as he knew it would be—with its elderly clerk behind the desk, two German officers writing letters, and the fat old woman knitting in the wicker chair by the door. It was exactly as he had seen it, with the broken chairs and the patches on the ceiling where the gilt had come off. He had not been in the hotel since before Austria had been invaded, since the days when the same lobby was filled with bankers and musicians and titled people and kept women returning from the *Festspiel*.

He had never seen it like this, yet the moment the orchestra began to play, he knew it at once. He had been here before and lived through this whole scene. He had come here because, as he felt the net slowly closing in, he knew that the Grand Brunswick Hotel would be the last place they would look for him. The Grand Brunswick would be the last place they would look for a British agent whom they had trapped at last. They would be searching all the buildings in the quarter and all the other hotels, but they would scarcely look in upon the headquarters of the Gestapo itself to find him. He had come in here to get his breath, to think out what must be done in order to escape. Boldness like this had turned the trick before and gotten him out of a tight place at the last moment. And so he had sat there in his black shirt and military belt, looking completely and thoroughly German, wearily trying to think of what to do before the moment arrived when they came in and recognized him and began the awful questioning.

But with the first strains of the "Intermezzo" he looked up from his newspaper and saw the orchestra and then the clerk behind the desk and the two German officers writing home and the old woman sitting in the cracked wicker chair by the door and he knew it was all up. There wasn't any use going on planning. It was all finished. In a little while Zosha would come in off the snowy street and walk past the old woman and go to the desk and ask the clerk something. Then she would come over to the one empty desk and on her way she would pass close to him and accidentally trip over his foot. Then she would look at him without any sign of recognition and say, *"Bitte entschuldigen Sie mich! Ich muss an den Bahnhof gehen."* Then she would look at the writing desk, and as if she had changed her mind suddenly, she would turn and go out the door again into the snowy street. And in a little while he would follow her and at the corner she would be waiting, like a prostitute, and as he came up to her she would take his arm and they would walk toward the Central Railroad Station.

But beyond that he could not see. The whole thing dissolved in a kind of mist with the silhouette of the Central *Bahnhof* fading out last like a building in the fade-out at the end of a cinema. But beyond, somewhere in that mist, was capture and death. It would be a triumph for the Gestapo—that at last they had run to earth and captured Eric North alias Henrich Hostaetter alias Emile van der Hoeven alias almost anything you liked, the most dangerous man in the service. Maybe a day or two and then a wall, a volley and blackness, oblivion—and rest!

It was an odd thought that death should be as young and pretty as Zosha and as sweet and gentle. It was odd that at last, he, the cleverest of them all, should have been caught by the oldest, the most melodramatic trick of them all, by a pretty counter-spy. Once or twice lately he had been suspicious. Once or twice in moments of clarity, when the weariness abated a little, he had told himself, "I must go away tonight and lose myself and never see her again." But he had fallen in love, something which had never happened to him before, something he had hoped would never happen because it rendered a man useless as a good spy. And so he had not heeded the warnings of the brain but gone on and on until now it was too late.

For he knew the truth the moment the drab little orchestra began to play. Zosha was in the counter-espionage. She would come in the door presently and when she went away again he would follow her and outside somewhere in the darkness between the Hotel and the Central *Bahnhof* two or three men would come up behind them and pinion his arms and take him away. . . .

But because he was so tired and because he was in love with her, he could not even feel any resentment or bitterness. He had been a fool, as big a fool as any novice. It would bring great credit to her if she delivered him up. He did not care. Let her have the credit. He was tired, so tired that he wanted to help her and then be done with the whole thing and rest . . . but it was odd that death should look as young and fresh and beautiful as Zosha.

.   .   .   .   .   .

While he waited, listening idly to the despairing music, he thought of many things, as he supposed men did who knew they had only a few hours to live. The thoughts came to him out of a paralyzing haze. He was unable to move or act, and curiously he had no desire to move or act. He only wanted peace and rest and freedom from the necessity of planning and plotting. It would be good to die and have done with it all, now that he knew that death looked like Zosha. You would never again want to kiss her or hold her in your arms, knowing that underneath that lovely face there was only an empty skull. Love, desire had already been killed. Physical death was only a little way beyond.

He knew now that he should have quit and made his way toward the border and escaped that time at Innsbruck when he felt the first sign of weariness. It was an old story. Always sooner or later it happened to men like himself. That awful paralyzing weariness overtook them. It was like a disease which destroyed their alertness, dulled their brains and made them useless. The service knew its danger from long experience. The orders were to return home at the first sign of it for a holiday or a rest, because when the weariness came on you, you were no longer of any use. Sooner or later you were caught and shot, or worse you were tortured and in the weariness your own brain betrayed you and you told them things which cost the lives of other men. That was the only thing which troubled him now as he sat waiting for her to come in the door. He might be so tired that when they tortured and questioned him he would no longer know what he was answering.

It could be very exhausting always hiding away, always tricking those who followed you, never really sleeping at all, always playing a role.

It was worse for him too, because he had this awful gift of second sight, the very gift which had made him more valuable than any other man in the service. It was, he knew, a thing of nerves, of super-sensitivity which made vast drains upon the vitality and health. And it was a terrifying thing—this fore-knowledge of what was to come, this recognition of people you had never seen before.

No, he knew now that on the night he had collapsed in the

little inn at Innsbruck, he should have fled as soon as he was strong enough, straight for the border. Or again in Vienna the time when he forgot which name he was using and what name was on his passport. They had very nearly caught him that time. Either the blond lieutenant was stupid or a little drunk or he had hated the Nazis and let him go, knowing who and what he was. He knew now that if it had been in the books for him to have been captured then, he would have known it despite his weariness. He would have seen it all just as he had seen it all now when the dreary music pulled everything together. No, it was not in the books on that occasion.

He was aware presently that the band had stopped playing. Then after a moment in which the thin old woman with the pince-nez shuffled some sheets of music about, they began again to play, this time the ballet music of *Coppélia*. That was right! That was exactly as he knew it would be! He would go to his death to the music of the doll-ballet *Coppélia*.

Then the old woman rose from the wicker chair by the door and crossed to the desk. She said something to the clerk who took out some letters from a pigeonhole, looked through them and shook his head. The old woman waddled back to her chair and began knitting again. One of the young officers left the writing desk and went to the clerk's desk and bought two stamps. All that was as he knew it would be. He had forgotten that part, perhaps because some portion of his brain was numb with weariness. But it was right—exactly right! That was how it happened. And now the door would open and . . .

The street door opened and Zosha came in out of the snowy street. She looked very young and very pretty in her blue Youth Uniform, her cheeks pink with the cold, her blue eyes shining. That is the way His Nibs said all Aryan German girls should look, only of course they rarely looked like that. Zosha was part Russian by blood, so she told him, but of course knowing now that Zosha was death and deception, you couldn't believe anything about her. There were snowflakes on the shoulders of her blue uniform. The sight of her freshness and beauty roused a sudden pang, even through the mist of weariness, the last pang perhaps.

The young officer smiled at her as he turned away from the

desk and she smiled back at him, that smile that sometimes
passed between young people of opposite sexes in Germany,
a kind of dedicated unnatural hysterical smile, denatured and
free of any sex feeling. It was no more than a sign of recognition between two individuals dedicated to the cause of Der
Führer.

He had seen it happen before many times. It had even protected him . . . being seen with her, so young and radiant in
her Youth Uniform. Only it was different this time. Always
before it had been a deception. She had deceived the very people who said, looking at her, "See! There is the ideal German
girl working for the Führer and the new order in the world."

Only this time it was real. It was true—that friendly, inspired
smile. He thought dully, "This time the laugh is on me!" Yet
he felt no bitterness.

Then she left the desk and came toward him and as she
passed she tripped over his extended foot and said, "*Bitte,
entschuldigen Sie mich! Ich muss an den Bahnhof gehen.*"
Looking up he smiled at her.

(Yes, that was right. A little comedy played against the
music of *Coppélia*.)

Then she went to the writing desk and quickly turned away
as if she had changed her mind. He watched her, fascinated
by the fidelity of the vision he had had. But as she turned away
something happened which he had not seen. She looked at
him swiftly and smiled as she had smiled at the soldier, the
same open, friendly, sexless smile. It was swift as a flash of heat
lightning and the sight of it made him suddenly feel sick in the
pit of his stomach. It was, he thought, the smile of a female
Judas.

Then quickly, exactly as he had seen it, she went out of the
door again and into the snowy street, and in a little while he
rose and followed her, not quite knowing what he was doing,
but dimly aware that whatever happened, it was better for her
to have the credit of his capture than simply to sit there waiting
dully until they came and arrested him. It could only be the
matter of a few minutes in any case, and by now the whole
thing was beyond his choice or will. He was little more than an
automaton.

The feel of the cold air was like a slap in the face and for one brief moment he thought, "I could destroy the pattern. Instead of turning toward the railway station I could turn and run in the opposite direction." But he knew that he would not get far because they were searching all the district for him. It was safe to go with her. As long as he was with her, he would be free. No one would stop him or question him so long as he was in her company—until she gave the sign.

The lethargy swept over him again and like a man hypnotized, he turned to follow her. Dimly he could see her trim figure ahead of him a little way. They were alone in the street. No other person was in sight. The police had given orders for everyone in the quarter to remain in their houses—all because they had trapped somewhere in the district a famous spy—Eric North alias Emile van der Hoeven alias what you will—who was himself.

"Important I am!" he thought grimly.

Then at the next corner she stopped as he knew she would stop and waited, and as he passed, she put her arm through his, just as she had always done when they had met before as lovers. Neither of them spoke but she swung into step beside him. Before them at the end of the street, silhouetted against the light of the stars, loomed the mass of the Central *Bahnhof*. From here on he did not know what was to happen, for the vision which came into being with the first bars of *Cavalleria Rusticana* had gone only this far. Beyond here lay darkness. He thought, "Perhaps I am already dead. Perhaps it is better that way." But against his heart he felt now the warmth of her arm penetrating through the cloth of his coat, and bitterly he thought, "The body of a pretty woman has warmth whether or not she is a Judas."

. . . . .

It had begun a long time ago, exactly when he could not remember save that even as a small child it had happened to him in occasional flashes, but he was too small then to understand what it was. The first time it had happened clearly he was fifteen years old and home in England on a visit from

Hamburg where his English father had a small exporting business. He had arrived in a house in Surrey which his grandmother had taken for the summer. It was a small house with a garden, set back from the road in a small grove of trees and approached by a winding drive. He had never been in the house or even in Surrey in all his life, but as the car turned in from the road, he knew it all very well, not only the drive itself, but the house which still remained hidden among the trees.

He saw not only the façade of the house with its flower boxes and old-fashioned Strawberry Hill Gothic gables but his grandmother herself whom he had not seen for six years. The odd part was that she appeared not as he had seen her last but much older and thin and quite feeble. He saw her coming down the short flight of steps to greet him, her face pink with excitement, her hands trembling. Then the car came round the corner of the lodge and there she was standing in the doorway exactly as he had seen her in the moment of clairvoyance. She had changed and aged and there was something indefinitely feeble about her—exactly as he had seen her during the sudden vision.

That night the vicar and his wife came to dinner and presently while they were sitting in the drawingroom, his grandmother had asked the vicar's wife to play something for them and the vicar's wife had gone to the piano and played a Chopin waltz and then "Für Elise." It was during the Beethoven piece that it happened a second time.

It was morning and he was in this same room but there was no one in it but himself. He was waiting for his grandmother to come to breakfast and idly watching a chaffinch in the cherry tree outside the window when he heard a voice behind him saying, "Excuse me for troubling you, sir" and when he turned he saw his grandmother's old servant, his face very white, standing in the doorway. "I would be grateful," he said, "if you would come with me. I think something has happened to your grandmother." And they went upstairs to his grandmother's room and there she was quite dead in her bed.

The vicar's wife finished playing "Für Elise" and presently

she and the vicar said good night and went home and he and
his grandmother had a glass of milk each and she went with
him to his room to see that he was comfortable. When she
had gone away he went to bed and read a mystery story until
very late, and forgot all about the curious vision he had had
while the vicar's wife was playing "Für Elise." In the morning he wakened and went downstairs to the drawingroom
and was standing at the window watching a chaffinch in the
cherry tree when a voice inside him said, "It is going to
happen. You must call a doctor before she dies." But before
he had time to turn he heard the voice of the old servant
saying, "Excuse me for troubling you, sir," and he knew that
it was too late. It all happened exactly as he knew it would
happen.

He said nothing of the experience to anyone, not even his
father when he arrived for the funeral, because to his sensitive
adolescent mind there was something peculiar and almost
indecent about the whole episode. And afterward he could
not himself be quite certain of the order in which the experience had happened. It was as if the time element had become
muddled and confused. From time to time similar experiences
occurred—small, detached flashes, without particular meaning. He would enter a shop and recognize all the strangers
in it—people he had never seen before, or sometimes in the
twilight borderline between sleep and wakefulness, there
would occur a sudden vision of a place which he had never
seen before and of people whom he had not yet seen.

More often than not these sudden flashes of clairvoyance
were forgotten but sometimes the memories of them lingered,
very clear and precise, so that he found himself waiting for
the pictures to become reality. Sometimes this happened
almost at once, the next day, or within a week; but with other
strange pictures, like the one in the Grand Brunswick Hotel,
they did not seem to arrive at realization at once but slowly
to fade into the mists of forgetfulness until one day perhaps
months, perhaps years afterward, a strain of music or the
sight of some unfamiliar yet familiar object would bring them
to life. In the very midst of some scene or action, he would

wake suddenly to the consciousness that he had known all this before and forgotten it all.

As he grew out of adolescence the experiences became less confused and more and more sharp in detail and outline. The tormenting thing was that he seemed to have no control whatever over the visions: they occurred without reason or logical succession. Once or twice he thought, "If only I could control this peculiar gift, I could conquer the whole world. I could win all bets at the races. I could make fortunes at investments." But there was no way to control these flashes of foreknowledge.

Once when he was eighteen and home in Hamburg from Oxford, he spoke of the experiences to his father while they were walking through the fields one Sunday afternoon. But his father, an unimaginative, materialistic man, had only laughed at him and said that all people had such experiences from time to time, especially that of entering a strange room and feeling they had been there before. It was nothing remarkable, he said. If it had been remarkable, he pointed out, some practical use would have been made of the gift long ago.

So he never again mentioned it to his father, not troubling to point out that doubtless only people of an imaginative, sensitive and inpractical nature were endowed with the gift.

But it troubled him, crippling and deforming all the ordinary relationships of life. How was it possible to embark upon a friendship with a man when suddenly without warning you knew how it was to end, in a betrayal of confidence or a bitter quarrel. How was it possible to marry or take a mistress with that awful power of foreknowledge perpetually making the relationship impossible. It made him shy with people and rather solitary by nature. All his natural sensitiveness became sharpened to a point where at times life grew almost unbearable. But worst of all was the confusion it produced in the element of time. There were occasions when it seemed to him that he lived simultaneously in the past, the present and the future, when his brain seemed divided into three parts, each dominated by a different place in time, operating without coordination. It was exhausting and when he was twenty-six the world seemed to collapse all about him and he had a break-

down and was sent to a remote village in the Tyrol to recover.

Here he met the scientist who made it possible for him to
regain control of himself, to order his existence once more and
to prevent the strange gift from ruining all his life.

The man was thin and tall and over fifty and had spent
all his life in surgery and physiology. He knew more than
any other living man concerning the human body, its muscles,
its bones, its nerves, its organs. He knew so much that he had
become aware of having reached the limits of the physical.
There was, he believed, nothing more to be learned from
operations and dissections; one had to go beyond into the
realm which science had always overlooked and neglected—
that realm of the mystical in which occurred such things as
clairvoyance and thought transference and that strange thing
the time element which had perpetually deceived mankind,
and distorted all conscious existence. His attitude was entirely
scientific, and he had come to the point where all the mecha-
nistic and physiological achievements of his celebrated past
no longer interested him. He stood at the threshold of a limit-
less world, veiled in mists into which few scientists had ever
looked.

The surgeon had come to the Tyrolean village to lose himself intellectually, to sever if possible all relationship with the
material world of his past achievement. No one knew he was
there. No one could find him. In this mood, at breakfast one
morning, he came upon the young Englishman who had the
strange gift.

That the young man was ill was apparent to him at once,
and that the illness was not of the body but of the sensitivity
he discovered before very long. The illness affected the body
only in so far as the strain upon it wearied the tissues and
the organs. The illness came not of the body but from outside it. After a day or two as they walked and ate together
it became apparent to him that the illness was born of what
might be described as mal-adjustment between the body and
the super-acuteness of the young man's perceptions. In their
conversations he discovered that the young fellow frequently
knew the end of a sentence the surgeon himself was speaking

—sometimes even a complicated sentence requiring thought—before he had reached the end. He had himself, something of the gift and so after a week he found that they were conversing and even exchanging ideas almost without speaking, certainly never in rounded completed sentences. To the scientist and surgeon, it was as if God had sent him a subject to work upon.

Then one night while they were sitting in the tap-room of the village inn, smoking their pipes and drinking beer, the young Englishman said, "The girl is going to sing a song called *Ein Kleines Hotel* and she will sing it to the young man over there by the window and when she has finished singing it, Fritz, the guide, will get up and go over to her and slap her face."

He did not know why he said it except that saying it brought a relief to his nerves and because the personality of the scientist seemed to make it possible. He could not have said it to anyone else in the world.

The scientist did not reply. He relighted his pipe and as he did so the girl took up her accordion and after a flash of notes, began to sing. The song was *Ein Kleines Hotel*. She looked directly at the young man sitting by the window and when it was finished, Fritz, the guide, rose, crossed the room and slapped her face. It all happened exactly as Eric had seen it.

When Fritz had been thrown out and the uproar died down, the doctor asked, "How did you know that?"

"I don't know. I saw it quite clearly."

"Did you see anything beyond that?"

"Nothing. After the slap the whole thing faded into a mist."

After that it was easier to talk and he told the scientist more and more of what had happened to him since that first experience with the death of his grandmother. And the more he talked the easier it became to talk, and the tension of his nerves slackened and health began to return.

There were many things which interested the older man—that there was no way of knowing when the flashes of foreknowledge were to happen, that there was no way of knowing at what point they would halt. Sometimes they seemed to carry on to an end, like a complete and isolated incident.

At others they went only so far and then seemed to dissolve in the wall of fog.

The scientist explained about the time element and the lag between an actual occurrence and the brain's recording of it—that the incident in the tap-room might only have been evidence of the boy's super-sensitivity, that what he had experienced was not foreknowledge but only came from the possibility that one part of his brain reacted much more quickly than another part, that the incident had actually occurred before it registered in the brain of the scientist, or in another part of the boy's brain.

The older man was not only brilliant, he was kind. He tried to help the young man while using him as a laboratory specimen.

"You must accept these experiences as a kind of special endowment," the older man told him. "You must accept them as simple ordinary facts. It would be best to control them if you can find any way of doing so. It would be a good idea to attempt turning them to advantage. In any case you must not again allow the experience to hynotize and paralyze you."

"How can I help it if always they turn out to be true?"

For that there was no answer save only the weak one the scientist gave. "Perhaps one day it will happen that you see wrongly—that the thing does not happen as you saw it."

Then one morning the scientist received a telegram and left. As he said good-bye, he added, "We must not lose each other. I will come back or you must come to see me in America. The rest of my life I am giving to finding out what I can about such things."

They planned to meet in a few months' time and they would have met but for forces far more powerful than either of them. The young man had a telegram calling him back to London and when he arrived, his uncle met him at Victoria Station. His uncle was in the Foreign Office and at lunch in his flat he told the young man that there was a job he could do to help his country. He knew Germany and especially Hamburg and Berlin. He spoke German like a German and French very nearly as well. He could pass as a German or a

Belgian. There were some things in Germany which the government wished to discover.

The young man thought it over for twenty-four hours. It seemed a wise thing to do. It might help him back on his feet. He might find in such a task some practical use for his extraordinary gift which would make it bearable and even useful.

And so he became a secret agent, the most remarkable one in the whole of Germany, because again and again, there occurred to him moments of clairvoyance which saved his life, or provided him with an extraordinary piece of information, or enabled him to discover and betray a counter-spy. But at last they tracked him down, into a block of buildings between the Grand Brunswick Hotel, and the Central *Bahnhof*, because he was tired, because even the strong, healthy body nature had given him could not longer endure the strain of his frightening gift.

.   .   .   .   .

And now here he was walking along the dark street toward the railway station and his death with indifference, almost happily because he could feel the warmth of her body against his arm. For the moment it didn't matter whither she led him as long as her youth and strength were there near to him. Once long ago when he had gone away to the Tyrol, he had been like this, dull and numb and indifferent to everything save the solace and relief of sleep which was next to death. It was like that now. Then he was aware suddenly that they had passed that point in the vision where it faded into mist with only the silhouetted mass of the railway station black against the night sky.

They were still walking and out of the doorways no men had yet come to step up behind him and pinion his arms and say, "Herr North—van der Hoeven!" but he remembered that he had not seen the men; that part he had only imagined, so there was no inevitability about it. That did not *have* to happen. She might herself lead him directly to the Central Police Station.

She did not speak save once when she said in her faintly

accented English, "Are you tired?" and he answered, "Yes, very tired."

They were walking very close to the buildings now—those great blank walls of Central European apartment houses which even in peacetime had an air of gloom about them—and suddenly by a gentle pressure she turned him and thrust him into a darkened doorway. It was not, he saw, the main entrance of the great building but a small door. Freeing his arm she took a key from a pocket in her trim blue uniform, thrust it into the lock and opened the door. Quickly they went through it into the darkness beyond. She locked it behind them and then said, "There are stairs. Be careful!"

Again with her arm through his, she led him down iron stairs until their feet struck a floor of concrete. He kept thinking, "It will come to me now at any second and I will know where I am and what is to happen." But he saw no more in his mind than he saw with his eyes. No clue came, no hint, no clear forewarning such as he had had swiftly at the first notes of the "Intermezzo."

Then she said, "Stairs again!" and they climbed another flight of iron stairs which rang beneath their feet and came after a little time on to a floor of tiles. She appeared to know her way well in the darkness for she did not falter nor grope with her hand along the wall. Then she unlocked another door and they went into a room. Here she withdrew her arm again, this time to strike a match and light a candle. The tiny flame illumined her face and he felt a sudden glow of feeling that was like a strain of music, like the swelling bell-music out of *Boris Godunov*. For a second he knew again what was to happen.

She would take the candle and place it inside the door of a cupboard built into the wall and then close the door a little way so that the flame did not shine directly into the room. Then she would return and say, "Lie down on the divan. You must be very tired."

It happened like that, exactly, but the vision went no further. The mist closed down again. He thought, "I am tired. That is why." But there was too the fact that one part of his spirit was stubbornly unwilling to see any further. It would not be possible to endure knowing exactly how the betrayal would happen. It would be unbearable. His body made him want to deny the vision in the Grand Brunswick lobby. His body, because it loved her, wanted him to go on being deceived until the very last second.

Then she sat down beside him on the edge of the sofa and began to stroke his forehead. Her hand was still cold with the cold of the snowy streets.

She said, "You must stay here. I must go now and you must stay here until I come for you. It would be unsafe to go outside. This room belongs to the concierge. He is a Communist. He is waiting for the Day to rise. They have already been here and searched the room. They will not come again, but outside they will be watching everywhere. Even your uniform would do you no good now."

He realized that her hand was trembling.

Then she bent down and kissed his forehead. In the darkness he thought, "The kiss! That was all that was needed." Aloud he said, "Perhaps it would be easier if I went out and gave myself up."

She laughed, an odd almost inhuman laugh. "No, you mustn't do that. Fabrizius wants the credit of catching you." Then she rose and went out the door. Dimly he realized that she turned the key in the lock on the outside.

Fabrizius! That was it! Just as he had imagined. She had saved him from the local Gestapo and Military only to save him for Fabrizius. Fabrizius was her chief. "They" had told him that when they had given him orders to meet her on a bench in the Tiergarten in Berlin. She was officially working for Fabrizius, but that meant nothing, "they" said. She was playing the most dangerous of double games—that of informer who had worked herself high into the confidence of the Gestapo. It was odd how intricately it worked, this world of double-cross and double-double-cross which Hitler and Himmler had invented. It was odd that even when agents saw him with her he was safe, because they believed she was gaining information from him. More than once before now they might have picked him up but for her presence. He wondered for how long they had been on his trail this time. Perhaps they had followed him to Flensburg and then all the way across Germany to Munich and then here into this Czech city. Perhaps they had been with him all along only waiting for her to give the sign to arrest him. One thing was clear. There was jealousy and intrigue at work inside the organization. The local crowd had gotten wind of his presence and tried to trap him and gain all the credit. Somehow she had led him out of the lion's mouth here to this janitor's room, to save him and the credit of capturing him for her chief, the dread Fabrizius.

But in his weariness he did not care what happened to him. He opened his eyes presently and regarded the room. It was cheaply furnished with a table, a few chairs, some photographs and a large picture of Hitler with a Nazi flag draped over it. What had she meant by saying the occupant of this room was a Communist waiting for the Day to come? Did she think him a fool or did she not notice that the picture was here? But almost at once he saw his own naïveté. Of course, if the man was an undercover Communist he would have a picture of Hitler and a Nazi flag—the biggest he had room for.

It was all so complex and complicated, this world into which he and Zosha had been born. You could trust no one. In their hearts, no one in Germany trusted any one else. That was why there was so much cruelty and fear. When you could not trust, you must dominate by evil, by force, by fear, by cruelty, however the domination might be achieved.

He remembered the day he was sent to meet her in the Tiergarten. She was, "they" said, young and blonde and beautiful. "Beautiful" was the word "they" used, not "pretty." They said, "She is not like the usual female agent. She looks her part . . . like a young girl who is an officer in the Youth Movement. But she is clever. She is half-Russian. We have investigated. She is absolutely trustworthy. She will be of good use to you. She will be able to get you into all sorts of difficult places and out of them. Everybody trusts her. She looks like Hitler's ideal 'Aryan maiden.' No one even suspects her."

So he had gone to the Tiergarten and there on a bench in the Siegesallé near the statue of Frederick the Great he found her. She was feeding the squirrels with crumbs of bread (even the poor squirrels were rationed). He knew that she was aware of him before he sat on the bench beside her. Anyone watching them would have thought it was a kind of healthy flirtation between two big blond Nordics—between Hitler's two ideals, the big blond Storm Trooper and the Aryan Maiden.

They talked first about the squirrels and then about the rather neglected condition of the park. "In wartime," she said, "there is neither time nor money for such luxuries as parks." And presently they allowed the casual pretense to drift away and she said in a low voice, "Where shall we meet again?" And he suggested a well-known restaurant in the Kürfürstendam. There, with lights and music, they would be able to talk. No one would suspect them. They would be two young Nazi fiancés having a dinner of celebration together. "My name," he said, "is Heinrich Paul." And she answered, "I am Zosha Hirth. I am part Russian. I speak Russian and Polish." She added, "That makes me valuable."

Then they talked a little longer, about what he could no longer remember for the spell had already begun to work and he was thinking, despite himself, that she was beautiful and had a lovely low voice. Presently she said, "I think we had better go now." It was growing late and people returning from work were beginning to cross the park. They stood up and she raised her arm and said, "Heil Hitler!" and he did the same. Then they went off in opposite directions to meet again at the Kürfürstendam restaurant.

But the thing had happened already.

He did not know how or why it happened but he did know that what had happened to him had never happened before. He had had other girls. In his work women were important. They were a part of the job, and for his age he was far more experienced than most men. And there was always that other thing of which most men had nothing—that curious vision which told him so much, nearly always too much, about them on a first encounter. But the thing which happened to him on the bench in the Tiergarten was like nothing he had ever known before. It was what was called "love at first sight."

His friend the surgeon had described it to him, analyzing it with the dispassionate detachment of a scientist. It happened, he said, when two bodies suited each other, when two minds and spirits were complementary. There was in it also the elements of chemistry and of mysticism, neither of which elements science had yet dealt with adequately. "Love at first sight," he had said, "is an experience which is scientifically possible, but very rare. A great many inferior people like to deceive themselves into believing they have experienced it, but in reality very few have ever known anything like it. The Greeks, the old poets, Shakespeare understood what it was. . . . They conjured up love potions and Gods and Goddesses to make the experience seem reasonable, because love at first sight was even to them a super-romantic and illogical experience. Nevertheless it existed and does sometimes exist. Take Tristan and Isolde. . . . There you had it. . . ."

Lying there on the janitor's cot in the darkness, he could hear the great man, disillusioned as scientists can be, but romantic as only scientists can be, talking on and on. Oddly enough the lecture had made no difference to his own emotions. It had made him neither disillusioned nor cynical. Not even the knowledge that there was no place for love in the hideous calling he practiced, that in the hideous calling love almost invariably led to betrayal and death, made any difference.

In the darkness he smiled, not without bitterness. He had believed that she too loved him. He had believed that she had arranged it so that she could be with him in Flensburg and Munich and now here. He had believed that she had protected and shielded him. And all the time she was acting on the orders of Fabrizius.

Suddenly through his thoughts came the sound of footsteps in the hallway outside the door. Someone knocked, once and then again. He sat up more out of long habit than because he was alarmed. He thought, "Now they've come. They followed us here. They'll take me first before she can lead me into Fabrizius' trap."

But it was not the Gestapo. They would have yelled, "Open up!" and beaten down the door. Once more the knock was repeated. Then the sound of footsteps going away.

He lay back again closing his eyes and wishing it were all over. It was odd that he felt no resentment against her. Perhaps it was because he was so tired, perhaps because he loved her so much. He thought, "It's all the fault of this damnable world into which we were born—a world of hate and misery." But for all this misery about them, they might have met and loved each other and been married and had a family and lived happily. At the back of the thought lay the memory of the three dreary musicians at the Grand Brunswick Hotel, fiddling and pounding dismally at the "Intermezzo" and the ballet music. They were the proper symbols of this tired world in which he and Zosha had met—the tubercular man, the ugly old woman, the old man with the folds of yellow skin hanging over his soiled collar. How could there be normal happiness in such a world? How could there be loyalty or decency? How could there be anything but despair and betrayal? Even hope became hysterical, like the insane cheering he had seen at Nazi party meetings, like the insane fervor which made a normal healthy girl like Zosha give herself over body and soul to a vile organization like the Gestapo?

"I am," he thought, "already dead. So what? What good is there to live in such a world?"

Then presently out of sheer weariness he fell asleep. For three days and three nights he had been fleeing, watchful, aware that any man he passed on the street might be the one who thrust a pistol into his ribs and said, "*Nun, Herr* Heinrich Paul." He dreamed that they came and broke down the door and took him and that when they went outside he found others kicking and beating an elderly man who they said was the janitor. They were kicking him to death because he was a Communist who pretended to be for Hitler. And Zosha was there, young and beautiful. She was standing by, saying, "Kick harder! Make him yell!" Only somehow, it was not Zosha but another young girl—a whole composition of young girls (the insane faces kept changing) whom he had seen screaming and yelling like mad women at party meetings.

.   .   .   .   .

It was dawn when he wakened, slowly, not knowing at first where he was or how he had come there. It was the large photograph of Hitler which made him remember all that had happened the night before. Slowly he went back over every incident, and now that he had slept a little it seemed to him that he had been a fool all along, from the very moment he sat on the bench beside her in the Tiergarten. He felt an odd sense of shame that he should have fallen into the oldest trap there was, and then found a little consolation in the fact that he had not been the only one deceived. "They"—the mysterious, powerful "they" who gave him orders—had believed in her too. But "they" had not been in love with her. There lay the difference.

The sleep had brought him no sense of rest and well-being because the weariness and the illness were of the spirit and the mind, an illness so great that he remained paralyzed and incapable of action. There was, he knew sitting there on the edge of the janitor's cot, nothing to do but wait. "Wait for what?" he asked himself and the answer came back, "For death!"

He considered the prospect dully and without emotion. He had been like this before, that time in the Tyrol, when he did not care whether he lived or died. Death would mean rest, release from being hunted, release from those sudden flashes of clairvoyance which made life unendurable. If only once what he saw in the visions had been wrong, he could have endured it, but what he saw was always right. It always happened exactly as he saw it. Now he knew he was too tired for the visions to trouble him. They would not come when he was like this, numb and exhausted.

While he sat there in a kind of fog, the sound of footsteps came to him. They were her footsteps; he would have known them anywhere. Then the key turned in the lock and she came in, carrying a cheap paper suitcase in her hand.

She came over to him and stroked his forehead as she had done the night before. "Are you feeling rested?" she asked.

"Yes . . . and you? Have you slept?"

"A little. They are still watching but they are letting people go in and out now."

"What are we going to do?"

"I've a plan . . . a very old theatrical plan but it may work for that reason."

She placed the suitcase on the bed beside him, opened it and took out a man's suit of clothes, a shirt, tie, shoes and socks, an overcoat and a hat. "You are going to wear these," she said. "Better change into them quickly. You must go out at the hour when people are going to work. They will notice you less then."

He was aware of an odd theatrical quality about the whole scene. He might have said, "Why do you do this to me? Why trouble to deliver me to Fabrizius? Why not let the ones waiting outside take me?" But he felt an odd embarrassment. He could not ask her these things. Remembering the past and how much he loved her, he could not face the ugliness of accusing her. It was much better to let it happen the other way. It was better to go with her, letting her believe that he still trusted her. Then she would arrange it so that when he was arrested she would not be present. He would never see her again and after a little while they would shoot him and he would have rest.

It was much better that way, much better for her and for the love that had been and perhaps still was between them. It would have existed forever but for this other unnatural love of hers, this curious German devotion toward an idea. That was stronger in Germany than the love between man and woman, between mother and son. It was evil, fanatic, something he could never quite understand. In the end it would die because it was inhuman, like the fanaticism of some Communists, but before it died it would have destroyed many lives and made the whole pleasant world a wretched place.

No, he could not accuse her now. He was lost in any case, and so it seemed to him evil and needless to destroy all that had been beautiful by a moment or two of bitter ugliness. No, let her go on thinking that she had deceived him.

He began taking off his Storm Trooper's uniform and she said, "Give me your papers. I must have the photograph for the new passport."

As he changed into the dark suit of business clothes, he watched her working deftly on the corner of the janitor's table. She had stamps which she was transferring. She used the surface of a hard-boiled egg to transfer the inking of a rubber stamp. She worked surely and skillfully. By the time he had finished changing, she stood up, finished with her work. Handing him a passport and a wallet partly filled with money and papers, she said, "You are Swiss now. You are comptroller of a bank in Montreux. You are here to finish up some business for the estate of a Swiss who owned property here. You have been in Montreux?"

"Yes. Many times."

"Can you imitate Swiss German?"

"*Ein wenig aber nur ein bisschen.*" He spoke thickly. The thing had become a grim sort of joke which made him want to laugh.

"If anyone stops you," she said, "lay it on thick. I will keep your Storm Trooper's papers. Found on me they will mean nothing." She opened a small box. "There is one more thing. This is the funny part."

She took out a pair of spectacles and a blond false mustache. "It's silly but it may work."

With spirit gum she fastened the mustache to his lip. Then she took up the glasses. "I hope you can see through them. They are very thick—for a very near-sighted person. Dark glasses were too obvious."

He put them on and the whole room became a dark blur. The bed, the table, the portrait of Der Führer were barely discernible, little more than dim outlines.

"I would not know you," she said. "You are middle-class, bourgeois, solid, dull. You look like all bankers." She sighed, "It may work after all." Then she took the Storm Trooper's clothes under her arm. "We mustn't leave them here. If they were found it would be hard on our friend, the janitor."

That was like her, like the Zosha he loved—to think of the janitor.

"Come," she said, "it is time. Bring the suitcase. It is empty but that won't matter. If they question you it will all be over anyway."

Opening the door, she looked up and down the narrow hall-way and then beckoned to him. In order to see properly, he pushed the gold-rimmed glasses high on his forehead and followed her.

She went down a narrow iron stairway into a vast cellar. They had, he knew, come this way on the night before when they had vanished out of the snowy street. Now she took him to the far end of the cellar and opening a steel door, she said, "Be careful as you can. Don't get yourself covered with coal dust and soot."

The passage was narrow and low and filled with steam pipes. In the days when there was coal, the pipes had supplied the other great apartment houses in the block with heat from the central plant in the vast cellar they had left. Halfway down the long passage she stuffed his Storm Trooper's uniform behind the pipes. "When they find it," she said, "they will know the bird has flown."

At the end of the passage they came into another vast cellar. Crossing this, she led him again up an iron stairway and when she opened the door at the top they were in the main hallway of an apartment house.

Behind the cage of the elevator she handed him a railway ticket. "There is your ticket to Freiburg. I will be on the train but I will not be in the same compartment. If you see me remember that you do not know me. They may suspect that I am taking the prize to Fabrizius. They may be watching me. Now go!"

She did not offer to kiss him and he thought, "That is very decent of her. She could not bring herself to do it. Perhaps she is going away now. Perhaps this is the last time I shall see her. Perhaps on the way to Freiburg they will take me." It was better like that.

But suddenly she took hold of his arm. "Are you well? Are you quite all right? Can you make it alone?"

"I'm tired. That's all. I'm quite all right."

"Good-bye then."

"Good-bye."

It struck him that she said "good-bye" and not "*auf Wiedersehen.*" As she went through the door back again in the vast cellar, he felt his heart contract with a wild pang of sorrow and bitterness for all the delight, the happiness that should have been theirs forever, but which they would never know again because they were born of an accursed generation in an accursed world. What had been meant by God had been shattered by the evil in man.

Then squaring his shoulders as a kind of gesture because he knew it would take all the energy he possessed and all the cool-headedness to pass the line of guards in the street and later at the station, he pulled the thick glasses over his eyes, picked up the cheap suitcase and half-blinded, made his way toward the door.

It was simpler than he had hoped. At the end of the street two men stopped him and demanded his papers. He could not see their faces. The thickness of the glasses blurred them, and he thought, "Perhaps the glasses have changed me too." It was odd the confidence the glasses gave him. It was not only that they changed the whole world, they seemed to change himself blurring his personality, dulling him.

"And your business?" one of them asked.

"Banker, here to settle an estate."

"You have visited the police control?"

"My passport has the stamp . . . see?"

The man asked, "That is your photograph?"

"Yes . . . without my glasses." He knew he had made a slip there, but there was no other way out. He continued to speak with what he hoped was a thick Swiss accent.

"Take off your glasses."

He took off the glasses, blinking and peering realistically and was relieved to see that he had never seen either agent before. Sooner or later he came to recognize those who followed him. The man who questioned him had a rat's face— like Goebbels. It was astonishing how many of them had that rodent look, like weasels.

"And the mustache . . . does it come off too?"

"*Bitte* . . . " he said stupidly.

It was a bad moment.

"What were you doing here in this block?" the man asked.

"I spent the night with my cousin Herr Luckenback. He lives in the flat at Number 33."

"*Parlez-vous français?*"

"*Naturellement. Je viens de Montreux.*"

That seemed to do it. Why, he was never quite certain. The man gave him back the passport. He put down the suitcase and readjusted his glasses. He took his time about it. He must save himself for Fabrizius so that she would get the credit of having captured the prize.

The man with the weasel face said, "Another banker pig!" Then they turned and left him suddenly before he had adjusted the glasses again and picked up the suitcase. He was deliberate and slow.

Not until he reached the railway station did he feel safe once more. It was all right he knew now unless he met some agent who had actually seen him before and might recognize him. The glasses made him dizzy and produced an awful aching in the top of his head.

At the railway station there appeared to be quite a crowd leaving. The police control seemed to discover nothing suspicious. The fat lieutenant only asked, "Your business here?"

"To settle an estate."

"Finished?"

"Yes."

"*Gut.*" He snapped the passport shut and returned it but the word "Finished" echoed after he had gone through the gateway. "Finished" that was it. Even if he had had a desire to escape, he was finished. He would never again be any good. It was easier to heal a terrible wound than to heal shattered nerves. But he felt a kind of odd perverse pleasure at having tricked them thus far. Perhaps it was only habit, the long habit of the satisfaction the hunted felt in outwitting the hunter.

The weariness came over him again, a strange numbness which seemed to paralyze all his actions. On the train he found himself a place in a second class compartment, and almost at once he closed his eyes. He dared not take off his glasses and the lenses tortured him, aggravating the sharp pain in the top of his head. Suddenly he felt consciousness slipping from him. It was not sleep. He was fainting. The blurred world about him whirled and faded into mistiness.

.   .   .   .   .

When he wakened he was aware, slowly at first, of the sunlight coming in at the window on the opposite side of the room. It was a room he had never seen before but he knew it at once by the pattern of light on the ceiling. It was sunlight reflected from water and it danced in a crazy pattern which at first hurt his eyes. Then slowly he knew what he would find in the room. Opposite him there would be a carved heavy wooden cupboard with figures of elves and gnomes dancing across the top, and there would be a table with a white lace cloth and an Aspidistra and a red carpet and two small chairs and a heavy deep Victorian chair upholstered in red plush and in it she would be sitting occupied with some sort of needle-work . . . knitting it was. He did not know in what town the room existed nor what had happened before or what was to come afterward. The room, as he saw it, was simply there isolated in time and space.

"Perhaps," he thought, "I am already dead."

The most remarkable thing was her presence in the room. She had said "good-bye"—not "*auf Wiedersehen*" but "good-bye"—there in the bleak hallway of the apartment house and gone away forever, closing the door. She had gone away forever, leaving Fabrizius' gang to pick him up on the train.

But if he were not dead, it was clear that they had not arrested him for this room was no prison cell. Before he could summon his courage to look away from the sun-speckled white ceiling, he tried desperately to remember what had happened after he went aboard the train. But he could remember only as far as the compartment. What had happened after that, how he came into this room, he did not know. In his brain there seemed to be only a swirling mist out of which faces emerged from time to time, faces of strangers mostly but once or twice her face appeared vaguely for a moment or two.

He thought, "I must have been very ill. Now I must look at this room."

He turned his head and there it was exactly as he had seen it and she was sitting there in the big old-fashioned plush chair, knitting, turned so that he saw her profile against the bright sunlight. Only she was not wearing the familiar blue uniform. She was dressed in a cheap, rather ill-fitting jacket and skirt. There was something dowdy and domestic about the scene, as if they had been happily married for a long time, so happily married that she had ceased even to care about her appearance.

He waited, watching her for a long time, aware of a vast inward comfort and happiness, afraid to speak lest he would shatter it only to discover that the whole thing had no reality. But at last, summoning his courage, he said, "Zosha." His voice sounded weak and strange, but it was strong enough to rouse her. She turned toward him and said quickly, "Eric! Are you all right, my sweetheart?"

She rose quickly out of the chair and came over to the bed. Beyond her through the window he saw painted high on the building opposite—"ZÜRICHER BÄCKEREI," Zurich Bakery. Zurich was in Switzerland. Zurich!

"I'm all right, I think," he said. "Why are you here?"

"I brought you here. We are in Switzerland. You are safe now, my darling. Never again must you go back into that poor, accursed country."

"Tell me . . . you said 'good-bye.' You went away."

She began stroking his forehead with the old gesture. She who was so calm had discovered long ago the relief it brought his nerves.

"Don't try to talk now," she said. "Listen to me. I will tell you everything."

"My darling," he said. And he was thinking, "What I saw in the Grand Brunswick Hotel was not true. For once I saw a lie. Now I am free."

"You must be very quiet," she said. He was aware that she had changed in some subtle way. Not only had her appearance changed but her very voice seemed different. She was talking now, telling him what had happened and how they came to be here in this shabby room in Zurich, safe and together.

She told it simply, as quickly as she could and as he listened the wonder and love in his heart swelled until it seemed to him that it would burst.

She had, she said, got aboard the train in a suburb of the city and by some good chance she chose the coach in which he was traveling. Inside the coach she found excitement be-

cause a man traveling in a second-class compartment had
fainted. When she discovered that it was her Swiss banker,
she said, "I am a nurse, I will take charge."

She was afraid of many things—that there might be a
Gestapo agent on the train, that some stranger might go
through the pitifully inadequate papers with which she had
stuffed his wallet, that the absurd mustache might come off.
When the train started moving again, she made the most of
the situation, asking the other passengers to leave the compartment so that the sick man might have quiet. Closing the door
and drawing the curtains she placed a pillow beneath his head
and sat with him. Now and then, she said, he had recovered
consciousness and talked for a little while although of this he
himself remembered nothing.

Sitting there beside him she had plotted desperately, working
out plot after plot only to reject each one because of some
flaw in it. It was impossible of course to take him to any
hospital because the police would come in at once and begin
asking questions. As far as Freiburg there would possibly be
little difficulty. She could go on in her uniform pretending
she was a nurse. So long as he slept or was unconscious, they
would probably leave him in peace. If any of Fabrizius' men
were about they would not trouble him, believing all the time
that she was taking him to Munich by a roundabout way to
deceive the other faction. But from Freiburg on, when they
took a train for the border instead of for Munich, there would
be trouble at once.

So, after a long time, she decided that there was but one
course to take—a bold one. It was to play upon his illness, to
exploit it; but in order to do this she would herself have to
find a new role, and at last she settled upon what it was to be.
In Freiburg she would have to buy clothes, dowdy Swiss
clothes, throw away her neat blue uniform and become his
sister. She had her own forged passport, prepared like his own,
by one of Fabrizius' own men. They were both tall, blond
and blue-eyed. It was easy to mistake them for brother and
sister. She would be his sister who had come from Switzerland
to take him home. She invented a whole story, down to the
most minute details, a whole family history with marriages and

divorces to explain the difference in the names on their passports. So long as he remained in a dazed and incoherent state,
there would be no danger of his being questioned. They could
not discover from his answers that she was lying.

On the train no one troubled them. Twice the conductor
and once a policeman opened the compartment door to ask
after the sick man. Each time they had gone away she had sat
up stiffly and said, *"Heil Hitler!"* If they had had any sus-
picions—and in Germany there were few people and no officials who did not have them—they were allayed at once by
the picture of the blonde Nordic girl in party uniform, raising
her hand in the party salute.

At Freiburg she managed to rouse him sufficiently to get
him to his feet and recruited the aid of the ticket comptroller
to get him off the train, through the gate and into the station.
Anyone seeing them could not doubt the genuineness of the
sick man's condition. The girl and the ticket comptroller were
forced to support him between them. People stared at them
but now in the stares there was no suspicion but only curiosity
and sometimes sympathy.

In the big waiting-room she found a porter, a kindly old
man, and paid him to keep watch over the sick man while she
went into the town to do some business. She took the cheap
and empty suitcase with her and in a department store she
purchased a shoddy suit, a hat and a blouse. Putting these into
the suitcase she went to a public lavatory and there changed
from her uniform into the new clothes.

"It was an extraordinary feeling," she said. "It was as if I
had become a new and different woman. Whatever remained
of the old life seemed to be washed away. It gave me fresh
courage. I was sure then that the plan I had worked out would
go through, unless one of Fabrizius' men was still following
us. If he saw me buying tickets for Zurich or saw us get on
the Swiss train, then we were lost."

He listened to her story in a kind of daze, confused and
puzzled, and only clearly aware of the fact that she was sitting
there on the bed beside him, her hand in his. That to him was
all that mattered. He was aware vaguely that what she was
telling him was an heroic story, because at each stop she

risked torture and death, but the elements and motives in it were still confused in the weariness of his brain. When he looked at her, he was aware again of the great change in her. She was no longer a young girl, but a woman. She was older and more subdued but also more tender. This too puzzled him, for although the rescue and escape was in itself a nerve-wracking experience, it was not enough to have changed her so profoundly.

Suddenly she bent down and kissed him and he felt her tears on his cheeks. Then she sat up very straight again and went on with the story.

When she returned to the station she found him still sitting on the bench where she had left him, awake now but staring in front of him into space. The old porter looked at her and remarked that she had changed her clothes.

"Yes," she told him, "I am crossing the border on a mission. Our uniform is not welcome on the other side of the border."

"Perhaps one day," said the old man.

"Perhaps one day," she echoed. "*Heil Hitler!*"

"*Heil Hitler!*" said the old man.

Then she bought the tickets, studying the people about her and those waiting in the station. She could discover no one who seemed to be one of Fabrizius' agents, no one certainly she had ever seen before. Smiling to herself, she thought, "He must have trusted me to have let me go unwatched." It was rare that he did not have an agent engaged upon important business shadowed by another agent.

Luckily there had been little time between trains, barely enough for her to hurry into the town and effect the change in her appearance. Now with the aid of the old porter she managed to get him through the gate, past all the officials and safely onto the train. Neither the police nor the railway officials made much show of inspecting their papers, again perhaps because they both appeared to be so blond and such splendid specimens of the race which the small, dark Goebbels extolled. But there was another element which protected them, the potent fact of his collapse and nearness to death. It had blotted out all else. People had gathered about them curiously, the way she had seen cattle in a field gather about a sick and dying animal, the way cattle gathered about the spot where an animal had been slaughtered.

When the stationmaster had remarked, "The young man is ill. You had better take him to a hospital," she had said, "Yes, utter collapse. The doctors said the only chance of saving him was to take him home at once."

"He was a flier?" the man asked with sympathy.

"Yes . . . a flier. A Stuka."

"Ach . . . that is bad. And so young too."

Then he had helped them—the traitress and the spy—into the train and himself fetched a pillow to place beneath the head of the sick man.

The fact of his illness blotted out all else, perhaps because it brought madness and death painfully near to all those who stood like cattle in a field, watching. It occurred to her that if the illness had been faked, the effect would have been lost. The very illness had a power of its own. It was as if it surrounded them in its own protective aura.

The rest of the story was simple and brief. In the night she had thrown her party uniform out of the window somewhere between Freiburg and the border, and at the frontier there was little trouble. It was four in the morning, the hour when death comes to the ill and unwary. The officials tried to rouse the sick man to ask him one or two questions but it was clear that he was beyond the possibility of being roused to consciousness and after a little while, sympathetically, they went away.

As the train pulled over the frontier into Switzerland she began to cry. She wept uncontrollably for a long time until she thought of Fabrizius in his office in Munich when the news came that not only the most famous foreign secret agent in Germany had again escaped but that one of his own agents had disappeared with him. Fabrizius would scream in his high-pitched voice and smash with his riding-whip anything breakable in his office. And then—she shuddered at this—he would go down to the prison and wreak his sadistic vengeance on the helpless prisoners. And presently she began to cry again, all her courage and daring melted and collapsed now. She wept for the prisoners of her beloved lacerated Germany, for herself, for what she had believed, because for a little time she had come very near to committing the greatest crime a woman can commit.

.   .   .   .   .

When she had finished she kissed him again and said, "But we are not free yet. The police here will come and question us about our papers."

He scarcely heard her for what happened to them now did not trouble him. They were over the border out of that monstrous country of suspicion and death. It seemed to him at times that there was in all Germans something decadent which worshipped death and looked upon suicide as an honorable and courageous thing. Had not the whole nation itself again and again since the time of Hermann the Red committed itself to suicide, binding its citizens together with ropes of deceit and vanity and injured pride to march to death against the legions of the world?

It was not only Germany she had escaped but this other corrupting thing—the love of destruction and death.

But he was puzzled still and his spirit, he knew, would never have peace until he understood what it was that happened on the night he hid himself in the very heart of the enemy in the lobby of the Grand Brunswick Hotel. He had to know. He had to believe that once what he saw was wrong. And so he said, "But you came to the hotel that night meaning to deliver me up to Fabrizius."

She looked away from him. "Yes," she said, "that is true. How could you know that?"

"I saw it as I sometimes see things. I knew that you were not what they believed. You were not 'one of us.' Before you came in I saw it all and I *knew*."

She began to cry and presently she said, "Yes, that was true. For hours before I fought with myself. My brain and my heart fought, like wild animals, inside me. On the one side there was duty and family and country and the ideals they had taught me—the only ones I ever knew. I had lived for this triumph, this splendor of my country. I had risked my life for it many times. It was for the New Germany, the new order that I lived. On one side there was all that, on the other there was only . . . you, ill, hunted, trapped beyond escape. I thought, 'there is no way of saving him in any case. The best I can do is take him to Fabrizius. There I have a little power. There perhaps I can help him.' And so at last with my heart beaten and choked I went to the hotel and passed you and said, 'Excuse me. Now I must go to the railway station.' That was my Judas kiss."

She was silent for a moment staring away from him out of the window at the brilliant sunlight over the lake. Behind the lake the great mountains rose, white with snow against the sky. He did not press her to go on. He waited, watching her, understanding a little now why she was so changed, so still, so dignified, so much more beautiful.

Presently in a low voice, still looking away from him, she said, "It was a little thing that changed it all. It came the moment I put my arm through yours and felt the warmth of your body through the cloth of your uniform. Something terrible happened. It was like the opening of the sea or the falling away of the mountains. Quite suddenly we were the only two people left in the world. In time and space, in the darkness of that narrow street there was no one but you and I. And a voice said, 'I will not do this thing. I will save him— God alone knows how—but I will save him, and myself too if it is possible!' Suddenly I hated passionately all those things in which I had believed, all that world which had once seemed to me so glorious. I hated the men I had worshipped, the men I had cheered. I hated everything which before that moment had been my life, because you and I and the thing between us suddenly became more precious to me than country or family or party or anything in the whole world. You and I—walking along the dark street in the snow—were more important than politicians or parties or wars or the German Reich. We were a man and a woman who loved each other standing alone at the beginning of the world, alone in time and space. No state, no party, no ideas had any rights which we were bound to respect, because we stood there together, a symbol of all humanity. No power had the right to destroy our happiness and our right to live. The same voice said, 'You may not be able to save him, but if he is caught you will be caught too. He will die but you will die with him,' and that was better than the other thing."

She was silent again for a moment. Then she said, "From that moment there was no longer any doubt. Now I am like a little naked child. I have left everything. I have nothing now but you, nothing on earth. I have betrayed everything I ever was before." Then she smiled, "But I do not mind. I am happy."

He pressed her hand against his cheek and said, "I am sorry now that I asked you. But I had to know . . . whether for once I had been wrong."

"No, you were not wrong. I came there meaning to betray you."

Then suddenly a flash of vision came to him. There would be a knock at the door and when she opened it there would be two Swiss policemen outside in long capes, one tall and heavy with a red mustache and the other a small dark man. And the tall one would say, "Excuse us, but we have come to inspect your papers." And they would look at the papers and say, "You will have to come with us to the Inspector." Then the picture faded into a fog and after that he did not know what was to follow.

But it did not matter, even if they were interned and separated. They had escaped that awful nightmarish world. And what had happened to them had happened to very few lovers since the beginning of time. Some day somewhere, when all the misery and suspicion and hate had abated a little, they could find a place where there was peace and decency and they could have the happiness God had meant for them since the beginning of time.

There was a knock at the door. She rose swiftly and went to open it. Beyond her in the hallway he saw two policemen in long capes, one tall and heavy with a red mustache, the other a small dark man. The tall one said, "Excuse us, but we have come to inspect your papers. . . ."

DAUGHTERS OF MARS

Miss maria's earliest memories were of the tramp of soldiers' feet and the rattling of gun caissons over a rutted road as General Sherman's Army marched through Georgia to the sea. During the middle years of her life the memory wasn't very clear, but as she grew older and older it regained something of its childish clarity. There were moments in the long evenings in the little house when, shut up at sundown by the Germans, with no radio and no telephone, she grew confused and was again a little girl of four hiding in the underbrush beside a Georgia road of red clay. And old Martha, who had gone on the visit with her, was there, black and big-bosomed and comforting, holding her close and saying "Doan you cry! Doan you make no rumpus, or the Yankees'll git us." And so, listening to the sounds from the road below where the dirty blue-coated troops passed, she had clung to old Martha, choking herself not to make any noise lest the Yankees find them and cook them and eat them.

Sometimes in the long still beautiful evenings which even the Germans were not able to desecrate or defile, she would talk childishly to Miss Susan or Miss Ellen and one or the other would say gently and patiently, "Come now, Maria. We aren't in Georgia. We're in the Department of the Oise and the Civil War is over and old Martha has been dead for fifty years and you'll be eighty-two on your next birthday." And Miss Maria would chuckle and return to her book again until from outside in the village street, beyond the garden wall, would come the sound of tramping German feet, and she would fall again into a faint doze and in spite of every-thing be back again in Georgia hiding in the underbrush with old Martha. It may have been that this happened because she was old and frail or it may have been because it seemed to her now that since the very beginning there had always been war in the lives of herself and her sisters, interrupting it always just at the moment when things seemed to be going well and peacefully.

And then perhaps it would be Miss Emmeline who roused her and she would have to pull herself together to remember about Emmeline. Emmeline was only seventy-three and the baby of the family and she alone of all of them had married and lived away from home for nearly fifty years. She wouldn't be here now except that she had been caught while on a visit. Emmeline had always been a problem, going out in the world so much and living in England and reading modern novels. Emmeline, a British subject, was still a problem, being caught here while on a visit, with the Germans all around them.

Then there was a knock at the house door and she heard the rheumatic footsteps of Nicolas as he went to open it and admit the German sergeant who came each evening to see that they were all in the house and not listening to a secret radio. Miss Susan said, "Emmeline!" and Miss Emmeline rose, as a British subject, taking her novel with her, and went into the cupboard, closing the door behind her.

The outer door opened and the sergeant came in, a young peasant with sausage hands and enormous feet who seemed a monster beside the fragility of the three visible old ladies. Even the old major-domo Nicolas, his face as blank as a white wall, seemed dwarfed as he stood beside the sergeant. The sergeant was embarrassed, his big blond face scarlet. He was all elbows and feet, stupidity and awkwardness. He did not like his task. Even to his slow-moving disciplined mind, it seemed silly to be perpetually spying upon three old American ladies; but those were his orders.

"*Guten Abend, gnädige Frauen,*" he said.

The three old ladies replied in French, "*Bon soir!*" They had no rancor against this young lout. If they had any feeling at all, it was one of pity because the boy seemed so out of place standing there in his clumsy uniform when he should have been peacefully at work among the cows in some high field in Bavaria. If the gentle old ladies hated anything, it was something called the German spirit which to them meant everything brutal and uncivilized and crude in the world.

The sergeant, clicking together the heels of his clumsy fabricated boots, read off their names, "Maria Wingate, Susan Ann Wingate, Ellen Margaret Wingate." With his horrible Silesian accent (for he came from Silesia and not Bavaria) the names were unrecognizable, but they knew what he meant to say and after each name, they answered politely in turn, "*Oui.*" Miss Emmeline's name, which was Mrs. Eric Chalmston, he did not, of course, read because she was hiding in the cupboard and neither he nor the German staff had any knowledge of her presence. As the elderly widow of an English General, they might have suspected her of anything.

When he had finished, he clicked his heels once more and clomped out of the door. Miss Maria returned to her reading, and Miss Susan and Miss Ellen to their knitting, and at the sound of the bell attached to the garden gate, the door of the cupboard opened and Miss Emmeline came out of her hiding place and returned to reading her wicked modern novel.

· · · · ·

Only Miss Maria was old enough to remember much about life in America, for Miss Susan was only four years old and Miss Ellen three when they went aboard the packet-boat at Norfolk to leave America forever. Sometimes Miss Susan pretended that she remembered the Yankee soldiers at the docks and Major Wingate's sulphurous rage at sight of them, but Miss Maria never believed her. She was certain that Susan couldn't have remembered going through half-ruined Richmond on the way to the packet-boat nor what the big house and garden in Savannah was like. She had simply heard Maria tell about it all so many times that she had come to believe that she herself remembered all these things.

Again and again, more and more frequently as they grew older, the sisters would ask Maria to tell them about America; but what she remembered was, of course, very little like the America they had not seen for seventy-five years. The things she remembered were all about the South in the last agonizing days of the Civil War when half the South and their father's beloved Savannah were dying, and the women were tearing their fine bed sheets into strips for bandages and there wasn't much to eat but hominy and corn meal and wild rice from the islands.

Emmeline had less curiosity than the others but that was perhaps because she had been born in France and never knew anything about America, and she had been married and even though she never had any children, she had after all had a life away from the rest of them and from their father. Only Emmeline had ever been rebellious.

All of them of course knew and remembered their father because he had lived to be eighty, but only Maria could remember him as he had been in America—young Major Wingate with the blackest hair and bluest eyes and finest figure in all the South. Only Maria could remember him as he rode over the plantations on his black stallion with herself trotting along at his side on a gray pony. Only Maria could remember him coming home in his gray uniform with his arm in a sling, telling the frightened women in the drawingroom of the Savannah house, with tears in his eyes, how badly things were going for the Confederacy. Only she could remember, far back out of the misty past, the full terror of his rage when the cause was lost and the carpetbaggers came down from the evil North to mingle their insolence and vulgarity with that of the ignorant freed "bad niggers" who swaggered along the waterfront and through the old streets lined with great houses and gardens filled with azaleas and magnolia and wistaria. Her sisters loved to hear about those houses and gardens. In an odd way as they grew older they sometimes lived in the ghost houses and gardens which they were only able to remember as fragments out of a dream, for now as old ladies, they kept returning more and more to their beginning and asking Miss Maria to tell them all she remembered.

What she, in her gentleness, could not convey to them was the terrible rage of her father on the morning two carpetbaggers—lean-faced, evil-eyed Republican Yankees accompanied by an officer of the Union Army—came to say that they meant to stay as guests in Major Wingate's house. He bade them to return the next day and when they arrived the house was empty; there remained not so much as an old broom or a crust of bread, for Major Wingate had moved out of it overnight with all his family and belongings, leaving a house where his family had lived since before the Revolution. By nightfall he and his wife and two servants and three small children, Maria and Susan and Ellen, were on their way to Norfolk. The Major had taken an oath that he would leave his country and never again set foot on its soil so long as the Yankees were in power.

What lay behind his fearful decision was something which his daughters, and even Major Wingate, never fully understood. They were witnessing the death of a civilization, of an old and leisurely way of life at the hands of a new order based upon machinery and thievery and greed. The new order was to create a slavery as bad as the slavery which had been destroyed and a way of life infinitely more ugly, not based upon wide fields, but upon slums and tenements and filthy factories. It was a lingering death at which the Major could not and would not assist.

And so he had taken his three small daughters and his gentle brow-beaten wife to live in France where it was possible for a gentleman to live like a gentleman. He had kept his oath and his daughters had kept it after him. Not one of them had ever again seen their native land. Miss Emmeline, born on the eve of the Franco-Prussian War, had never seen it.

Often during the long slow evenings in the north of France when until eleven o'clock, time seemed to stand still and every creaking in the old house made itself noisy and insistent, they talked of "dear Papa." Of "dear Mama" they spoke rarely and then only in a casual way, perhaps because she had faded out of life when Miss Emmeline was a baby, perhaps because she had never been a very vivid person but only a kind of appendage to the flamboyant Major Wingate.

In those days Papa had been a rich man, for he had a fortune from the sale of cotton tucked away in gilt-edged consoles in England and he owned property in New York administered very shrewdly by Cousin Gerald Wingate whom fate had placed on the northern side of the Mason-Dixie line during the Civil War. Papa, indeed, had found life very agreeable in the Paris of the Second Empire, with a house in St. Cloud and another in the Rue Faubourg St. Honoré. He had a fine carriage with high-stepping horses in which he drove with his wife and four daughters up the Champs Elysées, a dashing figure with his curling black hair, his flashing eyes and his mustachios and imperial. He had a second carriage and pair, used by a handsome and giddy lady who was a friend of Cora Pearl and Hortense Schneider who had all Paris worshipping her in *La Belle Hélène* and *La Grand Duchesse*. She was a friend too of Miss Howard, the English mistress of the Emperor himself.

But of all this world neither "dear Mama" nor the daughters knew anything, for nearly all their life was spent at the house in St. Cloud where they lived in a genteel and feminine way as Southern ladies should live, a life secluded and dull, away from all excitement, shielded from knowing anything which ladies should not know. It was only after "dear Papa" was dead as an old man of eighty that Miss Maria discovered about the questionable lady. She found the evidence in the form of letters and daugerreotypes in an old black metal box in the attic, and as she went through the letters reading the passionate words of a woman long since dead, she grew bewildered, partly by the passion of the letters themselves and partly by the awful discovery of her father's secret life. She was nearly sixty at the time and at eighty-two she had never revealed the secret to her younger sisters, not even to Baby Emmeline, the worldly one who had been married and knew about such things.

In the house at St. Cloud they had lived very nearly the same life they would have led in Savannah, for the house was furnished with the things out of the Savannah house and old Martha was with them, taking care of baby Emmeline by that time, and with her were two black servants called Toby and Evangeline. The children had a French teacher but they seldom saw other children and rarely spoke French. The Major had determined when he left Savannah to bring the life he loved with him and to preserve it in defiance of the world; and so his family, even when he himself ran a little wild, lived in the suburbs of Paris exactly as they would have lived in Georgia.

For the children it had been a life that was happy since they knew no other. There were four of them, although at that time Baby Emmeline was scarcely much good as a playmate, and the great excitement was the return from Paris of "dear Papa," the handsomest, the only man in their small world, with his dashing looks and fine waistcoats and the faint perfume of eau-de-cologne and occasionally something which years afterward Miss Maria realized was *patchouli*, a scent not used by men. But all that life had been interrupted brutally when Miss Maria was eleven years old by the coming of the Germans.

Again as in Miss Maria's earliest memories there had been wild excitement and women and children crying and the tramp of soldiers' feet and confusion in the house and the Major using bad language, and suddenly they had all been bundled into a kind of stagecoach with trunks and pieces of furniture on the roof, with all the other furniture piled into two carts which followed, and in the middle of the night they had gone off into the darkness through streets filled with tramping soldiers and galloping horses. The Major had angrily moved all his household furniture brought from Savannah because he did not mean to have destroyed the life which he meant to preserve and cherish. He was a proud man and a dandy. He had made an oath and he would keep it until he died.

On the long journey in the direction of Fontainebleau "dear Mama" caught a cold which settled in her lungs and a fortnight later she died, quietly, without a complaint, as she had lived. The Major was absent in the outskirts of Paris helping his "friend" to save her horses and furniture.

Miss Maria, the eldest, had cried now and then, less because she missed her mother than because that was the way good little girls behaved when they lost their mothers in the books "dear Mama" had given them to read. They all cried bitterly when a year later old Martha died, and Papa brought a French governess into the house; but being young, they all became used to these changes too and the French governess, Mademoiselle Choron, really made little difference, because she too fell to worshipping the Major, and because no one really mattered much so long as he spent part of his time about the house.

Otherwise, life was much the same. The presence of Mademoiselle Choron even failed to bring any change, because in her wild desire to please the Major she herself slowly became a Southern lady from Charleston and when she spoke English it was always with a Southern accent. She was, even then as a young woman, angular and thin and plain and intensely gallic in appearance and manner, but she came presently and with the most comic effect to call them Mis' Maria, Mis' Susan, Mis' Ellen and Baby Emmeline, and sometimes even "Honey."

So presently that war too was forgotten, with its terror of cries in the night and the sound of tramping feet, and the gray began to come in to "dear Papa's" beautiful black hair, but that only made him seem more handsome and more distinguished than ever.

Dozing now before the fire, her book in her lap, Miss Maria was seeing him like that, because she liked him best at that period, when she was a young girl. He had always protected them and made for them a quiet gentle life since the beginning. For his daughter Maria there had never been any other man so handsome, so fiery, so wonderful as "dear Papa." Once, long ago when she was in her thirties she had had a chance to marry, but when the moment came for decision, she could not bring herself to leave "dear Papa."

Now, half a century later, she could scarcely remember even the appearance of her one suitor. He had been a gentleman—if he had not been "dear Papa" would not have allowed him the house—but unlike the Major he was rather pallid and gentle. He had gone away, defeated, and a little later she heard that he had married his cousin in Richmond. She did not mind very much because she always had "dear Papa." She had him to care for and watch over until at last he died at eighty, a Savannah gentleman who had kept his oath of never setting foot in his own country.

· · · · · ·

Two hours or more after the clumsy young sergeant had gone out of the gate, the little ormolu clock on the Caen stone mantel struck ten and Miss Susan said, "Bedtime" and rolling up her knitting, glanced about the room at the familiar furniture.

She was worried tonight and the sight of all the old things in the room brought her a sense of security in what she was beginning to suspect at last was the most insecure of worlds. They had changed houses a half-dozen times since 1865 but the furniture had always remained, carefully salvaged by "dear Papa" in the midst of wars and riots. The last time, in 1914, when "dear Papa" died more of rage at the invading German troops than of old age, she and Maria had managed the salvaging. So it was still all here—and no matter how many times they changed houses the rooms always looked the same, like a drawingroom in the old South.

Miss Maria, as the eldest, had always been their father's companion. Whenever he was at home it was Miss Maria who was called upon to read to him, or ride out with him in the victoria or go for walks. So the housekeeping had fallen to Miss Susan, his second daughter and to housekeeping she had given the whole of her life and the energies which had no other outlet. In a way the big Duncan Phyfe sofa had become a husband and the great banjo clock and the chairs her children. She saw that they were waxed until they shone; she had the chairs and sofas recovered always in the same olive colored plush; when the backs and joints grew weak she had them strengthened. If "dear Papa" could come back now he would find his furniture and his house as well kept as it had been while he was alive.

Miss Susan was not like Miss Maria, thin and immensely wrinkled; she was plump and had a complexion like a girl. When people commented upon it and asked her the secret, she always said that nothing had ever touched her skin but soap and water. But that was probably not the reason. Its clearness, its fine texture, its delicate color came from some inward peace of which Miss Susan alone seemed to have the secret. She had never been emotional like Miss Maria, nor cross-tempered like Miss Ellen, nor adventurous like Baby Emmeline. Save for scratches on the furniture or a bald spot in the carpet, nothing had ever disturbed her calm. Her world was a small one encompassed by the walls of the houses in which she had lived with her sisters. Only twice had she been disturbed and that by calamities which did not concern her housekeeping—once when Baby Emmeline eloped and once when "dear Papa" died.

Each evening she sought mildly to induce the sisters to retire at ten-thirty but there was always trouble with Maria and Baby Emmeline. Maria was so old that she needed very little sleep and Emmeline, in the years she had been a General's wife, had grown accustomed to late and worldly hours. Maria preferred dozing before the fire to retiring to a "good night's rest," and Emmeline liked sitting up playing patience or reading her immoral novels. Nowadays since the Germans came, it was worse because the sergeant came in promptly at seven-thirty each morning to check on the old ladies, to see that they had not been out after curfew hours and were still behaving properly. That meant that they must be up and dressed and about the house at that hour. Receiving a man in their bedrooms was, of course, unthinkable.

So gently she again attempted to lure her sisters to bed. As usual Miss Ellen rose and putting away her book, went out of the room, but Miss Maria and Baby Emmeline said they would stay up a little longer.

As she poked the fire so that it would die down safely, worry took possession of her. Coal was precious now, not only because it cost so much but because each small lump stood between them and the discomfort of advancing winter. When the little they had in the cellar was gone, there would be no more at any price. Three months ago, she could have filled the cellar with coal at a cheap price, but after a conference with her sisters, they had decided against buying more coal than the normal amount needed at the moment. They would not hoard coal when their French neighbors in the village could not afford it. It would not be an honorable or ladylike thing to do. Now as she poked the fire, thinking about the winter, she was not so certain that it was always a good thing to be ladylike and honorable in a world dominated by Germans.

But her thoughts were interrupted by the faint droning from overhead which, despite its faintness, seemed to penetrate the very walls of the old house and vibrate in the wood of the floor beneath her feet. She knew the sound. It was the British bombers going to bomb Creil, the railway yards ten miles away. They came over night after night and dropped bombs on a French town while the French cheered. It was a puzzling world, the way things had gone lately, but it did not disturb Miss Susan much so long as the house and its furniture and dishes were safe. What troubled her much more than the bombing was the question of coal. In the last war life had been uncomfortable, but never quite like this. She did not trouble to look into reasons. Politics and economics she left to Ellen, the blue stocking of the family and Baby Emmeline who had lived in the world.

At the top of the stairs she said, "Good night, Ellen, sleep well," and received the same speech from her sister. For more than fifty years they had parted thus at the top of the stairs each night to go to their own rooms. "Dear Papa" had always insisted on each of them having a room of her own. That was the way ladies lived.

.   .   .   .   .

When Miss Susan and Miss Ellen left, Baby Emmeline put down her novel and said in a low voice, "Maria!" The older sister wakened out of a light doze and said, "Yes, Baby."

"I'm worried about Susan. She seems so vague at times . . . as if nothing in the world existed outside this house. Why, she doesn't even take any notice of this war."

Maria with the quickness of very old people was suddenly quite awake. "Susan seems to me to be failing."

There was a quiet note of triumph in the old lady's voice. She regarded her sister shrewdly. Of all of them she was fondest of Baby Emmeline, perhaps because she was so much older that there had never been any rivalry between them even for the affection and attentions of "dear Papa." Emmeline was the only one of them who ever had any trace of *chic*. The others just wore clothes, quiet, dun-colored clothes such as their father thought ladies should wear. But Emmeline always had style. Even as a little girl she had a way of putting on a hat or a ribbon or sticking a flower in her hair which made her look different. Maria thought sometimes that this was why Emmeline had attracted that rather fast young soldier more than forty years ago the summer they took the house at Dinard. That was why Emmeline eloped and "dear Papa" hadn't allowed them to mention her name in his presence until the rather fast young man had become a general.

Baby Emmeline at seventy-three was still the same, sitting there, rather thin and pert in her black dress with the white collar and a little black ribbon about her throat.

Maria knew that they were going to have a "talk" now that Susan and Ellen had gone to bed—a talk about many things, most of them reaching far back into the misty past. Distantly they heard the slow crunching sound of the bombs falling from the planes which had circled until they found their mark. The window panes rattled with the vibration.

Maria said, "I think it's very odd we haven't heard from Cousin Gerald. He's always been so particular about seeing our money came through."

"It's wartime," said Emmeline.

"In the last war he always saw to it, regularly."

"This one is different, Maria. You weren't living in a town full of Germans in a part of France occupied by them."

"Yes," said Maria quite reasonably, "I hadn't thought of that."

"I'm sure he's doing all he can," said Emmeline.

There were three Cousin Geralds in their lives. The first had been their father's roommate in Harvard before the war separated the North and the South. Somehow the cousins had remained friends, and after the war "dear Papa" had left all his American affairs in Cousin Gerald's hands. He had done well with their money for nearly thirty years, and then he had died and afterward his son, Cousin Gerald Number Two, had taken over, and after that things hadn't gone so well. The English consoles had been sold and the money invested in American stocks, and so began the long era of slipping down-hill from one house to another, each smaller and less pretentious than the last, until since 1930 they had been living in this small house in a village in the Oise.

They hadn't much left, only about three hundred dollars a

month, but it did very well in a village like Aumont with old
Nicolas and Marguerite, the cook, to care for them. They had
never seen Cousin Gerald Number One. Cousin Gerald Number Two had visited them once, just before the last war—a
rather red-faced, vulgar man who talked a great deal about
money and didn't seem like a Wingate at all. "Dear Papa"
hadn't cared for him at all. And now there was a Cousin
Gerald Number Three whom they had never seen, a young
fellow about twenty-four or five. They supposed that if they
went on living, he in his turn would go on looking after their
affairs. That was the arrangement their father had made and
nothing would have induced them to change it.

"I feel," said Emmeline, "that I am being a burden to the
rest of you, having to be hidden every time a German comes
into the house. I think we should have gone when the order
of evacuation came instead of hiding away."

"We're quite comfortable, Emmeline," said Maria. "Now
there isn't any more fighting in the street, it's almost the same
as before. It's quiet and comfortable. What could we have
done on the road with all the refugees? I don't believe Susan
could have survived it . . . and with Ellen's short temper it
would have been very troublesome."

"Anyway, it's too late to do anything now," Emmeline
sighed. The bombs began scrunching again. "It's the winter
I'm worrying about. Poor old Nicolas has to stand in line to
buy everything. There isn't any more sugar."

"We'll be all right. We did very well in the last war and in
1870 although you were too small a baby to remember it.
And Mama used to tell me about Savannah when there really
wasn't enough to eat. Sometimes it seems to me that we were
always mixed up in wars."

Emmeline began thinking about her husband who had died
of pneumonia contracted in the harsh Flanders winter of 1916.
"Sometimes," she said, "I'm glad that Eric is dead. He could
never have endured sitting by and watching the mistakes made
this time."

The bombing was finished now and from overhead came
the fine drone of the bombers going back to England. In
Creil, ten miles away, more houses had been smashed, those

new model houses built during the last ten years by the Communist Mayor and his friends. Maria always thought of them as "those horrid Communists." Now she only thought what a pity it was that all those nice new houses were being destroyed.

The noise of the bombers died away and Maria said, "I just discovered a scratch on the sofa tonight. Nicolas must have done it. Susan will be very cross. Nicolas is failing, I'm afraid."

From the distant end of the village came the sound of a German bugle—a long, lonely and faint sound. Emmeline did not refer to it. She only said, "Perhaps we had better go to bed, Maria."

She rose and put out the old-fashioned oil lamp which had furnished light for the four sisters through the long tranquil evening. There was no longer any electricity. Soon perhaps there would be no more oil. The sisters did not mind the lamps. They rather liked them, since the sight of them carried them back to their childhood.

The moonlight coming through the fan light above the main doorway showed them the way to the stairs. It had been a fine, clear night, wonderful for bombing.

At the top of the stairs the oldest and the youngest of the sisters kissed, a mere touch of cheeks that was like the brush of one withered leaf against another.

"Good night, Maria," said Baby Emmeline.

"Good night, my dear," said Miss Maria. "Sleep well." And as an afterthought she said, almost to herself, "I think it is very odd that we hear nothing from Cousin Gerald."

But Baby Emmeline did not sleep. With the moonlight streaming across her bed, she listened to the sounds of the night, the hooting of an owl from the edge of the forest, the clatter of hooves as a German cavalry troop passed along the cobblestones beyond the garden wall, and once again the far-off plaint of a bugle. She was disturbed, by what she did not know. Tonight she felt very alone, as if in her long sojourn in the world of reality, she had become a stranger in this enchanted world in which her sisters lived, a world which had not changed for them since "dear Papa" had brought them as little girls from Savannah, a world which he and, after him, his daughters had managed miraculously to preserve. Tonight they had spent the whole evening in a drawingroom in Savannah before the Civil War.

Just before she fell asleep at last, she sighed and thought, "Perhaps they have been lucky, for nothing has ever touched them."

.   .   .   .   .

The next morning there was something about the sunlight, the very clarity of the air, the etched sharpness of the naked beeches against the blue sky that seemed cruel and obscene beside the misery of the little village. Three weeks earlier it had been bombed wantonly by the Germans while its narrow little streets were jammed with old men and women, nuns and children, farm horses and carts. Ten of the little gray houses with red roofs along the *Mairie* and the schoolhouse had been smashed, the wreckage littering the little gardens and the narrow streets. The rubble was still there except where the Germans had cleared it away to allow passage for their troops. In the whole of the little village there were only a dozen or more old men too feeble to work. All the younger men were prisoners or beyond the barrier which separated occupied from unoccupied France, or dead. No one knew their fates, and so in every household there was always a faint hope, better than food, better even than the brilliant morning sunlight, that some time the door would open and Emile or Jacques or Pierre or Jean would walk in and take his wife and children or his mother into his arms.

On their way to the little market Miss Susan and old Nicolas had to climb over piles of rubble and pass great smears of blood on the gray walls—the blood of small children and old women and nuns. They passed them without comment, thinking, if their tired old brains thought at all, how lucky they were that their house had escaped with a few broken window panes. They were old and they accepted what came and both of them had been through so many wars.

It was nearly eight o'clock and they walked along as rapidly as rheumatic legs could carry them because the earlier they arrived at the market the better would be their chances of finding something good to eat. Nowadays the little market, under its roof of red tiles, appeared a bare place with only a few stands set up, each bearing a few cabbages, and some bunches of turnips and carrots. The Germans had requisitioned all the available butter, and eggs no longer appeared. There were still potatoes to be had but the price had risen to a point where Miss Susan refused to buy, believing always that if she waited the price would go down. The peasants who came to market were beginning to hoard things, even burying them in the forest in order to defeat the Germans who were stripping the whole countryside. Some of them did not trouble to come to market at all.

This morning the peasants greeted Miss Susan with the same affection and good humor they always showed for the sisters. Everyone in Aumont and the country knew about them, respected them and loved them for their goodness and innocence. The peasants knew what ladies were and they knew that the three old maids and the sister who sometimes came on visits from England were ladies. And they thought it amusing that the old ladies had hidden themselves away when the order of evacuation came, instead of taking to the road to be starved and bombed and machine-gunned like sheep. When the riff-raff broke into the house to pilfer it as they had the other houses in the village, they had found four old ladies, an elderly man servant and a cook, living behind the closed shutters as if nothing at all were happening outside. The old ladies were seated about the fire knitting and reading and taking no notice of the bombs or the tanks that rumbled past beyond the garden wall. The sight so awed the intruders that they went sheepishly away.

It was a good story. Peasant told it to peasant chuckling, even in these evil times.

But the rest of the morning was not so pleasant. The lines in front of each shop were longer than the day before and housewives came angrily out of the shops saying that there was no more sugar or pepper or tapioca to be had at any price. They grumbled against the Germans and against their government. Political quarrels broke out among friends, and women shouted recriminations against Laval and Blum and Daladier and Reynaud according to their own political beliefs.

Miss Susan and Nicolas made the rounds of four shops, standing in line at each one before they turned toward home at last, their basket only partly filled. Half the things they wanted were not to be had. Poor Miss Susan felt faint and her feet and knee joints ached by the time she reached the garden gate of the house where *les Mademoiselles Wingate* lived. But worst of all there were doubts in her heart, tremulous and disturbing doubts which it would take great courage to mention to Miss Maria and Miss Ellen and Baby Emmeline.

Her heart kept saying, "This is only the beginning of winter and there is not enough of anything. What will it be like when winter comes. Perhaps we should leave the house and go into the other part of France or let Cousin Gerald rescue us."

But she knew that this was a thought which she dared not even to mention to her sisters. She was the timid one, always bullied by Miss Maria who was dominant because she was the eldest and "dear Papa's" favorite, and by Miss Ellen, who was the intellectual one, and even by Baby Emmeline because she had been married and lived in the world. They all treated her as if she were not very bright.

And anyway they hadn't had a word from Cousin Gerald in New York for nearly four months. He might even be dead. As she limped into the garden, that thought made her tremble with fright. If anything happened to Cousin Gerald what was to become of them?

Inside the house, she came upon signs of fresh catastrophe. In the hall she found Miss Maria and Miss Ellen talking to two men in German uniforms—one tall, thin and hard, with cold blue eyes, and the other, a plump ugly man with a hard jaw and loose fleshy lips. She thought at once, "They have come to take Baby Emmeline away to a concentration camp."

The conversation was a mixture of French and German. Miss Ellen knew German about as well as the two officers knew French, but as Miss Susan, trembling, listened, she was able to make out what it was all about. The two officers had come to claim rooms in the house. The German forces in Aumont had, they said, been augmented. They were forced to demand two rooms from the American ladies.

Miss Ellen and Miss Maria kept insisting that they were not French but American and that the officers had no right to intrude on the premises. But the two men remained firm. They made insolent apologies but ignored the protests of the two old ladies; if they did not obey gracefully, then the officers would be compelled to take over the rooms by force.

Miss Maria at last led them upstairs and craftily conducted them to the third floor. She planned to put them in the room occupied by Nicolas and the cook. Them she would shift to the little salon and the pantry belowstairs. But the two officers refused the rooms and demanding to be shown the other rooms, selected Miss Maria's own room and the one occupied by Miss Ellen.

Miss Maria felt her heart grow small. It would mean that for the first time in their lives the sisters would have to share rooms. And it was very dangerous—all of it—with Baby Emmeline, a British General's widow in the house. And having strange men living in the house with them. The idea was appalling. Papa would have been shocked and indignant. In all the wars they had been through since childhood no such thing had ever happened!

But Miss Maria did not lose her dignity nor forget that, whatever the Germans were or did, she was and always would be a Savannah lady. Gravely she and Miss Ellen made the officers understand that by evening the rooms would be ready for them.

Then the Germans went away, rudely, without so much as thanking the old ladies. Miss Maria stood in the doorway watching them go down the garden path. As the gate closed, she said, "I don't suppose any people could be as different from Papa as the Germans."

Then the two sisters went into the salon and summoned Baby Emmeline from her hiding-place in the cupboard, and then, with the door locked, they sat down surrounded by all the Savannah furniture, to hold a council of war.

Miss Susan broke to them the news of the growing shortage of food—news which they received quite calmly.

Miss Maria said, "We shall manage somehow. There are always plenty of turnips and cabbages and sugar beets."

"But," said Miss Ellen, "the Germans are taking the whole sugar beet crop for alcohol which they need badly."

"As for fuel," said Baby Emmeline, "the forest is only five minutes away. We can burn wood and carry it ourselves."

Miss Susan murmured, "Perhaps we should write to Cousin Gerald for advice."

Miss Ellen, the tart one, replied, "What good is that? Apparently he doesn't get our letters and if he does it is evident we don't get his replies."

"It's you, Emmeline, that I'm worried about," said Miss Maria. "It is very dangerous now, with Germans in the house."

"Tut," said Baby Emmeline, "I can go on living as I have. We shall keep the salon door locked and when they are about I can stay in the cupboard. If necessary I can rig up a light and read in there."

"It'll be very stuffy," said Miss Susan.

"I can leave the door ajar."

It was all a futile, aimless, conversation since all of them evaded the real reason why instinctively they had come together for a conference behind locked doors. None of them mentioned the point. They kept veering about, avoiding it. None of them save Baby Emmeline faced the issue even in her own mind. Emmeline was the only one who had ever escaped out of that romantic unreal world in which they had spent all their lives.

Emmeline knew what was troubling them. She knew that they ought to go away now while there was still a chance, before they were utterly trapped by disaster, perhaps even by starvation. They could still, somehow, get word to Paris and the skeleton Embassy staff that four old American ladies were trapped here in the North in the Occupied Zone. She knew they had quite given up hope of rescue by Cousin Gerald. But above all she knew that they would not face the issue because they could not bring themselves to leave the Savannah furniture and all the knick-knacks with which, like crows, they had filled the little house over a period of years.

And there was always that vow of Papa's never to set foot

in his native land so long as it was ruled by Yankees and Georgia was united to the North. For Emmeline the power of the vow had gone a little vague but for the others it was powerful still.

In her heart she was terrified, because she was certain that none of them could survive the cold and hardships of the winter which lay before them. They were too old, too delicate, too accustomed to their ladylike sheltered life. One by one they would go until only herself, the youngest, the widow of an enemy General would be left alone.

The conference led nowhere. It broke up when Nicolas announced that lunch was ready. Throughout lunch Emmeline, usually so worldly and full of chatter, was silent, thinking how she could shatter that unreal world in which her sisters lived and force them to leave. She tried to think of some way of enlisting the aid of Cousin Gerald, but there seemed to be no way. Certainly with only a British passport for papers, she could not make her way to Paris to the American Embassy.

．　　．　　．　　．　　．

It was arranged for Miss Maria and Baby Emmeline to share one bed and Miss Susan and Miss Ellen another. It came out this way because Miss Maria the eldest and Miss Ellen, the one with a bad disposition, could never have got on together. They sat up late that night, planning to go to bed after the two German officers came in. With the door of the salon locked they sat about the tiny fire, Miss Maria reading, Miss Susan doing household accounts, Miss Ellen knitting and Baby Emmeline trying to fix her attention on a book. At the usual hour, the red-faced sergeant came to read off the names of three of them while Baby Emmeline hid in the cupboard. Afterward it grew to be nine o'clock and ten and finally eleven and no sign of their officers, so at last Miss Maria led the way and they went off to bed.

A little after midnight, one of the men came in. He slammed the door, stomped up the stairway and made a thundering noise going to bed, and a little later the other one—who occupied Miss Maria's bed—came in drunk singing loudly. In their beds, the old ladies lay awake listening, for none of them was able to sleep. Somehow they did not mind so much sharing beds. It made them feel less lonely and less uneasy. After the troublesome and annoying day, what disturbed them most was the thought of two brutish German officers asleep in the beds Papa had brought from Savannah.

.   .   .   .   .

Cousin Gerald II had not forgotten them. At the very moment the second German officer came in drunk and singing, his son Cousin Gerald III arrived at the Gare D'Orsay.

It had been an awful trip, all the way from Lisbon, through Spain on the broken-down Spanish railroads. And at the border he had waited baffled and angry, first with the moronic adenoidal customs officers on the Spanish side and then all over again on the French side with pompous self-important Germans. The train going toward Paris was almost empty and unheated, but at the stations on both sides of the frontier were hordes of frightened people trying to escape out of a dreadful and terrifying world which held for them only possible torture and death. Like trapped animals they were all heading for the one porthole that remained in the doomed ship—Lisbon.

It wasn't so bad traveling on an American passport with all the proper stamps and seals from the French and German Embassies in Washington. You finally got through, even though you had to put up with stupid delays and rudeness and to exercise an iron control on your temper. The man who occupied the compartment with Cousin Gerald III from Biarritz to Paris was clearly a Gestapo agent assigned to follow him and discover what he was *really* up to. The story that he had come to rescue three old ladies who had not been in America for seventy-six years was too impossible. He said *three* because neither he nor his father really knew where Baby Emmeline was.

Cousin Gerald III was a child of "the bad period." At twenty-six he had never worked seriously at anything. There had always been enough money to get along on and no prospect of a serious job. He "worked" after a fashion in his father's brokerage office, but there was very little work to be done and he was not a young man who took any special pleasure in work. And so a good deal of his young life had been spent at Southampton and Palm Beach, in El Morocco and the Stork Club. Sometimes gossip columnists referred to him as a "glamor boy" which annoyed his father but rather pleased Gerald III. He wasn't a bad sort, only a little irresponsible and a little cheap and not blessed with very good manners. There were a good many like him, products of the "bad period" all over America. Whether they hung out in the Stork Club or clustered about the pin-ball machine in the corner drugstore, did not much matter; they were under the skin, all very like each other.

It was Cousin Gerald II's idea to send his son to rescue the old ladies whose property he had managed for more than thirty years. It would be a tough job and a responsibility. The boy, with his brashness and good looks and easy-going ways, might succeed where a more serious-minded fellow would fail. And the mission would keep him out of trouble for at least a month and the expenses could be charged up to the estate of the old ladies.

When the project was proposed, Cousin Gerald II told his son the whole story of the old ladies for the first time, but his son did not altogether believe the story. Until now he had been aware simply that there existed somewhere in France four old ladies who were distant cousins of his father, who looked after their affairs. He had never heard of the fiery Major Wingate of Savannah and his oath. The whole story was too silly and improbable—that they had never returned to America in seventy-six years, that one of them had been born there and had never seen America! He took the whole story with a large helping of salt, but he would, he said, be delighted to rescue them. The idea appealed to him and it would make a great story to tell over bars. When he told the story to his friends while he waited for his traveling papers, they thought it as preposterous as he did himself.

And now here he was stepping out of the train in Paris,

for the first time in his life—the Paris he had always meant to visit when he had time, the Paris from which his friends had brought home wonderful stories of drinking and night clubs and bars and women. Probably it wouldn't be too dull after all.

The German *contrôle* held him for nearly an hour, going over his papers and asking him dull questions in broken English. He found it necessary to tell in detail the history of the old ladies, and the Germans seemed to find it as improbable as he himself and his friends had found it. But at last they allowed him to go, not alone, however, but accompanied by a soldier who would conduct him to the Hotel Bristol where he had been instructed to go and where the German *contrôle* said all Americans were segregated. No foreigners and no Frenchmen were allowed on the streets after sundown. That was why a soldier had been sent with him.

He had somehow expected Paris to be a city of light and gaiety. He was a nice fellow, but not too clever, and so the image of lights and gaiety still dominated him as he stepped out of the great railway station, carrying his two suitcases and accompanied by a strange soldier clad in clumsy ill-fitting gray whose only means of communication seemed to be a series of grunts.

What he looked out upon across the darkened Seine was a dead city. The bare trees along the border of the river raised their naked branches against a starlit sky. There was no moon but so clear was the night that the stars themselves cast a kind of faint phosphorescent glow over the whole city. On the opposite side of the street walking up and down along the balustrade along the river, a single figure—that of a German soldier—moved like a toy against the filigree of naked branches. A single car, an old-fashioned, rather high-built affair, slipped past and vanished into the dark reaches of the Quai de Voltaire.

For a moment he felt a sense of shock. This was not the Paris his friends had described. He hadn't expected it to be exactly like that, but he had not expected anything so terrible as what he saw now. For there *was* something terrible about it—the darkness and the deserted streets and the lonely figure of the sentry opposite. He thought, "This is not going to be fun!" And then he was aware that there were no taxicabs, no car of any kind in sight.

To his dumb companion, he said, "Automobile . . . taxi . . . car," very loudly as if that would help the man to understand.

The soldier grunted and replied, "*Keine automobilen. Laufen.*"

So that was it. He'd have to walk, carrying two suitcases. He wanted to ask how far it was, but couldn't trust his college German. Instead he said, "Okay! Come on!" and stepped into the street. The soldier went with him.

They walked across a bridge and he stopped to look down at the river but there was nothing to be seen, only the reflection of the stars drowned in the slow moving water. At the end of the bridge, the soldier indicated with a grunt that they were to turn to the left and for a long time they walked along an empty street with a high wall at their side. Then presently the wall ended and they were in a great open space—a vast space dimly lighted by the stars. A car rushed past them and out across the square and seeing the black outline of a stone needle against the sky, he thought, "This is the Place de la Concorde." And almost at once, "This is a hell of a way to see Paris."

It was a long walk and by the time he reached the Hotel Bristol his arms felt as if they were wrenched from their sockets. It was a dull walk for on the opposite side of the great square the starlight scarcely penetrated the dark narrow streets lined by steel-shuttered shop windows. Inside the hotel door his guide transferred him to the authority of a small dark German who looked like Goebbels and once again he had to show all his papers and explain that he had come to rescue three old American ladies.

But at last that was finished and he sent his accursed suitcases to his room and went to the bar for a drink, thinking, "If it's as tough as all that for a fellow to travel alone, what is it going to be like with three old girls."

In the bar he found something approaching the Paris his friends had described to him. It was brilliantly lighted and filled with Americans—men and women from the Embassy, newspaper correspondents, a few others who were old Parisians or there on odd missions like himself. They were playing backgammon or talking. There was one table of poker. Most of them were quietly getting drunk. They were all prisoners here, of the little man at the door who looked like a rat.

At sight of him those at the table nearest him looked up and one of them said, "A new prisoner! Come on, brother, have a drink!"

Before an hour had passed he knew nearly everyone in the place. They were a good lot, but all a little hysterical, with nerves on edge and all hating the Germans. Some of them were quite drunk. When he told them why he had come and repeated the improbable story of Major Wingate's daughters, they all laughed and told him to tell them another. The Civil War was far away, something which existed only in dry pages of school books. Why, nobody could still be alive who remembered anything about the Civil War.

. . . . .

At about three in the afternoon, old Nicolas came, pale with excitement to tell Miss Maria that there was an automobile at the gate and a young man getting out of it. He was suspicious for he lived always in the terror that one day a car would drive up and the Germans would take possession of the house, putting them all into the street. So Miss Maria went to the upper floor with Nicolas and, like Sister Ann in the Bluebeard story, looked out to discover the meaning of the cloud of dust.

What she saw was a rather battered car with an American flag flying from the hood and a young man descending with a suitcase. For a moment her heart stopped beating and she thought, "They have come from the Embassy to take us away." And then seeing the suitcase she thought, "He is coming to stay." And then with wild excitement she thought, "Maybe it is Cousin Gerald's boy." She heard him say, "Okay! See you Tuesday. Better bring another car to fetch the old gals." But in her excitement she scarcely heard the last sentence. She was already hurrying down the steep stairs. By the time she reached the drawingroom she had convinced herself that the young man was Cousin Gerald's boy—a relation coming to visit them! A Wingate! What wonderful news!

Miss Susan and Miss Ellen and Baby Emmeline received the tidings with a sense of shock and then, recovering, clustered like a covey of fluttering birds about the window. They saw old Nicolas open the gate and take the suitcase and lead the young man up the path to the house.

By suppertime the flutter among the old ladies had died a bit and afterward they all sat about the fire among the Savannah furniture. The red-faced sergeant arrived as usual to call the roll, and the discovery of a strange young American he had not counted upon upset him. After a long time he came to the conclusion that Cousin Gerald III would have to accompany him to headquarters, although he had already been there and registered and been told that he could remain for only two days.

When he and the sergeant had gone away, Baby Emmeline came out of the cupboard and they sat around the fire again, talking about Cousin Gerald III. Now that the first excitement of the visit was over, they all succumbed in their various ways to a period of calm, almost of reaction.

Miss Susan, the most placid and stupid of them, said, "He seems a very nice boy . . . so kind to come all the way here to rescue us."

The remark was met by a silence, for each of the other three, having formed opinions of their own, not wholly favorable, were unwilling to cast the first stone. The truth was that they found Cousin Gerald III rather a shock, and not at all a Wingate. It was the tart Miss Ellen who spoke first. "I must say he does seem rather breezy and common . . . and rather free and easy and familiar, even if he is a cousin."

No one denied this, not even Miss Susan, who now began slowly to see that what Miss Ellen said was true. It had not occurred to her before.

Miss Maria said presently, "He did seem to me to drink a good deal of wine at dinner . . . and he showed no appreciation of its quality. He just gulped it down as if it was beer."

"He had a whole bottle to himself," remembered Miss

Susan, "and asked for more." Her gaze wandered to the portrait of her father hanging over the fireplace and she thought of how he had drunk his wine, sip by sip, savoring its excellence. He had taught her about good wine. It was true that Cousin Gerald III seemed to guzzle.

Again Miss Maria spoke, "We do have to remember that he was born and brought up among the Yankees. Papa always said they knew nothing about eating or drinking."

Baby Emmeline had been knitting silently. It did seem to her that they were ungenerous considering the boy had come all the way from New York to rescue them. But she had to admit to herself that she did not care for him especially. He was, as Maria said, too free and breezy. But perhaps all young Americans were like that. She had heard stories and read about them now and then in novels where they seemed rather free and easy and bad-mannered.

"I don't see what made him think we wanted to be rescued," said Miss Ellen. "It seems presumptuous." With an indignant thrust she put her darning back into the rosewood stand. She was in no mood for darning.

Then Baby Emmeline spoke for the first time, very sensibly, as she always did. "It's too bad," she said, "that he isn't better brought up, but that's not important. The important thing is that we plan about leaving. I've come to the conclusion that we should go."

The other sisters looked at her in surprise. They had considered the prospect but always distantly, in a kind of hazy dream, never as a reality.

"There is a good deal to be done," she said, "if we are to leave day after tomorrow. We must leave then or not at all. We shall have to close up the house and arrange for living expenses for Nicolas and Marguerite. We shall need a caretaker."

The mention of the word "caretaker" shocked them, especially Miss Maria. How could they go and leave Papa's furniture to be carted off to Germany by the first German who came to the house after they left.

"We must be sensible about it. I'm sure the furniture will be quite all right," continued Baby Emmeline. But in her heart she wasn't sure. She had never been attached to it like the others, having lived away for so long a time that its loss made less difference to her. She knew that if they went away and left it, they would never see it again.

"It's a question," she said, "whether the furniture is more important than what we'll have to face this winter." She kept thinking to herself, "I must persuade them. I must be sensible." But the more she talked the hollower sounded her voice. She knew that she was not even convincing herself. But she went on talking, telling them even lies and giving them false hopes, like the belief that the Embassy would take charge of the furniture and see that it was shipped to America —back again to America after seventy-six years. She thought, "They must go. They will never survive the cold and hardships of the winter."—Miss Ellen with her bad heart, Maria with her arthritis and poor stupid Susan with her bad kidneys.

She did not think of herself, perhaps because as she talked, she felt so much younger than all the others—so immensely younger. And so much wiser. They were so fragile and helpless, never having lived outside the world of this room. But all the time a very small voice kept saying, "Does it matter? Even if they leave they will not live much longer."

Even if they stay in Unoccupied France the change would not be so violent, but the Embassy had insisted on their going to America because in a little while Unoccupied France would be no better than the part in which they lived. Cousin Gerald III had told her that much in a private conversation in the upper hall; she hadn't yet broken the news to them. If only she could get them out into Unoccupied France that would be something.

Presently, by talking gently and reasonably, she induced them to consider the possibility of going away, to leave the Embassy to care for the furniture and the portrait of "dear Papa." Each of them, as they listened, began considering what they would take with them—which dresses and costumes and what knick-knacks out of all the collection which filled the house.

They could not take much since all of them, with all their baggage, would possibly have to crowd into a single automobile. It was a terrible problem—the choice after so long a time of exactly what they would take. Miss Susan began to cry and had to be comforted.

Nine o'clock came and then ten and eleven and still Cousin Gerald III failed to return.

"Do you suppose," suggested Miss Maria, "that there *was* something wrong with his papers and they have kept him?"

"Perhaps," said Miss Susan, "we should go and look for him." And the others very quickly snubbed her for being a fool. They could not go into the streets without being arrested.

"It would be terrible," she said, "if anything happened to him after Cousin Gerald sending him all the way here just on our account."

At the same moment a prodigious jangling of the garden bell answered her.

"That must be him now," said Baby Emmeline. "I'll go."

"You can't go," said Miss Maria; "you'd be arrested if it was anyone else."

Then they heard the slow cautious footsteps of old Nicolas and a moment later Cousin Gerald III was in the room. His face was quite red and he stood a little unsteadily in the doorway. When he spoke, his voice was unnaturally loud. It was very clear what had happened to him.

Miss Ellen pursed her lips with an expression of having tasted something disagreeable and drew her skirts about her. Miss Maria and Miss Ellen looked at him in silence with astonishment. It was the worldly Baby Emmeline who took charge.

She said, quite calmly, as if nothing were wrong, "Would you like to talk for a little while before going to bed?"

"Yes," said the young man. "The funniest thing has happened to me. I just met an old friend."

An old friend in a village like Aumont! Who could he have met?

Baby Emmeline said quite calmly, "How extraordinary!" The others regarded her with admiration.

"Could I have a little wine before going to bed?" he asked.

"Certainly," said Baby Emmeline and went to fetch the wine.

Cousin Gerald III sat in one of the old armchairs, throwing one leg over the arm, and lighted a cigarette. "Yes, sir, I met an old friend. Would you believe it, when I went back to headquarters the officer on duty turned out to be an old waiter I knew from New York. So we celebrated. He's living in a big white house in the center of town."

"That must be Monsieur Perrin's house," observed Miss Maria. "He was killed when the Stukas bombed the refugees."

"He has awfully good wine in his cellar," said Cousin Gerald III.

Then Baby Emmeline came back with the wine and five glasses. She thought it rude to allow Cousin Gerald to drink alone. Miss Susan was forbidden wine but for politeness sake she could take a little in the bottom of the glass.

Cousin Gerald rose a little unsteadily when she came in and said, "Can I help you?" But Baby Emmeline said that they were used to waiting on themselves. Nicolas was old. They never kept him up late.

Cousin Gerald raised his glass, "Here's to escape. . . . Here's to freedom and the new life in America."

The four old ladies raised their glasses, but their purple veined hands trembled a little. Cousin Gerald crushed out the end of his cigarette on the old silver tray brought long ago from Savannah by "dear Papa." Then an odd sneering smile turned the rather handsome mouth into ugliness.

"America," he said bitterly, "America has been ruined . . . by the Democrats. The damned fools have stopped everybody from making money."

Again the old ladies winced. Papa had been a Democrat. They were Democrats. A Republican was a carpetbagger or a thief, a pariah.

"Yes, sir!" he continued, "the Twenties were the good old days when everything was wide open. Why, Dad made a million dollars in six months. Now if he makes two hundred thousand in a year, he thinks it's a big year."

The old ladies could think of nothing to say. Two hundred thousand was a great deal of money. When Papa had had thirty thousand in a year they had thought themselves fabulously rich. And now for a long time the four of them had been living, quite nicely, on less than four thousand. Miss Susan, thinking of her housekeeping and how economically she did her buying, felt dizzy.

But it was evident that Cousin Gerald III was excited and talkative and used to staying up late. He went on discussing America, and they listened because they had never in all their lives talked with anyone like him. The things he told them were fascinating but frightening. They heard about the subway jams, and necking and the wild life of prohibition days and the persecution of Wall Street and glamor girls and the luxury of Park Avenue apartments and Hollywood and the movie stars. America, said Cousin Gerald, was a wonderful and exciting place with marvelous plumbing and wonderful night clubs and beautiful girls. He dropped the ashes from his cigarette on the carpet in a circle around his chair and filled his glass again and again until the bottle at his side was empty.

And at last, about one o'clock, he grew sleepy and suggested that they all go to bed. Miss Susan remained to put out the lights and Miss Maria went into the small salon to see that Cousin Gerald III had water and biscuits and fruit by the sofa where he was to sleep.

None of the sisters went to sleep until nearly dawn. A curious excitement and dread hung over them. About two o'clock they heard the German officers come in, together apparently, and very noisy, clumping up the stairs in their heavy boots. In their beds, Miss Maria did not speak to Baby Emmeline, nor Miss Susan to Miss Ellen. They lay side by side as quietly as possible so as not to disturb each other. They had no need to talk for each knew what the other was thinking. In the deathly early hours of the morning, the things Cousin Gerald had told them assumed strange nightmarish forms and were joined by the nightmarish forms of things they had seen or read about in occasional newspapers and magazines which came their way.

Baby Emmeline did not sleep at all for worrying and about daylight when Miss Maria had at last fallen asleep, she rose and dressed and went out to walk in the garden. It was the only time she was safe from being spied upon. In Miss Maria's old coat and hat, everyone would mistake her for her eldest sister. She was not so shaky nor so bent but otherwise they were remarkably alike.

She was trying to decide what they should do. With no sleep, shivering a little in the frosty early morning air, she felt old and tired, as old and tired as Maria, and twice as wise. As she walked back and forth beneath the pruned linden trees, she saw that her sisters were children; they had always been children, but they had not the strength or resiliency of children. She was the baby. At seventy-three she was still Baby Emmeline. She would have to look after them now until they died.

"What happens to me," she thought, "does not matter so long as I can keep alive until the last of them has gone."

The bell of the little church in the village began to ring for early mass and she knew that she would have to return to the house and hide in the cupboard until the sergeant had made his call and gone away. But she felt better now. Something in the clear crisp air of the October morning had made her strong again, and she was strong because she had made a decision.

.   .   .   .   .

There was no sign of life from Cousin Gerald III until just before lunch when he appeared and apologized for having kept the old ladies up so late. At lunch he was less noisy but he still talked about America. He meant, in a perfectly good-hearted way, to make them excited about the prospect of going to America, but everything he told them only frightened them.

When they left the table Baby Emmeline lingered behind and said, "I would like to speak to you alone for a moment if it's agreeable."

So they went into the small salon and the old lady, sitting on one of the Savannah chairs, told him that the sisters had decided not to be rescued. She talked very quietly, her voice soft with apology and the effort to make him understand. It was difficult, she knew, almost impossible, and as she talked, watching his young astonished face, she saw that he would never understand.

"You see," she said, "my sisters have lived a very quiet life. They have not been in America since they were children and I have never been there. They are too old to go now. It would be worse for them to try to become accustomed to America than to stay here. We are old and old ladies do not need much to eat. We may be cold but we can put on more clothes and burn sticks gathered in the forest. You see, we should have to bridge a gap of seventy-six years."

And then she told him about their father and how her sisters' life had centered about him until he died, and after that about the cherishing of his memory. "We were born in war," she said. "Four times our lives have been upset and changed by war." She smiled, "But somehow it has never touched us. We have managed to survive. We have even managed to be fairly happy. My sisters are not so frightened of bombs as of the America you told us about." Again she smiled, a little wearily, "I know we must seem very foolish, and we are sorry to have put you to all this trouble. Of course we shall settle your expenses out of our income. If I had known you were coming I think I would have cabled you that it was not worth the trouble."

"But the Germans . . . the men in your house!"

"We are not afraid," she said. "Papa always said that being a lady was the greatest protection a woman could have. We have always found it so. Somehow they do not bother ladies."

He tried arguing but it came to nothing. The thin little old lady opposite him was as willful as she was fragile.

"And please do not ask the Embassy to persuade us. It would be very unpleasant because we should resist being moved. We should use force if necessary."

Since there was nothing to be done and he could not leave until the Embassy car called for them in the morning, he went up again to the town to find his friend, the ex-waiter. When he had gone Baby Emmeline went into the drawing-room where her sisters were waiting, and as she stepped through the door she felt a strange surge of happiness and security. This was their world, the world their father had brought from Savannah long ago, the world they had managed to preserve through riots and wars and disasters. Here in the room they were secure.

She said, "I have told him that we are not going with him."

At the sound of the words the three old ladies began to cry, out of sheer relief and happiness. Miss Maria embraced her and said, "You are wonderful, Baby. I would never have dared to tell him. It would have been so difficult after he came all the way here to save us."

"It was not easy," said Emmeline, "but I felt that I had to be firm even if I was rude."

At six o'clock Cousin Gerald III came in very pleased with himself. He had arranged everything, he said. His friend, the waiter would look after them and call on them now and then to see that they were well. He had brought them two hundred pounds of sugar and nearly a hundred pounds of coffee. His good American dollars had made that possible in a town where there was said to be no coffee and no sugar.

And again Baby Emmeline had to be firm. Gently she said, "You shouldn't have done that. We cannot accept it."

"But that's nonsense. My father will be delighted to know that I have helped you."

"But that is not the reason," she said. "You see, the French are our friends. We have always lived among them. They have always been kind and generous. We would not feel right having sugar and coffee when they have none."

Cousin Gerald III could think of no answer. This lost world in which he found himself was beyond his comprehension. There was something frightening about the four old ladies sitting there in the dowdy old-fashioned room. It was as if the wheels of time had gone backward, as if this was all something which had happened to him before in another life. Suddenly, for no reason at all, when he tried to speak his tongue refused. A lump came into his throat and tears filled his eyes.

When he had gone out of the room, Baby Emmeline said, "I'm sure that is what 'dear Papa' would have wanted us to do."

Then suddenly the bell on the garden gate jangled and Baby Emmeline went into the cupboard and the red-faced sergeant came in and read off the names and the old ladies replied politely as each name was called.

.   .   .   .   .

In December Cousin Gerald II called Cousin Gerald III into his office and showed him a cable from the Embassy in Unoccupied France. It read:

Miss Susan died November thirteenth at Aumont Oise. Funeral service already held stop others still Okay.

The son looked at the father and for a moment again, as in the old-fashioned drawingroom in Aumont, he could not command his speech. Then he controlled himself, swallowed and managed to say, "Bravery is the damnedest thing." And then with an effort, "I'm glad Baby Emmeline is all right. She wanted to be left to the last so she could take care of the others."

THE GREAT FAÇADE

I SAW HIM FOR THE FIRST TIME ON THE CAMPUS OF STILLWATER University. I was a freshman, rather skinny and ill-favored, just up from Centerville, wearing one of the ridiculous freshman caps which they wore then. I was plainly a hick and knew it down to the toes of my round-toed yellow shoes. Before coming up to the University I had been outside the borders of the county but twice, once to go overnight to St. Louis and once to go to my Uncle's farm at Columbia. I was working my way through school by helping in the dairy barns of the Agricultural College and felt altogether like a worm, so the first sight of Duncan Allerton Masters was pretty impressive.

He was coming along the wide, diagonal path that led from the science building toward the town where I was bound to buy the twenty-cent meal the poorer students could get at Schultze's cafeteria. Although there was no football practice until four in the afternoon Duncan was already dressed in football togs. Why he dressed thus in the morning and wore the uncomfortable outfit all through the day I did not then understand. Any other member of the team doing such a thing would have been razzed but Duncan got away with it.

He was tall, blond and handsome, with fair curling hair and blue eyes. The football sweater with its shoulder padding made him seem even bigger and more impressive than he really was. As he walked, he was accompanied by a little court of admirers, mostly sophomores and freshmen, who appeared to be hanging on every word. It was evident that he was explaining some football play for he was punching and jabbing and using his hands altogether in an eloquent fashion. Even then, greenhorn that I was, it seemed to me that he was over-doing it, rather like a ham actor, but he was so good-looking and so physically radiant that I imagine the little court about him forgave him, if indeed they noticed

anything at all. They were boys who had not made the team
and I imagine they were identifying themselves with Duncan the great star of the University eleven. Anyway they
were lapping it up.

As the little group came toward me I tried to shrink aside
so that I could pass unnoticed. I was only a hick, a freshman, a worm. But I was not permitted to do so. When they
were only a few feet from me, the great Duncan interrupted
his discussion to smile in my direction. It was a magnificent,
warming smile with a brilliant display of flashing white teeth
accompanied by a Jovian nod. He not only smiled. He
actually spoke to me. He said, "Hello kid! How are you?"
The voice was as filled with eager concern as the mouth was
filled with perfect teeth.

I tried to pull myself together in order to speak. Warmth
spread through my spindly body. I had been spoken to by the
great Duncan. I managed to say, "Fine, sir, and how are you?"
But he and the group of sycophants had already passed to
leave me standing a little bewildered, looking after them.
The great Duncan had not even slowed his pace. He had not
even heard my answer.

It did not matter. I was still warm with satisfaction. The
great Duncan had asked me how I was—me, a wretched
freshman up from the country. Slowly through the crisp
October air I crossed the rest of the campus, thinking, "If the
great notice me I must have something. Maybe I can be a
popular fellow like that after I've been here for a time."

The inside warmth did not go away and when I reached
the corner, I crossed the street to Jake's soda fountain. I was
going to celebrate by blowing myself to a soda. I was going
to spend all of five cents, maybe even ten cents on a banana
split. If I had the banana split I could go without dessert
over at the cafeteria a little later. Five cents made all that
difference to me then.

As I swung open the screen door I saw Merle Jenkins sitting at the soda fountain. You could hardly call it sitting,
for Merle was a twisted little fellow with one shoulder higher
than the other and a curve in his spine. When he walked, it
was with a crab-like movement, sidewise with one hand on

his knee to help him along. Physically he was a kind of monstrosity but otherwise he was a wonderful fellow. Sports were for him out of the question, and that was a bad handicap in the days when sports rather than scholarship was the goal of most students. Merle made up for it by other college activities. He was nearly always at the head of his class, and in his second year (for he was a year ahead of me) he was editor-in-chief of the college paper. Yet he wasn't a grind. He had merry, bright, dark eyes and a sense of humor and a kindliness and simplicity which made him popular even among the more stupid of the athletes. Merle even had time for a hick freshman like me. His father was a lawyer over in Illinois, rather a notorious character in his way. He was a great Bryan man and one of the first syndicalists, even before that word was known among the intellectuals. He was always publishing pamphlets at his own expense on economic and political questions. Looking back on them, they were pretty good pamphlets, for the old man was a smart fellow. The only thing was that he was ahead of his times. His son Merle was very close to him and naturally absorbed a lot of his thinking and ideas.

As I entered the soda fountain Merle turned his head and said, "Hello, Cresswell! Come and have a split or something with me!"

Again I was pleased at being noticed, this time by so smart a fellow as Merle. It was certainly a fine October morning.

"Thanks," I said. "I just met Duncan Masters crossing the campus. He seems a good guy."

"He's all right," said Merle. "What are you having?"

I ordered a banana split because that was filling.

"How are you getting on?"

"All right. I'm gettin' used to things."

"It's always tough in the beginning. What are you planning to do—after college, I mean?"

"I guess I want to be a newspaper man."

Merle grinned, "Well, they say it's an interesting life, but it takes a lot of getting around and that's no good for me."

He shifted his position on the high stool. I think with his twisted body he could not sit long in one position without pain. The odd thing was that he treated his deformity perfectly naturally. He had no shyness about it, nor did he capitalize it. He treated it objectively, as if his body were a thing apart from himself and his spirit, simply the dwelling place of the mind and spirit that was really Merle Jenkins.

After the banana split we left the fountain and walked along the edge of the campus, Merle toward his fraternity house. It was a small, poor fraternity without much popularity or prestige but in its membership it had most of the brains of the college.

At the corner we parted and I went toward the cafeteria.

That was the beginning of the curious three-cornered friendship between Duncan, Merle and myself which went on until Merle's death.

·   ·   ·   ·   ·

The next stage of the story began in my sophomore year when Merle said one day, "How about going to Duncan's tonight for some beer?"

My heart leapt at the prospect. To go to the great Duncan's room and drink beer with the big shots. I felt I had to conceal my excitement so I said, "But I hardly know Duncan. I've only spoken to him a few times."

"That's all right," said Merle. "I'm inviting you. It's my party too. He'll be glad to see you."

"Well, if it's that way," I said.

I still could not make out how Merle, with his brains, had gotten mixed up in the athletic crowd. There didn't seem to be any connection.

In Duncan's room there were four or five other fellows. I don't even remember their names any more but at that time they were big shots in college. Freshmen talked about them in awed voices and wherever they went they were followed by other students. They were big, healthy, precociously developed fellows. I suspect that one or two of them were over twenty but were kept on by the faculty because they were good athletes and so good business for the school. There wasn't anything in the least adolescent about them. They had heavy beards and talked about women most of the time in a dirty, weary way.

Duncan was better off than most of the boys in the college. He had not only a bedroom but a living room in a house owned by a woman called Mrs. MacKenzie. It was a big old-fashioned house near the campus and Duncan's two rooms had an outside entrance right off the street. Mrs. MacKenzie was a widow who made her living by renting out rooms in the big ugly house her husband had left her. She and her daughter, a pallid girl named Agnes, cleaned the rooms and gave the boys their breakfast.

On the first evening I ever went there we drank a lot of beer and had some toasted cheese sandwiches made by Agnes MacKenzie. She brought them in herself and put them on the table. She was quite a pretty girl with blue eyes, a fair skin and blonde hair. I had seen her about the town but never really noticed her before or how pretty she was. She left the sandwiches on the table and went out quickly, blushing under the lewd eyes of the fellows in the room.

When she had gone they made a lot of cracks about her figure, her legs, her breasts. I had been brought up rather strictly and I didn't like that kind of talk. As a matter of fact, I don't like it today, even after about thirty years of fairly wild living. I think women are to make love to but not to talk about. The talk that followed was pretty rough and I could see that Merle didn't like it much better than I did. I must say that the worst of the talk didn't come from Duncan. He joined in but you felt he did it just because he wanted to keep up with the other fellows, the tough, older big shots. Anyway, the talk didn't seem to fit his clean good looks, his fresh color and fine teeth and look of health. He looked the sort of athlete who speaks to boys in the Y.M.C.A.'s encouraging them to lead a clean life and warning them of the pitfalls of disease. He actually did make speeches of that sort all during his career as a football star and later as a young lawyer.

We all drank a lot of beer. I got to feeling woozy but I didn't enjoy myself beyond the feeling of satisfaction at being out for an evening with big, popular famous fellows. I don't

think Merle liked it very much either. All that evening his
eyes never really left Duncan. They were bright, intelligent
eyes which clouded or lighted up according to his feelings.
That night I could see by his eyes that when Duncan made
a dirty remark it hurt him. I still couldn't figure out the odd
friendship between the two. I didn't try very hard because I
was pretty young and not very good at such things, but I did
see that Merle, with the crooked ugly little body, had a kind
of shining worship of the big, good-looking Duncan. He
wasn't like me, just flattered by being noticed.

A little later in the evening when we had drunk up all the
beer there was, they began talking about the Eureka Skating
Rink and the girls that frequented it. The skating rink stood
on the edge of town, a big barn-like structure with a polished
floor and bowling alleys equipped with a mechanical organ.
It was looked upon as a disgrace by the authorities of the
sectarian college and was considered out of bonds for the
students but that didn't prevent them from going there. It was
frequented not exactly by prostitutes but by girls from the
lower end of the town who came there to pick up the college
boys and weren't above accepting money for their trouble.

The talk grew hotter and at last one of the fellows got up
and said, "Well, I guess I'll go down and do a little roller-
skating, fellows. How about it?"

All of them, a little tipsy, were in agreement but Merle and
Duncan and myself. I know the expedition wasn't in Merle's
line and I was still so green that the kind of girl you met at the
Eureka would have scared me to death. Duncan said, "No, not
tonight fellows. I've got work to make up."

They urged him to change his mind, saying it was Saturday
night and he had a right to something, only their language
wasn't as decent as that. One of them said, "You always say
that. I don't think you've ever been to the Eureka. What's the
matter with you?"

The color came into Duncan's face, but he held firm and
after putting on their coats, the big, over-age "students"
clumped out, a little unsteadily, leaving Merle and Duncan
and myself behind. The beer had made me sleepy and I kept
dozing off and forcing myself awake and then dozing off

again. Through the haze of sleep I heard Duncan and Merle talking. They were seated side by side at Duncan's worktable bent over some sheets of paper, very earnest about some problem of physics or mathematics. There were a lot of formulas in question but what they were I did not know. They sat with their heads close together under the green-shaded lamp and once in a moment of consciousness I caught a sudden glimpse of Duncan's face turned toward Merle, and in the eyes there was that shining look of admiration I had sometimes seen in Merle's eyes when he looked at Duncan. Even through the haze or perhaps because of it my green perceptions were heightened and I realized that of the two Merle was suddenly the dominant one, the strong one, although he was an ugly little fellow with a tragically twisted body. Merle kept talking earnestly, explaining some very complicated thing to big, good-looking Duncan who had become suddenly like a worshipping child or dog.

Then I fell sound asleep and did not waken again until I felt Merle shaking me. It was one o'clock in the morning and he said it was time to go home.

The fresh cool air cleared my brain and I said I didn't much like the fellows I had met that night. Merle agreed with me, saying, "I didn't like that dirty talk."

"Why does Duncan like them?"

"I don't know that he does," said Merle, "except that they're on the team with him. He's awfully broad-minded," he added. "He likes everybody and he wants everybody to like him. I wish I was a little more like that."

"Maybe he just doesn't notice the differences between people."

"Maybe he doesn't," Merle echoed and didn't talk any more about it.

I got the impression that he was troubled by what I said. You must understand that a lot of these impressions were not very clear at the time and were without much significance. They only became clear and fell into the proper perspective long after when I understood the whole story.

We walked in silence for a long time, Merle limping painfully along beside me and at my corner I turned off, thanking him for the party.

"Would you like to go sometime again?" Merle asked.

"Yes. I think I would." I wasn't at all certain that I should like to go again, but I was already beginning to be something of an opportunist, with the opportunist's policy of never really closing a door behind him.

*   *   *   *   *

After that night I noticed the MacKenzie girl when I passed her on the street or when I went now and then with Merle to Duncan's rooms. As I told you, she was pretty in a rather anemic way. It was the kind of prettiness which instinctively made you feel pity for her. Why, I do not know but there are women like that and it is just as well to avoid them for they can fasten upon you helplessly, a millstone about your neck.

She never talked much when she came into Duncan's room but into her eyes there came a cow-like look of adoration. He seemed to give her no notice at all. The mother was a big, powerful, aggressive woman of great energy. I think that largely explained the girl's look of meekness and submission.

In the spring of that year Duncan's mother and sister came to see him. His mother was a big, full-breasted, handsome woman, richly and rather fussily dressed. She wore what you might call "expensive" clothes. Everything about her smelt of money. The sister had had no luck. She was five years older than Duncan, plain, sallow, angular and a little sullen. If she and her brother could have exchanged their looks it would have been much better for both of them.

It was clear that both mother and sister worshipped Duncan and had always spoiled him. They brought a whole basketful of cakes and cookies and a couple of roast chickens.

When I remarked on the worship, Merle said, "Yes, you see Duncan's father died when he was five years old. He got all the attention from both of them after that. They're quite well-off, you know."

I didn't like either of them very much. The sister obviously hated anyone, male or female, who shared anything of her brother's interest or affection. The "expensive" mother obviously thought I was pretty poor potatoes and that Merle was beneath contempt. She had no appreciation whatever of his quick, bright mind and it certainly never occurred to her that he was of much use or service to her handsome, adored son. On that visit and subsequent ones, Merle and I learned to keep out of the way as much as possible.

Mrs. MacKenzie didn't get on with them too well and the daughter Agnes they treated as a servant which she certainly was not.

Although I didn't admire either his mother or sister I was glad to know them for it served to fill in the picture of all that went to make up Duncan. To me at that time it seemed that Duncan had been given almost too much in life—good looks, health, friendliness, wealth, the capacity for being loved and admired. He was an excellent athlete and had apparently a mind that was bright enough. There was in him at the age of twenty that kind of shining quality which young men of that age sometimes have. He never seemed to be ill-at-ease or to lack confidence. He could talk to the president of the college or any visiting celebrity without awkwardness or self-consciousness, as an equal.

A little while after his mother and daughter left, just before examination time, I went one night to Merle's room and walked in to find Duncan there sitting in a chair tilted back against the wall. Merle was sitting saddle-wise on a second chair facing him and as I came into the room I heard Merle saying fiercely and impatiently, "Come on now. You ought to know that, I've explained it to you twenty times."

As I entered they turned to look at me. It was clear that I wasn't expected and that my presence wasn't especially welcome. In the fraction of a second before the mood of the room changed, I saw an extraordinary thing. It was this—the handsome, all-conquering Duncan was humble and browbeaten. All the "glow" was gone out of him. He looked tired and worried and ashamed. It was Merle who was in the saddle. The small twisted body was tense, almost vibrant with vitality. It was something you could almost *feel*. The small face with the bright intelligent eyes was filled with light. It was for a moment almost a beautiful face.

Then at sight of me the whole mood collapsed. Merle threw down with a gesture of annoyance the paper he was holding and Duncan leaned forward and put his feet on the floor; the big handsome face relaxed again into its usual lines of perfect sympathy and charm.

I said, somewhat tactlessly, "It looks as if I was butting in on something."

Merle was surprisingly abrupt. "Yes, you are. If it isn't important, go away again and come back."

"Okay," I said and went out closing the door behind me.

In a little over an hour I returned and found Merle alone. He was in an odd mood of irritation. I had never seen him like that; usually his manners were perfect and his temper unruffled. Now he was hunched up in a morris chair pounding the arm of it with a ruler. He must have been pounding before I came in because the varnish on the arm of the chair was all worn away and the wood itself had begun to splinter.

I said, "Were you helping Duncan out for exams?"

Merle stopped pounding the arm of the chair and said, "Yes and that's the dumbest sonofabitch I ever knew."

There was a silence and nervously I asked, "Do you help him much?"

Then Merle flared up. "Help much? That's the only way he gets through school. If he had to do it himself, even this corrupt faculty couldn't have the face to keep him on here—not even as a crack football player. What do you think? When he makes one of those elegant, graceful speeches he does so well, who do you think wrote it? I did. I make him learn it by heart. Who do you think taught the mush-mouth how to speak, even to articulate? It's worse than if he was just plain dumb. He thinks everything should come to him handed out by God. He doesn't even know how to make an effort. All he wants is to be loved and popular, the dumb sonofabitch!"

I couldn't think of anything to say, and after a little silence Merle said, "The worst trouble is at exam time. I have to make him memorize everything." He sighed and threw down the ruler. "Sometimes I think it isn't worth the effort."

Then we went out to supper at the cafeteria and didn't discuss the thing any more. I had wanted to say, "Well, why do you go on with it?" but I was always a little in awe of Merle and his brain and character, and fearing another outburst, I dropped the subject.

One more thing happened before the three of us left college. It was our last year there, for Duncan and Merle were seniors and I gave up the struggle after my junior year and went to Chicago to get a job on the *Daily News* as a cub reporter. At commencement, Duncan was one of the speakers and he made a speech which overshadowed all the others, even that of the president of the University and the visiting politician orator who, it must be confessed, didn't do a very good job. After he spoke he was applauded and cheered. It was easy to see he was the most popular man in the whole college. Afterward he was surrounded by a small army of students and even professors wishing him well. The scene was like that of a newly elected politician surrounded by office-seekers. He was all graciousness and charm and I remember thinking he was the handsomest man I ever saw. I still think he was one of the handsomest.

At the exercises, Merle, by his own request, had been placed in the back row of the class. You couldn't even see him behind the taller men.

The mother and sister were there, dressed more "expensively" than ever. For three days they hovered about their paragon at dinners and commencement parties of all sorts. This time they had come from St. Louis in an automobile with a chauffeur. It was one of the first automobiles ever seen in the town and it attracted a good deal of attention. They brought with them a very pretty girl called Gracie Herman. She was rather German in appearance, opulent and blonde. She was very rich. Her father was a brewer. Just before he left, Duncan told me that he was going to marry her, even before he finished law school. Merle already knew it.

Certainly Duncan seemed the darling of the Gods during that bright sunny week in June.

After all the celebrations were over, Merle and I stayed on to do some summer courses. I moved into a room next to his with a connecting door. I think I really got to know him that summer—all the brilliance of his mind, the wisdom, and curious maturity of judgment and understanding which crippled and handicapped people have if there is any basis of character in them. In the intimacy that grew up between us, I learned many things I had not known about him before.

The relationship between himself and his father was a curious one. They got on badly, perhaps because the eccentric, brilliant father and the crippled clever son were too much alike and saw through each other. Merle admired his father but resented him.

One night he said, "My old man could have been anything. He could have gone anywhere but he had no balance and no common sense. He's twice as smart as Bryan ever was. Bryan got a lot of ideas from the old man."

He was silent for a moment. Then he sighed and said, "I'm as smart as he is but I've got more sense. I could do all the things he failed at except for being born like this."

It was the first time he had ever referred to his handicap. It made me feel embarrassed and I said quickly, "You can do it anyway with your mind. That can't make any difference."

"I could do it if I wanted to be a scientist, but it's something else I want."

"What?"

Bluntly he said, "I'm not going to tell you that. I've never told anyone yet. I'll probably never tell anyone." Then after another sigh he said, "Maybe I can do it anyway."

A couple of nights later I was wakened by the sound of a woman's voice in Merle's room. Drowsily, I listened, thinking at first that I was dreaming because I had never seen Merle with any girl. I had never seen him speak to a girl except the clerks in the bookstore and the girl behind the soda fountain.

This woman was crying and saying between sobs, "You've got to help me! She'd kill me if she ever found out. You've got to help me!" Then I heard Merle's voice speaking so low I couldn't understand what he said, and then the girl's voice saying again, "I'll kill myself, if you don't help me! That's what I'll do! I'll kill myself!" And then Merle's voice again, low and rather soothing.

It went on for a long time and presently the girl stopped crying and I heard the door open and the footsteps of the two going out. You could always recognize Merle's footsteps by the limp. Ten minutes later I heard the limping step mounting the stairs. He went into his room and closed the door and then crossed the room and opened my door very quietly. I knew what he wanted—to see whether I was awake and had heard what they were saying. The light fell full on me as I sat up.

He looked at me for a moment and then said, "Did you hear what was going on in here?"

I said, "Yes. Some of it. It wakened me."

He came in with his curious rolling gait and sat down on the edge of my bed.

"It was Agnes MacKenzie," he said.

"Agnes MacKenzie!"

"She's going to have a baby."

I was certain it couldn't be Merle's child. I said, "Why did she come to you about it?"

"She didn't know anybody else to come to. She's scared to death of that dragon mother." I didn't say anything but he added, "I suppose you want to know who the father is?"

"Did she tell you?"

"Yes. It's Duncan," he said in a low voice, very tense, as if he were suffering.

"Duncan," I repeated, and then naïvely I added, "I thought he was engaged to that St. Louis girl."

"He was . . . all the time," said Merle. "He has certainly messed things up."

I thought for a moment and then said, "Why, he never went out much with girls. He never even went down to the skating rink with the other guys."

"No," said Merle and the bitterness came into his voice. "No. That wouldn't be the way he operates." The light shone full on his face and from his expression and his voice it was almost as if he hated Duncan. I have never seen more contempt in a human face.

"What are you going to do about it?" I asked.

"I don't know. Only Duncan can't marry her. That would ruin everything. She's a simple, half-witted little fool."

Then he rose painfully and said, "Remember you never heard anything about this. You're not to tell anyone."

"Of course not. Who would I tell?"

"Okay." He placed one hand affectionately on my shoulder and said, "Good night, Frank."

"Good night."

.　.　.　.　.

Duncan and Merle went off to the same law school and for the next five years I saw them only once or twice, and then casually. I never heard from Duncan but I used to get letters three or four times a year from Merle. There was never very much in them concerning himself. The letters were usually filled with discussions of politics and national issues. They were brilliant letters. I wish I had saved them all but a newspaper man isn't generally very much of a collector. If he starts to collect anything he loses it the first time he moves. A couple of these letters still remain, however, written in the naïve period before the First World War when this country still wasn't quite a grown-up nation. But about Merle's letters there was nothing that wasn't grown-up. Even in the two letters I still have, he showed more understanding of our problems than any statesman since that time, with the possible exception of Woodrow Wilson.

Once or twice in the letters he mentioned Duncan, saying that he was getting on very well and was president of this or that organization. Once he wrote, "I think he has a great political career ahead of him." Knowing the world a great deal better than I had in college, this struck me as so much malarkey. I couldn't see how Duncan could get anywhere in politics. His good looks and his money and his physical charm would carry him a long way but when these things were ended, he was certain to come a cropper. That's all there was. There wasn't any more.

In one letter, Merle said that Duncan's wife, the rich brewer's daughter, was living in a suburb near the school and that she had just borne a son. Eighteen months later she gave birth to a daughter. Everything was going fine and according to plan. It seemed that Duncan was one of those beloved by the Gods who never had any bad luck.

There was, of course, the business of Agnes MacKenzie, but even that never seemed to amount to much. After that night when she came to Merle's room, I never heard anything more about it. All I knew about it was that she went off on a visit and returned after a couple of weeks and went on just as if nothing had happened. Mrs. MacKenzie's ugly house, where Duncan had lived, had a new coat of paint and some of the jigsaw work on the turrets, which had rotted, was replaced at the same time. I waited for Merle to tell me more of the story but he never did.

The year after they left law school, Duncan and Merle went into the law business in partnership in Zenith City and a couple of years later Duncan was elected to the State Senate. He was only twenty-six years old, the youngest senator in the history of the state. From that moment on, it was Merle who ran all the law business. Duncan for the rest of his life just went on getting elected or appointed. And the law business grew. It wasn't long before Merle was trying cases in very big cities and even before the Supreme Court.

I saw him now and then in New York or in Washington. He hadn't changed much. He had the agelessness of certain cripples. The twisted under-developed body did not change at all and the face seemed only a little older after ten years. It was clear that things were going well with him.

"And Duncan?" I asked.

Merle grinned. "He's doing fine. They all love him. You remember how it was in college. He was always the most popular fellow in the class. He was always nice to everybody."

"Yes. He certainly was." And suddenly I found there wasn't much more to say on the subject. There was a silence and then I saw a grin on Merle's intelligent monkey face. He understood the silence but wouldn't admit it in words.

"He's going to go a long way. He's running for Congress in the autumn."

"How's your father?" I asked.

"He died last summer."

"I'm sorry."

"You needn't be sorry. It wasn't your fault. He was disappointed and bitter. He always tried to make the world suit him and his ideas instead of trying to fit himself and his ideas to the world."

"That's the difference between being an honest man and a cheap politician."

"I suppose it is."

"What method does Duncan use?"

"Something in between. I don't think he quite knows himself, but it seems to work. They like him even in a normally Democratic state."

Merle went back to Zenith City and I didn't see him again for two years. But I ran into Duncan and his wife in the Mayflower in Washington.

He hadn't changed a great deal. He was a little heavier but still had the same smooth unlined handsome face. There was a little gray around the temples. His rich wife had, on the contrary, fined down. The voluptuousness had gone and she was smartly and, like his mother and sister, in the past, "expensively" dressed. He wore a "statesman's" white waistcoat and carried himself rather pompously. He was what you might have called "an impressive figure."

We lunched together, the three of us, the next day and of course talked about Merle.

"He's certainly doing well," said Duncan. "He's a very clever fellow and it's wonderful how he's overcome his handicap." He said this in a rich and sonorous voice, the voice which everyone loved, the voice for which he was famous.

I couldn't quite make out the wife. When she talked at all, she made intelligent rather biting remarks. I would have said that she wasn't any longer in love with him and that whatever love she had for him was born entirely of his good looks and physique. At that time he was still new in Washington and people turned to look at him just as they had done when he was a boy in college, only now he had acquired that air of studied indifference that marks the manner of a professional beauty accustomed to being stared at and discussed. Already the society editors and gossip columns writers had noticed his looks and written about them. They always spoke of him as "the good-looking new Congressman from the West."

I asked him how he was getting on in Congress.

"All right," he said. "You have to take things easy at first. It's a pretty intricate business."

"That was a remarkably good speech you made on the tariff —especially for a Republican."

"Yes. I thought it pretty good myself. Some of my colleagues didn't like it but it got a lot of attention. I told them it was time to bring some of our party ideas up to date."

When I read it, I had a strong suspicion where it came from, out of Merle's dead and disappointed father, by way of Merle.

I told him about spending an evening with Merle in New York and Duncan said, "Yes, he gets down here about once a month. I've talked to him about opening an office here in Washington but he likes Zenith City—says the Capital doesn't suit him."

Then his wife spoke up, "Of course Duncan talks to him three or four times a week by telephone. They have to do that to keep up to date on the law business, don't you, *dear*?" In her voice was the shadow of dripping acid.

"That's right, *dear*," said Duncan.

I am always suspicious of couples who "dear" each other too much in public.

I asked him what he thought about the international situation. (It was in June, 1918) and he said, "I've been giving it a good deal of attention lately. I'm still studying it but offhand I'd say that it didn't concern us."

It wasn't a very interesting lunch. The food was good but the conversation had a curious strained, tentative quality. It left me feeling exhausted and with a sense of having wasted a couple of precious hours. Of course it may have been the impression of boredom given by Duncan's wife. It seemed to stifle everything. It wasn't that she yawned or made it evident in any obvious way. You just had the impression that for a large part of the time she wasn't there at all and when she was there that she didn't care for any of it. Her rather small mouth drooped at the corners.

I left them in the lobby and went for a long walk up Massachusetts Avenue and after that I felt better.

.   .   .   .   .

Well, Duncan went on from success to success. He went to the Senate and became known as a great orator, but unlike most orators when he made a speech he said something. I heard him more than once from the gallery and as I listened I found a curious thing happening to me. While the magnificent voice rolled on, coming from the handsome figure with the graying hair, I found myself becoming hypnotized by the performance so that I really heard nothing he said. It was like a magnificent ballet or an opera in which there are no words or words that do not matter in the least. When he finished there was silence and then a burst of applause from the galleries, but I doubt that anyone in the galleries knew what he said. It got so people came to the Senate just to watch the performance and listen to the voice.

The odd thing was that if you read the speech afterward it was usually brilliant. Yet no one paid much attention to it. It never got proper notice in the press and seemed to have no effect upon Congress itself. As I listened I remembered again the days at college. By now I knew who had written the speeches—all of them.

Back in the home state Merle had everything under control. The law business now represented a half dozen big corporations and politically Merle had a machine that was functioning perfectly. For the first time in many years the Republicans dominated the state. But Merle got none of the credit. It went to Duncan. Politicians began to say that Duncan could swing the whole state any way he liked. It was about this time they began to talk of Duncan as "favorite son" presidential material.

It was about this time too that things began to go wrong for Duncan. In the first place, his wife left him and presently sued for divorce. The real circumstances never appeared in the papers, but everyone in Washington and most of the home state knew them. Actually she ran off at the age of forty-two with the family chauffeur, a husky fellow, ten years younger than herself. The same year his son was mixed up in a New York shooting scandal which involved a chorus girl. That appeared in the paper but was hushed up. It was at this time that instead of running again for the Senate or taking a chance as a presidential candidate, he went instead to Transylvania as Minister. Transylvania was a small post and not very important and for three years he rather disappeared from sight. While he was there he married a forty-year-old school teacher who came to Transylvania on a summer tour. She met Duncan at an official tea given at the ministry.

The year before he returned, Merle made his first trip to ministry. He visited Duncan at his post but he did not stay long. I saw him in New York on his return. For the first time he looked ill and showed his age. And there was a spitefulness in him, which some people associate with cripples, but which I had never before seen in Merle.

We lunched together and he seemed to have no desire to talk about Duncan. When I asked about him, Merle said, "He's got a swelled head. I thought his being away from the public for a time would chasten him but it hasn't. It's only made him worse. The Transylvania people have been feeding him flattery in the hope of getting better treatment on their debt payment, and that woman he's married just sits around worshipping him and telling him how wonderful he is. I suppose by the time she'd reached forty she'd given up all hope of marrying a handsome fellow like Duncan. So now she's taking no chances on losing him." Merle put down his coffee and said, "Let's not talk about it. Let's go and see a show. I'm going to Washington tomorrow. I've got some business there."

We went to a musical show but it wasn't much of a success. The depression didn't leave him and when the show was over, he said, "If you don't mind, I think I'll go to bed."

I left him with a feeling that not only his body but his spirit was ill. I think that when I left him that night I realized how fond I was of him. We didn't see much of each other, meeting only once or twice a year. I saw Duncan much more frequently, but for him I had no feeling of any kind. That night I lay awake thinking about Merle, his courage, his bright mind, his puckish humor, his generosity to me in the days when I was a hick. I couldn't help thinking that if only he had had a normal body there was nothing he could not have accomplished.

Duncan came home and ran again for Senator. Merle was ill and Duncan made it by a narrow squeak. In Washington I went into his office three months later to congratulate him.

He received me in his office beneath a portrait of Lincoln and as he rose to shake my hand pompously, a flash of intuition came to me out of the blue. I thought, "He really thinks he's like Lincoln. It's almost impossible to believe but he really thinks that."

He asked his secretary to fetch whiskey and soda for us and we settled down to talk, and in a little while I had again the exhausting sensation of feeling that everything he said was of no importance, I found myself *making* conversation, without any interest whatever, almost forgetting in the middle of a sentence what I was saying.

Just as I was preparing to leave the door opened and a rather plain, middle-aged woman came in. She was dressed badly and fussily. I can't describe the hat or costume. My impression was simply that both were covered with things, too many things. She had on too much make-up; her whole manner was that of a woman much younger. There was a sort of desperate, forced air of youth and coquetry about her.

Seeing me then, she said, "Oh, excuse me." And to Duncan, "I thought you were alone, dear."

Duncan stood up with an air of deference and said, "It's all right. Frank is an old friend. We weren't talking about anything important." Then he turned to me and said, "This is my wife," and to her he said, "Frank and I went to college together."

"How nice," she said.

"He's a great friend of Merle's as well."

She merely said, "Oh!" and then as if to dismiss Merle she said, "I won't interrupt you. I just found that I'd come all the way from Georgetown without any money. Could you let me have about twenty-five dollars?"

He took out his wallet and gave her the money. Then with

a sort of forced smile he said, "Go easy on it until the first of the month, dear."

"Of course, dear," she said. Then she turned to me and said, "It's so nice to have met you. I hope that Duncan will bring you to dinner some time."

Then she blew a kiss to Duncan and went out with the air of a chorus girl who has just been given a bracelet by her sugar daddy. There was something inexpressibly painful about the scene. I felt a little sick and rose as if to go. Then as I looked at Duncan I realized that he had seen nothing revolting in the little scene and dialogue. His broad, handsome, empty face was the very mirror of smugness and satisfaction.

"A mighty fine woman," he said.

I managed to say, "Yes, isn't she?"

"A mighty smart woman too," he said. "She helps me with my speeches. She used to be an economics teacher, you know." It seemed to me an odd admission since in all the years I had known him, he had never once mentioned either to me or to anyone else, so far as I knew, the fact that Merle had always written his speeches. Then he added quickly, "Sit down. Have another drink."

We had already had three. I didn't want them much. I was just keeping him company.

"No. I have to go," I said.

Then someone knocked and Duncan said, "Come in," and through the opposite door another woman came in. She was a rather faded middle-aged blonde and her hair hung down in wisps. She had, I remember, a very small mouth and the look of a woman who believes she is martyred. I noticed her because although I was certain I had never seen her before, there was something hauntingly familiar about her.

Duncan again introduced us, saying, "This is Mrs. Downing, my right-hand woman." And he smiled at his little joke. She said, "How do you do?" and placed some papers on his desk. I stood looking out of the window toward the capitol while Duncan put his signature on the papers, and suddenly I felt that someone was staring at me. Absently I thought that Mrs. Downing had gone and that Duncan was watching me. I turned but the starer was not Duncan but Mrs. Downing. Dun-

can was still signing papers beneath the portrait of Lincoln.
As my eyes met the dim gray-blue ones of Mrs. Downing, she
flushed and turned away.

When she went out I said firmly that I wouldn't have another
drink and that I had to make an appointment. I had an odd
feeling that he wanted to keep me on because he did not want
to be left alone.

I went to the Mayflower Bar, again glad to get away from
Duncan. I don't know why I went on seeing him through all
those years. I never got any pleasure from it, but only that
peculiar sense of emptiness, futility and boredom. Lately even
his extraordinary good looks had begun to sag a little. Small red
veins began to appear on his nose and in his cheeks and puffy
bags beneath his eyes. He had, however, the kind of good looks
which could never go altogether because they are built upon
a fine bone structure. The perfect profile only a little wrecked
still remained the best in Washington. The professional "statesman" carriage did not sag. But the wonderful booming voice
began to grow a little hoarse.

That year he was defeated for re-election and the party took
care of him by making him Governor of Alaska. He spent little
time there, always finding reasons for returning to Washington.
After eighteen months he resigned. It seemed that his wife
didn't like being in Alaska. In Washington she was still "somebody." She belonged to all the clubs and the organizations of
Senator's wives. I saw them a couple of times in Washington
and I got the impression that she was devouring him. His
vitality seemed to wane as hers seemed to increase. She dressed
more extravagantly than ever. In political circles she got to
be known as "the Duchess."

The party, still believing perhaps that he had some political
influence in his home state, made him Director of the Mint.
That of course was an awful comedown from the position of
once having been presidential material, but he accepted it. I
think that by this time he had got so that what he wanted most
was a title, any kind of a title. About this time one of the political column writers gave him a name which stuck—"The
Great Façade"—"A magnificent classical ruin with nothing
behind it."

In the same year the law partnership of Masters and Jenkins was dissolved back in Zenith City. I wasn't surprised.

As for Merle, the illness had grown upon him and he had to spend most of his time in bed from where he directed all his law activities brilliantly. He had by now a staff of three younger men, all intelligent and able, and he managed them as a skilled driver manages a tandem.

I stopped that year in Zenith City on my way west to Los Angeles and of course went to see Merle. He lived in a modest house in a nondescript part of the city. I found him in bed with a pretty trained nurse taking care of him. There were two brisk-looking young men in the room, just leaving as I arrived. Merle introduced them as his partners. Then he dismissed them and told the nurse to bring a bottle of Scotch, some ice and glasses. Grinning a little, he said, "Mr. Cresswell and I are going to have a long session. We haven't seen each other for a couple of years."

He looked old and withered and ill, so much so that I was aware of an effort not to betray by my expression any sense of shock. But I did not deceive him. You couldn't deceive Merle about things like that. He said, "I know I look pretty awful. Just try not to look at me."

I said I thought he looked well and probably would be well very soon. I noticed how twisted his poor body was—that he could not even lie in the bed very long in the same position.

He looked at me sharply and said, "I'm not going to get well. I'm going to die. I've got everything the matter with me. There just never was room in my twisted body for all my organs." Then after a sigh he added, "Now that we've got that over, pour out a good drink and we'll talk."

We talked a good deal about politics and the world in general, and a good deal about old times which seemed to give him pleasure and presently he said, "We probably won't see each other again, Frank. I'm going to tell you something. I know that a lot of things have puzzled you for years and I know you've been awfully decent about not butting into my business. I think you have a right to know some things and anyway I'd like to tell you. It's kind of like a confession. I've never told anybody about it."

There wasn't anything to say. I fancied that I knew more than he suspected. He told the story very simply.

He said, "I don't suppose you know what it is like to be born a hopeless cripple and to be ambitious. At the same time I think I knew I was ambitious when I was about thirteen or fourteen years old. I think I loved my father but I hated him too. He was a pretty good-looking fellow when he was younger. He could have had anything or done anything if he'd been a little more human, but he really hated the human race and held it in contempt. He was a smart fellow and even when I was only a kid he used to talk to me as if I was a grown-up man. Being a cripple I was naturally precocious and I knew him better than he thought. I think that's one of the reasons he disliked me a large part of the time."

Painfully he changed his position in the bed and lighted a cigar. Then he said, "By the time I was eighteen I knew what it was I wanted. I wanted to be everything my father had failed at being. I wanted to be Governor, a Congressman, a Senator —even President. I wanted to run things, I wanted to mold the destinies of my country." He looked away from me out of the window suddenly, "And by the time I was eighteen I knew I'd never be able to do it because I was a cripple and I didn't have the physical strength and I knew too that being a cripple would be a handicap. People just naturally like politicians to be big and handsome and pompous. And then at college I met Duncan. One of the faculty asked me to tutor him, to help him along with his classes so he could give more time to sports. I worked with him for a time and suddenly one night after he'd gone home an idea came to me out of the blue. I saw how the ambition I had could be satisfied. It was to make Duncan a part of myself, a kind of instrument, a tool which I could use."

At this part of the story Merle pulled himself up in the bed and something of the old fire came into the small, bright, intelligent eyes.

"You see, God had given him everything I didn't have and he'd given me everything Duncan didn't have. He was big and handsome with the kind of looks that made everybody, both men and women, like him on sight. And he had nice manners and he wanted everybody to love him—it was pitiful how much he wanted people to like him. But he was dumb. On the other hand, I had the brains. I could learn anything very quickly. I could think. I could plan. I knew what people were like. You see it was a wonderful combination. Together we made a whole person, an irresistible person when it came to politics—if only I could use him and make him absolutely dependent upon me so that his only thoughts were my thoughts, his only speeches were my speeches. He could use my mind, but his body, his appearance was to be mine."

Merle smiled a twisted smile, "I imagine you've guessed some of the story but you never had any idea how terribly close, how terribly close the combination was. It was as if what happened to his body happened to me, and certainly all that happened to my mind, happened to his. He got so he couldn't think without asking me what he was to think. He used to call me a dozen times a week from Washington. That part of it might have gone all right but it was his body being me that made the trouble. Of course what happened to his body couldn't always happen to mine. There was the business of women." Again he looked away from me out of the window. "When he made love, when he got married, it happened to him but not to me. I'm a virgin, Frank. I never thought that any woman would ever want to touch me, and because all that side of life was shut off forever, a lot of things grew twisted inside me. There were times when I hated and loved Duncan at the same time. I hated his wife although I never dared to show it, because I think, she had at times possession of his body—that body which properly belonged to me, which for a large part of the time *was* mine. Yet what happened to it where women were concerned couldn't happen to me."

He looked at me piercingly, "Do you understand what I mean? It is terribly difficult to explain. It was all twisted and sinister. It used to torture me. It was all the more terrible because women, oddly enough, didn't mean much to Duncan. He just accepted their adoration and love as a matter of course. He wasn't a passionate man or a very good lover. All the good looks were in a way wasted on him and I would have given all my brains, all my cleverness to have had those good looks just so that one woman would have loved me. I can tell you now, because it's all over and I'm going to die anyway, but I used to be tormented—I *was* tormented most of my life by ideas of women and voluptuousness. And there was never any satisfaction. The only way out for me, the only way to go on living, was to work harder, to make more money, to win more cases, to use Duncan more and more as an instrument of power. You remember the night Agnes MacKenzie came to my room and you heard her talking? That night was torture for me."

Quietly I said, "Yes, I remember. I couldn't very well forget. I always wondered how you straightened that out."

"It was simple enough. I was pretty green in some ways but I knew that somehow babies could be got rid of. I went down to the skating rink and picked up some of the girls there and found out about a woman who took care of them and I made up a lie for Agnes about my sister asking her to come on a visit and then fixed it up for Agnes to be taken care of. And then I went to Duncan and got money from him to pay expenses and twenty-five hundred dollars besides. And when Agnes was all right again, she came home and I gave the twenty-five hundred dollars to her mother, saying that Duncan appreciated how good she'd been to him for the four years he lived in her house and that he wanted to make her a gift. She didn't argue about it. I don't know to this day whether the old dragon knew the truth. I suspect she did and was simply glad to have the trouble taken care of and gladder still to have the money.

"What I did was a shocking thing and at times it's haunted me ever since, because in a funny twisted way that child was *my* child and Agnes MacKenzie had been *my* mistress, even though I hated her for owning even for a little time part of the Duncan that properly belonged to me. I did an awful thing. But I had to do it. If Duncan had broken his engagement to the rich girl he had promised to marry and married Agnes instead, it would have made a scandal. But that wouldn't have been the end of it. If he'd married that anemic complaining MacKenzie girl, he would have been saddled with her for life, and so my life and my ambitions would have been saddled with her. She'd have defeated any politician's career.

She was mediocre and common and poor. There wasn't any place for her in the scheme of my ambitions. On the other hand, the girl he was marrying was exactly right for him, for *us*. She was good-looking, she was rich, she made a good impression. She would grow into exactly what a Senator's wife, even a President's wife ought to be. Because it didn't turn out that way wasn't my fault. What happened was beyond anything I could control."

He poured himself another drink of the whiskey, which I divined slowly was keeping him alive.

I said rather trivially, "It must have been very convenient to Duncan to have you get him out of the mess so easily."

"He never even thanked me," said Merle. "He seemed to take it for granted, the way he did everything else. I suppose because everything always seemed to be done for him."

Then he went on with the story. "His wife was really a very nice woman, not stupid at all, but she and I just didn't get on. I suppose under the circumstances it was impossible. As things went on, it got so that Duncan couldn't act or have an opinion unless he called up or saw me to ask about it. It got so bad that he really couldn't answer some of the things she asked him or plan anything without talking to me first. That was enough to make any woman resentful and jealous.

"After a time she began slowly to understand what the game was—that she was married not only to Duncan but to me as well, and over me she had no control whatever. And so she came to hate me and in hating me she hated him as well. Yet she knew well enough that she couldn't get rid of me so long as she was married to Duncan, because by that time Duncan couldn't stand on his own. He was like a shadow without my existence. But it wasn't altogether that. She was a passionate woman."

As he talked I kept remembering the day long ago I had lunched with Duncan and his wife at the Mayflower—the day when it was like lunching with people who weren't there at all, the futility of conversation, the bitter droop of the wife's mouth.

Merle was saying, "She came to see me the day she ran off with the chauffeur. She came here to this house late in the afternoon and I knew something was up by the change in her appearance and the look in her eyes. She came into my library downstairs and said abruptly, 'I'm running away with Tony Galeazzo. I thought you'd like to know about it first.'

"She knew that I didn't want to hear of it at all, that I knew it was the worst calamity that could happen. It was just the moment when they were talking about the possibilities of running Duncan for President. The setup was just right. It looked as if neither of the two candidates could muster enough votes to be nominated and the nomination would fall to Duncan as a favorite son. What she was doing couldn't have been worse. By now things had developed so that what she was doing hit at me really more than at Duncan. Everything I had planned and worked for was about to happen and now what she was doing would ruin everything.

"I tried to argue with her. For two hours I talked to this woman who had been in a way *my* wife as much as Duncan's, although for a long time we had hated each other. She listened with a stony face and I knew after talking for an hour that it was no good. Nothing could change her.

"At last, when I had given up, she said, 'And now I'm going to tell you something, Merle Jenkins. I'm going to run off with Tony Galeazzo. He's a wop. He's ten years younger than myself. He can barely read or write. His parents are Sicilian immigrants. But he's a man, and I'm over forty years old and that's all that matters to me. It matters more than sitting in the White House beside a phony, an empty, a ghost.'

"She worked herself up and said a lot of things she could only have said in the white heat of her fury. She said, 'Duncan wasn't much to begin with. I don't suppose you can realize what it means to be married to a man who even made love to you as if he was doing you a favor, but that's the way it's been for twenty years. He acted as if he wasn't even interested. But whatever he was to begin with, you've made him into nothing —nothing at all, a man who can't even decide what suit he should wear without calling you up. I've not only been married to him but I've been married to you for twenty years, without being able to tell you what I thought of you. You've always been there with us, between us, no matter what happened and never any chance of getting back at you.'"

Merle grinned, a sudden devilish, bitter grin, that was blackening in effect. "I didn't tell her what I might have—that in all those years I had been married to her far more than she ever knew, that slowly I had become an evil lascivious fellow, who in his thoughts was always with her no matter where she was or what she did, that in my thoughts I too had lived with her for twenty years because I had long since identified myself with Duncan's body, that in all these thoughts I *was* Duncan, married to a handsome, desirable woman who with my conscious mind I hated as much as she hated me, because like Agnes MacKenzie, she possessed a side of Duncan which could never belong to me, which I could never dominate. I wish now that I had told her all that. It would have made the scene in my library all the more fantastic."

Then Merle sighed suddenly and looked so old and ill and bitter that for a moment I thought, "He is going to die—now." But he took another drink of whiskey and went on talking.

"I doubt," he said, "that you have ever seen anything like the fury of that woman. She called me corrupt and vicious and perverted and evil. I think she divined but never wholly understood why and how Duncan had always belonged to me far more than to her, how she herself belonged *through* Duncan to me. In the end, she said, 'I'm going to run off with a cheap and handsome wop and I'm going to be free and I'm going to live and that's all that matters and to hell with you and Duncan —both of you! It may last only six months but it's worth it. If I don't do it I'll go crazy.'"

Merle grinned maliciously, "Well, she did it and it didn't last," he said. "On my advice Duncan let her divorce him. She married Tony Galeazzo and in about two years he got five hundred thousand dollars out of her and cheated on her the whole time. And then he ran away and left her. She was in California and wrote me that she was ill, asking me to come and see her. She died out there in a little house in Balboa. She just didn't want to live any longer. By that time the world had forgotten all about her."

Outside it was getting dark. Merle said, "Will you put on

that lamp beside you and turn the shade away? I can't stand much light directly in my eyes. I hope you won't mind."

I said, "Of course not." I had the impression that he didn't want me to see his face too clearly—that face which had once been so different.

The rest of the story he told in a voice which grew weaker as he talked.

He said, "The scandal never really got into the papers but it got around enough to ruin all Duncan's chances for the nomination. But the party consoled him by making him minister to Transylvania. I saw to that. I thought it was best for him to get out of the country for a time until everything died down and he had a chance to get hold of himself. He was terribly upset by his wife's running away, not because he loved her especially, but because it was inconceivable to him that any woman could prefer another man to himself—especially an almost illiterate man who had been his own chauffeur. The night he got the news, he cried all night. It was a pitiful, shameful sight, especially when you knew that he wasn't thinking about her or even minded losing her, but only about himself and his hurt vanity."

As he talked and the light outside faded into darkness, his face grew dimmer and dimmer in the shadows. Only the eyes seemed to remain, the burning frustrated, bright eyes which now, as always, seemed so alive.

"Being a minister," he said, "was the beginning of the end. I couldn't be with him there and he began to get out of control. It's true that he did cable me often enough and occasionally telephoned me whenever there was an important decision. But that wasn't good enough. They went to work on him, flattered him. The high officials, the Duchesses, the rich industrialists took him over in as shrewd a campaign as you ever saw. They wined and dined him, published his picture everywhere, until he gave them everything they were trying to get, as far as he could give it. He made recommendations that always favored the country where he was representative rather than the country he represented. When he was recalled the President told him that he had behaved as if he were the minister of Transylvania to the United States, rather than the other way round.

"In Transylvania the second wife came in. If I'd been there it would never have happened. You've seen her. You know that she wasn't young, she wasn't even good-looking. She just went for him. She flattered and worshipped him and he fell for it. If he'd fallen for a young chorus girl you might have understood it. There would have been something normal and expected about it, but to fall for a middle-aged virgin just seemed ridiculous. And did she take possession of him!"

He paused for a moment and then whispered, "I'll go on in a moment."

"Maybe I'd better go," I said, "You've been doing all the talking."

"No," he whispered, "it just comes and goes, and when it comes it's pretty terrible. It keeps me from talking."

We sat silently for what seemed an interminable period and then suddenly the twisted body relaxed and he said, "It's all right. Now I can talk again. Anyway, there isn't much more to tell. That woman—that second wife—wasn't like the first one. I think that by the time I first saw her she had a pretty good idea of the situation. Anyway it was clear that she hated me and was determined to break the whole thing up. She wasn't very subtle or clever about it. She just went to work on him telling him I'd make a slave of him and that he ought to stand on his own. She wouldn't let him telephone me and presently she began changing the speeches I wrote for him and even helping him to write his own.

"That was the real beginning of the end. I was tired and I was beginning to be ill and I didn't fight the way I might have done. Anyway, I hadn't much heart in it because I knew that my plan—the plan on which I'd spent all my life—had ended in failure. We'd gotten just to the threshold of success. He had one foot in the door of the White House when everything collapsed. It wasn't just an accident. By then I knew that. It happened because he was what he was and I was what I was and because the first wife was caught in between us. It just couldn't happen any other way. The trouble was that the material wasn't good enough. I knew it by that time. There and then I began to see that not only had I failed in the plan I'd given my life to but that I'd destroyed three people as well—

Duncan and his first wife and finally myself. It didn't matter that I was a good lawyer and made lots of money. That wasn't what I wanted. I wanted to be popular and loved. I wanted to have power. You see, Frank, I wanted from the time I was a boy to be President of the United States, and the only way I could do it was through Duncan." In the shadow that hid his face, he laughed and the laugh had a horrible sound. "You see, the joke was on me in the end. I blunted and destroyed my own instrument by working it too hard. By the time he came back with that second wife he was just a pompous self-important half-wit, and she took over what I threw away."

There was a knock on the door and the nurse said, "I'm sorry, Mr. Jenkins, but your friend has been in here for more than two hours and the doctor said you weren't to see anyone for more than twenty minutes."

Merle's voice came out of the shadow. It sounded suddenly stronger. "It's all right, Miss Janeway," he said. "I feel much better. Mr. Cresswell's visit did me good. You see, I got something off my chest. I promise to send him away in ten minutes."

She went out again and when she had gone he said, "There's one other thing I forgot to tell you, Frank. The MacKenzie girl—Agnes—turned up again a long time afterward. He got her a government job as his file clerk and he got a government job for her husband and her daughter. He arranged it so the taxpayers supported the whole family of the girl he had seduced between making speeches to young men on clean living. Of course, it didn't cost him anything. Maybe you saw her around his office?"

"Yes," I said, "I did see her once. . . ." I knew now she was the pallid dumpy woman who had brought in the papers for him to sign. She was the woman who had stared at me.

"I suppose," said Merle, "it wasn't really Duncan's fault at all. If I'd only let him alone, he'd be a dumb good-looking old man, living on his income and carrying the plate on Sundays in the Presbyterian Church. I guess you shouldn't meddle in other people's lives."

I said good-bye and told him I'd stop off on my way back from California. He took my hand in his small, nervous intense one and pressed it.

"Good-bye," he said, "and good luck to you."

When I stopped off on my way back from California he was already dead. He had died the night before I arrived. I stayed for the funeral and at the church Duncan and his awful second wife showed up. All the leading politicians of the state were present and a lot of big lawyers from as far away as Chicago and New York were there too. Duncan looked old, older than his age. He was a little bent and the pouches under the eyes and the veins in the cheeks and nose had spread. But the handsome profile remained unchanged. The ruined façade still kept its remarkable beauty.

"The Duchess" looked a harridan with dyed hair and even more things on her hat than had been there before.

I think she knew how far down the scale of things her husband had slipped. She had become very eager and "rattly" and after the funeral she stood in the entrance to the church, bridling and tossing her head in withered coquetry at the prominent men as they came out. Some of them spoke politely but coldly to Duncan, some of them did not even remember him. He stood at one side, rather pathetically, his head and hands trembling. I had the impression that he was a little drunk, even at Merle's funeral.

Well, that's very nearly all of the story, except that yesterday I saw Duncan's obituary in the *New York Times*. It occupied only a paragraph or two beginning: "*Duncan Allerton Masters, former United States Senator and Minister to Transylvania died in Washington yesterday after a long illness. He had held as well the posts of Governor of Alaska and Director of the Mint.* etc."

The "long illness" was simply drink. It had begun at the moment Merle Jenkins gave him up. From then on he had been afraid, like a man with no soul in his body, like a Zombie.

"UP FERGUSON WAY"

TWICE BEFORE IN MY LIFE I HAVE WRITTEN STORIES ABOUT
Zenobia, once more than twenty years ago and again a few
years later. Both times I was forced to give her a different name
from her own for she lived to a prodigious age and was still
alive. Once I called her Zenobia White and once Zenobia Van
Essen and both times I invented certain details to disguise
her as much as possible—something of course which could not
be done because there was never anyone I knew or heard of
who was quite like her. Both times I invented the end of her
life and both times I was wrong. The first time, being a young
writer and still romantic, I gave her a dramatic death. The
second time a commonplace one. The whole point of what I
am going to tell you is that while they found a body in Zenobia's cottage and buried it, she never really died at all.

The longer I live the more I am inclined to believe in forces
which we do not understand, which compel our destinies along
other courses from those we have carefully planned. I can't
help believing too that these same forces entangle our lives with
those of others, although they may be strangers or persons only
encountered casually two or three times in all our lives. Something like that happened with Zenobia's life and mine. I never
knew her very well for she was already an old woman when
I was born and I saw her only casually in my youth, but in a
life spent largely wandering about the earth in meeting thousands of people of every race, nationality and creed I never
met one who left upon me so profound an impression. She
compelled me to write of her at least twice and still, even after
they buried her, she compels me to write of her again. And I
have the impression that the story of our vague but strong
relationship is not yet finished. I am aware of her presence every
time I go "up Ferguson way." You see her real name was
neither White nor Van Essen but Ferguson—Zenobia Ferguson, a rich, pretty name.

The first time I saw her I could not have been more than seven or eight years old. My father, a Democrat and somewhat of a politician in his small way, used at election time to drive out over the country visiting farm and village people, seeking the assurance of their votes, either for himself or for some fellow Democrat. He rode in an old-fashioned buggy, driving a team, and very often he would take me with him for company. For a small boy it was always an exciting adventure. We visited very nearly every farm in every township, driving up remote narrow lanes that led from the rich valley farms into the hills.

My father was a pleasant man. Nearly everybody loved him and called him Tom and when noon came or darkness fell we were always invited to sit down for noonday dinner or to spend the night. Going about with him I came to know every farmer and every lane in the whole county, a beautiful county I never forgot in all the years I spent away from it. Irresistibly I found myself comparing other landscapes to it and never for myself did I find a more satisfying one.

It was a country of rich, flat valleys between wild wooded hills with springs and streams everywhere. You could leave a rich valley and driving up a narrow wooded lane leave civilization behind you and climb into a wilderness of tangled ferns and trees, wild grapes and dogwood. Sometimes after climbing for a time through a forest you would come upon a kind of small rolling plateau where there was a lonely hill farm with the house built beside a spring. It was the kind of country where over each hill a new and romantic world appears, different from the country you had left behind. That kind of country makes romantic people. Flat country makes dull, prosaic and material ones. Zenobia lived all her life in one of those lonely farmhouses. If she had lived in flat country her story would have been different. People would never have referred to her lonely farm as "up Ferguson way" as if there were something high and strange and mystical about it.

She was a kind of vague relation of my father's and mine because her grandfather and my father's great-grandfather were brothers. Her ancestor had married an Indian woman of the Delaware tribe who on the frontier at that period was known as a Princess because she was the daughter of a Chief. Despite the remoteness of the relationship she called my father "Cousin Tom" and because it pleased her he called her "Cousin Zenobia."

On the first day I ever saw her the weather was bright and the air clear and brilliant with that peculiar brilliance which comes to our country in the month of October. My father and I had risen while the frost was still on the fields of the valley and all morning we had followed the valley road stopping to talk with farmers, sometimes taking a hand at husking corn or ringing pigs or driving cattle while we talked. A little before noon we reached Ed Berry's place and he invited us to stay to dinner but my father said, "No, thanks just the same, Ed. I want to drop in on Zenobia and get down into the other valley before noon."

At the mention of Zenobia, Ed's face relaxed into that peculiar special smile which came over the faces of people when they spoke her name or thought of her. It was a smile in which humor and affection and pity and patronage were all blended, the kind of a smile people have for a beguiling child. Yet it was more than that—an indescribable smile, reserved for Zenobia alone by the people of the county.

Ed said, "So you're going up Ferguson way?" And there was something in his voice that even as a child I recognized as special and different. It was as if he had said, "So you're going out of this world for a time?"

Then he added, "Give Zenobia my best. Tell her we'll be up to get her corn out before Thanksgiving."

It was then the middle of October with Thanksgiving more than a month away. It was odd that Ed didn't count on seeing her in the meanwhile when he lived only a couple of miles away.

We said good-bye and my father spoke to the horses and turned from Ed's lane to the old township road which led from the valley through the forest "up Ferguson way."

Even at that time the road really led nowhere except to Zenobia's place. It was an awful road, full of holes with ridges of red sandstone cropping out of the dark soil here and there. A little way from Ed's farm the road led into the forest up and up winding its way through the thickly growing trees. It was in the days before caterpillar tractors existed and the country was so wild and rough that even if one cut the trees, there was no practical way of getting them out and so much of the forest was virgin, the same forest which had existed there since glacial times. The oaks and beeches and maples rose straight up like Greek columns to a height of a hundred feet or more and underneath them grew a jungle of dogwood and iron wood and wild grapes and ferns and snakeroot. Along the sides of the steep rough road springs gushed out of the sandstone among clusters of maidenhair fern. There was a peculiar almost tropical luxuriance about the forest bordering the road that led "up Ferguson way" and there still is today.

For nearly half-an-hour the horses struggled up through the tunnel of trees and vines and then we came suddenly into the open in a high pasture with a broken gate. The blue grass was still green with the autumn rains and all along the fence rows the sassafras and sumach were flaunting their brilliant autumn foliage against the bright blue October sky. The road had become little more than a trail.

We drove on and presently we came out upon the bald top of a very high hill. It was as if we had reached the top of the world. Above us there was nothing but the clear October sky and below lay valley after valley, big and small, all bordered and intersected by forests of beech and oak and maple which had turned red and gold and purple. Far below in the checkerboard of the valley lay golden squares of shocked corn bordered by other squares green with the brilliant emerald green of winter rye and wheat. In the distance the whole faded imperceptibly into the blue autumn mist of infinity.

My father pulled up the horses and said, "Take a good look, son. You'll never see anything more beautiful than that." It was a bold statement for a man who had seen so little of the world, but nearly forty years later his son who by that time had seen most of the world, knew that he had been right.

We sat there for a long time and presently my father slapped the horses with the reins and without a word drove on. Even then I guessed that he had come all the way up over the awful rough road as much to see the view as he had to call on Zenobia Ferguson. We started downhill again along the wild road and

as we rounded a clump of flaming sumach we came full upon
a pair of woodchucks and an extraordinary thing happened.
They did not scamper off in their heavy, alarmed fashion.
They merely sat up on their hind legs like two plump little old
people and stared at us. One of them chatted a little as if
scolding us. But although we passed not ten feet away from
them they did not stir but only turned their heads to follow
us out of sight.

I said to my father, "Why don't they run away?" But the
only answer I got was, "I don't know. Maybe they don't see
people up here very often and aren't afraid of them."

Then the road curved and we came in sight of a cottage set
against the hillside below the crest of the high bald hill. It was
small and, never having been painted, was the earthy silver
gray shade of wood weathered for many years. It seemed to
grow out of the hillside and the vines which climbed over
the little porch heightened the illusion. Enclosing the little
garden was a rather bedraggled picket fence overgrown with
vines and before the door stood the inevitable pair of tall Norway spruce that stand before every old farmhouse in our part
of the country. At the sound of our approach a white yearling
colt ran over to the fence to whinny at sight of the team, and
three big dogs, one a very old hound dog and two others that
were just farm dogs came running and barking. Then as we
pulled up to the hitching rail a strange figure opened the door
and came down the path toward us.

At first I thought it was a man for it wore a man's clothes—
blue denim pants and a man's checked shirt open at the throat.
The figure was slim like a man's and very erect, but the face
was too feminine for a man's face and the black hair drawn
into a knot at the back of the head killed the illusion.

My father said, "Hello, Cousin Zenobia. We've come to pay
you a visit." And she said, "You're surely welcome, Cousin
Tom. Hitch the horses and come in." Then as I climbed down
from the high buggy she laid her hand on my head and said,
"Is this your boy?" And my father answered, "Yes, this is the
middle one."

"I don't recall ever having seen him before," said Zenobia.
Then she held my head between her hands and looked at me

for a long time, and at last she said, releasing me, "Yes. He'll do. He has the right kind of eye." To my father she said, "You know, you can tell people and animals by their eyes, Tom."

I hadn't the faintest idea what she meant. I only knew that I had had my first and only experience with hypnotism. Long after she turned away from me, even though I was looking up into brilliant October sunlight I saw nothing but the eyes of Zenobia Ferguson. They were black Indian eyes, pupilless and opaque and in them there was a fierce intensity, not that of madness, as I understood later on, but the intensity of someone who sees beyond present things into a world beyond.

I know now that I was puzzled too by her sexlessness—that she seemed a very handsome, fierce creature who was not quite like any man or any woman I had ever seen. She was at least sixty at the time, yet she had the figure of a boy and her hair was still quite black. I suppose this, like her eyes, was a heritage from the remote Delaware chieftain's daughter.

The dogs gathered round us sniffing and wagging their tails and the white colt came away from the fence and rubbed its muzzle against my head. I was small and a big colt that behaved like a dog must have startled me for Zenobia said, "Don't worry. He won't do you any harm. He's just playing." Then she gave him a push and said, "Run along, Willie."

Willie ran away and Zenobia said, "Sure, you're staying for dinner, Cousin Tom."

My father protested but it did no good. Zenobia said, "You come in, Tom, and talk to me while I get up something. The boy can play around outside."

They went inside the cottage and I wandered off into the jungle of a garden which surrounded the house. Looking back now that garden seemed to one small boy as romantic, as full of adventure as any jungle in Sumatra. In October few flowers remained save wild asters but the whole place was a ragged mass of iris and old-fashioned rose bushes, grapevines and fruit trees. I helped myself to great bunches of purple grapes and ate them as I wandered about the bushes. The three dogs followed me and Willie the colt, and presently I lost all uneasiness of them. They became suddenly old friends and when the white colt nibbled at my hair I only laughed, with that curious satisfaction which a boy knows in his relationship to a pet raccoon or puppy.

Among the ragged lilac bushes I came upon an old spring house where the water gushed out of red sandstone outcrop into a great stone trough. It was cold, clear water and for a long time I held the grapes beneath the stream for they tasted better when they were chilled. Behind the spring house stood the old log house built there beside the spring by Zenobia's grandfather in Indian times. It was a tiny cabin not more than fifteen by twenty feet in size made of hand-hewn logs with mud plastered between them. I went inside and saw that the old house was now the home of the white colt Willie and the dogs. Behind the cabin I came suddenly on a Jersey cow with a new-born calf that was like a young doe. At sight of me the cow showed no alarm but only stared at me out of her great sloe-eyes while she licked the calf. I went up to the calf and rubbed its brown nose and still the cow showed no uneasiness.

These were the things which I saw with my eyes but while I wandered about something else was happening to me; something which I did not fully understand then save as a sense of childish ecstasy. I think it began when we emerged from the rough road tunneled through the woods to that high plateau under the brilliant October sky. I know now that it was like coming out of one world into another in which the senses were heightened and sharpened. I seemed to belong here very near to the two woodchucks who regarded us so humorously without fear, near suddenly to the old dogs and Willie the colt.

In that jungle of old lilacs and rose bushes the birds came very close. A robin sat on a lilac bough not three feet from me and watched while I ate the grapes. A squirrel sat without fear on the eaves of the old log house and chattered and made faces at me. And the sight of all these things made the heart of that small boy sing, I think because all these living things seemed so near and so without strangeness or fear. It was as if this little world existing high against the blue October sky were a small paradise, a little world that was what all the great world should be.

I was playing on the edge of the little duck pond below the spring house, rapturously happy, when I heard Zenobia's voice calling me. It was a deep pleasant voice with a curious bell quality. Ed Berry said he could sometimes hear her calling home the Jersey cow from down below in the valley more than two miles away. It wasn't that her voice was loud but it had a clear quality which, when the wind was right and the evening clear, could be heard a long way off. All the neighbors down in the valley knew Zenobia's voice. It belonged in that wild, pretty, tangled spot.

．　．　．　．　．

There were no screens on the doors or windows and although there were, at that time of the year, only a few sleepy flies to annoy us, Zenobia kept a small branch of lilac in her hand which she waved over the table from time to time. Then I noticed her hands for the first time—big and work-hardened but long and beautiful in shape. She wore a lot of rings on them—old-fashioned cameos and amethysts in heavy gold settings. I think she had put them on in honor of the occasion just as she had put on in place of the man's clothes a complicated and elaborate dress of some purple stuff.

It changed the whole character of her appearance for it made her into a great lady—I think really the first great lady I had ever seen. The rather bold Indian features seemed softened and no longer savage but noble and splendid. She was decidedly not a pretty woman; that was too mild and milksoppy a word. She was decidedly handsome. And she had something which I did not understand then, being a small boy, although I was aware of it. As I grew older I came to know what it was, something which a woman does not acquire. She must be born with it. It has a great deal to do with her figure and a great deal with her spirit. Here on this lonely farm against the sky was a woman who had both distinction and what the French call chic.

The dinner was good. There was squash and beans and cabbage and cheese and milk and jam made of wild grapes and honey and homemade bread and butter cold and fresh out of the icy water of the old spring house. Only one thing puzzled me. There wasn't any meat and when Zenobia went into the kitchen to bring in the frosted pawpaws she had for a desert, I said to my father, "Why isn't there any meat?"

He looked at me quickly and said, "You mustn't speak about that. Zenobia never kills anything."

She came quickly into the room and that day I heard no more of the story. I did not hear it until long afterward, perhaps because my father thought I was too young.

When lunch was over, Zenobia said briskly, "The boy ought to have his nap, Cousin Tom, and I'd not be surprised if you'd like one too."

We had eaten a great deal and my father was sleepy. I said, "I don't want to take a nap. I want to go out and play." What I really wanted was to re-enter that enchanted world where there were no annoying grown-ups and all the animals and birds were companions. I had never before been any place like that strange wild thicket of old-fashioned flowers and shrubs.

They didn't argue with me. My father said he'd like a nap and disappeared into the parlor to lie down on the sofa. Zenobia began clearing away the dishes and I went back to the pond below the spring house.

I began digging in the mud while the ducks swam in close to watch me, turning their heads on one side in duck fashion to satisfy their curiosity. They chattered a great deal among themselves. The cow came down to the pond to drink, the new calf teetering on its long legs, moving forward in jerky sudden movements. I stopped digging to watch and suddenly the calf became my brother, a small creature for whom I felt a sudden intense love, quite different from the sort of love I felt for any person, even my own parents or my brothers or sisters. It was as if we were both a part of something which other people did not understand, a whole world apart in which there were sounds which no human could understand. I knew suddenly what the ducks were quacking about and understood the look in the great brown eyes of the Jersey cow. The squirrel came down to the edge of the pond and did a curious thing. He dipped both his tiny paws into the water and then put them into his mouth and cleaned them with his tiny pink tongue.

And while I was watching him I felt that someone or something was watching me. The sensation became so intense that I turned and so discovered Zenobia standing near the spring house among the willows, in the old-fashioned purple dress. She was smiling at me and suddenly I had for her the same feeling of fathomless understanding I had experienced for the ducks, the cow and the squirrels. For a long time we stared at each other and then she said, "That one over there—the squirrel. That's John. He's an impudent bad character but very comical."

Then softly she said, "John . . . John! Come here, you rascal!"

The squirrel sat up, cocked his head, and then came round the end of the pond, passed very close to me and scampered up the purple dress to Zenobia's shoulder where he sat up again, chattering, his tail curled up over his back.

She looked down at me and said, "You see what they're like. We can talk to each other." She turned her head a little way and said, "How about it, John? Can't we?" The squirrel made a chattering noise and Zenobia said, "He's asking who you are and what you're doing here." Then to the squirrel she said, "It's all right. He knows what we know. He may forget it some day but in the end, it will come back to him. He's one of those that is teched like us." The squirrel turned toward me exactly as if he understood what she was saying. He remained quite still for a time as if studying me, and then suddenly he began to chatter again and scampered down the purple dress across the path and up on to the roof of the old cabin, swearing angrily.

Then I saw what had happened. My father had wakened and was now coming toward us out of the tangle of bushes. Zenobia said softly, "It's no good now. He's spoiled it."

We bade Zenobia good-bye, hitched up the horses and drove off, leaving her standing at the gate in the purple dress with all the rings on her fingers. We drove up the rise of the bald hill and down the other side through the dark tunnel through the forest out into the world again. On Ed Berry's place we passed two hunters, their bags heavy with slain rabbits.

My father said, "They won't go up to Zenobia's place."

"Why?" I asked.

He chuckled. "Because she'd get out her own shotgun and drive 'em off. They all know about her. Once she did kill a man. They all know about it."

We drove for a time in silence and then I asked, "Dad. What does 'teched' mean?"

He looked at me quizzically, "It usually means somebody's a little crazy. Why did you want to know?"

"Because Cousin Zenobia told the squirrel it was all right, I was 'teched' like her."

My father chuckled, "Sometimes I think maybe she's right."

I punched him on the arm and he added, "I wouldn't let it worry you. Most people think Zenobia is 'teched' but I think she's a mighty smart woman." And then he sighed. Why, I did not know then. I only suspected there was something he envied Zenobia.

. . . . . .

I don't know when exactly I heard the beginnings of Zenobia's story. Very likely I never heard it all in one piece, but in fragments, absorbing it and fitting it together in my own growing mind as children absorb folk-tales and the stories of their countryside. Zenobia was very definitely a part of the county, a part of its life and its history. As I grew older I used to see her sometimes on the streets of the town, for she left the Ferguson place about once a month to make the ten-mile trip as best she could, hitch-hiking her way on wagons and in buggies to buy spices and coffee and things she could not raise with her own hands on that high bald hill. Sometimes she bought a ribbon or two and when the first five and ten cent store came to the town, Zenobia was in heaven. She bought all the cheap jewelry she could afford out of the meager income left from her peach orchard and grapes and apples after the taxes were paid.

No one in the town took any special notice of her but upon strangers the sight of her, wandering along Main street in her bizarre clothes with a basket filled with spices and trinkets over one arm, was startling. For these monthly trips into town she dressed with the greatest care and always she wore the same dress and hat and lace mitts.

The dress, I think, must have been one she made for her marriage. The material was yellow taffeta and the design included many ruffles and pleats. It had a train and the faint suggestion of a bustle. On her head she wore a big black picture hat covered with whatever flowers were in bloom at the moment in the woods and fence rows of her high pastures. When winter came she adorned the hat with heads of wheat and the immortelles which grew in her garden. All these she sewed on fresh each time she made the expedition to town. The effect, you might think, was bizarre and sloppy but this was not so. If you saw her in the early morning before the flowers had wilted, the effect had the same indefinable chic which touched her whole appearance. Sometimes she used bunches of brilliant blue bachelor's-buttons, sometimes two or three large sun flowers, occasionally a cluster or two of scarlet geraniums. She would have made a great milliner. I think in New York or Paris she would have made a fortune.

On her fingers she wore innumerable cheap rings and over these she always wore black lace mitts. The yellow taffeta dress had a train which she rarely troubled to pick up and as the years passed, the dust and moisture created a band of brown at the bottom of the slowly decaying material which made up the skirt. You would think that she had a mad appearance but neither was this true. The upright dignity of her carriage, the strength of the hawk-nosed face, the intelligence of the opaque black eyes gave her both distinction and presence.

To the townspeople who knew her story there was nothing wild or strange about her. And when strangers who had been startled by her appearance, heard her story, she lost her strangeness for them.

Zenobia was born in the cottage where I first saw her just after her parents had moved out of the old log house which later became the barn. When she was four years old her mother died and from then on she lived with her father in that cottage on the high hill close to the sky with its wide view of three counties. In those days the farm was even more remote than at the time I first knew it. In winter it became isolated altogether by snow and mud which made the first crude roads impassable. And so she did not go to school. Her father taught her everything she knew and that was a good deal for her father, although an eccentric man, had an education far beyond that of the neighboring farmers, and he passed it on to her along with all the old books I saw in the cottage. It was a lonely life and she grew up nearer to the birds and wild things than to the people who lived in the valley below.

And then one day when cholera swept through all the county, her father ate a fresh peach on a visit to the county seat and returned home and died before Zenobia had time to go down to the valley for a doctor. She was seventeen when he died, a tall, straight, self-reliant girl with blue black hair and black eyes. The neighbors helped her bury her father and then proposed that she come down to the valley and teach school, for she had a better education than any of them. They proposed that she live with them in turn. They were kindly people and would have welcomed her and all of them, none too well educated, wanted their children to have the benefit of Zenobia's knowledge.

But Zenobia would not leave the farm high on the hill against the sky. Perhaps it was the magnificence of the view or her own nearness to nature and all wild things which held her there. No one ever knew, for she never told them. She only said that she "had to look after Pa's farm." No amount of money or entreaty had any effect.

"It's my land now," she said stubbornly. "I can't leave it after Pa worked so hard to get it cleared." It is possible that even then there was in her Indian blood and in her upbringing something which made her wild and shy of towns and places where people gathered.

But the old men who knew her as a girl and talked about her and as they grew older told her story over and over again, said there was never anything queer about her as a young girl. She was very handsome, they said, and smart as the crack of a whip. And she could dance wildly and well for after she fell in love with Aaron she sometimes came down from the farm to the Square Dances held in the valley. The old men all said that they would have married Zenobia gladly and that they envied Aaron his luck: "A handsomer or a smarter woman there never was in all the county!"

When her father died, the neighbors volunteered to help her with the farm, working for nothing or for a share of the wheat and corn because they all felt friendly toward her and had a curious awe for "education." That is how Aaron came to meet Zenobia.

He was the son of the miller who had the big mill on Honey Creek. The old men who knew him said Aaron was the strongest man in the county. He stood six feet four and was broad and muscular and when he first went up to the farm on the hill against the sky to help with the harvest, he was a year older than Zenobia. He had blond hair and blue eyes and a straight nose. The old daguerreotype which they found after Zenobia was dead shows him sitting up very straight with hands on both knees staring straight into the picture-taking machine. But for all the woodenness of the pose there is in the faded gold-framed picture a twinkle in the eye and a cockiness in the carriage of the head. It is clear that he must have been, as the old men put it, "quite a fellow with the girls." The old men said he liked to joke and had a laugh you could hear half a mile away. His heartiness, his cockiness, were probably just what a wild, shy girl like Zenobia needed and was looking for. Anyway they said that she changed mightily after she fell in love with Aaron and that she came down from the hill farm to go to dances and parties and for a year or more was the belle of the county.

I don't know how they met—perhaps when he came in to the dinner she had cooked for the harvest hands or perhaps they met in the old spring house when he came there for a drink of the cold water that poured into the great trough of pink sandstone. Anyway it happened a very long time ago, well on toward a hundred years. And Zenobia is not really dead yet, or Aaron either for even today young people born after she has been dead have heard their story and know their names.

It was one of those passionate love affairs watched by the whole world around them. Never, the old men said, had two young people ever been more in love. They said that Aaron would sometimes sit out a square dance just for the pleasure of watching Zenobia as she danced with a special wild grace that none of the other girls displayed. The Indian in her gave her not only a gypsy look but a gypsy wildness.

And when the dance or sociable was over Aaron and Zenobia would go back together on horseback up that long tunnel through the woods until they came out on the high bald hill. Sometimes there was glistening snow on the ground and sometimes the night was soft yet brilliant with stars and the air scented with the perfume of wild flowers or the musty smell of the wild grapes which hung down over the road.

Sometimes, the old men said, it was whispered that Aaron did not return to the valley the same night. But the odd thing was that in so respectable a world as the valley the whispers caused so little disapproval and resentment. I think it must have been because even those people understood that there was something special about Zenobia. It was as if she belonged to another world with her strange wild, lonely life. I do not know—perhaps no one ever knew—whether Zenobia and Aaron were lovers but it seems unlikely that they were not. He was a handsome, wild young man and she lived alone without restraint high on her lonely hill.

As one of the old men called Mr. Charles said to my father, "I hope they were lovers. They should have been. It was wrong and bitter cruel if they were not."

They would have married as they planned to do but for the fact that Aaron had a plan. He meant to go out to the West for he wanted to get ahead in the world and he wanted to be established before they married, and so one day he left filled with the idea that he would find a gold mine there and then come back and marry Zenobia and take her with him back to the West.

When he went away Zenobia returned to her old solitary way of living. She never went down into the valley to the dances and sociables, but remained on the hill girded by forest.

While Aaron was away dark things began to happen in the

county which have since become legendary. There appeared
from nowhere a band of highwaymen and robbers. In those
days farms were far apart. There were no telephones and
horses were the only means of transportation. The robbers
were three in number, one tall and two short men. They
dressed in dark clothes and never were seen save in the darkness and with their faces covered. They would appear on a
lonely road through the woods or on a covered bridge to stop
a family or perhaps a lone traveler and rob them. After a little
while it became evident that they were not a band of outsiders
for they remained there in the county and it was clear that
they knew who were the rich and the poor. They knew, too,
many other things like the Christian names of their victims.

After a time the terror grew so great that no one ventured
out on the road at night and then it was that the highwaymen
took to descending on lonely farmhouses to break their way
in and rob and terrorize the inmates. The sheriff organized
special posses to patrol the roads and made up search parties
but the efforts of the posses came to nothing and after a time
it became clear that someone was informing the highwaymen
of the activities of the posse in advance, for they never appeared or robbed anyone on the nights the sheriff and his men
went out on patrol.

Of all these activities Zenobia Ferguson on her lonely farm
took no notice. People tried to persuade her to leave the place
and come down into the valley but she only said that she had
no money anyway and the farm was so remote that it was safe.
Anyway she meant to stay there until Aaron came back. It
may have been that she was not afraid or more likely that
between her and that piece of land high against the sky with
all the wild things that dwelt there with her, there was some
special bond which other people did not understand. In any
case she stayed stubbornly in the cottage, coming down only
once or twice a month dressed in her finest clothes to buy
what she needed in the village.

What she did not know or ignored was the legend that she
was rich, that she had money hidden away which her father
had left her. To many people it was the only answer to all
the books—people who had libraries must be rich—and to the

fineness of Zenobia's clothes. They didn't understand her liking for jewelry and ribbons nor the fact that even in a calico frock, she appeared better dressed and more stylish than the banker's wife in her furs and broadcloths. Simple people said, "Zenobia Ferguson has a pot of gold hidden away somewhere."

And so one night when the sheriff and his posse were not out on the roads, the highwaymen came up the tunnel through the forest up to the high farm. It was a still bright night like the nights Zenobia and Aaron had ridden up the same primitive path. Neither Zenobia nor her father had ever had a lock on the doors of the cottage and when the highwaymen entered they found Zenobia asleep. They woke her and, standing about her with handkerchiefs over their faces, told her they wanted the gold she had hidden away. Zenobia, truthfully perhaps, told them she had no money. They found her cheap jewelry— mostly cameos and garnets and a few amethysts set in silver. But that didn't satisfy them and presently they bound her and burned matches against the soles of her feet to force her to tell them where her money was hidden.

It did no good. She did not cry out and afterward in court she said there was only a few dollars in the house. She would have told them where it was, she said, but she hated cruelty and was determined not to give them even the satisfaction of those few dollars. She did not scream. She would not speak to the robbers at all and when the daylight came they went away, baffled.

A week passed before Zenobia's scorched feet were healed enough for her to hobble down into the valley to tell of the highwaymen's visit. The old man said that she always walked differently after that terrifying night. They said that was one reason why, even to the day of her death, she carried herself very straight, with a peculiar air of fierce pride.

Even after the robbery she would not leave the Ferguson place. She did have locks put on the door and she bought herself a pistol and a shotgun and a dog. Later at the trial she said, "I didn't buy the guns to protect myself but my place. I didn't want strange people wandering about all over it. It was my place and I loved it and all the animals on it. I wasn't harming anyone and no one had any right to come up there raisin' hell."

It was a crude explanation, perhaps because she hadn't the words to explain more clearly what she meant, but more likely because she did not believe people would understand how she felt even if she explained. I think it was the first time people began to understand about Zenobia—that she was different and a little "teched," that it was different "up Ferguson way" in that world against the sky. Among the Pennsylvania Dutch settlers people began to whisper that Zenobia Ferguson was a "hex."

In the meanwhile out in the West Aaron had, he wrote, found a "pardner" and was prospecting. Each week now she came down from the hill to get his letter at the post office. It wouldn't be long now, he wrote, until he'd be coming back to fetch her.

She kept all these letters. Mrs. Berry (Ed Berry's daughter-in-law) found them when they went up to bury Zenobia more than three quarters of a century later. I have them now along with Zenobia's journal. They are extraordinary letters, not too well spelled and not always grammatical, but filled with passion and tenderness and a strange, direct poetry and mysticism. In the robust, good-looking young Aaron there must have been a streak of that "fey" quality which Zenobia had all her life. In one letter he wrote, "It's fun out here. You can go all day and never see a house or a man. It ain't crowded like it's getting to be back in the valley. Out here you and I can have the world to ourselves with nothing around us but the trees and the wild flowers, the birds and the beasts. I am coming back soon. I will write you when I am coming. I want you to be there waiting for me when I come up out of the woods. I want it to be evening with the sun going down behind the hill, and we'll walk up and up to the top of the hill overlooking the three counties and then. . . ."

Sometimes he quoted passages from the Bible but they were always the wild pagan, passionate parts. I remember that among them he quoted often enough the Song of Songs, as if he felt his own ardor and words were not enough. He wrote, "How beautiful are thy feet with shoes, O Prince's daughter!

The joints of thy thighs are like jewels, the work of the hands of a cunning workman.

"Thy navel is like a round goblet which wanteth not liquor; thy belly is like an heap of wheat set about with lilies.

"Thy two breasts are like two young roes that are twins.

"Thy neck is as a tower of ivory, thine eyes like the fish-ponds in Heshbon, by the gate of Bath-rabbin; thy nose is as the tower of Lebanon which looketh down toward Damascus.

"Thine head upon thee is like Carmel, and the hair of thine head like purple; the king is held in the galleries.

"How fair and how pleasant are thou, oh love, for delights!"

They were a strange pair to be bred among the staid, straight-laced people of the valley. Out of the ashes of Aaron's old faded letters there still arises after nearly a hundred years a kind of wild and glorious passion. I think that all along until the end Zenobia knew proudly that God had somehow set her aside, that there was a richness in the strange lonely life which the other women in the county never knew.

At last Aaron wrote that he and his pardner had found a good thing and that he would be coming home soon. In the cottage Zenobia began to pack up the books of her father's library, not without sadness, for only Aaron and his love could ever have made her leave the Ferguson place.

In the county the three highwaymen were still at large. Their depredations had spread now into adjoining counties. They worked on horseback and struck now here, now there, at places far apart. The people of three or four counties began to talk of calling out the militia to guard the bridges and the lonely stretches of road.

And then one night a little after midnight Zenobia was wakened by the barking of her dog and in the darkness she heard the sound of footsteps going about the house from one door to another. As she described it at the trial, she was not frightened. She was only angry again at the invasion of her world. She got out of bed and picking up the clumsy old pistol she pointed it at the door calling out, "If you don't go away, I'll fire." For a moment she waited and then she heard the sound of a man's low laugh, and pulled the trigger.

For a long time after she had fired, she waited listening. The laugh was not repeated and there were no more sounds of any kind outside the cottage and at last she went back to bed. But she did not sleep. At the trial she said she lay awake for the rest of the night, not through fright, but because she was haunted by the sound of the laugh. It kept coming back to her, as if it were the laugh of someone she knew. She kept hearing the laugh, interrupted by the sound of the pistol's explosion, checked before she could really recognize it. Then as the sun came up she dressed and unlocked the door and looked out. There on the doorstep, lying dead face down, was Aaron.

.   .   .   .   .

It was late on the same evening before Zenobia appeared at the home of Ed Berry's grandmother. What she did during the long hours of that day alone with Aaron's body, no one ever knew or will ever know now. Ed Berry's grandmother said that Zenobia's face suddenly appeared in the doorway. The lamps were already lighted but even their rosy glow did not change the chalky whiteness of Zenobia's wild young face. The black eyes had a curious hard staring look in them.

Ed Berry's grandmother said, "Come in and sit down, Zenobia. What is it? What's gone wrong?"

Zenobia, without speaking, sat down and stared in front of her. For a long time she was silent, so still that Ed's grandmother thought she had gone mad.

Then very quietly she said, "Aaron is dead. I killed him. I didn't mean to."

Ed's grandmother brought her a glass of blackberry wine which Zenobia drank meekly. Then with the same tense quietness she told her story. She understood it now. Aaron had come home without telling her, to surprise her. She said, "I know what he meant to do. He meant to come into the house quietly and waken me, as he used to do sometimes before he went away, but while he was away after the robbers came I put a lock on the door. He didn't know about that and he went all the way round the house trying to find a way in. That was when I heard him and took up the gun. And when I called out, he laughed thinking I would know who it was . . . and I didn't . . . I didn't . . . not till afterward when everything was still and I kept hearing the laugh in the stillness and I thought 'It sounded like Aaron but it couldn't be.' That's what kept me awake till morning. I told myself, 'If it was Aaron he would call out!' "

Then she covered her face with her hands but no sound came out of her. There were no wracking sobs. She kept that same awful stillness about her. Presently she said, "Will you send one of the boys for the sheriff and a preacher and come and help me with Aaron?"

Ed's grandmother said that for the first time on that evening she saw the mad, fixed look in Zenobia's black eyes. It never again left them until the day she died.

The sheriff came and the preacher and after they had gone away a strange thing happened. Zenobia said to Ed's grandmother, "The sheriff is the leader of the robbers. He has the same eyes and the same voice and the same way of breathing. I saw his eyes above the handkerchief when they were torturing me. That man is the leader."

But no one paid much attention to her, thinking that Aaron's death had driven her crazy. But the odd thing was that Zenobia was right. A month later a woman came to the police in the county seat and betrayed the sheriff. She was the wife of one of the other highwaymen and when her husband left her for another woman, she told the whole story. Only then did it become clear why the robbers never operated on the nights the sheriff led the posse. It was one of those stories which became legends in a frontier country. And in a way it was the sheriff-robber who had really killed Aaron for if the band had not come to Zenobia's cottage to torture her, there would have been no lock on the door and no pistol and Aaron could have walked in as he had planned to do.

They buried Aaron in the old orchard there on the hill because that was what Zenobia wanted and afterwards they held a kind of trial of Zenobia. It was never more than that, for no one really believed that she had murdered Aaron with intent. She would have no lawyer to defend her but simply told her own story, very quietly, and in all the court there was not one person, even the prosecuting attorney, who did not believe her. She walked out of the court and went back, riding in Ed Berry's buggy, to the Ferguson place high above the woods close to the sky with its view of three counties, and there she lived until she died.

But from then on she no longer lived in this world at all but in a world of fancy, nearer to the trees and the water, the rain and the snow and the birds and beasts than to anyone on this earth.

She was over sixty when I first saw her on the day my father took me through the green tunnel in the woods "up Ferguson way." After that I saw her many times, sometimes on the street in the town moving along with her strange air of dignity and chic in the yellow taffeta gown, the black picture hat and the black lace mitts. Twice I saw her at the cottage "up Ferguson way" when my father covered the county electioneering, but never did I quite recapture that strang sensation of moving out of this world into another in which trees and streams had meaning and where animals were not animals, inarticulate and shy, but companions whose language one understood. Perhaps it was because as I grew older I slipped out of that childish simplicity in which I could pass so easily through the wall that separated Zenobia's strange world on that high lonely hill from the world of dull reason and what we call perhaps oddly and wrong "reality." I think Zenobia knew this for she did not appear again in the ragged, jungly garden in her fine purple dress to accept me into her world because I was "teched."

From the day Aaron died, Zenobia never killed anything, not even a fly, and she would allow no one in her world on top of the hill to kill or harm any living thing. Hunters in the county knew that she might kill a man. They remembered Aaron. And when she appeared armed with a shotgun, they did not argue with her. Once in the early morning while it was still dark she very nearly frightened to death two boys whose hound dogs had treed a raccoon on her land. She came crashing out of the underbrush in her man's clothes with a shotgun under her arm and at sight of her wild black hair and wild eyes they dropped their lantern, left the hound dogs and ran. After a little time no hunter ever went near the Ferguson place. And Zenobia and her animals were left in peace.

I saw her for the last time when I was about seventeen years old. I left the county then and did not return for twenty-five years. During all that time I went through two wars and saw most of the countries of the earth but I never wholly forgot Zenobia. I thought of her at the strangest places and times. At least three or four times I dreamed of her, seeing her always as she stood in the purple dress, with the squirrel on her shoulder by the spring pond. There was no reason for this save for that bond between us which she had recognized when she said to the squirrel that I too was "teched."

I have never been a hunter. I have never shot a rabbit or a quail or any small living thing. Although I have killed lions and tigers, panthers and leopards, I never did so with any pleasure but only out of politeness to my host. It took will-power to force myself to kill the first leopard I ever saw, spitting and snarling at me in the tall elephant grass beneath the howdah. And I felt sick the first time I shot a great tiger, for it was like destroying beauty and magnificence itself. Once I infuriated a fellow hunter when he was about to kill a superb *Gaur* in the bamboo and teakwood jungles of Mysore by crying out, "You can't kill anything as splendid as that!"

I am even an indifferent fisherman when it comes to keeping the fish. Although I love the sport my impulse is always to throw back the fish. I suppose that is what Zenobia meant by saying I was "teched." In any case, I know that on the night I killed the tiger in far-off India I dreamed of Zenobia standing by the spring in the purple dress.

When I came back to the county it was to buy land and settle there for the rest of my life. Zenobia was dead by then but the strange thing was that the only desirable piece of land was Ed Berry's farm and by then the farm beyond the woods and against the sky had become a part of Ed Berry's place. It had to be sold together and so I came into possession of the Ferguson place and many strange things which went with it.

The place, Ed Berry's widow said, hadn't changed much except that Zenobia's cottage had burned down.

"It wasn't much of a loss and it wasn't fit for anything by

the time Zenobia died. She got poorer and poorer and couldn't pay the taxes but nobody made any fuss about it. The auditor— it didn't matter whether he was a Democrat or a Republican— just let it ride along. She finally got pretty old and feeble but she wouldn't leave the place. We tried to get her to go to the County Poor Farm but she said she couldn't. She was pretty spry though and could take care of herself right up to the day she died. Some of us neighbors used to bake things and make pots of baked beans and things and take them up to her once a week. She had an old cow and she managed to get along. She always seemed happy but when she got to be very old it seemed like she didn't belong to this world at all. She wasn't much interested in what we had to say but she'd talk to the birds and animals just like they were people. I was the one that found her dead—I went up with some baked things and some fresh meat and found the door open—you know she never locked the door again after that thing happened about Aaron—and there she was lying on the bed dead; she was all dressed up in a purple dress with all her jewelry and gimcracks on and her hair neatly done just like she knew she was going to die and prepared for it. Maybe that was something she learned from the birds and animals. It was a funny thing . . . the room was filled with birds of all kinds. They flew out the door when I came in.

"No," the widow continued, "the place ain't much changed except the house is gone. Some tramps must have stopped there for the night and set fire to it. It looks kind of ragged and the old orchard don't amount to much any more. We just use the whole place to pasture cattle. A car can't get up the road any more—it's so worn out. You got to go on foot or on horseback."

"Where did you bury her?" I asked.

"Right there on the place in the orchard beside Aaron. It was kind of against the rules but nobody made any objection. The county had got used to her. I guess most people were kind of proud of her. It was Ed's idea to bury her up there. He said she wouldn't rest quiet anywhere else." She sighed. "Ed always had good ideas like that."

.　　.　　.　　.　　.　　.

It was a bright morning in early May when I went "up Ferguson way" again for the first time in more than twenty-five years. I went on Tex, a big Kentucky mare, because, as Ed's widow said, it wasn't possible any more to get through the lane in a car or even a horse and buggy.

The woods on either side of the lane was little changed save that the wild grape vines grew in a thick tangle almost closing up the road here and there. The white blossoms of the blood-root were nearly gone, but the banks on either side of the lane were bright with hepaticas and yellow violets and spotted yellow Canadian lilies and trillium. Among them the ferns thrust up their first tender green fronds and now and again in the openings of the tangled grape vines I caught glimpses of splashes of white made by the dogwood beneath the tender green and pink of the new foliage on the oaks and maples and beech trees. The clouds of white blossoms seemed to give off light and the whole woods was alive with the sound of wild birds. The rich growth gave the whole forest that air of tropical luxuriance which marks the woods of glacial Ohio.

I thought, "Maybe there is something special about this place. Maybe because of Zenobia things grew more luxuriantly here." And then I put aside the idea as nonsense.

At the top of the lane I came suddenly out of the woods again on to that high open hill against the bright warm sky of early May and as I climbed up, the view of the three counties lay spread out before me once again, only this time the colors were not the bold reds and yellows and purples of October but soft shades of green with the ponds and lakes and deep stretches of Honey Creek reflecting the blue of the sky above.

I reached the top of the hill where the Berry cattle were still grazing and then down below me in the protected hollow by the big spring I saw what remained of the Ferguson place.

The house was gone and only a hollow, grown over with honeysuckle, remained where the cellar had been, but the old log house where Zenobia had kept the cow and the dogs and the white horse was still standing. The tangled garden had spread out, seeding itself across the slope. The two ancient Norway spruces still stood by the gate of the broken fence.

One side of their trunks had been scarred by the heat of the fire that consumed the cottage but the trunks were healed again. Up one of them climbed a trumpet vine.

I tied the mare to the old hitching post and went through the gate. All the earth was yellow with daffodils and above them bloomed the huge old purple and white lilacs. The biggest Japonica I have ever seen seemed like a bush of flame. The spring house was still there, completely hidden beneath the overgrowth of vines and shrubbery, and outside it the little spring pond. One whole bank was covered by the little cool ice-green old-fashioned flowers of the Star of Bethlehem.

I drank out of my hands of the cold water gushing out of the rock and lay down on the bank near the pond, experiencing a strange feeling of happiness and peace. It was not only good to be alive, it was good to be alive in this particular spot on the surface of the earth. And slowly I began to feel again that sensation I had known as a small boy, of coming up out of the valley into another strange world that somehow existed on a different plane from all other human life. I did not fall asleep yet the sensation was that of being suspended between sleep and consciousness when everything becomes amazingly clear and one's senses are awake to things which at other times go unseen and un-recorded. I was very near again to the trees and the flowers, to the rock, to the water that gushed from it. It was almost as if I could understand what the birds were saying as they chirped and sang in the ruins of the old garden.

Then suddenly I felt that I was being watched by someone or something, exactly as I had felt on that October day as a small boy when Zenobia appeared suddenly among the bushes beside the spring house in the purple dress. I turned and found myself saying "Zenobia." It was the strangest sensation I have ever experienced, of reaching into another world, of being almost at the brink of understanding. At the same moment I heard Tex, the mare, neighing exactly as a horse calls to another horse. She did it twice and then three times. I thought, having somehow lost myself in time and space, "She has seen Zenobia's old white horse." And then, expecting fully to see

Zenobia in the purple dress, I turned a little further. But in the spot where she had stood with the squirrel on her shoulder, saying, "He's teched like us" there was only a red fox sitting perfectly quietly, his big bushy tail curled about his feet. For a moment we both stayed there, very still, watching each other. Then after a little time he yawned, stood up and with a final look over his shoulder at me, he trotted off through the daffodils under the shrubbery. The mare called again twice and then everything was still but for the noisy chirping of the birds.

I don't know how long I stayed there, perfectly happy and still as if I had become a part of infinity, but when I wakened the sun was already down behind the top of the hill. I had no consciousness of having dreamed yet I was aware that something had happened to me, some experience which I could not quite recapture, some experience that was rich and satisfying.

I thought, "I must get home for supper." And after a final drink at the spring I turned past the hole that had once been the cellar and came upon the great flat rock which had been Zenobia's doorstep. It was charred and chipped by the fire that had destroyed the cottage but that made no difference to me. I saw the cottage again as it had been with the little porch covered with trumpet vine and suddenly I thought, "Here is where she must have found Aaron, lying face down dead as the sun came up." And for the first time I knew the full horror and tragedy of what happened there. Until then it had only been part of a story. Now, suddenly, I *knew* it, almost as if I had been Zenobia, opening the door to look out into the garden.

Tex had broken loose while I slept and was up near the top of the hill feeding on the fresh new blue grass. I caught her without difficulty and we set off down the ruined lane through the woods back again into the world. As we entered the green tunnel she neighed twice again and turned her head to look behind us. I too turned, believing that I would see Zenobia's old white horse trotting up to follow us. But there was nothing there in the green-hued twilight.

. . . . . .

I went away to the East and two months passed before I again went "up Ferguson way." This time I went on foot accompanied by Rex, Prince and Regina. They are big Boxer dogs and when I am at home they go everywhere I go and sleep at night in the same room with me. They do not go away from the house unless I go with them. They are as much my friends and companions as any living person, and so it never occurred to me that I should never take them "up Ferguson way" because that was a wild world in which they did not belong.

It was midsummer and the woods were full of damp heat, of ferns, of lush growth and dancing deer-flies. The climb up the long ruined lane left me breathless and dripping but at the top where one came out into Zenobia's high world, there was a breeze and the air was fresh although the whole panorama of the three counties lay blurred and dancing in a haze of midsummer heat. Again I had that same sensation of entering another world.

We followed the lane over the crest of the hill and as it descended the other side, I saw ahead of me on the edge of the winding lane a woodchuck, descendant no doubt of the pair I had seen years before at the same spot while Zenobia was still alive. He sat up very straight watching me and the dogs. He did not scamper away as I came nearer and then I thought, "Let the dogs give him a run. It'll be fun for them and they'll never catch him." He sat up there on the edge of the lane not twenty-five feet from the safety of his burrow. They couldn't possibly catch him before he ducked out of sight.

Boxers are not hunting dogs. They are essentially watch dogs. Their noses are not good and their eyesight is scarcely better. They hear everything even at a great distance but they did not *hear* the woodchuck. They were running about, their blunt noses to the ground, scarcely a dozen yards from him.

Suddenly I said, "Look!" and the three of them raised their heads and saw the woodchuck. From three sides they ran for him but still his way of escape was open. He was safe.

But a strange thing happened—something I have never seen before or since. He did not run. He only sat there, upright, chattering a little, full of trust, as if he had no fear of anything. In a second the three dogs had him and in a second it was all over and suddenly I was sick.

I had done an awful thing. I had betrayed Zenobia and the squirrel. I had violated all that world of which I had been permitted to be a part . . . a world into which I could enter because I was "teched." Even today, three years afterward, I feel shame and disgust over what I did without thought on a shallow impulse. The sight of the comic woodchuck sitting there full of trust and without fear will always be with me. I had done a dreadful thing.

I did not even go on to the garden and the spring house although the heat and climb had given me a terrific thirst. Instead I turned back, leaving the dead and mangled woodchuck for the buzzards, called the dogs and set off again down the hill.

But I never again took the dogs when I went "up Ferguson way."

. . . . .

The next morning George, the postman, brought me a heavy package. It came from Abilene, Washington, from Ed Berry's daughter-in-law. Inside it was a letter from her. It said simply that she was sending me some old letters and a journal which she had found in the cottage after Zenobia died. Now that I owned the place and was vaguely Zenobia's only relative she thought that I should have them.

The letters were Aaron's love letters written while he was in the West, the ink on them long since yellow and faded on the rotting paper. As I have told you, they were passionate letters, pagan and wild, strange letters to have been written by a young fellow born and raised in the straight-laced atmosphere of the valley. It was clear that he and Zenobia knew a strange satisfaction and glory that was very near to the woods and birds and streams and remote from the everyday lives of the valley people. In these letters there was the feeling of Pan, of Dionysus, of Diana of Ephesus.

Of the Journal, Ed Berry's daughter-in-law wrote, "I can't make out what is in it. A lot of it sounds like nonsense and none of it makes much sense. I thought that, being a literary man, you might understand it."

The Journal took a little reading and a great deal of understanding, but after a while it became clear. The names Zenobia used were not the names of people but of animals. The conversations were not conversations with people but with the birds and the beasts of the fields and the forests. There were even recorded conversations which must have taken place with spirits—the spirits of trees, of stones, of waterfalls. There on the high lonely hill in the midst of the forest, Zenobia had lived in a world peopled by friends which none of the others of us could ever know or understand, unless you were, like Zenobia and the squirrel, a little "teched."

There is only one more incident to tell. I have a daughter, now eleven years old, who has grown up largely in the valley. She is tall and like Zenobia, very straight. But unlike Zenobia she has blonde hair and very clear blue eyes. She has a horse and caracul sheep and rabbits and pigeons and she knows all there is to know about animals and farming and the earth, for she has a feeling for these things and without that feeling, no one can ever understand about animals or how things grow. A friend once said, "She is a disconcerting child. When she looks at you out of those clear blue eyes you know that she knows things you don't know and never will know." It is what Zenobia undoubtedly would have recognized as a "teched" look.

She has a friend called Mary, unlike her as possible. Mary is small, and plump, and merry, and gossipy, but they understand each other and a lot of things some of us older people do not understand. When they were eight, they took to going off for the day, sometimes taking sandwiches with them. Where they went was a secret. Sometimes they begged sandwiches from the kitchen and stayed away all day. There were many places to go—the woods, the creek, the wild tangled swamp called in the family "The Jungle." There were caves and waterfalls. Neither of them had any fear of wild things, even of snakes.

One evening they did not return until after dark. I went out to find them and after searching for an hour, returned home to find that they were already in the kitchen having a late supper.

I said, "Where were you?"

Sally wouldn't say anything but her friend Mary said, "We stayed to see the raccoons come out. They don't come out until after dark."

"Did you see them?"

I saw Sally give Mary a black fierce look to enforce silence but Mary was already talking, "Yes, we saw a mother raccoon and a whole family. They came to the spring and the mother raccoon washed everything she gave the babies to eat before she gave it to them."

"If it was dark how did you see them?"

"We saw them all right," said Sally stubbornly.

"Weren't you scared coming home after dark?" I asked.

And with scorn, Sally asked, "What is there to be scared of?"

A little later when I was alone with my daughter, I said firmly, "I must know where you go. You must say where you're going. It's a big place and I must know where I should go to look for you."

"We didn't go any place."

"That's a silly answer. I must know or I'll have to forbid you to go out alone."

The clear blue eyes were filled suddenly with anger and resentment, "We can't do anything around here without everybody butting in."

"Why can't you tell me where you go?"

"Because it's a secret."

"Why is it a secret?"

"Because it is. . . . Because if you knew, you'd spoil it for us."

I knew it was no use going any further. There was behind the blue eyes a determination which was more than a childish whim. I don't know why it never occurred to me what lay behind it. I should have known.

After that Sally was forbidden to go off for the day unless I knew where she was going. For three days she stayed around the house, miserable, sullen and resentful, and on the fourth day she came to me and said, "I'll tell you where I go if you'll promise not to tell anybody else."

"I can keep a secret. I promise. Where do you go?"

She looked away from me and was silent for a moment. Then she said, "Up Ferguson way."

I didn't answer for a moment because the phrase seemed so startling. I hadn't heard it since I was a boy. She could never have heard it, for by now all the old people who had ever talked about "up Ferguson way," were dead . . . all, I thought, but Zenobia. She went on living. I said, "Why do you call it that? Where did you hear it called that?"

"I never heard anybody call it that. We just made it up. It was a secret." She looked at me strangely for a long time. Then she said, "Do you call it that too?"

"Yes. That's what they used to call it when I was a child."

Then she dismissed me, "Can I go now? Mary and I haven't been there for a long time."

I wanted to ask her what she found there and why the place so fascinated her but I knew I wouldn't get any answer. I had never told anyone what I had found there. Why should she? She'd think as I had always thought that to talk about it, to tell anyone would spoil everything. I had so nearly spoiled it the time I thoughtlessly took the dogs with me.

I did not ask her. I only said, "Yes, I like it up there too."

She glanced at me quickly out of the clear blue eyes and as our glances met I knew that she too was "teched" like Zenobia and Aaron, the squirrel and me. And I knew that she suddenly understood about me. She said, "I'm glad you put up those 'no hunting' signs." And in the blue eyes there was a sudden glint such as I had once seen in Zenobia's eyes and I knew that she, like Zenobia, would run any hunter off the Ferguson place with a shotgun. I knew too that Zenobia wasn't really dead at all, that she was still there and Aaron with her perhaps now, in the trees and in the spring, in the animals and in the waterfall, of the earth itself far more than she would ever be in the grave in the orchard where she lay beside Aaron. She was still alive in my consciousness and in the eyes of my daughter with that kind of immortality which she understood perhaps better than any of us. For me she is always there on that high hill against the sky when the rain falls there, or the wind blows, or the evenings are breathless and still high up above the three counties. It is the kind of immortality I should like to know, to find my place forever in God's scheme of life and sky and sea and earth.

Sometimes I hear again Zenobia's voice saying to the squirrel, "He knows what we know. He may forget it some day but in the end it will come back to him." It may be that we have to lose that knowledge and understanding which children have and then perhaps it comes back to us through living experience and wisdom. Maybe that is what Zenobia meant.

THOU SHALT NOT COVET[1]

SAINT-FIRMIN IS A REMOTE SWISS VILLAGE THAT LIES JUST beneath the Pic du Diable. It was never a fashionable winter resort with the Americans, English, or French—not a place like Gstaad or Saint-Moritz or Davos or Villiers. It was frequented almost entirely by Germans or by expert skiers who knew that it had some of the finest ski slopes in the world and that the village was the home of a whole tribe called Zupper who had produced from among its members a dozen of the finest skiers in the world.

The village lay sprawled across a kind of saddle between two mountains, the Pic du Diable and Mont Noir, and there were long, sweeping, sometimes savage runs from the peaks of both mountains down into the town itself. One ended near the railroad station, another just at the door of the Kulm Hotel, which had once been a huge sanitarium for sufferers from tuberculosis, and a third came to an abrupt stop just outside the Kurhaus. Swooping down these long runs one had the feeling of surveying the whole of the world, a white world, sometimes glittering in sunlight with blue shadows along the glaciers and the projecting cliffs, sometimes clouded and veiled in falling snow and mist, sometimes warm and damp, when the warm foehn blew up from Italy, with the thunderous sound of avalanches everywhere in the still air.

You had to climb for your skiing. There were no ski lifts and no funiculars. Perhaps that was why it was never frequented by the fashionable international world. Also it was difficult of access. One went to Zurich and changed trains twice, climbing up and up along frozen chasms and waterfalls and winter glaciers, through mist and snow, to arrive at the little old-fashioned station covered with tiny gables ornamented with jigsaw ornaments and carving. On the long journey up, especially if you left Coire at dusk and started as the day faded

[1] Copyright, 1943, by Armin L. Robinson.

into darkness, you had a terrifying sense of having died, of making a journey into another world. And when you wakened the following morning and looked out of your window into a white and glittering creation, the sense of having gone overnight into another world still persisted. The little village with its scattered houses, its two hotels, the gay Beau-Site and the vast Kulm, the boardinghouses and the Kurhaus, seemed to hang in some remote part of the skies with only the two great mountains above it.

.   .   .   .   .

We came there because an Austrian in New York, a crack skier, had recommended it. "It is a dull place," he said. "But you'll find the finest skiing in the world. The people aren't very interesting—at least those who don't ski are not."

It was the kind of place we were looking for—not Saint-Moritz with its bars and international glitter, not Davos with its hordes of young Englishmen and sporting, husky, rosy-cheeked girls—but a kind of lost place where we shouldn't know anyone, where the company was neither glittering nor interesting, where I could work and the dogs could run and the children could spend the whole day out-of-doors.

It was a long journey from New York, dully long with a caravan including nurse, children, dogs, and even a canary bird. We landed at Genoa, and went from there to Zurich and from Zurich to Coire and then to Saint-Firmin. There was an endless tangle of passports and visas, frontiers and changes, so that the last stage of the journey came as a relief. Yet there was something frightening and primeval about it, despite the wild, unreal beauty, which was spiritually more exhausting than all the nightmare of baggage and complications which preceded it. On the last stage of the long journey there was a full moon, obscured from time to time by wild scudding white clouds, lighting up the glittering waterfalls and throwing the deep gorges and the wild, wind-torn pines into black shadows. The tiny mountain train skirted gorges that dropped away two or three thousand feet into the obscurity of eternity. I do not like great heights and whenever the moon flashed out to reveal the great depths below us, my heart stopped for a moment and there was a sudden sickness at the pit of my stomach.

It was a wild journey through country which did not exist outside the imagination of Wagner or Gustave Doré. Halfway there, I wished that we had never embarked for this lost place.

A little before midnight the train came suddenly into a high wide valley where a half-frozen stream ran between forests of stunted pine. Above the valley the glittering snow swept away in the moonlight up and up to join at last the milky colorlessness of the frozen moonlit sky. And then quite suddenly we were in a village and the train stopped and the train guard, a short, thin, sallow man with a limp, called out, "Saint-Firmin! Last stop! All out!"

The little station, with its gimcrack gables fringed with icicles and all the signs in both French and German, was a cheery place, like a toy. There was a buffet with all sorts of rolls displayed and piles of fruit and bottles of Swiss wines. The sleigh from the hotel was waiting and the driver, in his blue cap with Hôtel Beau-Site in gold letters on it, stood by while we had cups of hot Swiss chocolate. After that we drove in the big sleigh behind four steaming horses up the steep streets to the hotel. It was late, but in the little chalets and the pensions an occasional light gleamed yellow against the blue white of the moonlit snow. The terror and exhaustion of that final lap of the journey wore off a little but a kind of dread, indefinable and uneasy, remained. Perhaps foreboding was a better word. It was as if unknowingly I had brought myself and my family into a strange world where we did not belong, a Gothic world, disordered and grotesque as a German folk tale.

The proprietor of the Hôtel was a tall, heavy German-Swiss by the name of Turnbaum. He had sloping shoulders, a potbelly, and a long nose, with blond hair cropped short above pale-blue eyes set too near together. His coat hung on him like a tent and when he shook hands, the palms were damp. The hotel appeared neat and new and well kept, but that night we saw little of it but the entrance hall. We fell asleep, exhausted, almost without being aware of the rooms we were given. They seemed pleasant enough with bright chintz curtains and big bay windows.

. . . . .

I was awakened by a brilliant light in my eyes, a light so violent that it came through the drawn curtains, as if a powerful searchlight had been turned full upon the windows. Putting on a dressing gown, I pushed back the curtains and was forced to close my eyes against the brilliance of the light. There was nothing supernatural about it—only the reflection of the brilliant morning sun against the snow-covered mountain directly opposite. When my eyes became accustomed to the glare, the whole immense landscape appeared—snow, snow, mountains of snow, without a tree or a house or a break in the whiteness and glare. I thought at once, "The Austrian is right. It is God's own skiing country." The excitement which only a skier can know rose up in my heart. This was paradise. I hurried through bath and dressing.

Downstairs I found the hotel empty, with only two other people in the dining room, a dark woman and a blond man of about forty. The odd thing was that I knew them. They were not married. It was clever of them to have come to this forgotten place, and only the strangest of circumstances had brought here someone who knew them. We shall call them Herbert and Maggie. Herbert was in business of some sort—a businessman with the businessman's air of omniscience. Maggie was a rather ugly but a clever, smartly dressed worldly woman of thirty-two or -three. That is good enough. They play little part in the story. Neither was romantic, and I did not believe their escapade had anything to do with romance. It was—as you might say—practical, almost utilitarian.

It was idiotic to pretend that I did not recognize them. Perhaps if I had been French I should have gone through the formality of pretending that I was blind and did not see them. But all three of us were Americans. Neither my wife nor myself had strong feeling about people enjoying themselves. We believed that sexual morality was people's own affair, so long as it did not corrupt the decency of their relationship with outsiders. That point has a certain bearing on the rest of the story.

They saw me and grinned, and the woman, Maggie, said, "Dr. Livingstone, I presume."

We had breakfast together and presently my wife joined us. It was a gay breakfast, for, oddly enough, we were all glad to see each other. I felt a curious pleasure in their company, as if it relieved a little the feeling of loneliness and dread in this wild, beautiful place. It was a little like coming across old friends in purgatory.

Very quickly they explained the emptiness of the hotel, "Old Uriah Heep Turnbaum tells us it's because the season hasn't begun. He says, 'Wait until the fifteenth,' and the whole place will be teeming. That's when we clear out."

"How did you ever hear of Saint-Firmin?" my wife asked.

Herbert beamed at us through his clear, shining glasses. "I heard about it in Germany," he said, "from a manufacturer named Hagen in Stuttgart. He says it's a place that is very popular with Germans—rich Germans."

"I didn't know there were any rich Germans."

He laughed. "Boy," he said, "you'd be surprised. I've just come from there."

Maggie added, "They're not very popular anywhere just now. It's too soon after the war. They all huddle together wherever they can find a resort where they aren't treated as pariahs. When they appear, I'm clearing out. Herbert doesn't mind them, but I can't stand them. One or two Germans are supportable, but in crowds, nothing doing—I suffocate!"

"You talk about them," I said, "the way some people talk about Jews."

. . . . .

It was the time of the ghastly inflation in Germany, when no money had any value, when people were starving and it needed ten million marks to buy a newspaper. I simply did not believe we would be overrun by Germans once the season began. How could there be Germans with enough money to come to Switzerland, a country on the gold standard with a terrifically high rate of exchange?

I had not been in Germany since the fall of the first postwar government. I had never liked it very much. I am not much of a mystic and have no special belief in reincarnation save in the strong intuitive reaction which I feel for countries and people, as if I had known them before in some previous existence. I always felt when I was in Germany that it was a country I knew very well but that something dreadful had happened to me there in some previous existence. I did not, like many people, find even Munich a warm, gay, and fascinating place; to me it always seemed a liver-colored false Florence dominated by the memory of an insane king, where one grew surfeited with heavy rich food and beer. For me the Black Forest, with the mists drifting through the tops of the black pines, seemed a place fit only for Fafnirs and Alberichs. For me Germany was always the same, under any government, a place where the sinister lay just beneath a façade of medieval towns and gaily painted cottages. Berlin was a horror. I was always glad to cross its frontiers and go into France, into Austria, into Holland, even into poor wretched Poland.

I didn't say much of this. Herbert was an intelligent fellow, a very smart businessman, and he was inclined to see things only in terms of business, a point of view which can be very shortsighted and limiting and at times even disastrous. There are so many elements besides columns of figures or records of profit and loss—things like human emotions and character, famines and fanaticism, things like Hitler. But at that time the world hadn't even heard of Hitler.

Sometimes in the evening the four of us played bridge by the fire in the big empty hall of the Beau-Site, but more often we talked. There was always a pleasant drowsiness after a day spent out-of-doors in the magnificent snow and sunshine which kept the conversation from being as violent as it might have become under more normal circumstances. Herbert and Maggie weren't much as skiers. They were learning and they stuck to the nursery slopes along with the children. My wife isn't an athlete, so for company I hired a guide called David Zupper. I hired him too because it was dangerous to go out alone into all that gigantic expanse of snow.

Zupper belonged to that great tribe of skiers, all called Zupper, like most of the inbred inhabitants of the village. He was everything that Herbert was not, and vice versa. David was built like a panther and for him skis were wings. He did not think or concern himself with problems. He lived by instinct, knowing the signs of an impending avalanche or a blizzard, or the sudden softness which preceded the coming of the foehn. For him there was no sense of dread over Saint-Firmin. The great mountains were his home as they were the home of the shy wild ibex.

With David and sometimes one or two other boys from the village we would climb up and up from eight in the morning until noon, through clouds and blizzards, until at last we reached the hut at the top of Mont Noir. Then, after eating the lunch we carried, we would set out down the mountainside, swinging back and forth across the endless expanses of clean, powdery snow, down, down, down, coming at last to the tree line, just above the railway station. Then a final dangerous swoop in and out among the trunks of the trees and we ended up in front of the Friedl Bar to have a hot grog with lemon in it and a big sausage sandwich. It was a wonderful life and David was a good guide and companion. He was clear-eyed and untouched by what was happening in Germany or Austria or Russia.

So the days were spent in the glittering white wilderness with David and the evenings, after a hot bath and a good dinner, with Herbert and Maggie beside the fire.

Herbert, in his expensive tweeds and his shining gold-rimmed glasses, confided in us that he had been spending much time in Germany on a mission that was a secret one. It concerned a complicated deal which on one end involved the Farbenindustrie, a combine of chemical interests, and on the other two of the biggest German and one of the greatest of heavy German industrial units—the Hagen Iron Works of Stuttgart. It was the period before it was discovered that all bankers and industrialists were not minor incarnations of God, and I was impressed by the grandiose schemes and plans which Herbert discussed. Neither my wife nor myself was much at business and so we believed not only all that he presented as facts but a great deal which time showed was sheer fancy. Maggie, who was a buyer and had to deal with some pretty crooked, shrewd people, was nobody's fool and seemed to take some of Herbert's more grandiose world schemes with a whole shakerful of salt.

Idiotic or not, the schemes and theories had a melodramatic and rather terrifying quality, like so many of the stories, true but surpassing belief, that were typical of that mad period between the two wars—like the stories of Rasputin and Kreuger and Stavisky and Daladier and Reynaud and their mistresses and many others—stories that one dared not to write as fiction because people would only say they were trashy and sensational and untrue.

Herbert said, "Things are not so badly off in Germany as you think. We must help Germany to her feet because she is valuable. We must do business with her big men in order to make money. Germany is an enormous market. If we let her sink down she will only go Bolshevik and infect Europe and the rest of the world. Some of the ablest financiers and industrialists in the world are in Germany. We must work with them."

I know that all this sounds rather stale now, but at that moment, high up in the wilderness, it sounded interesting and new and persuasive. If I had lived by my instinct as David Zupper did, I should have said, "I don't believe this. It is rubbish. It can only lead to disaster." But I only listened and was impressed as most of the world was at that time by men like Herbert.

For certain men in Germany he had a kind of worship. They had managed somehow to keep great organizations intact through inflationary chaos. They had managed to place great assets through strange and intricate deals in countries outside Germany.

Maggie asked flatly, "Do you like these men?"

"Yes, certainly," said Herbert. "They are fine fellows, most of them, and very clever. Now, you take Hagen himself—the Baron, the older one . . . the one who told me about this place."

He was always "taking Hagen." There seemed to be something about Hagen which fascinated him. Herbert was very good with words when it came to describing grandiose plans but he wasn't very good about people, and so the only picture

I got of Hagen was that he was tall and thin and had a big house in Stuttgart, a kind of palace in Berlin, and a huge estate with a medieval castle on it in Bavaria. And he was "awfully smart" as a businessman. That was about all I could get out of Herbert as an impression of the Baron Hagen.

In those quiet evenings before the "season" began, Uriah Heep Turnbaum, the proprietor of the Beau-Site, was about a great deal. He was always coming in, rubbing his moist hands together, to ask if we had everything we wanted or to poke the fire. Two or three times, he himself appeared behind the little oak bar in the place of the bartender, to mix our cocktails before dinner. He was always respectful, although oily, and rarely joined in the conversation. He appeared to enjoy listening to what we were saying. He was not an agreeable companion even on the other side of the bar, and his interruptions were always annoying. He was at once groveling and arrogant in the most peculiar fashion. It was this combination of qualities which made me suspect his Germanic origin.

Maggie said, "I don't believe he's Swiss at all. I've never seen or heard of a Swiss like him. The Swiss may be tiresome and disagreeable at times but they are independent always. The Swiss are by nature a free people."

. . . . .

The bright days and the pleasant nights went by quickly and then one night by chance, Maggie and I found each other alone at the bar just before dinner.

She said, "I'm going away tomorrow."

"So soon?"

"The Germans are due to arrive on Monday. I can't take them. I'll just get mad and make a scene or something." She drank her Martini and then said, "And I've had enough of Herbert. I'll go nuts if I have to spend another forty-eight hours with him."

I smiled, and she went on, "He couldn't be nicer and I ought to be ashamed of myself, but that's how it is. He's so damned nice he's driving me crazy. I can't cope with that child's mind any longer. I can't hear him say once more 'now take Hagen' when my instinct tells me that Hagen is a crook and a son-of-a-bitch."

I couldn't help asking, "How did you ever take up with him in the first place?"

She made a curious answer. "He was so nice and clean and simple. I'd just had a goings-on of the other kind—fascinating, subtle, devilish, etc., etc. Herbert seemed so nice and simple and American. But, brother, I just can't take any more simplicity. It's driving me nuts."

"I get what you mean."

"Herbert wants to stay on. We had a row tonight while I was dressing—as much of a row as you can have with Herbert. I said I was going to leave and he said I didn't care for him and didn't show him any consideration and when I didn't deny either thing he got mad. He wanted to stay on until his rich German friends turned up. They're due to begin arriving on Monday, so Maggie's out of here with the larks tomorrow. I don't want any part of them."

"He's going to take it hard. He thinks you're fascinating."

"He thinks I'm fast and wicked. But living in sin isn't any fun unless you get a laugh once in a while and Herbert hasn't a laugh in a carload."

"Where are you going?"

"Straight for Paris and the Ritz Bar. I feel as if I'd been living for a month in that country that lies backstage in the last act of *Walküre*, way up behind Brünnhilde's rock. When the *Walküre* begin to arrive it's time for Violetta to get out."

"Funny—I have the same feeling about this place. It's all unreal."

"It's that old Wagnerian aura. The Boches have left it behind them here. I wish you luck with them."

Then Herbert appeared looking pink and clean and innocent and sulking a little. He looked so clean he seemed almost shiny.

.   .   .   .   .

We said good-by that night and when we came down in the morning Herbert and Maggie were gone, but in their place had arrived the first of the German contingent. Oddly enough,

I took a liking to them on sight. They were both past middle age and both had a look of distinction. The man was small and dark and rather finely built with a hawklike nose and a strong, wide mouth and high, intelligent brow. He was dressed quietly in dark rather shabby clothing. He might have been of any nationality. One might have encountered him in London or Paris or New York or even India.

The woman was unmistakably German or Swedish, taller than the man and very blonde. She, like the man, must have been in her fifties, and there was something in her carriage and splendid figure which made me think at once that she must be a singer. She was beautiful in a fine Junoesque fashion.

At breakfast they sat at a window quite a distance away from us. The man was reading the German newspapers he had brought with him from Zurich, and now and then he read her something of interest or put down the paper altogether to discuss something with her. The woman kept watching us and turning away whenever I glanced in their direction.

I thought, "They appear charming and intelligent. If the others are like them Maggie is quite wrong about the invasion."

That evening when I came in I found the two of them talking to Nannie and the children. Dogs and children have the most astonishing way of picking up strangers and making introductions. I think half the interest, half the people in my life have come into it through my having had children and dogs. They are able to break down all reserves, to cross barriers of race, creed, and color.

When I came up, Nannie said, "These are the newcomers." And turning to them, she said, "I'm afraid I don't know your names."

The man brought his heels together and said, "Herr and Frau Oberregierungsrat Moll."

And from that moment we were friends. They had the simplicity and assurance of intelligent people who have accomplished something in life, who knew the world. There are people in the world whom one might call "the elect"—people who are decent and dignified, warm and human, who have a sense of values which never permits them to be rude or avaricious or vulgar, but whose greatest characteristics are generosity and the simplicity born of experience; and that, my friends, is something quite different from Herbert's kind of simplicity. One learns to know them almost at sight, for all these things are written in their faces. One finds such people anywhere in the world. They are confined to no country or civilization. Herr and Frau Oberregierungsrat Moll were like this.

I noticed that the dress of Frau Moll was *démodé* and just a trifle shabby and that Herr Moll's tweeds were worn beyond the point of shabbiness which the Englishman cultivates deliberately. I wanted to see more of them and asked them to meet us in the bar at seven-thirty. They accepted so quickly that I got the impression that they were very lonely, not only in Saint-Firmin but at home in Germany as well.

When my wife and I entered the bar, the Molls were already there waiting for us and rose as we came into the room.

They did not have cocktails but each took a glass of sherry. We talked of the skiing, of the wild beauty of Saint-Firmin. They had known it for many years. They both spoke excellent English; Herr Moll, without any accent at all. When I asked for the check, a strange thing happened.

Herr Moll said to the barman, "Please may I have the check for the sherry?"

"But I invited you for a drink," I protested.

"Please," said Herr Moll, "I will explain later."

I allowed him to pay for their sherry and when the barman had gone, Herr Moll said, "I was not being ungracious. I must explain to you." A curious look of pain came into the dark, intelligent face. "You see, we cannot afford to buy drinks for people and so we cannot accept them. You see, the money I earn in Germany has no value outside Germany and almost none inside. We are only here because my wife has a little money which comes from what she had saved and invested in London. It is very little but enough to bring us here if we are very careful for ten days or two weeks. We stay as long as it lasts and then go back to Germany." Then he said a curious thing, "It makes the rest of the year possible. You see, we have to get out of Germany for a little while each year."

He spoke perfectly simply, as people do who look upon

money as a convenience and a means to personal liberty but as no more than that.

"I understand," I said, "if you like it that way."

We dined together and slowly bits of their two lives came out casually to form at the end a kind of beautiful mosaic. They lived in Cologne, where Herr Moll was a judge of the Supreme Court. They had a house there and a small place in the Palatinate where they went in summer. The Ober-regierungsrat collected old editions and fine bindings, although lately, because of the inflation, little had been added to the collection. He said quite simply, "If ever you come to Cologne, you must come to see us."

I was right about Frau Moll. She had been a singer and still sang two or three recitals a year, mostly for her own pleasure. She had sung in Vienna, in London, in Paris, and of course nearly every German opera house—no big roles except in the smaller opera houses like Hanover or Württemberg, where she had sung Brünnhilde and Sieglinde.

With a smile she said, "I was never a great singer but I have always been a fine musician. One can lose one's voice but not one's musicianship."

They were unhappy and there was sadness in the dark eyes of the Judge and the blue ones of Frau Moll, even when they smiled or laughed. For the first two or three evenings they were reticent, but slowly they began to open up. They had come early, they said, before Saint-Firmin became crowded. It was not so nice then. They liked the villagers, gnarled, ugly, and inbred as they were. And it was a change. They always kept coming back to that without, I think, realizing how much they talked about a change.

In the meantime, a few more Germans arrived with each train, morning and evening, now four or five, now as many as ten a day, and slowly I began to see what it was Maggie meant about clearing out before they arrived. They were not what you might call nice types. Physically they had a look of coarseness, like a breed apart. One had a dim impression of a herd of cattle. They were noisy. Of all ages, from children to grandparents, they trooped in and out. They were rude to the servants and quarreled over the food and the service at the table. And they had a way of staking out preserves in this or that corner of the hotel public rooms. If you entered their preserves even by accident, they glared at you or made rude remarks. Worst of all, the older women had a way of taking possession of all the best chairs and the most comfortable corners and keeping possession of them by depositing a book or a knitting bag in a chair. This was supposed to stake out a permanent claim. If you moved the book or bag and sat in the chair, sooner or later you were told rudely that the chair was engaged and were asked to get out. This was a curious convention I had never before observed. It seemed to be a German custom.

Gradually, the Molls and ourselves were thrust into a corner, the most obscure and uncomfortable corner of the room, away from the fire, away from everything. It became apparent that in such a world we simply did not know how to take care of ourselves. Once I heard one buxom, masculine woman say, "Well, at least this is one place where Germans have some rights. If only the whole world were like this." And her male companion, a tall, heavy man with a thick neck, answered, "One day it will be. One day we'll have everything the French and English have and more too."

I am a good-tempered fellow, but I felt the blood rushing into my face with apoplectic force. I suddenly knew exactly what Maggie meant.

In the streets and the shops, the same behavior prevailed. The bus became impossible. After each run down the mountain I came to prefer walking up the long steep slope from the station to the hotel to losing my temper over the struggle and the rudeness one had to encounter to find a place or even get aboard the vehicle. Again and again I heard talk about "the rights of Germans." It seemed to be very nearly an obsession.

In the meantime our friends the Molls grew more and more depressed. They had neither the coarseness of their country-men nor the will to combat their methods, and like ourselves they were pushed into a corner. They rarely spoke to their compatriots and never held any conversation with them, but they never betrayed to us their dislike of the other Germans in Saint-Firmin. Because we had grown very fond of them, we never discussed the question with them except on the basis of individuals, as if they were not all of the same nationality. We came to have special names for certain particularly obnoxious ones. There was the Old Sow, the Wolf, the Chambermaid, the Prussian, and so on. To the Molls, the Prussians were a race of foreigners who had nothing to do with southern Germany. More and more the Molls disappeared in the daytime, going for long walks, each armed with a walking stick, down the mountain below the timber line. They even took to carrying a lunch packed for them.

As each train came in with new Germans, I became aware of an increase in the unhappiness of our friends. I knew suddenly that one day it would reach a point where they could no longer stand it and would go away, and that filled me with regret, for then we should be left alone among the wolves. Once or twice I considered moving all of us to some other part of Switzerland where we would find British and French, Americans and Austrians, but my wife objected.

"After the New Year," she said, "it will be better. They will thin out. I can't face moving dogs, children, and luggage all over again. Anyway, we couldn't get in anywhere at this time of year."

It was the argument about moving dogs and children which won me over to her point of view. I could not face another trek before the final one homeward to France at the end of the winter. It was clear that we were trapped. It was extraordinary how members of the human race could befoul a corner as wild and beautiful and clean as Saint-Firmin.

Then one night, two days before Christmas, as we sat in an obscure corner, huddled into the only chairs which had been left us, Herr Oberregierungsrat Moll said, "We are going away tomorrow. This afternoon we went down the mountain to Flensdorf. It is a tiny place. We found a room there in an inn. It is quieter. We could not bear to spend Christmas here."

What he was saying very clearly was, "We could not bear to spend a German Christmas here among these Germans."

We expressed our sorrow at having them leave. My wife said, "We shall be very lonely without you"—lonely in a crowded hotel, in a crowded village.

We talked then of other things for a time, but you could see that all the time Herr Moll was troubled by something. At last, when it was nearly midnight, he suddenly sighed as if the effort was great, stiffened his thin body, and said, "There is something I have wanted to say for a long time. I feel that we owe you an apology for our own country people. I hope you won't think they are all like this. There are civilized, nice Germans but you don't see them outside Germany now. They haven't the money. They're starving to death at home. We were lucky—Anna's having a little money placed in London. We have nice friends at home I should like to have you meet. It would give you a little different idea. Also, they are imprisoned inside Germany—all of them ruined because they believed in their government and its banks and currency." A look of utter contempt came over the lean, dark face. "These people here are all connivers and speculators. They have speculated in the currency of their own country. They have made fortunes out of the misfortunes and tragedies of Europe. That is why they have money outside of Germany."

Frau Moll said, "Yes, you must come to Cologne just to see for yourself. We aren't all industrial people and bankers and shopkeepers there. Some of us are quite civilized."

It was the first hint I had had of how the industrial and banking people really linked up with Herbert and his giant projects, with his deals with the Farbenindustrie and Baron Hagen, the steel king. But it was not quite clear to me then. It only fitted into the pattern later on as events became history and history in time clarified the interlocking pattern.

Judge Moll said, "Most of the industrialists and bankers have taken care of themselves. They've made deals with Schneider and Vickers and the big American oil companies, and the speculators are all right for the moment. And a lot of political adventurers are getting on. There are some of them here now —take Heintzlemann, that big fat brute with the red face. He's here for some reason, to see someone, to plot about something. He's no more than a gangster." He sighed and pressed his thin hands against his temples for relief. "I don't know what is happening in Germany. No one does. But it appears that all the wrong people are coming out on top."

Frau Moll said cozily, "If only you could have known Cologne before the war. You must at least come and meet some of our friends."

Then suddenly Oberregierungsrat Moll began to talk, passionately, intelligently, with a curious and scholarly objectivity, about the German people. He said many things that I was to remember long afterwards, perhaps for as long as I lived. What he said made me understand many things I would never have understood otherwise.

He said, "There is a curious fundamental curse of envy in so many Germans. And there is much self-pity. They envy Britain her power, America her wealth, France her civilization. They want all these things but they are not willing to earn them. They want to take them by force—things which can only be earned since force only weakens everyone and destroys the very power, wealth, and civilization they covet. The trouble is that Germany got started too late in the race. Their leaders, the demagogues, play upon the natural envy and the covetousness of the people. They always preach force and unscrupulousness. And they play upon German self-pity, which is very strong. They are always talking about German rights and the great debts owed to Germany. We are, alas, inclined at times to whine."

A little later he said, "The German and his country are both handicapped by being provincial. You rarely meet a German who is cosmopolitan, really interested in his mind. He is nearly always rigidly German—harping on German *Kultur*. Science to him is not an abstract thing belonging to all the world. There is only German science, only German music, German art. Even socially he is provincial. You'll see that in the diplomatic world. There is always something especially German about German diplomats. They are always asserting their Germanism, always putting a wall around themselves." He sighed again and pressed his temples. "The demagogues have all these things to play upon, to exploit. That is what is so frightening now with the worst people in Germany coming into power. There is a kind of innocence, a kind of bucolic ignorance about so many Germans. Above all people in the world they are material for the demagogues to work upon."

Before we retired, he said only one more thing I remembered long afterward, "Sometimes I think the German people are under a curse which works only for their destruction. It is as if they were a people bent perpetually upon suicide."

He might have said more but for the fact that the door from the bar was suddenly flung open and into the room came the red-faced Heintzlemann. He was roaring drunk and was leaning upon a younger man with a round face with pale-blue eyes and straw-colored hair. Heintzlemann kept bellowing something in German which I could not understand because he spoke in a low Silesian dialect.

The pair swept through the room, treading on the feet of the Old Sow, who rose indignantly and began to berate them in the coarse language of a fishwife. She followed them, cursing at them until they reached the door at the far end of the sitting room. There Heintzlemann turned and spat at her. He called out, "You think you're better than I am, do you, you old swine? Well, just wait! You'll see! You'll see!" Then he bent down, kissed the young man with the pink face and straw-colored hair on the cheek, and, still bellowing, turned and continued on his way.

The scene had a paralyzing effect, even upon the coarse Germans who filled the sitting room. There was something animal and inhuman about the spectacle. Oddly enough, it was the kind of scene you would expect to see only in Germany. It could never have happened among Frenchmen or Englishmen or Russians or Americans or Austrians. It could have happened only among the people in that room. There was something sickening about it.

Anna Moll rose and said quietly, "I think we had better go off to bed."

We rose to join them and I said, "We will come to the station to see you off in the morning."

They did not protest. They only said, "That will be very kind of you."

It meant that I would lose nearly a whole day of precious skiing because the climbing was easiest and the snow best in the morning. But it did not matter. I felt their loneliness very keenly. They suddenly appeared to have turned very old,

older than their years. I was aware that, in their shame, they
wanted to run away now, out into the night, anywhere at all.
I thought, "If Germany is like this, I see why they talk so
much about getting a change."

My wife and I went to bed without talking at all, and for a
long time I lay awake thinking about the gentle Molls and the
other Germans in the place, so brutal, so incredible, so frightening. I was filled with a sense of dread for the future, vague
and indefinable. What it was I feared, I did not know, but the
scene was filled with potential, explosive terror.

Long afterward, looking back, I understood what it was.
All the people in that room, save the Molls and ourselves, were
Nazis—the coarse ones, the speculators, the conniving money-
makers who had saved themselves and built up their own selfish
interests with the brutality and envy and coarseness of potential Nazis. Only at that time there was no such word as Nazi
and Hitler was a name unknown but to a few outside of
Germany.

I had forgotten even that Herbert had talked casually about
a new political party called the National Socialists in which
Baron Hagen was interested as a possible instrument for "saving Germany."

The next morning, accompanied by the dogs, we walked to
the little station to see the Molls on their way. The sun was
shining on new powdery snow. The pines below the station
looked like Christmas trees with the snow still lying on their
flat, outspread branches.

It was a gay morning, but there was no gaiety in the hearts
of any of us. The Molls looked tired and pale, as if they had
not slept at all. When we talked, the conversation was stiff and
forced. I was aware that they were still ashamed.

Mercifully the little train appeared, late, sneaking up through
the snow-covered pines. As it drew into the station I saw that
it was crowded with more Germans arriving for Christmas.
They were peering out of the windows and crowding the plat-
forms. There seemed to be hordes of them, and the sight did
not raise our spirits. The moment the train stopped they began
crowding off, many of them already in ski costumes, all of
them wearing too many things, too many scarfs and badges

and fancy jackets and furs, in the way Germans have. They shouted and quarreled and all tried to get their skis out of the baggage van at once.

When they had all descended, Herr Moll said, "We'll go now. There's no use in your standing about until the train leaves."

"Yes," said Frau Moll, "go along. Get your day's skiing before the crowd gets started."

You could see that they wanted to be on their way down to the peace and quiet of the obscure little inn in Flensdorf. I shook hands with them both and then Anna Moll did a curious thing, she kissed my wife on the cheek and said, "Forgive the familiarity. We shall miss you." There were tears in her eyes.

They climbed aboard the train and looked back once and smiled.

Then we turned away and as we came round the station the two dogs, Hustler and Dinah, began to bark wildly and strain at the leash. What they saw was another dog, a Scotty like themselves.

The stranger belonged to a young woman standing on the edge of the platform with a middle-aged man. They were a remarkable-looking pair. The girl was pretty in a rather buxom fashion and very young, not more perhaps than twenty or twenty-one. She was dressed in a shabby coat of some unnamable dyed fur and on her head was the German's idea of a chic French hat—a kind of "Dorothy Vernon of Haddon Hall" contraption in brown velvet with a brown ostrich plume trailing down the back. The fur coat was short and from beneath it hung the brown velvet of the suit she wore.

The man gave the impression of a prosperous provincial French undertaker—one of the sort with a clientele which demands only funerals of the first class. He was tall, with a long, narrow face. The complexion had a waxy pallor darkened where the heavy black beard showed through the skin. His eyes were a yellow brown and he wore an absurd overcoat, very long, of black material with a collar of expensive black mink. Topping it all was a stiff bowler hat. Against all the panorama of snow and mountains and forest and in the midst of all the crowd in skiing clothes, the pair looked absolutely preposterous.

The three dogs kept up their barking, and once again my pair performed their service of introducing me to remarkable and unlikely people. This time not only were they encountering another dog; this dog they encountered was of the same breed.

The girl looked toward us and smiled. It was a frank, simple, warm smile which made you like her at once. Then in very good English she said, "Let them get acquainted."

So still on the leash, the three dogs were introduced. Oddly enough, Hustler, my male Scotty, instead of attacking the newcomer according to his habit, wagged his tail. It was evident that he liked the stranger.

"What are they called?" asked the girl.

"Hustler and Dinah."

"Mine is called Runty. He was so little when I got him. I love Scotties. They're so little and so brave."

I laughed, and my wife said, "Our two run away every time they get a chance. Yesterday they turned up at a village six miles away. How they got there through four feet of snow, I don't know."

The dogs kept on sniffing and wagging their tails, and the man simply remained standing there watching us without saying anything.

"We're waiting for the big sleigh from the Beau-Site," said the girl. "It was full before I got my luggage out of the van." Then she said, "Excuse me, my name is Baroness von Schildsen." Then the color came into her face. She was shy and what she said next appeared to cost her great effort. She turned and said, "This is Baron von Hagen." And after a second she said as if to explain the situation, "He is a friend of my husband. We came across each other on the train."

It took me a moment to recover from the shock. From all Herbert's talk about him I had formed a picture of the powerful Baron Hagen which was quite different. I hadn't expected this rather dank undertaker. He didn't at all fit the idea of a powerful king of heavy industry. We shook hands, and his face for the first time showed any expression. It relaxed into a smile which had a certain charm. Then the big sleigh appeared and was at once rushed by an army of Germans.

Out of experience my wife and I drew back rather than be trampled and gave up the whole idea of the sleigh. But the girl and von Hagen were able to hold their own. Something about the Baron's appearance and manner or the mink-collared coat struck awe in the other Germans. Coldly he said, "*Bitte!*" and stepped forward, looking formal and imposing, to take the best seat. He put the girl in beside him, but she did not keep her dignity. She snatched up her dog Runty and shouted a long string of indignant German words at the jostling, elbowing mob. It was in coarse, slangy German which I cannot remember and did not wholly understand. But it was something like this, "What goes on here? What a bunch of bums! You ought to be ashamed to call yourselves Germans! Get out of the way!"

As the sleigh drove off she turned and, smiling quickly, waved to us. The Baron sat looking straight ahead.

The sleigh, with much jangling of bells and cracking of the whip, dashed off up the hill toward the hotel, and I thought, "It is very odd that a man with all that power and money didn't hire a private sleigh but waited for the hotel conveyance."

·   ·   ·   ·   ·

The next night was Christmas Eve. There was a big Christmas tree and much singing. Three of the younger Germans brought out guitars and sang old German folk songs. Several barrels of beer were drunk and everything turned *gemütlich* and sentimental and all the Germans suddenly loved each other. They even relaxed their rudeness toward the non-Germans in the hotel. The Old Sow and the Wolf and all the others became close friends. It was all overdone and hysterical, as overdone as the rudeness and ruthlessness which had preceded it. There was an unbalanced quality about the whole thing. It became a kind of sloppy, indecent orgy of sentimentality, as if they were saying, "Christmas is a German festival. It belongs to us alone. Only we know how to celebrate it." For once there was something they need not envy others.

Before going to bed I noticed one remarkable thing—that for the first time, the red-faced, odious Heintzlemann was not drunk, and the younger man with the straw-colored hair, the pale-blue eyes, and the pink cheeks was not with him. Early in the evening we had a drink with Baron von Hagen in the bar. After that he joined the singers and was as well behaved as any small-town German shopkeeper on Christmas Eve.

For a little while after dinner we stayed downstairs, fascinated by the exotic quality of the medieval love feast which had overtaken our fellow lodgers, and about ten o'clock we went to our own rooms to decorate the Christmas tree for the children and arrange the gifts for Christmas morning. A little while later, one of the maids knocked at the door and said that David, the guide, was waiting downstairs to see me.

I found him standing in the hallway, very tanned and wiry and straight, with his cap in his hand. He was watching the orgy of *Gemütlichkeit* through the doorway, so absorbed that I had to speak twice before he noticed that I was there. He grinned and the blue eyes twinkled with mockery.

Then he said, "I just came to tell you that we can't go out in the morning. A storm is blowing up—a bad one—the kind nobody could go out in and return alive."

We went into the bar and had a drink, finding a corner for ourselves where we hoped to be unmolested. We both had *Schnaps*, I think as a kind of protest because all the others were drinking beer. It was difficult to hold a conversation in the face of all the singing and uproar, so we just sat there watching. There was a kind of grossness in the spectacle, of the kind you see in the pictures of Breughel. David's rather cold, clear blue eyes were very steady. Once he turned and said in his very bad Swiss French, "*Ces ne sont vraiment que des cochons!*" And suddenly I understood for the first time how he really felt, along with all the other guides and all the villagers. Each year they tolerated the invasion because it meant prosperity for them for the rest of the year. There was a kind of hatred in his voice that tied in with the curious aura of Saint-Firmin itself and that sense of dread which I had felt from the very first. I began to believe that it was the presence of the Germans in the place rather than the wild scenery which brought the sense of wild, Gothic unreality. I do believe that fierce and concentrated hatred and contempt can create a kind of intangible intensity in an atmosphere, like electricity.

Then I saw Uriah Heep Turnbaum coming toward us, washing his hands like Lady Macbeth. He was always bad news, but I hardly expected what was coming. He bent down and whispered in my ear. At first I did not catch what he was saying and, despite the menace of his bad breath, I was forced to ask him to repeat it.

This is what he said, "I am sorry but there is a rule against bringing guides into the bar of the Beau-Site. Someone has just complained."

I am usually a quiet, peaceful man, but certain things are likely to bring up sudden almost apoplectic attacks of temper. I felt one coming now. I could feel the blood rushing into my face. It was incredible that any of the coarse people in this room should object to the presence of a sportsman, a swell fellow, a gentleman like David. Such an issue was never raised among people in other skiing resorts where skiers looked upon men like David as a race of aristocrats.

I said, "Who objected?"

"That I cannot tell you," said Turnbaum.

"You will tell me or I will stay right here and if there's any more trouble I'll smash the whole place to hell."

This appeared to awe Turnbaum, who seemed to think I was drunk.

"I will tell you if you don't make trouble."

"I only want to know. I don't want to be mixed up with these swine if it can be helped."

At the word "swine" his face changed color. He said, "It was Herr Heintzlemann."

"That pederast! That perverted hog!"

Turnbaum shrugged his bottle-shaped shoulders. "He is with the Baron Hagen, a very important man. What can I do?"

David was still watching. Fortunately he appeared to believe that our conversation was a private one and none of his business.

I said, "Very well. We'll go up to our rooms and drink. I'd prefer not to mix with this company."

"Thank you," said Turnbaum. "It is not my fault, you understand." But I could see that he hated me, and I was more certain than ever that he was no genuine Swiss at all but one of them.

He went away and I said to David, "Let's get out of here. Come up to the sitting room and have a Christmas drink with my wife."

We left the noisy room and upstairs found my wife decorating the Christmas tree. It was pleasant up there, away from the obscene celebrations going on belowstairs, celebrations which seemed to me to have very little to do with the spirit of the Christ child.

Following up his remark, I led him to talking about the Germans downstairs. The *Schnaps* rather loosened his tongue and he talked more easily than I had ever heard him talk. Out of his heart came all sorts of things. When I asked about the people belowstairs, he said, "They are a new kind of German. In the old days they were mostly young and came here only for the skiing. They weren't so bad. These are mostly little people who have got rich somehow. I don't know how. But they hate and envy everybody who is not German. Why should they hate and envy us poor mountain villagers? They are *bad* Germans. Not all Germans are like them, but most Germans have something of that in them. They are a resentful and envious people who want the whole world!"

Later on, he said, "Something bad is going on in Germany. I don't know what it is, but my grandfather who lives in Zurich says all Swiss know the signs. They have lived through them before. He says it's a kind of deviltry that gets into them —that it comes out of the swamps and forests, out of the blood and soil, just as it did in Roman times."

I was interested in the speech but I did not remark at the time a curious phrase which later became a kind of slogan of great significance. I only remembered it years afterward when it became the favorite phrase of Alfred Rosenberg, the philosopher of all these people belowstairs. The phrase was "blood and soil."

Outside the rising wind howled louder and louder. Once I pushed open the window to see if it were snowing. The gale threw the sash back into my face, almost knocking me down. Before the window closed, the snow swept into the room, carried across the floor as far as the Christmas tree by the wild fury of the storm. Certainly there would be no skiing in the morning, perhaps not for many days.

Then David suddenly rose and bade us "good night" and "merry Christmas."

After we had gone to bed and the lights were out, I lay in the darkness for a long time, unable to sleep, listening to the howling of the storm. It was an odd, unnatural Christmas. Here in our own rooms, it was peaceful and secure enough, but all around that sense of dread kept creeping in. As I lay there awake, the memory of the scene belowstairs became fantastically important and rather terrifying, like a nightmare in which the overdone *Gemütlichkeit*, the Old Sow, the Wolf, the unspeakable Heintzlemann, and the Baron all played roles.

*   *   *   *   *   *

In the morning, the wind still howled and the snow beat against the windows, but in the sitting room it was warm and the children and the dogs played and barked about the Christmas tree while we drank chocolate and ate hot Swiss rolls covered with butter and mountain honey. I had the feeling that we were in a kind of warm and cozy pocket in the very midst of a wild and hostile universe.

After breakfast I dressed lazily and went downstairs to let the dogs out for a run. When I opened the door they ran barking to disappear into the driving snow. Waiting for them, I stood in the doorway. Evidently our German friends were sleeping off the effects of the Christmas Eve celebration, for the lower part of the hotel was completely empty. There was not even a servant in sight and the great hall was a picture of desolation with torn paper streamers, confetti, stale stains of champagne and beer on tables and floor. The whole place had a curious dead, acrid smell.

I was glad of the cold, clean, snow-filled air. The Scotties stayed away for a long time. I whistled, but still they did not appear. Dogs are likely to become intoxicated by a snowstorm.

I gave up whistling and waited and then out of the snowstorm I saw a figure coming up the drive. As it came near I realized that it was the Baroness, the girl we had seen briefly at the station. I recognized the pretentious, shabby fur coat. She came out of the falling snow on to the portico and I saw that she was crying and upset at finding me there.

I felt like apologizing for my presence and said, "Is there anything I can do for you?"

She blew her nose and said, "It's my dog, Runty. I let him out and he ran off into the storm. I called and called but he didn't come back. I've been looking for him for the last hour. I've been all the way to the station. I can't whistle very well and in the storm, it's no good calling. He can't hear my voice. I'm afraid he'll lose his way and not be able to get back. He has such short legs and the snow is so deep."

I smiled, "Mine have done the same trick." Then to reassure her I told her again of the escapades of Dinah and Hustler, how somehow they made their way through deep snow to the other side of the mountain.

"It looks as if I'd have to go look for them. Would you like to come along? Maybe we'll find Runty at the same time."

She could not answer me at once for sobbing. There was something hysterical about her grief, out of all proportion with the loss of a dog—a loss which was only possible and not probable.

I said, "Perhaps you'd better have a drink first and warm up."

"No! No! I don't want to go in there. I want to find Runty."

She wouldn't even come into the great hall while I went to fetch a hat.

When I returned she had managed to control her sobs and was waiting in a sheltered corner of the portico, the shabby fur coat pulled up about her ears. When she saw me, she said, "I'm ashamed. I won't cry any more."

"That's all right."

I confess that I was worried about our own dogs. The blizzard was like nothing I had ever seen. I did not see how even a hardy Scotty could stay out in it for long and survive. We set out down the drive toward the town, our bodies

thrust forward into the wind. Any conversation was out of
the question. Now and then I turned with my back toward the
wind, put two fingers into my mouth and whistled shrilly,
without any response from the truant dogs.

Thus we continued all the way down the hill through the
empty village. Now and then a single figure would emerge
from the blowing snow, pass us without looking up, and disappear again like a ghost. When we reached the station I
shouted, "We'll go in and have something hot to drink."

Inside the little *buffet de la gare* was warm, like most Swiss
interiors, much too warm. We both had hot chocolate and
rolls, and as she drank, the girl began to thaw out a little. She
was very pretty in a Gretchen sort of way, with her cheeks
aflame from the heat after the biting wind.

Shyly she said, "I'm afraid I seem a fool."

"No. Not at all."

"If I lost Runty I don't know what I'd do. You see, I was
very lonely. It's the first Christmas I've spent away from home,
and it was awful at the hotel last night. I've never seen a
Christmas like that. I went up to my room early and went to
bed but I didn't sleep all night. That's why I'm so foolish this
morning, I suppose."

"You should have joined us," I said.

"I didn't know you well enough."

"We would have been glad to have you."

I was interested to discover that she was not traveling with
Hagen as his mistress. That was perfectly clear. There was
something innocent about her which made deception out of
the question. It did not even seem to occur to her that anyone
should suspect that she was traveling *with* Hagen. It still
seemed very odd that she was traveling alone, that she should
have come to such a place as Saint-Firmin, knowing no one.

"What about having Christmas dinner with us?" I asked.

Her face was suddenly radiant. "That would be wonderful."

Then I fancied suddenly that I heard barking and even went
to the window to discover that I was right. Outside in the
blizzard were the dogs, not only Hustler and Dinah but the
Baroness' Runty. They were playing and barking wildly,

obviously enjoying the storm like true Scotsmen. For a second I felt an impulse to wring their necks.

. . . . . .

It was Gretl who, in her innocence, brought us together with Heintzlemann and the Baron. It happened like this.

When we returned from the station with the dogs, Gretl had Christmas dinner with us. That, she said, was what she was called—simply Gretl. Her name was Margaret, but Gretl suited much better the fresh, naïve, healthy quality of the girl. We had champagne for lunch, and she was excited and happy and kept giving out fragments of information about herself, small odd pieces unrelated, like a heap of pieces from a picture puzzle. She was already divorced from her husband, who had been a man thirty years older than herself. She occupied a tiny cheap room built for servants' quarters on the very top floor of the hotel. Her father, who had been a Lutheran pastor, was dead. She was not of the nobility but of the solid German middle class. The title had come to her by marriage. She was twenty-three years old. Life was very hard in Germany. Honest people of the solid middle class actually had not enough to eat, or clothes or shoes. She could not believe her eyes when she came out of Germany and found that other people had fine, warm clothes, and not only food but things such as champagne and caviar and *pâté de fois gras*. She had gone first to Vienna, where she got a job as a chorus girl in a musical show.

"There," she said, "I met my fiancé. He is coming here after the New Year. You will like him. He is an Italian from Milano."

She had saved the money she had earned as a chorus girl. That was what she was living on now.

It was a strange, disconnected, incongruous chain of isolated incidents which she revealed—a picture of a life utterly disrupted and cast adrift on the turbulent sea of that afterwar period. I kept thinking that in normal times she would have been the wife of some solid good citizen and the mother of two or three children by now. But all that had been changed by the ambition and envy of power, by men she had never seen—the Kaiser and a lot of other Germans who wanted to devour the whole world. I don't think any such idea ever occurred to her. In her simplicity she simply accepted what came along without questioning or thought. At any rate, she appeared very happy at our family Christmas dinner. She fitted into it as simply, as naturally as any girl from my home town in Ohio. The tears, the loneliness vanished, for the moment at least.

From then on she became a part of our lives in Saint-Firmin, like the children and the dogs. We were all fond of her. She had no interest in me save as a friend. She was equally fond of my wife and myself.

On the third night after the dog episode she said, "Baron von Hagen has asked me to have brandy with him after dinner and asked me to ask you both to join us."

I accepted because I wanted to know better what this industrial genius was like. He seemed so unlike what one expected of a "big shot" in America. As I said, he gave the impression of a provincial French undertaker. We saw him about the hotel or in the village street, a sallow, rather dreary fellow always in his mink-collared, black broadcloth overcoat, without flair, without personality. Wherever he went the other Germans treated him with the groveling servility of a nation for which *hochgeboren* is one of the key words. Hagen was not very *hochgeboren* but he represented what was even more important to the Old Sow, the Wolf, Heintzlemann and the other Beau-Site Germans. He was rich and he was powerful and he vindicated their sense of defeat and bafflement among the other peoples of the world.

It was a strange, unreal evening. I discovered that Hagen had a soft voice which had the quality not of velvet but of plush, as if at some time his vocal cords had suffered an injury. At times it was difficult to understand what he was saying. This forced you to listen carefully and give great attention while he was speaking. The hands, rather clammy to touch, were small and rather oily, with heavy blue veins. They inspired a sense of repulsion. His eyes were not, as they appeared from a distance, dark brown or black but of a yellowish-green color.

He addressed Gretl as "Baroness" and it was apparent at once that he was attracted by her. I thought at first that it was the attraction of opposites—that of a perfectly ageless, embalmed man for a healthy, simple, rustically pretty young girl. He spoke English with a heavy accent.

At first the conversation was stiff and slow, not, it seemed to me, because there was any shyness or awkwardness in any of us, but because his mind was elsewhere. Presently I divined that Gretl was the source of his distraction. One had the impression not simply that he was disrobing her mentally; it was something stronger, more intense and complicated than that.

After three glasses of brandy he seemed to relax a little and to grow more human and warm. I observed that we had a mutual acquaintance, Herbert, and at once he brightened a little when I told him that Herbert had been here a little while before, embarked upon a love affair.

"Yes, he is a clever fellow," said Hagen. "We are working on two or three projects together. They promise rather well. German industry needs help from the outside. It will work toward the mutual good. We have great plans. If only industrialists could manage the world, it would be quite a different place and the danger of war and the Bolsheviks would be greatly reduced. The rest of the world has never properly appreciated German genius, especially in industry."

He had barely finished the speech when Heintzlemann joined us. He came up to the table behind the Baron's back so that the Baron did not see him until he had finished speaking. At sight of the newcomer, the Baron frowned. He did not acknowledge Heintzlemann's greeting. It was Gretl who introduced us.

It is almost impossible to give an impression of the animal vitality of Heintzlemann. He was a big man, heavy to the point of obesity, with a round red face and great hands like clusters of sausages. The grossness of the body was redeemed only by the shrewdness of the small blue eyes. He sat down and ordered a round of drinks and a double brandy for himself.

He spoke no English and although my wife and I could speak and understand German, the conversation continued in English at the will of Hagen, who, I think, sought deliberately to snub his companion and exclude him from the conversation.

Heintzlemann appeared not to notice the snub but sat leaning forward, straining to understand and now and then when he fancied he understood some remark of the Baron, he would nod his head vehemently and interject some approving remark in guttural German. There was in his manner the same obsequiousness which marked the attitude of most of the other Germans.

Most of the Baron's talk was along the same line—that the Germans were unappreciated, that they wanted to be friends with the rest of the world, that they were not understood.

Presently, with a certain venom, I asked, "Are all Germans like these in the hotel?"

But the Baron missed the point entirely. He said, "Oh, no. This is the new Germany you see here. This is the coming Germany—the Germany of vitality and force and skill."

He was approving of them. As he spoke, it became apparent that Heintzlemann understood more English than we believed, for again he nodded his head violently and made some guttural remark about "*Verdammte Juden.*"

We met with the Baron on two other evenings, partly because he sought the meeting and partly because I was myself fascinated by both Hagen and Heintzlemann. They were unlike any people I had ever met before, outwardly friendly, yet remote and strange and unreal as mad or morosely drunken people can be. Their standards, their reactions, were utterly unexpected, completely incredible. They each had a hate— Heintzlemann's was Jews and the Baron's was the French. He could not seem to forgive them their civilization.

The conversation was no more inspiring than it had been on the first evening and upon much the same level. Once or twice I was tempted to argue, but it seemed only a useless expenditure of energy. My wife, less philosophical, now and then grew angry and made remarks which would have been insulting to any other people in the world. Perhaps Heintzlemann, sitting there all flesh and grossness, did not understand them. The Baron's complacency was so great that they slipped off his pallid, waxy skin like water off tallow. Both men gave the impression of sexual abnormality. In Heintzlemann's case we knew what it was, for before the arrival of the Baron he had made no effort to conceal it. It was the animal kind of homosexuality which one finds often enough in Germany: there was no effeminacy about him, only brutality. With the Baron the analysis was more difficult to achieve, the effect more obscure. There was something definitely wrong, but what it was could not easily be defined. It simply made one uncomfortable.

One thing which became clear was that his inner, sinister passion for Gretl seemed to grow stronger. She appeared to be aware of this and always stayed close to us as if we were protection.

On the last night before his departure, after we had said good-by and accepted vaguely his invitation to visit him if we ever happened to be in Berlin or Munich, Gretl stopped off with us in our sitting room on the way up to her servant's bedroom. As I poured a nightcap she flung herself down in a chair and said, "Pfui! I'm glad he's gone. He wanted me to be his mistress. He has been after me for a long time."

"They're a funny pair. Heintzlemann is easy enough. I can't make out the Baron."

Then Gretl said a surprising thing, perhaps born of harsh experience on the side of her life which she had hinted at but never revealed.

"It is easy. Did you ever notice his eyes? They are the eyes of a man who gets pleasure out of inflicting cruelty. I know —my husband was like that. He and Hagen are friends. They used to go on orgies together. That is how I met Hagen first. My husband had the same kind of eyes. That's why I left him. I couldn't stand it. That is why Hagen goes for me. He knows I understand what he wants. He would not be embarrassed by having to tell me. We understand each other."

As she talked, her gentian-blue eyes grew dark and the color came into her face. Then a kind of hysteria seemed to seize her and she began to talk wildly.

"His wife puts up with him. She is a beautiful girl. She doesn't seem to mind. Maybe she puts up with him because she likes the wonderful jewels and furs he gives her." She laughed. "Maybe because he keeps her tied on a string. Each night when they come home he puts all the jewels in his safe and locks up the furs so she can't run off with them. When he goes away on a trip he locks them up and she has to go about just dressed in ordinary clothes like anyone else." She laughed again. "He is fantastic."

That was all that came out of Gretl that night, except when I said, "Hagen and Heintzlemann seem an odd pair. They don't seem to have anything in common. Why are they so much together?"

Gretl smiled a little tipsily. "Some sort of dirty work. That's why Hagen came up here. There's a lot of that going on today in Germany. In Munich there's a funny little fellow called Hitler who's got some sort of movement. He goes about preaching. Heintzlemann is always with him."

The name of the "funny little fellow" struck some faint chord of memory, but I didn't think any more about it. At the moment Gretl seemed to me far more interesting. In her innocence she seemed the clue to a great many things which puzzled me about that strange, foreign people—the Germans. Heaven knows, she was not profound. The world in which she lived was a superficial world, all surface. Her concern was with gossip like that about Hagen and his beautiful wife and the jewels which were locked up when she was not wearing them. Gretl never thought out anything to the end. She never looked beneath the surface. She seemed to accept what came her way without much question or complaint. Yet there was something warm and simple and kindly about her which grew into our hearts. I found myself thinking again and again what a pity it was that the life for which she was meant should have been so completely disrupted by men and forces of which she understood nothing.

The next day Hagen left, after sending flowers to my wife with a message repeating his invitation to let him know if we were ever in Munich or Berlin or near his *Schloss* in Bavaria. The gesture rather astonished me, for there had been no real intimacy between us, but only a kind of veiled, fundamental hostility based upon the striking difference of manners, ideals, and background. I could only think he believed that somehow, someday, in some way, I might be useful to him.

After he had gone, the young man with the straw-colored

hair and pale-blue eyes reappeared again in Heintzlemann's company and each night they got drunk and sang and made a rather repulsive spectacle of themselves. The most astonishing thing was the indifference with which the other Germans accepted this behavior. Even the hand-washing Turnbaum did not seem to object. One change, however, was noticeable. This was the change in behavior of the other Germans toward ourselves. It was quite evident that our connection with Baron von Hagen had impressed them. They no longer pushed us about and jostled us out of the best seats. They even said, "Good morning" and "Good evening" very politely.

When I spoke sarcastically of this to Gretl, she said, "Sure they think you're important since they saw you with Hagen. They think you might be able to do something for them, and they're afraid of you too. They're all afraid of everybody else. It's like that in Germany now."

. . . . . .

Then Luigi, Gretl's "fiancé," appeared. Without any pretense he simply shared Gretl's attic bedroom.

Luigi isn't worth more than a paragraph. It was easy to see at the first glance what he was—just another Italian gigolo, a young man, probably of peasant or lower middle-class stock, whom nature had endowed with vigorous black hair, a handsome face, large black eyes, and a magnificent physique. He wasn't the usual sort of night-club *thé dansant* gigolo. That had gone out of fashion three or four years earlier. He was another type altogether. He skied like a demon and had the energy of a horse, and he used the prodigious endowment bestowed on him by a kind nature as a way of making his living and leading an easy life. I know Gretl was in love with him in her curious, easygoing way, and he must have been a little in love with Gretl to have left his easy life in more luxurious, attractive, cosmopolitan winter resorts to come to Saint-Firmin to spend a week with her in an attic bedroom.

He was our first experience with Gretl's extraordinary capacity for always picking the wrong man. He had no more brains than Gretl. He was, like her, just a kind of natural phenomenon. He left without creating any impression stronger than that based upon the fact that he was a remarkable athlete and a hell of a good skier. Gretl said he had to leave to go back to his business in Milano. I really think she believed this. She had a remarkable capacity for deceiving herself when her affections were involved. She really thought, while she washed her stockings and underclothes in that attic room, that they were going to be married.

After he had gone, we saw more of Gretl than ever. As the holiday season passed, the Germans began to leave—the Old Sow, the Wolf, and all the others. Heintzlemann and the straw-haired boy were among the first to go. As they left, the place began to grow more pleasant and that feeling of sinister fore-boding, which was like a kind of obscure, lingering, physical pain, disappeared altogether at times.

Slowly, bit by bit, in her casual, disjointed way, Gretl came to reveal more and more of her story, so that by the end of January, when the money she had saved gave out, and she left for Vienna to go back to work as a chorus girl and to "meet Luigi," we knew all about her and the picture became clear.

It was a curious story. She came of a perfectly respectable German family on the edge of being *hochgeboren*. She had a widowed mother, two aunts, and a smaller brother and sister. They were all utterly ruined by the inflation and reduced to that respectable destitution which is the most horrid of all poverty. They did not actually have enough to eat, yet their position, which was all they had left, would not permit them to stand in a soup line or even to apply for the full amount of public relief they might have received.

Not far away from their house in a middle-class Berlin suburb there lived a rich and eccentric older man called Baron von Schildsen. He lived in a great house, surrounded by a walled garden, and since Gretl had been a little girl he had shown an apparently kindly but actually sinister interest in her, giving her apples and pears and candy and arranging to meet her as she came out of the *Hochschule* and walk part-way home with her. Only her childish instinct told her that there was something odd about him and made her always refuse his invitation to come into his garden.

When she was eighteen, her mother fainted one day from hunger in the doorway of a department store. It happened twice more, and then Gretl, in her simple, straightforward way, hit upon a solution. Anything, she concluded, was better than living always with an empty stomach and seeing her mother dying of starvation and her small brother and sister crying themselves to sleep with hunger. So one afternoon she walked into the house of the old Baron and quite simply said she would marry him if he would see to it that her family had enough to eat. It did not occur to her to ask him for a settlement. She simply wanted her family to have enough to eat and that was the way to get it.

The old man was only too delighted to marry her, and she went to live in the great house surrounded by the walled garden. He had only one servant, an old woman, who went home every night.

The life was a nightmare. What happened in the big house must have been terrible, for each time she spoke of it she looked suddenly pale and ill.

"I stood it for nearly a year," she said, "and then I went to a judge and said I wanted a divorce. When I told him as much of my story as I could, the judge said, 'Of course, my girl. And under the circumstances, he will have to make you a good settlement.' "

She got the divorce and the settlement, but as the inflation increased it didn't mean very much. What had seemed a big fortune dwindled in value to little more than enough to keep her family in the coarse, common kind of food which would keep them alive, and Gretl was very nearly back where she started. It was then she decided that the thing for her to do was to leave Germany and earn money outside. A franc or even a krone or a lira could be translated into thousands of marks.

So she had gone to Vienna, where her healthy good looks and un-German figure got her a job in the theater. What happened to her did not matter too much so long as her family in Berlin had enough to eat.

The story was just as simple as that. The extraordinary thing was that she seemed so untouched. It was, on the face of it, a horrible story, but Gretl herself seemed to have been unscarred by its horror. Perhaps it was that curious simplicity and super-ficiality which saved her. The past did not trouble her. The present was good enough. She lived always in the future in a kind of fairy-tale belief that someday there would turn up some fairy-tale prince, good-looking, charming, and rich, who would solve everything.

Our fondness for her increased, and on the day she left we went to the station with her and Runty to see them off. She said, "I'll look you up when I get to Paris. That's where I mean to end up."

As the train pulled out, we walked back up the hill in the belief that very likely we should never see her again. We had a kind of nomad philosophy about such friendships. But it was not to be so. We were to see her again and again. I had a letter from her only the other day, a letter smuggled out of Paris into Geneva and thence by plane to Ohio. It was as if there was something in the stars that drew us together, or it may have been that at times she grew weary and disgusted with her strange, disorderly life and sought the stability which our household and family represented. In any case, the curious, unlikely friendship has survived for nearly fifteen years.

*   *   *   *   *

With the coming of the avalanche season, I began to grow tired of the monotony of life in Saint-Firmin, and all of us began to feel a homesickness for the farm in France. We wanted to be home in time for the spring planting and the moment when the whole floor of the forest was covered with daffodils. Even my own passion for skiing waned before that homesickness. I wanted to see the gray walls and red roofs of Senlis blossom with the yellow wallflowers, the poplars turn green and feathery against the blue sky of the Oise. But most of all, after the strained, sinister winter, I was homesick again for my neighbors—the farmers, the simple people one met at the market, the Archiprêtre, the Mayor, the *petite noblesse*—all those French people who were so civilized, even the hum-blest and poorest of them.

I knew I would never again see Saint-Firmin, with its gorges and glaciers and wild beauty. I felt a little sad. It was not the wildness of the beauty that had ruined the place for me, but the aura of people at the Beau-Site. Somehow they had brought all that was sinister in Germany with them.

. . . . .

A year later from Vienna we had a letter from Gretl. It was written in rather stiff, formal English, completely contradicted by the ending, "Your warmly affectionate Gretl." It contained not very much of interest to us, save that even trivial things which happened to Gretl, such as a quarrel with the laundress or a proposition from the stage manager, had an interest. We had never known anyone quite like her. She had been home for a visit to her mother, who was well. She had not stayed for long as she did not like what was going on in Germany. It was, she wrote, no longer like Germany. She had not married Luigi. "He was no good," she wrote simply and directly, "what you call a bum. I guess I was lucky." The Baron Hagen had turned up in Vienna. "He is still after me," she wrote, "but pfui!" Hagen, she said, was one of the backers of that man Hitler she had told us about. At the end, she wrote, "I have got a job in a musical troupe going to London. If I have time while passing through Paris, I will telephone you."

Apparently she did not have time, for we never heard from her. She disappeared, apparently in the direction of London, leaving no address.

. . . . .

Three years passed before I again saw Hagen. In the meantime much had happened, for "the little man called Hitler" was no longer someone unknown and insignificant. He had become a power in Germany, backed by a gang of cutthroats and sadists and adventurers. The feeble attempt at democracy in Germany had broken down, sabotaged and wrecked on the side of Germany by all the elements which hated democracy, and sabotaged and wrecked from the outside by elements within the democracies themselves, who valued wealth and power above decency and sought to build up in Germany "a bulwark against Bolshevism." They existed in England, in France, even in America. I am afraid my friend Herbert, who so admired Hagen, was one of them. For these elements, "the little man called Hitler" was a wonderful instrument. To a Germany shattered, confused, and in despair, he promised everything. He promised employment, a sound currency, food, the destruction of the Bolshevists and the destruction of the capitalists, the end of the Jews, and the elevation of all true Germans to the wealth, the power, the civilization they coveted. It was a neat but sweeping program for a wrecked and despairing nation, choked with revenge and envy. And in the weakness and confusion of Europe, he had help from the stupid and the avaricious outside Germany.

I came to Munich from the sad loveliness of Vienna and stopped at the Hotel Vierjahreszeiten. Vienna was depressing, but in a nostalgic fashion, like the sound of a waltz associated in one's youth with a love affair, but Munich was aggressively depressing. It was never a very gay city, and its bilious-yellow neo-Florentine squares seemed charged with a kind of desperate vitality. Everywhere there were men and boys in brown shirts saluting each other with outstretched arms, filling the sidewalks in the crowded parts of the city, marching in columns, singing rather fierce, wild songs. The singing and marching went on at intervals all through the night beneath the windows of my room in the Vierjahreszeiten. Once in the street I stopped to listen to a brown-shirted spellbinder haranguing a crowd of brown-shirted boys and a few civilians. It was a familiar harangue, in Germany a very old one. It followed the lines of the talk I had heard in the Beau-Site in Saint-Firmin. Germans were a superior race. They had never had what they deserved. The Führer and the Nazi Party would give it to them. They would have power. They would have wealth. They would ride other inferior races. The Jews must be exterminated. Germany would be supreme.

And all the familiar and fantastic discourse, punctuated by the *Heils* of the crowd, seemed to be believed by them. Indeed, they were hungry for it.

The same night in the open street before the hotel I saw two men kicked and beaten by twenty men in brown shirts and two or three civilians. I was told that the victims were simply anti-Nazis.

All these things were terrifying, for what I was witnessing was not at that time even the operations of a government, but of a secret government inside the government. Hitler was not yet in power, but only the head of a political party. Munich already belonged to the Nazis. They ruled it.

I had expected to stay only a day, but the brown-shirted spectacle fascinated me, even in its more revolting aspects, and so I stayed on for nearly a week, aware vaguely that somehow what I witnessed concerned me as well as everyone else in the whole world. It was the brutal vitality of the spectacle that made it important.

On the third day as I stepped out of the lift I found the hallway filled with men in brown shirts. They seemed to be gathered about two or three important figures, being received by the manager of the hotel. Discreetly I turned to discover who they were, and succeeded. One was von Hagen, the second was Heintzlemann, and the third was Dr. Goebbels. It was my first sight of him. The face was that of a rat. You might have seen it in any criminal court in New York or Chicago where gangsters were on trial. It was exactly that—the face of a shrewd criminal who fancied he could outsmart the whole world.

Heintzlemann was still gross in appearance, although thinner than he had been in Saint-Firmin. He was dressed in riding breeches and a brown shirt with a leather belt. He carried a heavy riding crop. I looked for the boy with the straw-colored hair, but he was not there.

Von Hagen looked much the same. It was summer, but even without the long black overcoat with the mink collar, he still resembled a prosperous provincial undertaker.

I went up to my room and wrote him a note. It was brief, saying simply that I was in Munich and would like him to dine with me. I scarcely expected an answer. He gave the impression of being immensely important and immensely busy. But in the afternoon I found a note from him, saying he could not dine with me but could I dine with him. It was his habit to see certain people during the dinner hour, he might be interrupted from time to time, but if I did not mind that, he would be delighted to see me.

Of course I accepted. There were so many things I wanted to know.

. . . . .

We dined not in the Walterspiel belowstairs but in his own suite, the suite reserved in the old days for minor members of the Imperial family passing through Munich. It was a dreary set of rooms, with a salon furnished in clumsy furniture made of dark wood, upholstered in dusty-red plush. The walls were hung with second-rate tapestries and adorned with the heads of stags and wild boars. I believe it was called the Hunting Suite. The dining room was done in much the same manner, with immensely heavy, grotesquely carved chairs upholstered in machine-made needlepoint. It was all luxurious in an *echt Deutsch* fashion.

Von Hagen greeted me with as much warmth as his dank nature could summon. His hands were still waxen and damp. It was a great pleasure, he said, to find me in Munich. How were my wife and the children?

Then as the cocktails he ordered were brought in, another door opened and a very beautiful woman came into the room. She could not have been more than thirty, with dark hair and blue eyes and a fine figure. She was dressed with great chic in a simple black gown with wonderful pearls.

"This is my wife," said Hagen, and to her he said, "This is a great American friend of mine. We met in Saint-Firmin."

I remembered all that Gretl had told me of the clothes, the jewels, the cruelty and avarice of von Hagen in relation to this woman, and until we had finished cocktails and were halfway through dinner my interest was almost entirely in her.

It was not only that she was beautiful. She had as well a great air of distinction. She left the conversation to Hagen and me, herself scarcely speaking. Once or twice when she did make an observation, Hagen cut her short with an air of contempt and cruelty. He treated her as I have seen men treat dogs which they value more for breeding and the value as show animals than as friends or objects of affection. She did not appear to resent the rudeness. There was something still and quiet and mysterious about her, as if she were quietly enduring her present position, secure in the knowledge that elsewhere, outside the world of Hagen, there were happiness and satisfaction. I thought, "This woman has a lover somewhere whom she loves passionately."

The conversation of Hagen was obviously made to please me. That, the world learned later, was part of the technique. They believed that if they could make you like them, they could deceive you all the more easily. But there was, too, the pitiful desire of the German to be loved. I was aware of an echo of the speech so often heard among the Germans at Saint-Firmin, "Why does the world dislike us?" Yet Hagan's conversation was cynical, too, as if, I think, to show that he took me into the confidence of the Nazi Party. It was the sort of technique which would have worked admirably with Herbert. For myself, I found something repulsive in it, as if he were betraying the secrets of his side and saying at the same time, "You and I know what they are like. They aren't quite gentlemen or decent." It was a method, a habit, I have encountered in many Germans, even in very different times.

The conversation turned to Saint-Firmin, and when I said, "I saw Heintzlemann today. He seems to be quite important," he answered, "He is. He is head of the special guard of the Führer."

I asked, "What has become of the boy with the straw-colored hair?"

Hagen grinned—the grin of an undertaker taking you into his confidence about some scandal in the family of the bereaved. "He disappeared. I believe it was a matter of jealousy."

"You mean liquidated?" I asked, using a word just then coming into usage in Europe.

"He disappeared," repeated Hagen, and I knew what he meant. "But he has been replaced," he added, "several times over, I understand. It is very difficult to resist a man with Heintzlemann's power."

Then a little later I chanced to remark that an organization like the Führer's must need a lot of money and expressed curiosity as to where it came from. Hagen grinned again. "That is where I come in," he said, "myself and many others."

And then I understood. The remark explained a great deal—that men like Hagen, the big bankers and industrialists, had put their money on Hitler, not only the bankers and industrialists of Germany, but men outside, in other countries. I felt a little sick.

But Hagen was saying, "All this competition in the world is a terrible waste. The cartel idea is the solution. If bankers and industrialists could control the world, there would be no wars, but only prosperity for everyone. There would be no Bolshevism." He paused over his pudding and said, "You know, men like you could do a great service to the world by explaining such things." And then I knew why I had been asked to dinner and been treated so cordially. I understood too why, although he had asked me to dine with him because he had two or three rendezvous, we had never been interrupted.

He said, "I would like to show you about—to take you on the inside of the movement. If you could stay a few days. I shall be going to Nuremberg and then Stuttgart. I would be glad to have you go with me."

My curiosity prompted me to accept the invitations, but a sense of aversion made it impossible. I could not picture myself spending several days in the man's company. I heard myself saying, "I should like nothing better but I must be in Paris on Thursday."

"Another time then. Write me at the Stuttgart office whenever you feel inclined to come. I will arrange it."

"Thank you."

Then he turned to his wife and said, "You may go, Lisa, whenever you like."

She rose and bowed toward me. "It has been a pleasure to meet you," she said. "The evening has been very interesting."

It was a formal speech, spoken mechanically. She obviously had no interest whatever in me or in our conversation. I bowed and said I hoped we should see each other again, and she went out quickly. Hagen watched her with a curious look of obsession in his yellow-brown eyes.

When she had gone, I said, "May I say that your wife is a very handsome woman?"

He grinned, "Yes, she is good-looking, although not very clever. Politics bore her. She has not the mind for it."

There was one more question I wanted to ask. I asked it. "Tell me, what is the Führer like?"

He did not answer me at once. He took a sip of brandy and turned it over on his tongue. Then he looked at me for a moment, as if speculating upon how much he dared to say. When he spoke, he said, "That is a difficult question to answer. He is a little man—a hysterical fellow. He is important only because he expresses something very profound in the German character and because the times are made for him—or for a man exactly like him. In another time, in different circumstances, he would be only a ludicrous figure."

Now, long afterward, I still think that Hagen's description, perhaps sincere at the time, perhaps uttered only to mislead me, was an excellent one.

I had had enough and felt unbearably restless as one does in the company of people whose every speech is calculated and devoid of all sincerity. Conversation with Hagen was difficult because it was like talking to a dead man. There was no warmth in it, nothing to kindle the excitement which is the essence of good conversation. I made the excuse of having work to do and said that I knew he was a very busy man.

As I was leaving, he asked, "Have you seen our friend Gretl?"

I said that we had heard from her but had not seen her—that she was in London.

"I know," he said. "She was in Germany a month ago. I saw her. She was prettier than ever. I don't think she likes me very much. I am trying to make her like me." He smiled as he lighted a second expensive cigar. It was the smile of a man who had been used to having his own way, even if he had to buy it.

From the street, below the window, came the sound of the Horst Wessel song and the sound of marching feet—that heavy tramp! tramp! with which every steet in Germany was beginning to echo.

Hagen turned toward the window. "Come," he said. "Look!"

We went to the window and below in the street we saw a column of young men all in brown shirts, marching and singing. They were marching with that rhythm and precision which only German troops manage to achieve. It is a terrifying thing—the utter absorption of the individual into a machine, born of desire of the individual to be absorbed, to lose his own identity utterly in the machine—the *will* to be a cog.

Every other man in the procession carried a torch, and the wildly flickering flames gave the whole scene a barbaric appearance. For a long time we watched in silence and I thought, "Exactly like that they came out of the swamps and forests of Germany to fight Caesar—tied together with ropes to be slaughtered by the Roman legions. Perhaps it will happen again." And as I watched them, memories of the war came back to me, memories of German troops advancing arm in arm, shoulder to shoulder, singing as they came, to be mowed down by machine-gun bullets. I thought, "It is going to happen again. There is something in the German nature which finds an ecstasy in suicide."

The column passed, and the singing of the song glorifying a pimp began to die away. Hagen turned toward me, "Impressive, *nicht wahr?*"

"Yes," I said, "and a little frightening." I looked at him. "It will be a nuisance if the world has to defeat you again."

His face did not change expression. "This time," he said, "it will not be defeat. Victory for us will benefit the world. We have so much to give it."

· · · · ·

I went away the next day, happy once again to cross the bridge into Alsace.

My wife was in Paris to meet me. "Gretl has turned up," she said. "She is dining with us. Something has happened to her."

"What?" I asked.

"I don't know exactly, but she's different. She looks almost chic. But that's only the outside. There's something inside, too."

We dined at Maxim's, where Gretl met us. The fourth was a

young man whom she introduced as "My cousin Eric Nattle-man." He was tall, very blond, good-looking, and, as it turned out, rather dull. He had some sort of job in the German Foreign Office.

As soon as Gretl came in, I saw what my wife meant. Gretl was dressed smartly, yet the effect was not of smartness. Her clothes were as good as any of those of the women in the room, yet she did not look chic. Underneath, she was still Gretl, the Lutheran pastor's daughter. She was spontaneously happy to see us and kissed us both. She had been in London, she said, where she had had a small part in a play.

The evening was not remarkable, perhaps because of the presence of the cousin. He was definitely a defeating young man, taciturn, pompous, and, like so many Germans, on the defensive. Conversation with him was impossible. Maxim's that night was filled with spectacular people of every nationality. As a spectacle it was remarkable, but Herr Nattleman regarded the whole scene with a priggish contempt, refusing to become a part of it or even to regard it objectively, as the spectacle it was. Perhaps he was right. Perhaps that was a part of the Nazi strength. Perhaps it was something the rest of us had to learn through the bitterness of war.

At any rate, we were rid of him by the end of the evening. When we came in for a night from the country we stayed at an expensive but curious hotel. It was called the Suffolk, and one was as likely to encounter there Kipling or Lady Reading as the Marquesa Casati or a Hollywood actress. It was a small hotel, but many mysterious people came and went. The proprietor was Swiss. His wife was Dutch. It was luxurious and beautifully run. When the Germans entered Paris six years later, the officers went directly to the Suffolk, where they were expected. Everything was in readiness for them. It was all a part of a well-worked-out scheme.

That night Gretl was staying at the hotel and her cousin left us at the door. Inside, she said, "Pfui! What a prig! And I used to be in love with him. I guess my taste for Germans is spoiled."

She came into our room for a nightcap and stayed a long time to talk. It was true that something had happened to her. She was a little wiser and a great deal harder, yet at moments she was the old simple *gemütlich* German pastor's daughter. I had the impression that she was tired. Something about her made you want to weep, and while she talked, I found myself thinking again, "She should never have left Germany. She should have married a nice, middle-class German and had a whole family by now." If things had been different, I kept thinking—if the Kaiser had not coveted the whole world. If the Germans had only been content with all the power and wealth they had. And then I thought of Munich and the Vier-jahreszeiten and von Hagen looking down into the street at the Brown Shirts marching past, carrying torches, singing a song that glorified a pimp. And I thought, "It is beginning all over again. And a whole new generation of young people like Gretl will have their lives ruined." No, Gretl was never meant to be a trollop. She was very bad at it.

Then suddenly she said, "I forgot to tell you something very interesting. You remember, I told you about von Hagen's wife?"

"Yes," I said, "I met her in Munich. I dined with them. She is very beautiful. I can't see how she puts up with him."

"Oh!" said Gretl, with something of the old innocence. "She doesn't love him. My cousin Eric is her lover. That's what I meant to tell you."

I thought, "So I was right when I saw her in Munich." I asked, "Does von Hagen know it?"

"No," said Gretl. "If he did, he would kill one or both of them—in some way nobody would ever discover. It would be an accident or a strange illness. He told me once that is what he would do if any woman was unfaithful to him."

"He doesn't seem the jealous type," I said.

Then Gretl made an observation of great wisdom. "He's not jealous," she said. "It's different. It's vanity with him. He can't bear to think that any woman he had could find any other man more attractive. There are lots of men like that—most men are, I think. It comes because they know they're inferior. That's why von Hagen thinks of nothing but money and power. It's because he isn't much good as a man or a lover. Nobody in Germany likes him. They only show him respect because he's rich and powerful."

Presently, about four in the morning, my wife yawned and went to bed, but Gretl said she couldn't sleep, so we had another drink and went on talking, and then Gretl came to the point.

She said, blushing a little, "Could you lend me some money? I'm absolutely broke. I got here from London with nothing but my clothes and a few hundred francs."

Being in the money at the moment, I said that of course I'd lend her any reasonable amount, but I expressed surprise that she was broke since she looked so well and expensively dressed.

She laughed and in the laugh was the first bitterness I had ever heard in Gretl. She said, "The clothes are all right, but my boy friend walked out on me. He just went off to Australia and left me cold, without a cent but what I had in my purse."

"Who was he?"

"A stockbroker, about fifty-five. He was nice and kind of dumb but he certainly squeezed every farthing."

So she had picked wrong again.

In the hour that followed until daylight came up over the chestnut trees in the gardens behind the Suffolk, I gave Gretl a lecture, a wholly unmoral but realistic lecture. It might have come out of *L'École de Cocottes*.

"First of all," I said, "you're no good at this kind of life. You weren't meant for it. You ought to go back to Germany and marry and settle down and have a family. That's what you were meant for. Terrible things happen when people willfully distort their own destinies."

She frowned, and after a moment she said, "I know you're right. But it wasn't my fault. Everything got started off wrong. And it's too late to turn back now. I couldn't do that now. I wouldn't know how to live quietly." Then a hardness came into her voice. "Anyway, I could never live in Germany again. I'd suffocate. I'd go crazy. I couldn't go back there after I've tasted what it's like outside. No, it's no good talking to me about that—telling me to go back and be one of Hitler's brood sows."

She was perfectly firm about it, and I confess that I saw her point. It was too late for Gretl to turn back to nursing children and washing diapers. Her destiny was hopelessly twisted.

So I said, "Well, if you're going to lead this kind of life, at least use some brains about it. Get yourself a rich man who is generous too and get a settlement out of him. Get some jewels. Get something to show for it."

"The trouble is," said Gretl, "I always fall in love. I'm just a fool, maybe, but that's how it is."

"Even with the stockbroker?"

"Yes. Even with him. He was so dumb and he had such nice manners. And he didn't know anything about women at all. The only woman he'd ever known until he met me was his wife—one of those long-footed Englishwomen. He didn't go away because he was tired of me. He went away because he was ashamed. He was getting old, you see."

I did see. Gretl's simplicity never left you any doubts about things.

"Well," I said, "get yourself fixed with money and jewels and then you can afford to fall in love with somebody like Luigi."

At the mention of Luigi she blushed. "I know you didn't like Luigi," she said, "but you didn't understand him. He was a child." Then she said an astonishing thing, "Two whores couldn't marry each other. We both knew that always. I always felt sorry for Luigi."

Brutally, I said, "You've got to get over being sentimental. You're too damned nice for your job."

We had finished talking by daylight. I told her I would pay the hotel bill and gave her a check for ten thousand francs. "You can pay me back," I said, "when you strike it rich. Someday you'll come to your senses and get in the money."

She began to cry. She was a little tipsy. "You've both been good to me—so good to me. I don't know why you should."

"Forget it. I guess it's because we like you."

Then she went to her room, and as I closed the door, it seemed to me that Gretl was hopelessly German—nice German. She was a part of an extraordinarily confused picture of which von Hagen was a part, and Heintzlemann and even Herr Oberregierungsrat Moll and his wife were a part. Gretl and the Molls were the reason why so many stupid English and a few Americans were always saying, "The Germans are very much like us. They are so kind and homelike and solid." The same people were always overlooking von Hagen and Heintzlemann and the others, and the fact that people like Gretl and the Molls inevitably and periodically became their victims.

Later, as I fell asleep, it occurred to me that it was odd that Gretl had never mentioned having seen von Hagen on her visit to Germany.

A few days later Gretl left for Vienna. It was as if Vienna and not Germany was her spiritual home. Whenever she came to the end of her tether she went back to Vienna. She said she was going to the Festival in Salzburg. There would be a lot of rich foreigners there. We did not see her again for nearly two years, although we had letters quite regularly. She had fallen in love with a rich Czech from Prague. He was married and had five children, so it was not convenient to live in Prague. Instead, she stayed in Vienna, a city which she loved.

During this period she returned again to Germany to see her mother. Back again in Vienna, she wrote, "I did not stay as long as I expected. Germany is horrible. I shall never go there again. I was insulted and called bad names in the street because I wore good clothes and lacquer on my nails. My younger brother has joined the Brown Shirts and he would not speak to me much of the time. He called me *Ausländer* and worse things. It seems he forgot that he is alive today instead of starved to death because I went among *Ausländers* to make money to feed him. One night he called me all sorts of vile names. If my mother ever wants to see me again she will have to leave Germany. I hate it the way it is now—worse than I hated it when we were starving." Then she added, "I am very well and happy. I love Hansl [the Czech] very much. He is a very serious and respectable man." But she neglected to say anything about a settlement or any jewels. I said to my wife, "It's the same old story. She'll get nothing out of it."

Meanwhile, in Paris, you became aware on every side of the Nazi octopus. Its tentacles emerged now and then in the most unexpected way above the rubbish which coated the whole confused maelstrom of French and international life. Wherever they appeared, they corrupted. Among the rich you heard people saying, "I think this man Hitler must have the answer. There are no strikes, no popular fronts, in Germany. He has found the cure for Bolshevism." Even while the Church and the Jews were being persecuted in Germany, you heard rich Catholics and Jews in Paris defending the Nazis. "Oh," they would say, "the persecution is not real. It's merely political and made for effect. Hitler is really protecting them secretly. One of the secretaries at the German Embassy told me so himself." Or, "Herr Abetz told me confidentially that what Hitler wants most is a close alliance with Germany and France. We have never been able to count on England. We could count on Germany to help us put an end to Bolshevism." You heard the same kind of talk among high officers of the French army. Among English and American diplomats you heard quite often words of praise for the order that the Nazis were bringing about in Germany. I heard one military attaché say, "We need something of the sort in America."

Wherever the tentacles reached among the so-called "upper classes," they emitted a cloud of poison.

Von Hagen came and went from Paris. His name was always in the paper. He was conferring with Georges Bonnet or Flandin or Laval or the big industrialists. Once or twice I encountered him in the corridors of the Ritz, where he always stayed nowadays, abandoning Claridge's, which was the hotel usually frequented by rich Germans. On these occasions we had brief conversations and always he mentioned Gretl and asked if we had news of her. It was not merely the casual mention of a mutual friend to fill in gaps in conversation. He spoke of her admiringly. "She is the good German type," he would say. "I wish we had more of them." I had the impression that Gretl was almost an obsession with him. He mentioned the fact that he had seen her on her last visit to Germany, and again it occurred to me that it was odd she never mentioned having seen him, either in her conversation or her letters.

Once I mentioned Heintzlemann, saying that I understood that he had become very powerful in Germany.

"Oh, yes," von Hagen said, "very powerful. He is the head of all the Brown Shirts, but he is a stupid fellow. All egotist and ambitions. He will come a cropper. He has too many enemies. Lately he has been insufferable."

From the speech and manner I gathered that he and Heintzlemann were no longer having those little secret, intimate meetings at which they had cooked up so many things.

Then suddenly our old friend Herbert appeared in Paris
from New York. He was just as clean and shiny as ever, and
just as stupid in his intuitions and judgment of people. But he
had put on a little weight and definitely had jowls. This time
his wife was with him, a nice, pleasant-looking woman who
was president of her garden club in Long Island. There was a
suffocating sense of innocence about them both, especially in
comparison with von Hagen and some of the French and
German politicians with whom he was dealing as the purpose
of his visit. It was not the pious, smug stupidity of so many
Englishmen who contributed to bringing on the disaster, but
just plain innocence, of that American kind which cannot
believe that there are people as villainous as von Hagen or as
fanatic as Hitler or as depraved as Heintzlemann.

Herbert was excited during most of the visit about the
details of a gigantic deal he was putting over. In his innocence,
he liked to surround everything he did with mystery. He liked
to use the expression "big deal," with a comical look of mystery in his clear blue eyes. It never occurred to him, I think,
that every newspaper correspondent in Paris knew pretty well
what was going on and that he was in Paris to help bring about
a gigantic cartel of industrialists, German, American, British,
and French, which was to rule the world.

Before he left, he gave a dinner party to which he invited
me. None but men were present, some of whom I knew, some
I did not. They were big industrialists. The Frenchmen all
represented the *deux cents familles* hated by the men of the
Popular Front.

It was an extraordinary gathering, held to celebrate the conclusion of the cartel agreement and paid for, of course, by the
American. I heard frightening things that night, partly, I
think, because of two assumptions on the part of the French—
that I too was in the racket, and that being an American I
could not understand very well what they were saying. I heard
their willingness to sell out France as a nation. I heard them
talk not at all as Frenchmen but as creatures who were above

nationality, to whom money and power and property were the only values in life. It was the first time I remember having heard the name of Admiral Darlan. It was clear that he was working with them.

Of course, von Hagen was there, looking more than ever like a provincial undertaker in his tails and white tie. He was in a gleeful mood, making bad German jokes and telling disgustingly filthy stories, his opaque cat's eyes shrewd and cold with watching the effect upon the others. One had the impression that he was faintly hysterical now that the whole coveted world was almost in his grasp and the grasp of Nazi Germany. At end of the dinner, von Hagen, another German, a Frenchman, and an Englishman went off to a brothel—described by von Hagen as a very special sort of place, very discreet, where very special entertainment was provided.

Once in bed I could not sleep for thinking of the things I had heard and divined during the course of the evening. I felt a little sick and filled again with that dreadful sense of foreboding I had known long ago among the white peaks of Saint-Firmin. I wanted suddenly to return to America and escape from this sick, corrupt, dying Europe.

I wakened late and when I telephoned for breakfast, my wife came into the room holding a copy of the Paris *Herald*. She said simply, "It has happened."

"What?" I asked.

"What Gretl said would happen. Von Hagen's wife and Gretl's cousin have been killed in an accident in Germany. The *Herald* simply says their car ran into an obstruction on the road. The *Daily Mail* says it was a steel cable stretched across the road."

I read both accounts of the "accident." The *Daily Mail* reported that Baroness von Hagen, accompanied by Freiherr Eric Nattleman, were on their way in a high-powered sports car from Munich to the Baron von Hagen's *Schloss* at Titelsee when the car struck a steel cable stretched across the road. Both bodies were very nearly decapitated. Confidential sources in Berlin reported that very likely the "accident" was a plot on the life of von Hagen himself, who had many bitter enemies in

Germany. The murderers had killed Baroness von Hagen and Freiherr Nattleman by mistake.

Then slowly over the *café au lait* I began to understand the full horror of the story. If Gretl was right and von Hagen himself was the murderer, he had known what was happening as he sat at last night's dinner to celebrate his triumph. He had known it when he went off to the luxurious brothel to continue the evening's entertainment. It may have been the reason for his air of hysteria. To my wife I said, "It couldn't be true."

She was more skeptical. "Remember what Gretl said. Remember those people at Saint-Firmin. Any of them could have been guilty of such a crime."

But it was difficult to believe. No one, not even myself, believed a man at the top of the Nazi Party would be such an utter criminal.

A week later there was a letter from Gretl. Hansl, the Czech, had died suddenly of a stroke. There was no provision made for her. It was the old story again. Another love affair was ended and she was broke. She would, she wrote, see us in Paris as soon as she could get her affairs in order. At the very end she wrote, "You see, what I told you about von Hagen is true. He must have found out about his wife and Eric."

It was altogether a sickening world.

The third thing to happen was the death of Heintzlemann. We wakened one morning to find the newspapers filled with news of "the purge." It had happened swiftly, with a primitive and savage barbarity. Heintzlemann was one of the first victims. Hitler himself had gone to Heintzlemann's villa, where he found him with a boy. The boy, Hitler murdered himself, screaming with rage as he pulled the trigger. Heintzlemann, said the paper, was given a revolver and the choice of shooting himself or being shot. He was dead, although the press did not know whether as a suicide or against a wall. More than six hundred men and a few women were murdered on that day. Most of them had helped the Führer in his rise to power.

At breakfast in the dining room by the river, overlooking the soft green country of the Oise, my wife and I found conversation a little difficult. It was not because we minded the murder of all those people, or were in any way touched by them directly; it was something else that made us silent—the memory of all those people in the public rooms of the Hôtel Beau-Site in Saint-Firmin and the knowledge now that it was too late to stop them, that it would be only a little while until they let down the walls of pretense and hypocrisy, to spread murder and perversion and misery over all of Europe and perhaps the world. For a moment that morning I saw them through the big windows, coming out of the feathery green beech forest across the wide fields of wheat as I had seen them in 1914, as I would see them again in 1940, as the Romans who lived in that old town had seen them, sweeping down from the North to pillage and rape, burn and destroy, the coveted lands and civilization of the South. They had been going on in Europe since Roman times, these invasions, tinctured always with the peculiar barbarity of those people in the hotel at Saint-Firmin.

Presently my wife said, "Maybe now people will believe the savagery. Maybe now they'll do something to stop them."

But they didn't. In Paris and London, men like Chamberlain and Halifax and Georges Bonnet and Laval found excuses and justifications for Hitler and his barbarity and went on dealing with him. Small imitators and little bands of Fascists began to spring up in other countries outside Germany, and as the infection spread, it seemed to me that even those opposed to Fascism in Europe were touched by a kind of paralyzing stupidity. In Paris in certain high circles, it became fashionable to be pro-Franco and pro-Fascist. It became more and more clear that nothing could stop the Nazis or save Europe from destruction.

Then one afternoon as I came out of the Suffolk I noticed a huge and showy foreign car at the curb. It was a Mercedes, all black and chromium, and as I stood for a second looking at it, the driver opened the door and a woman smartly dressed in black stepped out. Behind her, in the car, sat very stiffly an elderly woman of unmistakably *hochgeboren* appearance, rather grim but rather smart, in a high-collared dark costume, with her hair strained high on her head, wearing a hat with a dead bird on it—a vision of stiffness, dullness, and respectability.

The young woman in black looked at me and smiled and started toward me, and then suddenly I recognized her. It was Gretl. As she passed me she said, "Follow me inside," and continued on her way into the hotel. Feeling as if I were a character in a spy melodrama I followed her. She was waiting for me in the little salon just off the hallway, smiling as if something amused her. At a second glance, I saw that she had changed enormously. The eternal "Gretchen" quality was gone. She looked very much a woman of the world, thinner and hard, much harder than she had been on her last visit.

She said, "Don't think I'm crazy. I'm getting married."

"To whom?"

She answered me very quickly, "I can't tell you now. That's my future husband's sister in the car outside. She's come with me to Paris to buy clothes. She doesn't know anything about the way I've been living. She mustn't know anything about it. She mustn't meet any of the people I know."

I shrugged. "It's O.K. by me. She looks pretty forbidding. Why can't you tell me whom you're marrying?"

"You wouldn't believe it if I told you. You'll know in a fortnight."

"Anyway, you seem to be doing all right by yourself. I hope you get something out of it this time. How about a drink?"

"I can't now. What are you doing about six?"

"Nothing."

"I could get away and come downstairs to the bar then."

"O.K. It's a date."

She hurried away and in a few minutes came out again and joined the *hochgeboren Dame* in the car.

A little after six she reappeared in the bar. She had changed her clothes and looked very smart and was wearing a ruby bracelet that cost plenty and a big emerald on her left hand. Over Martinis, I said, "What's all the mystery? Are you marrying Hitler?" And she answered me with a touch of the old Gretl's naïveté. "No," she said quite sincerely, "not him."

"Göring?"

"He's just gotten married."

"Goebbels?"

"He has a wife."

And then partly as a guess, partly by intuition, I said, "I know."

"You couldn't."

"It's von Hagen."

The color came into her face and she did not answer at once.

"Why can't you tell me?"

"I promised not to tell anyone. It's to be a secret until after the ceremony. I promised not to tell as part of the bargain. I promised I wouldn't see any of my old friends. In exchange I don't have to live in Germany. I don't even have to go there. He's very peculiar, but that's how it is."

For a moment I was silent, puzzled and thoughtful. Then I said, "Of course, you know you're marrying Blue Beard. Remember the first wife?"

"Yes. I know all that. I think I can manage that."

"And you know the other unpleasant things about him."

"Yes. I'm not a young virgin getting married. But I think I can manage that too. I've been through a lot of things—a lot more than I've ever told you."

I became relentless, partly through curiosity. "Why are you marrying him?"

"He is the richest man in Germany and one of the most powerful."

"You remember what happened to Heintzlemann?"

"It won't happen to him. Even if it did, it wouldn't matter."

"I still don't get it."

"He has been mad for me always, even when his wife was alive, even when I was married to my first husband."

"But you?"

"I'm tired of being a victim. I'm tired of falling in love." She looked at me with a hard expression about the eyes and mouth. "I'm taking the advice you gave me. This time I'm going to clean up."

I laughed. "The more you clean him, the better it will suit me. You ought to cut the pictures out of the frames and sell them."

She only said, "Watch me!" A curious silence fell between us. I think she was embarrassed at having suddenly revealed so much and I think we were both regretting the simple, warm-hearted Gretl who wasn't there any more, whom neither of us would ever find again.

"Well, I wish you luck."

"I'll be all right," she said.

"Why didn't you tell me you had seen von Hagen each time you went to Germany?" She didn't answer at once, and I added, "I knew it. He told me himself."

"I was ashamed."

"Is that why you told me the cock-and-bull story just now about promising not to tell whom you were marrying?"

"Yes." And quietly she added, "I must go now. The old dragon is waiting upstairs to chaperon me at dinner. The future Baroness von Hagen has got to be respectable now."

She rose from her chair. I got up too. "If you ever get into trouble, let us know. We'll always be interested."

She said, "I haven't forgotten the money you loaned me. I haven't had enough to pay you since then. I haven't even got it now, but as soon as I have, I'll pay you back."

"O.K. I haven't worried about it."

"Kiss Alice for me. I love her. I've never known any woman like her. To put up all these years with a tart like me."

"You're not a tart. You were never meant to be one."

The mouth turned suddenly hard again. "Watch me this time, baby."

She went away to join the *hochgeboren* dragon.

*   *   *   *   *

A fortnight later we received an overopulent engraved announcement with a coronet at the top telling of the marriage of Baroness von Schildsen and Baron von Hagen.

A little while later the Molls reappeared in the story in the form of a letter from Frau Moll. It contained only a line or two saying that Herr Oberregierungsrat Moll was dead in Cologne. Frau Moll wrote, "I know it may seem strange to hear from me after so many years, but my husband and I were always very fond of you both. In those trying days at Saint-Firmin you did much to make it bearable for us. We have thought of you often in the long years in between, and spoke of you often. Only a little time before he died my husband was talking of you. He said, 'I always like Americans. There is something bright and young and generous about them.' I thought you would like to know of his death and that he thought of you frequently."

I was sorry then that we had never taken the trouble to go a little out of the way and pay them a visit in Cologne.

But the letter did not end the story. A little while later a second letter arrived, this time bearing the postmark of Luxembourg. In it Frau Moll wrote, "A friend of mine is posting this outside Germany. There were many things I wanted to tell you in the earlier letter but could not, as everything I write and do is watched.

"My husband died, I think, of a broken heart. When Hitler came into power, they took away his judgeship because he opposed them. We were very nearly ruined and they continued to persecute and humiliate him in a thousand small ways. They took away his precious library of which he was so proud and worst of all they burned his books in the streets of Cologne. They had a special pile of rare editions with a sign on them, 'From the collection of former Herr Oberregierungsrat Moll, corrupted by foreign ways.'

"We could have gone away to England perhaps and have gotten along somehow, but my husband was born in the Rhineland and he loved it. He preferred to die there rather than as a stranger in a foreign country.

"I would like to see you both again but I am afraid it would be a shock to both of you. I am an old woman now. I live as quietly as possible, going out very rarely. It has been a long time since I have done any singing. Six years ago the Nazis forbade me to appear in public as a singer. I do not know what has become of our old Germany. It is not here any longer. I doubt that it will ever come back, for when we old ones are dead there will be no one who remembers it. It is not only that the Nazis have destroyed other people, they have destroyed the good Germans as well.

"I know you will be interested to hear that the one they used to call the Wolf is *Gauleiter* of our region now and that the Old Sow is called, 'Mother of the Woman's Youth Movement.'

They were all there that winter in Saint-Firmin for a purpose.

"I would like to have news of you. Occasionally a friend goes into Belgium or Luxembourg and I am able to post a letter from there. You don't know how much a letter from the outside can mean to us here in Germany. But you must write carefully—just news of yourself without any comment on politics. My pitifully few letters are all opened before they reach me, and it would be very bad for me."

We wrote, of course, simple newsy letters about ourselves and the children, the garden and the dogs. Very discreetly we suggested that she join us for "a long visit" but we only got an answer that she was too tired and ill to leave Cologne. She was too old to make the change. That was the last we ever heard of Frau Moll. I think she must have died or perhaps she was killed in the raids on Cologne.

. . . . .

The nightmare was closing in.

Austria was invaded and Czechoslovakia threatened, and then Mr. Chamberlain took his umbrella and galoshes to Munich and there was no longer any doubt.

For months we had no news either of the Baron or the Baroness von Hagen and then one morning the papers announced that the Baron von Hagen had fled to Switzerland. He had, it seemed, encountered the disfavor of the Führer and those about him. How he escaped was unknown, but he had been deprived of all his property, all the vast holdings in banks and industry. This was divided between the Nazy Party and the Hermann Göring Works. But more than this, there was an order for his arrest for the murder of his first wife and a man called Eric Nattleman.

Once more there swept over me the sense of living in a bad melodrama in which there was no sense of reality whatever. These were people we knew—von Hagen, Gretl, the Molls, all those people in the hotel at Saint-Firmin and at the banquet von Hagen had given in Paris. They were made of flesh, of blood. The strange things which had happened to them had really happened.

That afternoon I went into Paris and booked passage for my wife and children. I was aware that when people in Europe came to accept the fantastic things that were happening as simply the course of events, the jig was up. The Europe which I had loved for so long was doomed. It would continue a little longer and then suddenly go down into the abyss. The Europe I had known and loved for nearly half my life would never again exist.

I went to Le Havre with the family, depressed at their departure. The children were excited and the dogs barked a great deal. From the deck of the *Normandie* I looked down on the port and the many-windowed, dreary Hôtel Frascati, thinking what a splendid smash a bomb would make of its brick and glass. A little later as the ship slipped out of the harbor, I felt a sense of relief and a great satisfaction in being an American. My family was going home, out of an insane world dominated by a madman. I think home never meant so much to me before.

I took the evening train back to Paris and on arrival went straight to a small but expensive little restaurant called Tout Paris. At that time it was filled with Austrian refugees, mostly from Vienna—not as guests but as entertainers. It was run by an Austrian, the band and the waiters were Viennese, and among the clientele were many Viennese refugees who could not afford to pay their checks but who sang or danced for their supper. They were good singers and dancers, with all the nostalgic charm of Vienna. I went there, instinctively seeking a last remembrance of things past, in Sachers and the Bristol and the Café de l'Europe, of the Festival at Salzburg and the Mirabelgarten—all the good civilized things which had been destroyed forever by the covetousness of men like von Hagen and Heintzlemann and all the others. Well, I reflected, as I took a table alone in a corner, Heintzlemann is dead, murdered, and von Hagen is in disgrace. Maybe the others will go in the same way. Perhaps, after all, there is a law rewarding good and punishing evil. Perhaps, after all, there is in the end a universal decency.

Feeling depressed, I ordered champagne and as the waiter brought it, I heard a familiar voice—the voice of Gretl. She was standing by the table and with her was a white-

blonde Belgian trollop who looked a little like one of Frans
Hals' women. I knew her slightly. I had seen her plying her
trade in a dozen resorts and capitals. I was a little shocked to
see Gretl in her company.

Yet Gretl did not look down-and-out. She wore a short coat
of sable and three or four bracelets worth plenty of money.
She looked extremely well and seemed gay and excited.

The two girls joined me and sat drinking champagne while
I ate. We listened a good deal to the music, which was good,
and especially to the singing of a Viennese girl who had been
a star in Vienna. Gretl told me her story. She was in Paris
without money or home, bound nowhere. Her mother was a
Jewess, so there was no longer any place for her in any Germanic country. She sang all the nostalgic songs, *Ein kleines
Hotel*, *In Grinzing*, and, of course, *Vilia*.

Between the songs, Gretl talked in an odd, strained fashion.
Once or twice I looked at her suspecting that she was taking
drugs, but I think it was only a kind of overwrought excitement. The Belgian tart didn't say much. Her talents were not
for conversation.

When I asked, "Where's Hagen?" she said, "In Switzerland.
He's scared to come to Paris."

"Why?"

"He's afraid somebody will bump him off. He just stays in
the villa at Lugano. It has a wall around it. He has five guards
and a lot of big dogs."

"How did he let you out?"

"I didn't ask him. I just came. He didn't know I was coming.
Anyway, it's all finished."

"You've got a sable coat and some mighty fine jewelry.
Didn't he lock it up?"

"I just went to his room and took it while he was out driving.
It's only small stuff. The rest is locked up."

I thought, "She's learning." But now there wasn't even a
trace of the old Gretl.

"There's a lot more stuff—ten times this much. I'll get that
later."

"How?"

She giggled and looked at the Belgian girl. "Never mind.

We've got it figured out." The girl laughed too. She was obviously as much born to be a tart as Gretl had been born to be a good housewife and mother.

Then a dark, heavy little man came over to ask the Belgian girl to dance, and she left us alone.

"Now," I said, "what's the inside story of Hagen? Why did he scram from Germany?"

"They started cleaning him, and he got mad and fought them. Bit by bit they were taking away everything he had, his banks, his factories. . . . They were turning up under the control of Göring and some of the other boys."

"Sooner or later it seems to happen to all of them. Remember Heintzlemann?"

"That's what they'd have done to Hagen. It was all planned. He heard about it and pretended to go to the *Schloss* at Titelsee, and in the night he slipped over the border." It was odd that even now she always referred to him coldly as "Hagen." She never said "my husband" or called him by his Christian name.

"They never learn," I said.

"Who?"

"The people who think Fascism will protect them. They're always the first victims."

"I think he's gone nuts."

"How?"

"He saves wrapping paper and bits of string, and he has got uniforms for the hired guards and reviews them every morning."

"Is he broke?"

"No. He has plenty salted away outside. He is in a lot of deals in America and England that bring him in a big income. They're all like that—all the big shots in Germany. They don't even trust each other."

"I shouldn't think they would."

She wanted more champagne, which I got for her. Then she said, "Hagen thinks he's got all kinds of diseases, too. Sometimes he thinks he has syphilis and sometimes it's tuberculosis and sometimes cancer. There's nothing the matter with him but his imagination. He looks like a ghost. There are always doctors in the place. He thinks about himself so much he doesn't worry much about me any more."

I was silent for a time, thinking again that all these stories, all these people, were monstrous unrealities. I thought, "I've got to get out of here or I'll go nuts too."

The old sense of pollution, almost physical, swept over me to the accompaniment of Viennese music. It was extraordinary how easily people seemed to lose all decency and perspective in that insane prewar world. In a way they followed the pattern of Gretl's metamorphosis, changing imperceptibly without being aware of it. The corruption and despair, the cynicism, spread everywhere like a malignant disease. Perhaps, I thought, war and revolution are the only cures.

I asked suddenly, "Where did you pick up this tart?"

Gretl said, "She's all right. She's my adviser and manager. She's got a lot of smart ideas. We haven't finished yet with Hagen. He'll do anything I want except give me money and jewelry. I had to sell a ring to get the money to come to Paris. But he's got a lot of loot left."

"Well, you've earned it, I guess."

"I hope to tell you."

She talked just like that, using American slang she had picked up in the bars and cafés and restaurants—American slang was very fashionable then—American slang and cigarettes and cars and movie stars, from one end of Europe to the other.

The Belgian girl brought her friend back to the table and with him a middle-aged, shifty-looking man of undiscernible nationality who was introduced as Mr. Hoffstein. I didn't like either of them.

A little later I left them. It was the last time I saw Gretl.

. . . . .

The rest of the story which began in Saint-Firmin is brief enough.

Came the fall of France, which found von Hagen in Monte Carlo, where he had gone for his health. Once there in a rented villa surrounded by his dogs and uniformed guards, he was terrified to leave, even to return to Lugano. Then one day he was induced to go for a drive with his wife, and as they crossed the border on the road to Nice, the car was suddenly forced off the road by another car containing five men. They shot and wounded the one guard with him and dragged him into their car. That was the last ever heard of him.

Not quite a year ago I met Gregory Williams, an old newspaper-correspondent friend of mine, in "21." He was one of the last of the Americans to leave Paris, and we sat until two in the morning talking about all the people we had known in Paris, in Vienna, in London, in Berlin, and what had become of them. And presently the name of von Hagen came up.

"Certainly he is dead," said Gregory. "And they probably gave him the works before he died. I can't say I'm sorry. He was a rat if ever there was one. If they'd only kill each other off, the world would be a lot better place. I must say they've done pretty well and I guess they'll do a lot better before the thing is over."

"Did you ever know his wife?" I asked.

Gregory Williams grinned. "Sure I did."

"How is she doing?"

"She's doing all right. She's the queen of Paris now, living with the military governor in one of the Rothschild houses. They say she cleaned Hagen and took him for a ride and turned him over to the Nazis. She has cars and jewels and everything." He grinned again. "People over here won't believe some of the stories that happened in Europe. They just think you make them up. They say, 'Gee. You ought to write novels.'"

It was a queer end for a Lutheran pastor's daughter. But the end of von Hagen's story rather cheered me. It almost made me believe there was such a thing as Nemesis. I said, "Let's drink to the end of the rest of the bloody bastards."

We raised our glasses. "It won't be long now," said Gregory.

.   .   .   .   .

A month ago I received a letter postmarked Lisbon, bearing no return address. When I tore it open there fell out of it a letter and two one-hundred-pound British bank notes. The letter was in Gretl's handwriting. It read: "I took your advice. I'm doing fine. Here is the money you lent me long ago in Paris. It ought to cover the loan and the hotel bill and a little over. Good luck to you and Alice. See you after the war. Your affectionate friend—Gretl."